BLOOD LIBEL

BLOOD LIBEL

Philip Kerrigan

GRAFTON BOOKS

A Division of the Collins Publishing Group

LONDON GLASGOW
TORONTO SYDNEY AUCKLAND

Grafton Books
A Division of the Collins Publishing Group
8 Grafton Street, London W1X 3LA

Published by Grafton Books 1989

Copyright © Philip Kerrigan 1989

A CIP catalogue record for this book is available from the British Library

ISBN 0-246-13342-2

Printed in Great Britain by
William Collins Sons & Co. Ltd, Glasgow

For Ghosta

"The pressure of the past builds up like steam in a boiler. Unless the present gives way, there will be an explosion."

Carl Loftenburg,
Histories II

PART ONE

Pressure of the Past

1

He waited to escape.

I am an old fool, he thought. So old. My bones hurt my flesh, flesh hurts skin, skin like the pages of an old book. I am a bag of sticks and leather, yet I stand here, preparing to escape like some boy of fifty. I must be mad.

He shifted uncomfortably, afraid of losing his balance. To a man of eighty-four years, a fall from standing was as much to be feared as slipping from a high wire. Reason and weariness urged him to go to bed, as he had been told to. It was so late. The task was impossible. Much better if he took off his overcoat and scarf and returned to his bed.

Glancing back, he surveyed the room. It was pleasant, warm, nothing like a prison cell. There were his bed and personal belongings, his books, the piles of magazines and newspapers heaped on his desk. They reminded him of why he must try. This place was very fine; he was allowed to rise when he pleased, do very much as he wished. But it was a prison for all that. See what would happen if they caught him trying to leave.

He opened the door half an inch and peered out along the corridor. From a room several doors away came a long moan. He flinched back. Two uniformed women came out, talking over their shoulders to the occupant of the room.

They were familiar, he knew them well enough, but the uniforms started confusion swarming in his mind. He wavered on the divide between present and past. Clammy sweat started under his arms. He was in cramped darkness. Voices shouted, furniture tumbled and crashed. The children, the children . . .

9

He grasped the cold metal of his watch-strap, stared hard at its face, concentrated on the date. He must not become stupid now. He mouthed the words of a prayer, the soft clicks and partings of his dry lips and tongue as they pronounced the ancient words producing a feeling of certainty.

The uniforms whispered together, now and then glancing into the room. The voice still groaned: "Let me go home, please."

He thought: You have no home any more. None of us has. This place is our prison. The boy says I can leave any time I want, but what would he think of this?

Never mind about the boy.

Legs aching, he watched the uniforms go along the corridor. Lights went out. Their footsteps went down the stairs. A door closed. Only muffled snivelling remained. He stepped out of his room and closed the door. His tired blood stirred. Despite fear, he sensed possibilities where none had been for so long, a world outside memory. There was the rest of the house to pass through, but he was on his way. It was like a breath of childhood.

Twenty minutes later, he stumbled across gravel, ran face-first into the low branches of the cypresses that fringed the yard. He pushed them aside and forced his way deeper into cover, heaving for air.

The cold was intense. His breath rose in frigid clouds. Behind him the house lurked against the night. He turned back to the darkness, and was terrified again, sensing the world's enormity, seeing now the other side of countless possibilities: countless dangers waiting. He had known it before, and forgotten: the prisoner's fear of outside.

It would have been easy to turn back then, but he thought of Luba. Her face. He could not forget what he knew. Everyone else might, but he could not.

He straightened painfully. The chill already seeped into his hands and face. He pulled his hat down, dug gloves from his pocket and put them on, pulled his scarf tight. Now he must get to the road.

Rounding the east wing, he saw the window of his own room. No light showed. His absence had not been discovered. With luck, no one would think about him until morning. He

10

cut away towards the road. At least God was on his side in one matter; the grounds were not walled. When he reached the verge, he looked back through the trees at the house and lifted his hand. It trembled.

Then he stepped out onto the road, and was in the world again.

He came limping into the village. A pond flanked by darkened houses glistened in frozen starlight. A phone box stood on a triangle of grass by the water. He entered it, fumbled his spectacles on and searched for the number. He gave thanks that it was an old-fashioned phone. Bloodless fingers dialled the number, wasted the first coin when he forgot to add the code. He got it right the second time. It rang, bleeped, and he pushed the money in.

When he had finished the call, he remembered the letter in his pocket. He made his way along the road to a post box by a squat brick shelter. Grasped the envelope and pushed it through the slot. He was relieved. Now everything would be clear. He returned to the shelter, hoping he would not freeze to death before they came.

Lord, you pick your times in a strange way. I was young once, and of some use, but what am I now?

He thought of lying on a filthy bunk, shivering against bodies like stone. The rich stench of human dirt and sickness clogging the air. At least there was no smell here.

He huddled back in the dark; scared and exhilarated. Above all, he was angry. He talked to himself in his dazed state, fuelling the anger. It kept him warm. He had never stopped being angry.

2

Another evening.

Sarah was working at the dining-room table when David came in. She heard his briefcase drop in the hall.

"That you?" she called.

"Me?" His voice boomed. "I think so. Was when I left the office, anyway."

"Good. Do you think Madonna first or Lionel Ritchie?"

"When is this?"

"About twelve-thirty."

He hung up his coat, considering. "Why not the Beach Boys?"

"It's the middle of March, dear."

"Madonna, then, if you must."

"Fine." She pencilled it into the playlist. He was still pottering about in the hall. She glanced at the note she had scrawled for herself earlier, raised her voice again. "Are you going down to the boat this weekend?"

"What?" He was picking up his letters.

"Tony called. He wanted to know." She glanced at the framed photograph on the shelf nearby. A picture of them all lounging in the well of Tony's cruiser, wine glasses raised, sunlight flaring on the river behind them. All grinning for the camera because it was a good day.

"It's not April yet," David said. "The boats're probably still frozen in. He wants to spend Sunday in the pub, that's what he wants. Had a tough week in the House, doing his bit to ruin the country." He went into the kitchen. The fridge door slammed, a beer can popped. "Get you anything?"

"Not now. I'll wait till the party . . . I told Tony you'd call."

"See if I can fit him in, the old bugger."

He came into the room, carrying the beer and a sheaf of plans. He was immaculately suited, as usual, but had pulled off his jacket and yanked his tie adrift. He detoured to say hello, lightly kissing the top of her blond head. She turned in the chair, curling her arm round his neck, and stopped him for a real kiss.

"Good evening," he said, letting the plans slide onto the table. His dark face and deep blue eyes smiled at her. "How's broadcasting?"

"Same as usual. Are those the Wensum Mall plans?"

He snatched them back. "They *are*. And no journo gets a look at them till the unveiling tonight."

Sarah unfolded her long figure from the table and they headed through to the lounge. He piled the plans on his drawing board in the window and flung himself full length on

12

the settee. He had been out half the day on site and in the office for the rest. She could tell he was tired, but storing energy for the evening. She put some Mozart on the CD, turned it low, then she joined him.

He opened his eyes and winked at her, creating lines that made him look older than thirty-two. "What're you doing home so early?"

"Plotting the order of delights for Mike Proctor's Thursday jamboree," she said, smoothing the neat hair back off his forehead. "Had to do it out of the office, otherwise it won't get done at all."

"Anything momentous I should tune in for?"

"Local author talking about his new book on Norfolk steam engines."

"A treat in store." He seemed to be falling asleep. "Give us another of those kisses, will you. I'm in dire need."

She complied with the request, and it was soon clear that he was not so near falling asleep as she had thought.

After a while she said: "Oh, there's Crosby, Stills and Nash at about five to one."

"Which?"

"Our House."

"That's Crosby, Stills, Nash and Young," he said. "Why not play 'Helpless'? That's got some bite."

"It's the lunchtime show, pal. Can't have people committing suicide during the phone-ins."

He swallowed a mouthful of beer and rested his other hand on her leg, stroking her through the wool of her suit.

"Bad day?" she asked.

"Far from it. Pretty good, all things considered. Wouldn't tell you if it *was* rotten, anyway."

"I'd tell you."

"You wouldn't need to." He kissed her hand.

"What's that mean?" They had been serious less than a year. Hearing him describe her moods and characteristics still gave her pleasure.

"You know." He smiled. "I hear you coming from down the street. Your shoes need reinforced heels on bad days."

"What?" She pretended outrage, took his beer away and bumped her head against his chest.

"Then there's the hinge-rattling door slam," he continued,

13

"followed by the smash of briefcase on hall table, then the shoes kicked across the kitchen, all rounded off with a grunt for hello and the solo stampede upstairs for the splash-crash bath."

"I am *not* like that," she protested.

"It stays in the mind." He struggled up. "What's the time? Trevor'll start to fret if I'm not there before the bash starts."

She jumped up. "I need a bath. I'm wearing the blue tonight."

"Lovely." He stood and went over to the drawing table. She finished putting her papers away and came up behind him as he leafed through the plans. There was an expression of quiet satisfaction in his eyes. She looked at the plans.

"You're proud of it, aren't you?"

"Course not," he lied.

She jabbed him in the ribs. "You're smug all over."

"Justified, I think." He placed a photograph of old warehouses on the riverside next to his artist's impression of what would rise in their place. "Look at it. It's the nearest I can get to creating something out of nothing. Remaking those burned-out old relics from the inside, giving a lot of people who don't have work jobs to go to." She put her hand through his arm and held him as he talked about the shops and businesses which would open in the Wensum Mall development when it was completed. She liked to hear him so enthusiastic. There was something almost shy and embarrassed about the things he tried to say. "I mean, when I'm talking to Trevor and the others, it's all about costings and materials and long-term profits. But I just love it for its own sake; building something good where there were ruins before. It's not for outsiders, it's for people who've lived in Norwich all their lives. It's important." He caught himself, chuckled. "Going on again, aren't I?"

"You go on beautifully." She pulled his face round, and they stood for a while as the music came to a close.

"Okay," he said, finally. "Let's put the glad-rags on and get on with it. I hope there's sandwiches at this do. I'm starving."

They bathed and changed, and Sarah caught him watching her as she did her make-up and put on her jewellery. He sang a lot of old songs and asked her about her day, and she felt tiredness dropping from her because of his energy.

14

They were ready to go at seven-thirty. He helped her on with her coat and opened the door on the chill evening.

"Forward to the big push," he said. "You look gorgeous. I'd prefer to stay in and remove all those clothes you just spent so much time putting on."

"You dirty old man." She grinned, bumping her hip against him as she went out ahead of him. He pulled the door to, throwing his keys up and catching them.

"I think I'll go down and see Tony this weekend. After Grandfather. You want to come?"

She was about to say yes, when the phone in the house started to ring.

"Never mind," he said. "It won't be important. We have big fish to catch."

They carried on to the car.

3

The police constables looked out of place in the old, oak-panelled function room. But for a minute, no one but Sarah noticed them. The presentation party was nicely into its swing. A four-piece band worked through a catalogue of polite rock standards; the perfumed, polished company of councillors, businessmen and the city's well-to-do stood about in small groups, eating succulent morsels and talking of money, property and holidays. At the far end of the room, Trevor Games was holding forth from a raised platform. His red comedian's face shone like a stop light at the interested crowd as he wound up his speech.

"And so, ladies and gentlemen, I'd like to give you the man whose design skills are going to change a row of neglected riverside warehouses into Norwich's prime shopping and leisure facility. A man who's been all too modest about his part in getting this project off the ground, a good friend to many of you, Mr David Kalska."

David was chatting with an acquaintance from the planning department as the applause began. The mention of his own name caught him by surprise. He turned to Sarah.

"I told him not to do this."

"Go on up," she said. "Get some glory for yourself."

He took a deep breath, squeezed her hand, and mounted the dais. She thought how much more alive than everyone else in the room he looked. She was proud of him.

"I don't really need to say anything," he declared, with an awkward gesture of his hands. "You've seen the video and the presentation, and I'm sure you don't want me to waste good champagne-drinking time by waffling on."

"You waffle, we'll drink," Trevor heckled from the floor.

"Thank you, Trevor." He scowled. "Mr Trevor Games, ladies and gentlemen, one of Norwich's great visionaries. Especially after the first three bottles of champagne."

There was laughter, while Trevor spluttered good-humoured protests. Sarah noticed the policemen scanning the room.

"But, truly," David continued, more seriously, "there's no need for me to say any more, because this – " he pointed to the table, where a scale model of the Wensum Mall development was laid out for all to see " – says it all for me. I just hope you'll agree that it'll be good for the city and for the people who invest in it." He gave a half-wave and stepped down.

"A man of few words," Trevor declared, as hands came together again. He chivvied the band back into action with 'Isn't She Lovely'.

David returned to Sarah, reaching for a glass of wine.

"Public speaking," he growled.

She touched his cheek fondly. "Oh, you humble beast. You did all right."

He grinned. "Suppose I did, didn't I?"

Someone grabbed his arm and started congratulating him on the development plans. It gave her a chance to check the doors again. The policemen had taken off their caps and were speaking to one of the catering staff. Guests nearby eyed them in surprise. Someone laughed and asked his friends if their cars were double-parked outside. The policemen were still engaged in murmured conversation with the caterer when Trevor approached.

The scent of a story overcame her better instincts. Leaving David in conversation with an elderly lady, she drifted towards the door. She saw the senior policeman nod and say:

"Evening, Mr Games."

16

Trevor liked being recognised. He took the policeman's arm and turned him away from the curious.

"What's the trouble, officer?"

She missed the next few words as someone handed her a glass of wine and introduced himself as 'a great fan' of her radio programme. Trevor frowned, then brightened.

"What is it? One of his buildings collapsed?" He stood on tiptoe to look over the officers' heads. "Sarah, where's David gone to?"

"Over by the window, last I saw." She joined them. The younger officer smiled at her. "What is it?"

"These gents want to see him for a minute."

"Is it important?"

"'Fraid so, miss," the older policeman said.

"I'll get him."

The band launched into 'Say You, Say Me'. She went to the Wensum Mall model, but he was no longer there. Talk flowed easily around her, and she could not hear his voice. Then she saw the rich old lady holding him by the sleeve and explaining her fears about investment in developments like this. He was listening carefully to her. Friends were trying to draw him into their circles, but the old lady was obviously lonely, and he kept listening.

She touched his shoulder. He smiled when he saw it was her.

"Hello. Having fun? This is Mrs Archley."

The old lady inclined her head and Sarah said hello.

"I'm sorry, Mrs Archley, but I have to take David away for a moment."

Sarah led him towards the door.

"What's the problem?" he said.

"I don't know. There're some policemen."

"Gatecrashers. Want me to throw 'em out?"

"They're asking to see you."

"Me?" He had little chance to show worry, because people kept hailing him enthusiastically as he passed, and he was required to smile and wave back. She could tell he didn't take her seriously yet, but he was serious enough when they reached the policemen.

"Evening, officers. Did Willie Roach send you?"

"Sort of, sir. Is there somewhere we could have a word?"

17

"Out on the stairs. Come on."

Sarah let go of his arm as he ushered the policemen out. People's attention had been caught. They craned their necks to see onto the landing of the grand staircase as David went into a huddle with the blue uniforms.

Sarah remained by the door, watching David's face for information. The bore who loved her radio show was back again, asking her opinion on the future of local radio. She hardly bothered to ignore him. David's eyes narrowed, then the colour went out of his cheeks. He said: "What?" loud enough for her to hear, and the older policeman fidgeted uncomfortably. Unable to hold back any longer, she passed through the door and went to David's side.

"Your grandfather is Mr Josef Kalska, is that right?" the older policeman was saying.

"Yes, what about him?"

"He presently lives at the Brackford House Residential Home?"

"Yes. Will you tell me what's happened?"

"It's a bit difficult."

She slid her hand through David's arm, but he hardly knew she was there, he was so tense.

"Just tell me," he snapped.

"Well, sir," the policeman bit his lip. "It seems he's escaped."

4

They arrived at Brackford just after 8.45. The house was ablaze with lights. As they stepped from the car, ancient faces peered from the windows.

"Why do they look so scared?" Sarah said.

David did not reply. The journey into the countryside had agitated his temper. He strode up the steps and into the hall without bothering to ring.

A baggy middle-aged woman shuffled importantly towards them.

"Excuse me," she said.

David cut in: "Tell Mrs Hawkes I'm here, would you."

Disconcerted, but still game, she said: "And who – ?"

"Mr Kalska's grandson."

The woman coloured. "Oh," she said, fastening three buttons of her cardigan. "She's at home. In the lodge, I mean, having a rest. I'll see if I can get her."

"Thank you," David said.

She hurried away, and David turned to pacing the length of the hall.

"He'll be all right," Sarah said.

He took her hand for a moment, but could not keep still. Shifting anxiously from foot to foot, he paused outside an open door. Sarah followed. They looked in on a spacious lounge. A huge television warbled to a gathering of high-backed chairs. The chairs contained old, old people, most of them quite still. They watched a situation comedy programme with varying degrees of concentration. Beyond them, others were reading newspapers, talking or knitting. A couple of sagging gentlemen played chess and read fat library books. A lady sat in a corner by a big stereo system, wrinkled face beatific between the black knobs of headphones. She conducted gracefully with a pencil. A wizened little man with huge eyes stared at them.

David pursed his lips and Sarah heard a low growl turning in his throat. "Damn it," he said, under his breath. "Damn it, damn it, damn it."

Heels clicked along a passage. Mrs Hawkes set her face to look determined but optimistic. She came at them with a good deal of attack, hand outstretched.

"Mr Kalska," she said, too bright and hard. Sarah winced, almost wanting to warn her to play it differently.

"Mrs Hawkes," David said. "Why did you wait so long to call the police?"

Mrs Hawkes faltered. "Perhaps we'd better repair to my office."

They followed her to a pale green room with heavy curtains. Sarah hardly spoke. This was not really her business, but she had come because she knew and loved Josef. She kept her peace, watching David. He was drawn so tight with worry that his temper hovered every moment on the edge of explosion.

Mrs Hawkes called for coffee, but David was not interested.

"To repeat," he said, framing the question with his long,

19

expressive hands. "Why did you take all day to alert the police? Not to mention me?"

Sitting behind a big, leather-topped desk, Mrs Hawkes felt safer. She took up a paper knife and began toying with it.

"I don't believe you could call it all day."

"The police tell me that my grandfather's absence was noticed at eight-thirty this morning. You informed them at three-twenty this afternoon. And *I* only get to hear about it at eight this evening. What have you been doing all day?"

"Mr Kalska, I understand your anger, but surely there's no need – "

"There's every need. I pay you a lot of money to make sure my grandfather lives out the fag end of his life in a decent, comfortable way. Part of your duty is to keep him safe, and you've lost him."

"That isn't fair."

"Is it fair to let a sick old man go wandering out on a sub-zero March night?" He became amazed by it again. "My God, it's not as if he could run anywhere very fast."

"Mr Kalska, you said yourself, your grandfather is rather unstable." The paper knife flickered from hand to hand with increasing speed.

"That's why you're paid to look after him, Mrs Hawkes."

"You don't seem to realise – "

"I realise very well. You've mislaid a frail old man of eighty-four years so thoroughly that the police can't find him."

"Mr Kalska, please . . ." She dropped the knife and put a hand to her face.

Sarah was about to speak, but David realised he had gone too far. It damped his rage, and the worry seemed to hit him a solid blow at last. He sat on the edge of a chair, arms hanging between his knees.

Mrs Hawkes collected herself, head bowed towards some papers for as long as it took to clear her eyes.

"Pardon me," David said at last. Quietly now. Sarah wanted to take his hand. He did not willingly hurt people, but anything concerning his grandfather touched a raw nerve.

"I quite understand," Mrs Hawkes said. "It's been a very strenuous day. The police have been here . . ."

Coffee was brought in by the baggy woman. Sarah caught

the exchange of glances that passed between her and Mrs Hawkes as the cups and saucers were laid down.

When they were alone again, Mrs Hawkes said to her: "We weren't introduced. Would you be Mrs Kalska?"

"Sarah Lipman. I've visited David's grandfather."

"Ah."

David cleared his throat. "Shall we begin again, and I'll do my best not to shout."

Mrs Hawkes appeared almost grateful.

"Contrary to what you've just seen," he said, "I didn't come here to issue writs. I just want to get it clear what's happened. I got the bones from the police, but if you could give me the details . . ."

"I've made notes." Mrs Hawkes referred to the papers in front of her. "Last night, Mr Kalska went to bed at his usual hour – about nine o'clock. He needed no help to prepare for bed. As you know, he was usually quite capable of getting about by himself."

"More so than you thought," David could not resist saying.

"Be that as it may, he was in his room by nine o'clock."

"How was he?"

"His usual self, I'm told. You last saw him at the weekend, I think? Well, he was no worse. A tendency to become confused occasionally, no more than that."

"What about the trances?"

"Trances?"

"He goes blank, for hours sometimes."

"Oh, yes. Strangely enough, he's shown fewer signs of the problem lately. He's been quite as alert as I've known him in the past weeks. Reading and making notes, adding to his collection of newspapers and magazines."

"Nothing unusual, though."

"Not that the staff noticed. At quarter past ten, Mrs Wilmut knocked on his door to make sure he was settled. She didn't see him. As you know, we try not to make our guests feel like inmates in a prison. Their privacy is respected. However, Mr Kalska was in his room. He assured her that he had everything he needed.

"That was all, until this morning, when he failed to appear at breakfast."

"Eight-thirty," David said. "Why didn't you call the police then?"

"You don't understand, Mr Kalska."

"Spot on, Mrs Hawkes."

Sarah was tempted to interrupt, to moderate. But this was his affair. She wouldn't like him butting in on her arguments at work.

"You have to remember that many of our guests suffer from periods of disorientation," Mrs Hawkes said. "They often do things which give cause for concern. For instance, Mrs Hart-Robinson – you might recall her; the lady who did so much for the arts in Norwich in the nineteen-fifties. Every morning at half-past nine, she declares that she must be getting off to the city gallery."

"I presume you catch her before she gets too far."

"We've grown used to her. Unfortunately, other guests aren't so predictable. And it has to be said that if we were to increase security here, our guests would lose much of the freedom they presently enjoy. The very reason your grand-father, as I remember, chose to come here."

"A trip down to the village pub is one thing," David muttered. "Unplanned holidays are another."

"The moment Mr Kalska's disappearance was noticed, of course, I instituted a search of the grounds. At that point, I imagined that he might have become confused and wandered off into the woods. It sometimes happens. Generally, we find whoever has gone missing and bring them back with no harm done."

"You should've called me, Mrs Hawkes."

"We did try. First at home, then at your office. We wondered whether Mr Kalska might have taken it into his head to visit you. But you were unavailable."

Sarah put her cup down. A phone rang in another room. An old man called out. The phone was answered.

"I take it you've looked in his room for clues?" David said.

"We thought of that. But you know how your grandfather was. There are several maps and guide books among his papers. Whatever project he's been involved with these past four years, it must be wide ranging."

David placed forefinger and thumb just to the outside of his

22

eyes and pulled the skin back and forth. "Damn," he said, then nothing more.

"The police searched as much of the countryside as they could before dark," she said. "There's very little cover at this time of year, so they should have been able to spot him quite easily. They found no trace."

"Do they think he's close by?" Sarah asked. She wondered whether the newsroom had this story yet.

"They couldn't say. At any rate, no one's reported sighting him. It goes without saying that we're – I'm – very worried for Mr Kalska. He's been very well-liked here."

"Don't rent out his room yet," David said. "They might find him."

"I do hope so."

"So do I." He stared at her, and she glanced away, perhaps thinking of the consequences if they did not.

The wizened little man in the lounge saw them going across the hall. Mrs Hawkes followed in their wakes, trying to reassure them or herself. He lifted himself urgently from his chair, tried to call out. The movement sent a jab of white pain through his belly. He collapsed again. They were at the door. He licked his lips, made to attract their attention with a wave of his skinny hand, tried to call again. His voice was a whisper lost in raucous music from the television.

Mrs Hawkes let them out of the house. They passed from sight.

The old man slumped back, cursing.

Speeding flatly along the main road back to Norwich, the black countryside rose and fell around them like a petrified ocean. He drove with icy concentration, sliding the car around bends and other traffic as if in a race.

At last, Sarah said: "Did you notice something?"

"Notice what?"

"The way they think Josef got out. Down the back stairs and everything. It didn't look like an old man going loopy and deciding to take a walk."

"What are you suggesting, Holmes?"

"It was more like a deliberate attempt to escape."

23

He slowed to pass through a cluttered village street. "I think your reporter's brain's looking for a story."

"All right, where do you think he is?"

"Search me," he said. "Poland maybe?"

His face was sculpted by the dashboard light. Control snapped at last. "Christ! What does he think he's doing? In the middle of March! If he doesn't turn up safe, I'll sue that bloody Hawkes woman for the whole rotten place."

She kept her voice low. "She was right, David. She can't keep them locked up all the time. Josef would hate that."

"What the hell's she there for? It's bad enough people have to go to places like that. They should be looked after."

"It's a good place."

"It's an expensive dump bin." He snaked past a Volkswagen as if it were standing still, speaking mainly to himself. "Why did I let him persuade me? If he was still at home, none of this'd be happening."

She had heard the story of how Josef went to Brackford House. Heard it from David and from Josef himself. To listen to David, it was a case of letting selfishness get the better of him when Josef suggested it. Josef told a different story: how David tried to persuade him against it, but he had wanted to go; to stop being a burden on the boy, to be in a place in the country where he could please himself without worrying that his increasing frailty inconvenienced his grandson. The second time she visited him, while David talked with Mrs Hawkes downstairs, Josef held her hand and smiled with his small, kind eyes.

"You are my boy's young lady, that is right?"

She made a half-nod, feeling strangely shy of the description.

"I bet he tells you he threw me in this place like an old dog?"

"Not quite like that," she said.

"I bet he tells you how he took advantage of an old man to make me come here, eh? The bad grandson, locking me away here so he can have some peace and quiet."

"He doesn't, honestly." That was just what he had said once after a few drinks, in a brittle, jokey way that almost convinced her.

"I made him send me here," Josef said. "What use am I now? That he should work so much, and have to worry what I do alone all day. You know how much this place costs?" He threw up his free hand. "It's a crime, just that. I would go some place cheaper, there are many good places. But he tells me: 'Grandfather, either it is this place or no place.' So, here I am happy. I'm not alone all day. If I was in his house, I would be bored, and he would wear himself out looking after me. This way is best. He can get on with what he should have done already, finding himself a nice girl to marry."

She blushed as he gripped her hand.

"The boy is guilty because he cannot do everything," Josef said. "He talks very hard sometimes, but you must know by now, he is soft inside."

Not exactly the word she would use. Yes, he was gentle and considerate, but the professional side, the wish to control everything was real enough. She had wanted to ask the old man why this was, but David always seemed to turn up just as she was about to mention the subject.

Passing County Hall on the way into the city, he asked: "Your place or mine?" He always asked, although she had practically been living with him for months now.

"Yours?" she said, using the question mark in case he wanted to be by himself.

They were at the house on Brewery Quay in a few minutes.

"Are you coming in?" she said.

He drummed the wheel, looking sharply about the shadows and entrances of the luxury flats across the river.

"I'll drive round a few places. Maybe I'll spot the old fool."

"Need company?"

"It's okay," he said, and she knew he wanted to be alone.

"I'll stay up in case he arrives here."

"Check the Brewers as well. For all we know, he's holed up there with a pint and a pasty."

"One thing," she said. "Do you want me to give this to the station?"

He was dubious.

"Even if it's just the jockey giving it a mention," she said. "It might help."

He nodded. "Yes, do it, please."

She started to get out, feeling obscurely hurt.

"Sarah."

25

She looked back. He reached out and held the back of her head tenderly, moving his thumb gently in her hair.

"Thanks for coming. Hasn't been much of an evening, has it?"

She leaned back into the car so she could kiss him. He touched her breast and held her for a moment.

"You're good," he said. He often said this, just the two words, and she wondered what he meant by it.

"Don't get lost yourself." She lifted her head for another kiss.

"A short tour of Norfolk in the dark." He smiled, anxiety just underneath.

She slipped out of the car, adjusted her coat and waved as he backed up to leave the cul-de-sac. She watched until he turned the corner, then started across the bridge towards the pub.

5

David dropped in at the police station on his way out. There was no further news, and Willie Roach had not come on duty. He left a message and headed out of town again on the London road.

He oscillated between fear and anger. What he was doing – trying to find one man in the wide, empty spaces between villages – was probably a waste of time, but it gave him something to do instead of sitting at home, fidgeting.

He switched the radio on as he swept through Wymingham, listened to the 11 o'clock news. There was a mention at the end, just the basics. But as he reached for the knob at the bulletin's conclusion, he heard the jockey say:

"About that last item. We've had a message from Sarah, our lovely lady producer and presenter, asking you all to keep a special eye open for Mr Kalska. Seems he's a friend of hers, and she'd dearly like to have him back safe and sound before the night's out. So, keep a lookout for the gentleman if you're out and about round the county tonight. It *is* a cold one."

He smiled faintly. She was as good as her word.

He cut off the main road and drove between acres of dead winter fields toward East Bickstead. Images nagged him. Grandfather lying still and stiff in some ditch the police had missed. A blind, childish panic worked in his stomach, and he tried to stay angry, because anger meant everything would be all right. He worked on what he would say when the old man was sitting in front of him.

He knew that he would say nothing. He would not insult Grandfather by treating him like a child. Never in all his life, not even when he *was* a child, had Grandfather done it to him. Strict, yes, plenty strict enough, but always as though they were both adults. There was no little boy stuff between them. Maybe it was because there were no women.

The road ducked into Thaxton Forest. Fir trees rose on either side and swallowed the sky. He took the narrow lane toward Witherley Heath, passing great swathes of ground littered with piles of bulldozed roots. He wished it were dawn. The road was metalled, but so uneven that a sign warned 'Vehicles may ground on road surface'. He went slowly, fearing he might round a bend and find Grandfather in his headlamps.

He almost missed the woodyard. New trees had grown along the roadside, concealing it. He pulled over onto the grass and got out of the car.

A few arc lights ached in the dark. They picked out stacks of lumber, a few huts, a mobile crane. He stepped up to the chain link fence and stuck his fingers through, searching for configurations of the past.

This was where Grandfather had come with his single remaining child in the years after the last war. From the barbed wire of a camp in Poland to this place, enclosed by trees, which was rather similar in appearance. Grandfather, a man of forty-three years, and his daughter, Luba. David had seen the picture of them taken just after they arrived. Both of them weak and drawn, standing with cheap cardboard suitcases and bemused expressions in front of a wooden hut. Luba, a dark, starved-looking girl of sixteen, with eyes like flat black nails. Josef trying to smile and show his pride at a new start, Luba blank, like someone who could not wake. It was one of the few pictures of his mother that David had.

He walked along the verge beside the fence, trying to see the huts where the Polish and Ukrainian refugees had lived.

27

They used to stand off to the left of the yard, but he suspected they were gone now.

Returning to the gate, he looked for warning signs. There was nothing about guard dogs. He hefted himself up on the gate, dropped to the other side and walked across the sandy earth. The arc lights twinged in the corners of his eyes, burning purple streaks on the night.

He called out: "Grandfather?" Not Granddad. The old man never liked it, even when he knew English well. He always referred to himself as "your grandfather, boy," and it stuck. Early training goes a long way, David thought, checking the works office where Grandfather used to go every morning to be given his task for the day.

For twenty years, Grandfather – who was a bookseller in his former life – went out and cut wood for the country which had taken him and his daughter in. Through those early days in the huts and then the little council house by the church; through the years of trying to bring Luba back to life; through David's birth and Luba's death, he worked until there was nothing about his appearance to suggest he had ever done anything else.

David skirted the great piles of timber. The huts were still there, but unlived in. They hunkered low under the trees. They were so tiny, he could not believe it. They had lived here for, what, ten years almost. Until he came along and the council did something about their living conditions. He called out again, only heard his voice too loud in the frostbound forest. He rapped on the doors.

Which one had they lived in? He should remember. Grandfather had brought him here often enough, pointing it out, holding his hand tight and telling the story. "When we finally were free," he would say, "we came here. We lived here, and I worked, and your mother, ah, she tried so hard. But no good, no good, you see?" David would listen, not seeing. "Was I here then?" he asked once. "No, not you boy. You came later."

It was the second from the left. He went back to it and stood on the rotting porch. Then he tried the door and it gave reluctantly. He stepped inside.

"Grandfather, you here?" A rat scuttled. He went through each small room, stepping on bundles of old newspaper. The smeary windows showed abstracts of the lights outside.

28

His mother had sat here day after day, before she was his mother. A young woman with old eyes, rocking slowly in a chair bought from an auction in Thaxton. A big brown radio playing endlessly in the corner. Rock, rock, rock. Needles clicking in her thin fingers, eyes on the window, a view of green branches and passing faces.

David always saw this as if he had witnessed her long hours of loneliness for himself. Grandfather told him so many times that it became his own memory. "That is how she was," he would say, and break down quietly. David would put his arms round the old man's shoulders, trying to comfort him, even while the memory became so familiar that it ceased to have any meaning.

He closed the door, as if there were someone who should not be disturbed.

"Grandfather." His shout fell dead off the timber and trees and the freezing night air.

The church of Witherley Heath was just after the village sign. Next to it was the council house where he had lived until the age of eleven, when Grandfather retired and they moved to a flat in Norwich. Nothing seemed to have changed in twenty years. The village was still a long time dying. A single light glowed in the front bedroom of the house. This was what he remembered for himself. Not with his mother in it, though. She died when he was two years old. He believed that he recalled nothing about her, but the scent of honeysuckle always gave him a strange, warm feeling, because honeysuckle had grown in the back garden, and it meant being held, and a voice humming gently to him.

This was the place where, as Grandfather put it, Luba made a last bid to live a real life. It was Grandfather's sadness that he had not been the one who helped her to try. It had been a man, a lorry driver for some company up north. Grandfather hardly ever talked of it. As far as David had been able to discover, this man used to come down once a fortnight to pick up a load of timber. He noticed the silent girl who lived in one of the huts. Somehow he managed to draw Luba out of her loneliness. David had a sketchy picture of her standing on the porch, stumbling over English words she never learned to use well. His father was a shadow. All he knew was that there had been a brief affair of some kind, then pregnancy and the usual desertion by a man who already had a family back home. Grandfather obviously blamed the man for his daughter's death. He saw her betrayal after the effort to live again as the final blow. David gave up asking long ago, because of the pain in Grandfather's eyes at any mention. He knew his position in the result, because of the things kids shouted at him in the playground when he was a boy. He knew all about that.

There were so many taunts to throw, no wonder they could not resist it. A small, dark child who came to the school speaking bad English with a strong accent because Grandfather spoke mainly Polish or Yiddish at home. "He's a polish," Tommy Durrell would giggle, pronouncing it like furniture polish. "Hent got a dad, hent got a mum." "Talks funny." "Bastard." "Jew boy, Jew boy." "My mum says your mum was a prozzy." "Prozzy boy."

Not important now. He thought of it all with vague irony. It did not matter, as Grandfather used to tell him when he came home dusted over from another fight. Eventually, the jeers grew tiresome even for the kids throwing them. He saw how it was mostly boredom that made them do it, and a natural urge to attack the odd one out. That gave him an edge. It allowed him to operate on them without their knowing, so that eventually he led his own gang and found out how to make people do what he wanted. It left him with the feeling that familiarity did not breed contempt, only indifference, which is pretty close to acceptance.

But different then – the fact that everyone knew more of his parents than he did.

A car squealed past. He shivered and took a torch from his pocket, walked up the path to the church. He shone the beam on old graves. Where was Arnold Ginch? He had always thought of Arnold as his special concern. A plain headstone with the name on it, and a record of his having died somewhere in the desert in 1943. "Sorely missed." Not quite so sorely now. The stone was faded, the grave overgrown.

Half-hoping to find Grandfather slumped in the shadows of the porch, he grasped the rusted handle. No one bothered to lock the church now.

"Grandfather?" The question went out in the echoing dark

30

like a bat on the wing. The beam encircled threadbare matting and polished stone, cracked pews and damp walls.

Grandfather used to come here. Had to when he wanted to worship his God. The nearest synagogue was in Norwich. He never went to Christian services, but attended alone whenever he felt the need. It was God's house, he said, and it would do as well as any. Sometimes David would want to find him, and he would look in the church first. The old man would be sitting three rows back from the pulpit on the right hand side of the aisle, head down on the varnished wood, unmoving. David would tap him on the shoulder very lightly, and he would glance up with eyes very clear. He would ask the boy to pray with him. David always did, but he never felt anything. Grandfather would say: "Pray for your mother." He would recite the Kaddish, the Hebrew prayer for the dead, and David would listen, join in. But it was never real. His mother was nowhere; he did not know her except in a few blurred photographs. In a corner of his mind she had become like everything Grandfather told him. "Remember your past," he would say, "and the past of your people. Do not forget." He did not seem to realise that David could not forget what he never knew. The stories Grandfather told were of a country he had never seen, of a family he never could see, because they were gone. Kneeling beside the old man in the brown light of the church, he had chiefly felt a kind of bafflement. Later, this solidified into an intellectual attitude, and caused most of their rows.

The church was empty.

He closed the door, hearing again the alien sound of the Kaddish echoing up to the roof of Christian angels. It was all lost.

He drove next through Thaxton and on towards Diss, taking out his frustration in the empty miles on a lumbering container lorry. It sometimes occurred to him that his father might still be driving some fat rig around the country, but he could not say it bothered him. Grandfather was his father, if anyone was. His biological dad had probably clogged his heart to a stop on a diet of fry-up and Yorkie bars by now.

I want to find you, you old fool. I want to be the one who brings you home.

31

And there would be no more of that Brackford House rubbish. That was an experiment which was over. No matter what the old man said this time, he would come home, and staff would be hired to look after him, if that was what it took.

He barrelled north to the villages by the river, down the lonely spine of the Haverley road. The sugar beet factory across the marshes below shone like a miniature city. Nothing else for miles. The old church loomed out of the night. He passed it and went on down the farm track toward Haverley Staithe. When he got out of the car, the stony chill of the lowlands hit him. He could hear the factory working in the distance. The rest was desolation.

He climbed the path and shone his torch across the dyke. It was a depressing sight: boats parcelled up against the winter, their hulls like dead fish in the black water. Everything seemed to be in a state of disrepair. Landing stages leaned at crazy angles, bits of oily rope lay in coils in the stiff grass. Dismantled masts stuck out of drab tarpaulins. He walked slowly along the bank, calling out. The cheerful names mocked him. *Fortune*, *Daisy*, *Spirit of Freedom*. The dyke contained a good cross-section of craft, from little dinghies, to Tony Chandor's cruiser, *Calliope*.

"Grandfather?" He walked out on the stage marked *Marie Celeste II* and climbed aboard.

They bought her in 1977, after David caught the bug sailing with friends. A 26-foot Broads yacht with dish-hull, lifting part to the cabin top, and a draw of less than three feet. When he found her she was an ex-hire boat called *Angel Baby*. For several years she remained at the sailing club; then Tony Chandor had found a mooring here. They had put a lot of work into her. Nearly every evening for a whole summer, they drove out of Norwich in the old camper David had then, and cleaned her up. That was the part Grandfather enjoyed. David thought of him sitting in the cockpit, his long brown hands like part of the woodwork as he clutched a paintbrush and sang some old tune. He grew to love being out on the broad river between Norwich and Breydon Water. Even after he went to Brackford House, David took him sailing as often as he could get away from his work.

She was beautiful now, light as a leaf and fast-sailing in the faintest wind. Last summer, when Sarah was becoming a major feature, she also came along. The best times were when Tony could also free himself of business for a day and the two boats could sail downriver to Goldeston Lock, where the pub served a particularly rancid brand of cider that appealed to Grandfather. Sarah beside him, Grandfather hungrily watching the fields and woods sliding by, a bottle of some good wine hanging over the side to cool. And sunlight, to break the clench of this awful night.

The air seemed frozen to stillness. Stars were bits of white bone. He did not call out any more. He worked his way round the cabin, lifted the tarpaulin and peered in. It was all in order. No one had been here.

Trundling back up the lane, he noticed lights still on at the Hall. Although it was nearly two in the morning, he knew Tony's nocturnal habits well. He turned down the narrow track by the church and wound the car between bare black oaks.

The Hall stood half a mile away. It was a large farmhouse, parts dating back nine hundred years. The woods behind backed onto Haverley Marsh and the small river. Tony had obtained it cheap two years ago, after a publisher of glamour magazines was murdered there. He bought it partly because it was bang in the middle of his constituency, mainly because it was close to the rivers.

David stopped the car two hundred yards away and walked the rest. He headed for the front door rather than the entrance in the yard, skirted the garden to look in at the lighted window.

Through a gap in the closed curtains, he saw Tony, his great healthy frame stretched on the long couch by the embers of a big fire. Sal, the English setter, curled below him on a scatter of papers. Tony had his square-rimmed spectacles on. He thought they gave him an air of gravity in the House. He wore tweedy suits for the same reason. In fact, both ploys only made an observer think just how much of a young gentleman farmer he looked. He was holding a sheaf of papers at arm's length under the lamp, peering confusedly. He always seemed perplexed while reading reports, and that was another mistake his opponents made, because his brain was very quick.

David tapped on the glass. Sal got up, growling softly. Tony's head shot round so fast that he must have cricked his neck. He quieted Sal with a gesture and moved cautiously towards the window. He squinted out, recognised David and opened up.

"What the hell are you doing here?" he demanded, in a furious whisper.

"Sorry," David said. "Thought it was better than rousing the entire house."

"I assumed you were the ghost of the previous owner, for God's sake. Why didn't you bring a jemmy and break in through Julia's window?"

"She wouldn't understand."

"I'm not altogether sure I do." He gazed upon David like an exasperated but fond parent. "Are you coming in, or shall I hand your drink out to you?"

"If it's not too much trouble."

"Well clamber in. I'm not unlocking the bloody door at this time of night."

David entered. Sal growled again. Tony patted her head as he crossed the room to the drinks cabinet.

"Don't mind him, Sal. It's just our friend the cat burglar."

When she saw who it was, Sal came to David, tail beating the air.

"This isn't one of your ways of being spontaneous, is it?" Tony said, returning to the hearth with a couple of large whiskies. "I mean, two o'clock in the morning and all. Or were you just bored?"

They settled by the fire, Tony sprawled among his papers, David in a wing-backed chair. The grandfather clock measured time with heavy beats. He realised he had not eaten since lunch the previous day.

"Grandfather's disappeared," he said.

Tony paused in nibbling at his drink. "Oh, my Lord," he said, sitting up abruptly. "And I go yammering on like a fool. No wonder you look so foul." He rose. "Finish that drink up and I'll fix you another." He poured them and brought them back, cleared the papers and sat closer to David as he fired questions. When, where from, how? David filled in the details while the warmth of the fire and the whisky spread through him, adding to his tiredness. When he was done, Tony said:

"And you thought he might have turned up here? I see your point. But if he's been gone since last night – night before last,

34

rather – he should've put in an appearance by now. Even walking at his speed, Brackford's only fifteen miles from here."

"I don't know what to think."

Tony dipped a finger in his whisky and offered it to Sal. "I haven't seen old Josef since last summer. That day down at Reeford. He must have – grown quite poorly."

"They reckon not."

"Nevertheless, he buzzes off into the night without a word to anyone." Tony sighed. "Look, if you need an extra hand for the search, I'll get the car out."

"Can't think of anywhere else to look," he said, knowing he should have thanked Tony for the offer. But they had known each other for a long time, and most things did not need saying. "If I could snoop round your sheds, I'll push off."

"You're bloody exhausted. Why not bed down here for a few hours? There's nothing to be done till morning."

"I can't sit still. Besides, I want to check back with the police."

"Well, we'll give the outbuildings the once-over, but I shouldn't imagine he's there."

"Humour me."

"By all means."

Tony slipped on a pair of shoes and they went through the silent house, through the big, disorganised kitchen to the side door. Tony switched on the lights and they checked each barn and shed together. There was much farm machinery, plastic sheets, old straw and rat droppings, but no sign that Grandfather had been there.

As they closed the last door and Sal went ambling back to the house, Tony drew off his spectacles – he had forgotten them until then.

"My God," he muttered. "After all he's been through."

"I keep thinking that."

"Oh, look, he must be all right. You know what an old charmer he is. Some ancient widow's probably holding him hostage even as we speak."

David shivered. Then he said: "What'll I do if he's dead, Tony?" His voice had lost all colour. He stared hopelessly at the ground. Tony put an arm round his shoulder. They stood that way, not for long. Then David thrust his hands in his pockets and took a deep breath.

"He'll be fine," Tony said, his reassuring voice going up against the reality of the cold. "He's the toughest old bird I know."

"Yes," David said. He turned. "Thanks for not shooting me. I'll let you know if we find him."

"You'd better. I'm holding surgeries tomorrow, but Julia can always get a message to me. And if you need anything, anything at all, you know where I am."

"Thanks for the drink." David began to walk away.

"And when he does turn up," Tony called out, "tell him he's required to crew the *Calliope* this spring."

"I'll tell him." David tipped him a nod and went on.

There was one more stop to make: the council flat on Union Street where he and Grandfather had lived for ten years. He pulled up outside the building just after 3.30. Most streetlamps were out. The hospital gleamed orange above the rows of flats. He tried the double doors at the foot of his block. They were never locked. This building, and most on the street, housed pensioners. He went quietly through the stairwell to look at the back yard. Plastic dustbins and a washing line. After that he checked the first floor and the door of their old flat.

The day they had moved to the house on Brewery Quay, Grandfather was very doubtful. He liked the certainty of staying in one place. He felt safe in council accommodation.

"What happens if you cannot pay the mortgage?" he asked, as removal men took their belongings down to the lorry. "We always have a roof as long as the Government provides it." He always spoke of 'the Government' in trusting terms, because it had been good to him.

David several times explained how well he was doing, designing interiors for shops and businesses in the city, and how the property he had bought for a pittance had sold for a vastly increased sum. They could afford a proper place of their own. Brewery Quay was not expensive then. This was before the developers – he among them – converted the old warehouses and cleared the slums to make way for apartment complexes. At that time, it was a run-down piece of old Norwich, the river running past between walls of brick. The house itself was sprawling, in need of work. David got it cheap, knowing that it would be in the middle of the new building. "It's right on the river," he said. "We'll have space to moor a little boat of our own. It'll be great."

Grandfather shook his head, sorrowing mightily. For a long time after they moved, he would still talk about what would happen to them if the house was taken away.

A tortoiseshell cat with bright, suspicious eyes came up the stairs, surveyed him with streetwise insolence, and slinked through the catflap into the flat. David descended to his car, sat at the wheel staring blankly at the street.

A yawning sergeant sat behind the desk at City Hall station. David asked for Detective Inspector Roach, and was directed upstairs as usual. The squad room smelt of cigarettes and stale coffee. Two men in shirtsleeves were on phones. They turned bored eyes in his direction as he knocked on Willie's door.

"Yes?" The shout was a question joined with the invitation to enter. It suggested that here was a busy man with no time for fools. The man himself reinforced the impression. He crouched behind a stack of files, also using the phone. His long, balding head was youthful but sharp. He spoke in quick bursts of Putney-accented monosyllables. His eyes were piercing blue, his tie was neatly tied, and his jacket hung squarely from its own wooden hanger on the back of the door. He had been a friend since they met at the sports club in town when Willie was first transferred to Norwich, but these days they more often shared a drink than a game of squash.

David sat down and waited for the conversation to finish. The padding of the chair invited sleep, but he watched steadily until Willie signed off with a barked goodbye and replaced the receiver neatly in the cradle.

"Anything?" he asked.

Willie dotted the file under his hand with rapid stabs of a propelling pencil. "We've been trying to get hold of you. Phoned your place, got Sarah. She told us you were conducting your own search. I put out the word, but obviously no one saw you."

"That means you've got something?" David leaned forward.

Willie marshalled his thoughts. "You want a coffee? No? Well, we have it, fairly reliably, that a taxi picked your granddad up in Brackford on Tuesday night. Been asking around, but never got to this bloke till he came on duty this evening. I had a word with him myself. He wondered about the old man's accent, but as he said: he's a taxi driver, not a private detective. Here's the funny bit, though. He gave a fake name. Blum, he said he was. Any reason you know of why he should do that?"

"We don't even know a Blum."

"And he had a story about his car breaking down. Doesn't sound much like senility to me, more like a calculated escape attempt."

"So, where did he take him?"

"The railway station. Dropped him there at twenty past ten."

"The station?" David growled. "What did he go there for?"

"To buy a ticket on the last train for Ely." Willie pursed his lips and his eyes scanned the office window. "I hoped you'd know what it meant, but I see you don't."

"Any idea where he got off?"

"Haven't nailed it yet. Can't even be sure he got on in the first place. It's one of those two-carriage jobs; buy your ticket on the train. Only reason we know he might have been on it is that he tried to buy one at the office. The conductor doesn't remember anyone for sure – he was nipping it a bit in the guard's van between stops – and we haven't tracked down any passengers yet. Besides, he might've bought a ticket for Ely, then got off halfway."

"The line goes through Thaxton, doesn't it?"

"Wymingham, Attlebridge, few little stations, then Thaxton, Borden, Larkheath. I've got people checking them."

"He might have gone to Thaxton to reach where we used to live."

"The real stumper is that no one's stopped him yet. Someone should be down at Ely station now, seeing if he bought another ticket there, but you'd think someone'd notice an old man wandering about."

David stood. He did not know what to do with himself any more.

Willie left his desk and came round, pulling the wrinkles out of his waistcoat. "Go home, get some rest. I'll be onto you soon as we find out where he got off the train." He opened the door, took David's arm. "Believe me, now we've got the first lead, we'll have him in no time."

*

What's he playing at? David wondered, as he drove home. Taxis, trains, false names; none of it made sense.

He put the car in the garage and walked over the bridge to take a last look round. The pub was shut, the flats round the courtyard silent and dark. The river moved noiselessly beside his house, lapping a foot beneath the cellar windows. The house was deep. At the back was a railed-off patio. In summer, four people could squeeze round a table and watch the bridge and the river as they ate. A ladder went down to a mooring post where he kept a little motorboat.

Grandfather used to tend all kinds of plants on the patio, and had his bedroom-cum-study in one of the big ground floor rooms at the back. They had lived quite peaceably that way for five years, until Grandfather started to fall over rather often, and to ask where his wife and family had gone. His mind turned increasingly to the past, jumping back to a life he no longer possessed. David stood it for a long time, but not long enough to satisfy himself. He did his best to look after the old man, but his workload then was heavy, and he began to dread the moments when Grandfather's eyes unfocused, when he started calling him Aron or Ben. Coupled with the constant flow of books and magazines concerning the war, and the reminders to be aware of what had been done to his people, it became a dark motif in every day.

The repetition only reinforced his aversion. There was no point that he could see: he was not Jewish, not Polish. He had no country to return to. He was English, and bewailing the fate of a family he never knew would only have kept him from getting somewhere in the world he was stuck with. At first he argued with the old man, telling him that his obsession with the past was the cause of his wandering, but it did no good. After a long while, he sensed that he might soon begin to hate his grandfather because of what he was becoming in his decline. He was only twenty-eight then, not old enough to deal with it. So, when Grandfather, in one of his perfectly lucid moments, mentioned living elsewhere, he was more ready to listen than he would admit, even to himself. But he still hated himself for doing it. And if they found Grandfather now, he would not allow him to go away again.

He let himself in to the big house that he now shared, unofficially, with Sarah. She was not downstairs. He shrugged

39

off his coat, fetched a glass of water and some cold chicken from the fridge, and tiptoed down the hall to Grandfather's room. It was ready for him, as always. The books and pictures he had not taken to Brackford House, the Indian chess set on which they had played thousands of games, and a big reconditioned Murphy radio by the bed so he could listen to it when nightmares kept him from safe sleep. David sat on the bed and fingered the tuning dial. Luxembourg, Cologne, London, Athlone.

He closed his eyes on the dial's wide sweep of the world.

Where are you?

6

It wasn't right.

Blind darkness. A dull wind with ice in it cut Josef's face and hands.

He wandered across the bend in the road. His feet dragged, but he could no longer feel them. Tears ran down his face and froze in the seams of his flesh. He could feel nothing.

Oh, God, why has it gone so wrong?

The road climbed away from him on both sides. He was near the bottom of a hill, trees behind him, a wall in front, the faint trickle of water somewhere below. He was alone. He was frightened and raging at himself.

I have done nothing. I have failed.

He stumbled onto the verge and fell to his knees. Sobbing, his head descended until it touched the spikes of grass. He put out senseless hands and levered himself up, then turned over and sat heavily on the ground.

He had not eaten for over 24 hours, he had been out in the cold since last night, but he did not think of this. His mind burned only with his failure.

He raised his head, felt the tendons strain and the bones creak. He searched for some light, saw only a thin scatter above and far off. He was alone in all the dark world. And what had he accomplished?

All this way he had come, pushing his body on when he

thought he must drop, fighting the confusion which always threatened to engulf him, facing the onslaught of a world he no longer knew. And it was over in a moment, like the tides being stopped by one upraised hand.

"Sent me away," he whispered, the words dribbling out along with his tears. "Like some dog they sent me away."

"Papa!"

He jerked round at the cry. Luba? Or was it Ben? Where were the children? Behind him a dry stone wall glistened faintly, skeleton trees reared up against the stars.

"I tried," he said, and his heart shook in its cage of skin. "I don't know what happened."

"Papa."

"Get down," he warned. "They will see you."

"What happened, Papa?" Luba was close, murmuring in his ear, but he could not see her. "What happened?"

"Not strong enough." He clasped his left wrist. It was dead to the touch. Heart flickered thinly.

"Papa, what will happen to us?" The fear in her voice. It filled him with a terror of knowledge. He had failed to do what he spoke so bravely of doing. He was here in this loneliness with nothing left but certainty of what was to come. If only Yitzhak were with him. If only the boy . . . But the boy knew nothing.

"Please, Papa, I'm cold."

He saw Luba's face, thirteen years old. The colour gone, the grey eyes huge and dull.

He staggered up, whispering her name, and she flew from him. He lurched and almost fell again. One shoe scraping on the road, he turned in a circle, trying to find his children.

"No man knows what it is to fear until he has children of his own."

Who told him that? Uncle Mavro. How long was it since he saw him?

He lifted his eyes to the other side of the road. There was sound from above. Lights flared high up in the trees.

He thought: It cannot end this way. I did not come so far to lose like this.

"Papa, please . . ."

He tried to straighten his back, and the cold clutched him through his clothes. The lights were coming towards him,

41

flashing through branches. A roar began in his ears, and he believed it was the sound of his own blood, then the rumble of railway carriages. He willed his hands to work again, but they were useless. He started towards the narrow opening in the trees opposite. The light flamed from that opening now, and the roar grew louder.

"Papa."

All right, child, I'm coming now. Don't fear.

He saw them moving before him, his wife and children, and they were going ahead of him. He thought: This time I will keep them from harm. This time.

The light burst over them with lovely brightness, bathing him too in its warmth.

He threw up his arms and welcomed the light.

7

The alarm woke him at seven. Sarah reached over and silenced it, but he was awake as if a switch had been thrown.

He lay under the covers, unmoving, while Sarah slipped out of bed and put on her dressing gown. He was worn out, and could not remember why for a moment. Then she turned, smoothing her hair out, and looked at him with concern, and it all fell into place.

She knelt on the bed and kissed his cheek.

"Stay there. You must be shattered."

He watched her with one eye as she disappeared into the bathroom. She was brisk in the mornings. He listened to the sounds of water running and her toothbrush, wishing it had been the phone that woke him.

When she came back and plugged in her hot brush, he was out of bed and choosing clothes for the day.

"Aren't you staying in bed?" she said. "You came in so late."

"Things to do." He frowned at a black tie.

"What about Josef?"

Both of them were tired, and he should have kept it in mind. Instead, he shot back: "I still have things to do."

She sat at the dressing table and began to do her make-up.

David continued, hearing how matter-of-fact he sounded. "I can't do any more. Last night's trip into our humble past didn't get me anywhere." He pulled the curtains. He felt as if he had not seen daylight for weeks. He told her what Willie Roach had discovered.

Sarah examined her face in the mirror. "Are you going to ring him now?"

"When they have something, they'll ring me." He grabbed a shirt from the drawer. "One way or the other."

That gained him another accusing glance. He ignored it and sat down on his side of the bed again. None of what he was saying was true. He intended calling Willie, then rejoining the search. For whatever use that was.

Sarah was side-on to him, furiously brushing her hair. The rise and fall of her arm made the dressing gown tighten rhythmically against her breast, her legs were crossed under the dressing table. Desire stirred with the need of her warmth, and he wished he had started the day better, because a gentle interlude with her would certainly distract from Grandfather. But she had to be at the studios by eight.

Sarah picked up the hot brush. He wondered why they still had mornings like this, when they seemed to get up with the intention of grating on each other's nerves.

She pressed the steam button on the brush. Wisps rose from her hair. He wondered what they would be like if they were married.

He got up and matched tie with shirt. *We* didn't get up crabby, he thought. *I* did. He dropped the clothes and went over to her. He put his arms round her neck and looked at their reflections.

"Apology?" he said. "I'm all buggered up about Grandfather."

She held his hand. "I know. I'm sorry."

He kissed the crown of her hair. "I'm going to make a large breakfast. Care for some?"

"No." She never ate breakfast. "Be nice if you got the coffee going, though."

"Would, wouldn't it?" He pulled on his dressing gown and went downstairs. He switched on Radio Three and found them playing sixteenth-century lute music.

The rich smell of coffee began to fill the kitchen as he broke open eggs, bread and tomatoes. He did it to feed his hunger, also because cooking occupied and calmed his mind.

Sarah came down, poured her coffee and re-tuned the radio to her own station. She wore a dark blue suit and court shoes. She looked businesslike, but sexy too. She always looked a little more sexy than he thought would be good for his concentration if he were doing business with her. The first time he met her, when she interviewed him for a programme about local success stories, he had taken some minutes to gather his thoughts on the proper topic.

She sipped her coffee. On the third finger of her left hand, she wore a great opal ring that had to do with someone who happened before him.

The radio fanfared the news, a female voice launched into a familiar catalogue of gloom and doom. Trouble in the Gulf, a nuclear leak at Sellafield – officially regarded as 'unimportant', another scandal brewing in the city. Then:

"A Norwich man is still missing from home after almost thirty-six hours. Police are 'very worried' about the health of Mr Josef Kalska and are widening their search. Mr Kalska is the grandfather of Norwich architect and property owner, Mr David Kalska, who is the designer of the proposed new Wensum Mall development."

He stopped eating. His eyes were bleak.

She came round the table and took his hand. He followed her almost meekly to the couch. Sitting there, she hugged him for a time. Then she said:

"Tell me what you're feeling."

His head rested in the hollow of her neck. She wanted him to talk, but it was not something he did easily when the matter was serious. Self-sufficiency, learned early, was a difficult cage to break out of.

"I want to help," she said.

"You do, just by putting up with me. Don't worry, I'm all right." He pressed his lips to her forehead so that her make-up would be undisturbed. "You've got to go to work."

At the front door, she paused and turned to him.

"I feel wrong about going."

"Go and entertain the masses." He was in control again. It was better this way. "I'll call if anything happens."

"I'll try to get back at lunchtime."

"Probably won't be here."

"I'll call you then . . . Somewhere." She was outside in the hard white morning. Still uncertain.

He let go of her hand, and she tapped away across the pavement. Cold air pricked his face. A milk float trundled into the courtyard of the flats down the road. She glanced back as she turned the corner. He had waited to be sure he would be there if she did. He waved, smiled reassuringly. She looked unhappy.

The phone chirped in the lounge. He was on it before it could ring three times.

"David?" It was Willie Roach.

He tensed. "What's the news?"

Willie said: "He's turned up."

David knew it was not good.

"We've just had a report in. He's been involved in a car accident."

"Oh, shit." David sat down.

"Don't have many details yet, but he's in hospital."

"How bad?"

"Doesn't say . . ." He coughed, embarrassed by the attempt to deceive. "Pretty bad."

Several seconds passed before he could force himself to speak again. "Okay," he said, "I'd better get to him. Where is he? Norfolk and Norwich?"

"He's not here," Willie said.

Incomprehension. "Where then? He didn't get to Ely, did he?"

The line crackled. "I don't know how or why . . ."

"Willie, where is he?"

"Edinburgh."

8

He tried to get a flight from the airport, but nothing was going soon enough. He phoned the radio station, left a message for Sarah. Then he put together an overnight bag, threw it in the car and set out for Peterborough. He meant to pick up the

Edinburgh train there, but by the time he bypassed Bishop's Lynn, he had decided to drive it. The journey was more than 350 miles, and he had never been there before, but anything was better than twiddling his thumbs on a 125.

He stopped once for coffee and a bite to eat at a service station outside Grantham. Hitting the road again, he played Beethoven then Kate Bush loud to block out too much thought. But all the way up, as the country changed and the light shifted, he came back to the same question:

What was Grandfather doing in Scotland?

Big blue signs flashed by like frames from a road movie. Only the surroundings and the traffic changed. Just beyond Newcastle-upon-Tyne, the sky turned sour black and rain began to spatter the windscreen. By the time he neared the border, it was shovelling down. Redesdale passed in a mist, and Catcleugh Reservoir danced under the raindrops.

The hospital had refused to let much out. Grandfather was 'serious', but they would not say what his injuries were. They knew little about the accident. He was going to stop in Galashiels to phone again, but realised he was only thirty-odd miles from Edinburgh, and pushed on. The nearer he got, the more sick he felt. The rain slackened, leaving the empty hills under a pall of darkness like the coming of night.

Just let him be all right, he thought. Never mind that he's old and has to die some day. Just let it not be today.

A small, wiry-haired nurse caught him as he searched for the ward. He must have looked half-crazy; still frantic from driving round the city to find the Royal Infirmary, exhausted from running about the sprawling grounds. She started to tell him he shouldn't be here at this time of day.

"Josef Kalska," he panted. "Where?"

She scuttled off to find someone. David barged through double doors and found himself in a general ward. Rows of bed-ridden men stared at him. He let the doors swing back and went along the old corridor, checking names on doors. One of them did not have a name. He pushed it ajar.

Grandfather was in there.

He stopped. Shock went over him like a wave of dizziness. The door swung shut. He nudged it open again and went

46

inside. No one else was there. Just a clean, pale yellow room with partly-shaded window, a cabinet, a chair, and the bed.

He walked round it, afraid. Not of the bed or the shrunken figure stretched under the clothes. It was all the apparatus surrounding it. One box of lights monitored the heart rate, another thing on a trolley breathed quietly down a tube into Grandfather's mouth. A bag full of yellow liquid hung down at the bedside. He only realised it was urine after some time.

He was unsure how he recognised his grandfather. One arm was in a sling, the other wrapped with a blood pressure cuff. The head was encased in bandages and electrodes. Only the wrinkled eyelids, fallen back in the skull, and the great blade of a nose told him. This was his grandfather, who had been so strong. He was almost part of the machinery.

David pulled a chair to the bedside. He touched the right hand. It trembled briefly. He could hardly think an entire sentence. Memory threw up all the stupid things people said in hospital dramas on the television. He could not remember the last time he told Grandfather he loved him. He felt as if his head would burst.

The nurse returned with a fat Sister and a man in a crumpled brown suit. David cleared his throat, rose to meet them. The man stuck out his hand.

"You're Mr Kalska's grandson? I'm Mr Lymon, the ortho-paedic registrar. Shall we step out for a minute?" He was perhaps thirty-five, his voice a softened Glasgow burr. He needed a shave and about two days' sleep.

In a tiny office three doors down the corridor, Lymon said: "What've they told you?"

"Nothing. I've been all day getting here."

Lymon turned up the notes on a clipboard the Sister handed him.

"RTA, admitted at two twenty-five this morning. Fractures of both legs and left arm, three cracked ribs on the left side, lacerations to arms, legs, back and scalp, major fracture of the skull."

"Christ, what hit him?"

"I don't know that. The police have those details. They're with the driver now."

"Where?"

47

"Look, why don't you sit down again. You look all-in. Sister, is there any chance of a cup of tea?"

She nodded to the nurse.

"And one for me, please," Lymon called after her. "I beg your pardon, Mr Kalska. I'm parched. Been in surgery all day."

David sat by a narrow window, staring out at the old hospital buildings stained by the rain.

"There's also some internal injury," Lymon added. "Ruptured right kidney and spleen. We've done what we can."

"I think you're trying to tell me it's serious."

"I'm afraid so."

Tea arrived. Lymon accepted his gratefully.

"I take it you're offering no false hope?" David said.

Lymon stirred his tea.

"How old is your grandfather?"

"Eighty-five in a couple of months."

Eyebrows raised in surprise. "He's taken a good deal of punishment. Tell you the truth, I'm surprised he survived long enough to be brought here."

"Is there a chance?"

"He's alive now and he shouldn't be. He must have the constitution of a Chieftain tank. He's been under observation all day. I thought it'd be over by now, but he keeps going, so it's impossible to say. Must be a hell of an old man."

The pressure mounted in David's head. He wanted to get back to the room.

Lymon finished his tea. They left the office.

"I can't tell you anything for certain," Lymon said. "Not that he'll die tonight or tomorrow, or whenever. In view of the head injury, I tend to the belief that he'd be better gone, but we can't even be sure of that. He hasn't regained consciousness at all."

"I wish he would. Just so I could ask why."

"I heard. Norfolk to Edinburgh. That's some trip for an old man."

"He was always strong. Nothing wrong with him but his mind."

"Maybe that's the only explanation. The brain's a maze at the best of times." They paused at the door. "You can stay . . . as long as you wish. Would you like to be alone with him for a while, talk to him and so forth?"

David nodded.

Lymon beckoned the Sister. As he explained to her what was going on, David looked round the door at the bed. The fear of it still ate at him.

Heavy footsteps sounded in the corridor. Lymon swore under his breath.

The police had arrived.

"So, you've no idea why he might have come here, sir?"

"None," David said.

There were two of them: a Detective Inspector called Gilston and a Detective Sergeant Humbie. Gilston was brief, pale and balding; Humbie dark and hefty. Gilston spoke quickly, like a racing commentator, Humbie with the relentless steadiness of a steam roller flattening knobbly facts.

They had been questioning him in the little office for half an hour. His temper was shredded.

"As far as I know," he said, "he's never been here. He never even mentioned to me that he'd *like* to come here. Now will you fill in the details and let me go back to him?"

"Certainly, sir." Gilston coughed. His pale forehead flushed pink.

"I know there was an accident. What exactly happened?"

"Well, your grandfather was stumbling around on a deserted road near East Linton – that's out Dunbar way towards the coast – at about one o'clock this morning. Very cold, icy night. A Mr Richard Colvin was leaving the house of his father-in-law at that time. What seems to have happened – there being no witnesses – is that Mr Colvin came down the drive at the rear of the house – it's wooded and walled – and ran smack into your grandfather at the end of it. Mr Colvin must have tried to avoid him, but he hit him with the offside wing, then slewed across the road and collided with the wall on the other side."

David closed his eyes.

"He's also in intensive care," Gilston said. "The doctors aren't holding out a lot of hope."

"Damn it."

Humbie offered chewing gum. There were no takers. He settled back and unwrapped a sliver of spearmint.

"It's nasty," Gilston said. "His father-in-law is George Miller.

49

Very respected surgeon at this hospital. Neurology. He's here with the family now."

"And it was my grandfather's fault?"

"Everything points that way. Must've walked straight into it. Better for Mr Colvin if he'd kept right on and slammed on the brakes, but that's not an option when you see someone rear up in your headlights."

"Was there anything on him?"

"Your grandfather?"

Humbie turned to a page in his notebook.

"It's all in his locker, of course. I had a quick look this morning. A wallet, with several old photographs of women and children, thirty-five pounds in cash, a little book with writing in what we assume to be Polish. And a train ticket, Peterborough–Edinburgh."

"Single, by the way," Gilston added. "We've not nailed it yet, but we assume he arrived sometime yesterday afternoon, and took a taxi from Waverley station. Once we get the driver, it might give us an idea where he thought he was going."

David rubbed his eyes so hard that sparks and lights flared behind the lids. "I keep trying to think why, but nothing comes. There's no reason why he should be here."

Gilston stood up. "Perhaps if he recovers consciousness, he'll be able to tell us."

David started back to Grandfather's room. Humbie followed, to take notes if Grandfather did happen to speak. A group of people came out of a door further along the corridor. Humbie more or less pushed him into the room.

"What the hell – "

Humbie gestured with his sleepy eyes. David peeped round the door at the group. The corridor was quiet. A doctor talked to a white-haired old gentleman in an expensive camelhair coat. Two men about his own age supported a young woman who wept silently into her gloved hands. The old man's face was set. He listened to the doctor, muttered replies, nodding precisely.

"He must've died," Humbie whispered. "That's Mr Miller, the old chap. Two sons, and the daughter; deceased's wife."

David's attention was captured by the woman. Even crying, exhausted by grief, she was lovely. Her hair was the black of

50

washed coal. She bore a resemblance to the men, but where they were powerful, she was beautiful.

Miller raised his palm and began striking it with his left forefinger to punctuate his words to the doctor. The brothers listened. Miller was used to being listened to.

"He was the terror of this place," Humbie said, close to David's ear. "Saved my old mum's life in 1966."

The widow shook herself free while the men talked. She walked a few paces to a window. Night grew beyond the glass. She leaned against the sill, clenching her hands tight. Her profile was clear. There was something proud about her.

Miller noticed. He said something to the brothers. The big, red-haired one went to her. She began to cry again, and the group moved off.

"That's a shame," Humbie said. "Only been married five years. Mr Colvin was well-known in the city. Very successful in computers."

They reached the bedside. Nothing had changed. Grandfather lay still in the jungle of devices made to keep him alive.

"He won't wake up," David said, wanting to be rid of the policeman.

"I'll just sit by, if you don't mind."

He did mind. He wanted to be alone with his grandfather. But they sat down together, the policeman and the architect who was certain that he was a bad grandson, and Grandfather went on trying to breathe, fighting every inch against death as he had done before.

Lying on his hotel bed, a large whisky and soda in one hand, David called home. He fixed his eyes on the television screen in the corner. The pictures kept his head steady.

Sarah answered. She had been waiting.

"How bad is it?"

He told her how bad. "Trouble is, he's fighting it. He *could* go any time, but they told me to go away and get some sleep. Apparently, medical science is so advanced they can even predict the moment of death early enough to get you out of bed and across town in plenty of time."

"Where are you?"

He focused on his door key. "Albany Hotel. It's in George Street, downtown."

51

"I'm sorry."

"What for?"

"Not being with you."

"It's not an activity for pairs. Better solo."

"For not being there to take your call this morning, then."

"Oh, well . . ." He felt the urge to break the television screen.

"When he wakes up," she said, "you can tell him he's on all the news programmes. Not just ours. Even the television this evening."

"When he wakes up," he said. Someone entered the next room singing 'Luck Be A Lady' in a new arrangement for the tone deaf. He wanted to scream and throw his glass at the wall, but resisted that urge too.

"David?"

"I'm here. I miss you somewhat."

"Same here. I can come up, if you need me."

"No. It wouldn't . . . It probably won't be worth it . . . Doesn't that sound terrible?" His eyes burned, and he heard her gulp back tears, but he did not let go. "Is there anything going on I ought to know about?"

"Trevor Games rang up to give his condolences."

"Grandfather's not dead yet."

"Well, whatever you give when . . ." She trailed off, then re-started on a different tack. "And they really don't know why he did it?"

"No. But that doesn't bother me. *I* don't know is what bothers me."

He woke at six from a black dream. In the dream, Grandfather was dying and they were trying to contact him, but he was out sailing. He saw it like a film: he and Sarah laughing together as they tacked upriver towards Brundall, while the fat Sister in Edinburgh tried to telephone him. He jerked awake, convinced that it must all be over, called the hospital. A voice told him that Mr Kalska was still holding on.

Hardly rested, he breakfasted in his room at seven, having watched the news until he had been told everything at least three times. He showered, shaved and put on his clothes, then phoned Kate at his office to cancel appointments for another day. The back of his mind was grinding through business he should have done yesterday: meetings with the head of the Eastern Building Society, for whom he was designing new premises; lunch with Trevor. They would all have to sweat a little more.

He checked out at eight-thirty. The morning was sketchy, the traffic going through the city just tolerable. He asked himself what day it was, and nailed down Friday. Friday the thirteenth, which was some kind of rotten omen.

The hospital had a gritty, exhausted atmosphere left over from the previous night. He went straight to Grandfather's room and took his place beside the bed.

The machines did their work, and the face amid its network of tubes and wires was very pale.

He sat at the bedside, holding Grandfather's hand, wondering what to say. His mind was like the blank walls. He did ask the old man to keep trying, but he was not sure he believed that was the right thing. He talked about the disappearance, how he had looked for him in the old places. Soon the words were flowing gently, and he told him how Sarah was, what condition the boat was in, how business was going. Every now and then the pain would grow too much and he would walk away for a while. He did not know why, because Grandfather was eighty-four and very sick, but the thought of his not being around any more was intolerable.

Lunchtime came, and there was no change. He wandered out with the intention of finding a telephone. On his way past the desk, the Sister in charge came after him.

"Mr Kalska, excuse me."

He pulled up. "Do I have to go, Sister?"

"No, I just wondered . . . Is anyone else visiting your grandfather?"

"There isn't anyone else," he said. "Why?"

"Oh, just one of our night staff says she saw someone in there last night. The wee small hours, this was."

"No one else, Sister. Just me."

The Sister pursed her lips. "Probably some drug addict. We really need better security here. You get all kinds of strangers just walk in off the streets."

"He didn't do anything, this man?"

"No, not at all. I just thought I'd ask."

He went out into the streets with another worry on his

mind. After the Brackford House business, he was in the frame
of mind to sue anything that moved. Grandfather wasn't even
safe in hospital.

He picked at lunch in The Doctors, a pub across the road,
but his stomach was churning. He drank a couple of pints of
bitter and went out to a cardphone. After the usual three
attempts at getting through, he was in touch with Kate. The
news was not good. Every one of his most important clients
semed to have dropped out of the woodwork with a very
urgent problem that only he could solve. The phone, Kate
said, had not stopped ringing. He took notes from her until
the credits on his card ran out, promised to get back as soon as
he could, and returned to the hospital.

Grandfather was the same. Two nurses came to clean him
and change his dressings. The nurses kept including him in
their conversation, despite the fact that he showed no reaction.
David stared out of the window. The sight of the old man
being lifted and bundled was too much.

He stayed on, running out of things to tell. Sleep tugged at
him and he dozed off, and still Josef's heart beat on, the
machine pumped breath in and out and the ECG monitor
showed that his brain still worked in the dark of his skull.

It continued that way through the afternoon and late into
the evening. David rang the hotel and re-booked the same
room. He found a hamburger restaurant off Forrest Road and
forced something down for the sake of energy, then crawled
into bed at the hotel after midnight. Reception had given him
a whole sheaf of messages from clients who had tracked him
down. He thought of phoning Sarah, but it was late and she
would probably be asleep. He fell into a dead sleep, and woke
at three to call the hospital and ask the question.

Next day he tried to deal with some of his business from the
hotel. It was Saturday, and he ran up a huge bill tracking
people down at home or the golf club. He talked to the most
urgent ones, but the cry kept recurring. They wanted him on
the spot as soon as possible.

Sarah was home the second time he tried. She wanted to
come up. He told her not to, because it might end at any
moment. She was upset then, because of Grandfather, but also
because he put her off. He tried to make it clear that he did
want her with him, but he could hear the hurt in her voice

when she rang off. The truth was, he would have felt worse for her attending the vigil with him. This was his to do.

The rest of that day passed in a haze of sameness: hospital routine going past the door; the slow, excruciating rise and fall of Grandfather's chest. He looked through the belongings, which had been under lock and key, found nothing, worked over some figures and details he had gleaned from the phone conversations. Nurses brought endless cups of tea and sympathetic expressions, for both of which he was grateful. He wondered whether Edinburgh had a synagogue where he could pray, but that was as far as it went. He hardly knew the words any more. He would feel embarrassed, as he always had when Grandfather tried to make him aware of his religion. What use was Judaism to an illegitimate, half-English boy?

Sunday, he was nervous the whole time. Before coming into the hospital, he took a walk along Princes Street. The starvation of winter clung to everything. He thought of phoning Sarah, but couldn't face any more of the undercurrents. He took a taxi to the hospital, and listened to Radio Four on the headphones that hung on the wall.

Lymon popped in just before five. He studied the charts and the machines, lifted Grandfather's eyelids and shone a light in them.

"You amazing old bugger," he muttered.

"I wish he'd wake up," David said, rising to stretch his legs.

"You're not the only one."

A nurse appeared in the doorway, slightly out of breath.

"Mr Kalska, there's someone on the phone for you. They rang through to the desk. They say it's urgent."

Swearing dryly, he followed her out.

Trevor Games' voice crackled in his ear:

"David? Sorry to bother you at a time like this."

"It's okay, Trev, what is it?"

"You've got to come back."

"Take a running jump, will you?"

"I'm serious, Dave. There's a meeting with some council chaps. They're talking about making investigations into that development land Charlie Hogg's selling 'em. If Charlie drops out now, we'll be right up the creek."

"Trevor, I'm with my grandfather. I can't come home now."

"I'm telling you, I need you down here to strengthen the

sincerity quotient. You want this thing to fall through? The Mall's your baby more than anyone's."

"Trevor, I can't do it."

"You've got to, you silly bugger."

"I'm not one of your yes men," he snarled suddenly. "You talk to them like that, not me. Got it?"

"Yeah, I'm sorry." Trevor usually avoided the downside of David's temper. He sounded flustered. "But can't you just pop down tomorrow? It's important, I mean it."

"I'll talk to you later." He put the phone down. The nurses round the desk stared at him. His face was dark with anger. They had not seen that side of him before. He could see them reassessing the easy-going man they thought they knew. He stalked back to Grandfather's room.

Lymon was scribbling notes on a clipboard, studying them as if he could not read his own writing. "Nothing serious, I hope?"

"Business calling," David said, pacing restlessly.

Lymon studied him carefully. Then he said:

"Mr Kalska, why don't you go home?"

"I can't," he said.

"It's very hard for you, I know. But – " the hands came together again, "the way you're going, you'll be in a bed yourself soon. There's just no point."

"He might die while I'm gone."

"He might have gone when you stepped out of the room just now. His condition, in technical parlance, is critical but stable. You could sit at the bedside for a week, and he'd still be fighting. You're wearing yourself out. Why not go home and sort out whatever it is? I promise to have you called the moment anything changes, the slightest thing."

They talked it over at some length. David did not want to listen, but he could see Lymon was a good man. He would crack up if he had to sit like this for much longer, and Grandfather had never thanked him for letting business slide.

"If he wakes," David said. "Even a flicker – "

"You'll be told immediately. No guarantees. I can't promise that you'll have six hours' notice to get back here, but I'll give you my considered opinion, for what it's worth. He's stayed alive this long, he won't go just like that now."

David allowed himself to be persuaded. He said goodbye to

Grandfather, promised to come back as soon as he could. He just had to go home and fix things.

He felt that he was doing wrong as soon as he left the hospital. Self-reproach grew like a fat weed on the way to the hotel. It grew bigger when he checked out, and was blooming nicely by the time he climbed in the car to start the homeward journey.

What if he dies now? Never mind that he'd tell you to deal with business. You should be with him.

Two in the morning. Norwich was clenched in frost. Sarah waited, running *Mildred Pearce* on the video. She rose and came to him, tall and warm in her silk dressing gown. She kissed him, not minding what he said about his breath. He dropped his bag and held her. Under the dressing gown she wore nothing, and the smooth rise and fall of her made him excited. He did not know how to regard the arousal. He was so tired he could hardly think at all.

"Is he going to be all right?" she asked.

He shook his head. "I don't know."

She went to the kitchen to make him coffee. Spoon clinked on china and glass. He flicked through a stack of letters on the bookcase. All of it could wait until morning.

She came in again, and tears were rolling down her face.

He took the cup from her, made her sit down.

The crying lasted a while. All she would say was: "Poor old Josef." He tried to comfort her: eventually it worked. Then, by one of those mystical transitions that take place late at night, the comforting became caressing, and they made gentle, weary love among cushions on the floor.

They went to bed, lying close. Just before she fell asleep, she said again:

"Poor old Josef."

He lay beside her, watching a shallow gleam of light on the ceiling, a reflection off the river.

Poor old Josef.

The phone cut in on his darkness. He grabbed it, fear coming hard on the heels of waking. It was for Sarah: one of the presenters had called in sick – laryngitis, no voice at all – they

57

needed her. He tried to burrow back into sleep, but fright had shocked him awake.

She came down to find him eating, sorting through correspondence. He had already called the hospital. Situation unchanged.

"You may hear me today, if I can't get anyone to dep for Nick."

"You I'd listen to," he said.

He walked with her to the Anglian Radio building round the corner, kissed her goodbye. Home again, he changed into a good dark suit – perfect for convincing nervous clients of his reliability even under stress. He went to the office and proceeded to deal with as much of the talk as he could before eleven. A lot of time was wasted taking expressions of sympathy, but he noticed that no one let it deter him from voicing his own problems.

Then he went out to Sprowston Hall for the meeting with the council men. It went reasonably well, considering that some of those involved wanted to stop the Mall going ahead altogether. Afterwards he lunched with Trevor, who was golfing in the afternoon. David ate a light salad and a single glass of wine, while Trevor shovelled in steak and baked potatoes, wine, dessert and brandies. He kept apologising for bringing David home.

By half-past two, he was home again to do some work at the drawing board.

A Post Office van pulled up outside. There was a knock at the door.

"Mr Kalska?" The postman was a thin man with a big, equine nose. He handed over three white envelopes.

"You starting a personal delivery service?" David asked.

"Not so's you'd notice. Does this have anything to do with you?" He presented a larger brown envelope.

David held it like a sachet of poison. He was cold all over.

The front was quite a mess. His name was written at the top in wobbling letters. The address disintegrated into a crabbed scrawl.

"It's been going about for a couple of days," the postman said. "Finally turned up on my round." He peered at David curiously. "Is it yours, then?"

He said: "Yes."

"You all right?"

He managed to say "Yes," again. But he was not all right at all.

The letter was from Grandfather.

9

He mixed himself a drink. Hands trembling, he studied the envelope again. His name was legible, but the address was confused. The first part was the number and road of the council flat. The rest referred to this address, but was so wildly written that anyone else would have had trouble deciphering. It was postmarked the day after Grandfather disappeared, but from Norwich. He must have sent it before he left.

He was about to tear it open, when the thought that it might be some kind of evidence stopped him. He fetched a knife and slit the paper carefully, lifted out three sheets of a student notepad.

He thought: Oh, God. Hopeless sadness started again. The letter was worse than the envelope. A mass of words dragged across the paper, sloping every which way. There was Polish in it, and Yiddish; the changes seemed arbitrary, as if the old man's mind had slipped a cog and gone on with whatever came to hand. It began well enough . . .

> Dear David,
> This will be a strange letter for you to receieve from me. It fill me with fear only doing this.

The usual thing. In all his years in England, Grandfather never really grew comfortable with the language. Most of the time he was fine, but then he would falter badly.

> You must understand. I have to go from here. I cannot rest. This evening I go, because I see no one has maked the effort. It is like no one cares now. So I must do it.

Then it switched to Polish. David tried to remember, but the words were like code. His eye came upon *źli*, and that bothered him. He thought it meant 'evil'. After that there was a paragraph of Yiddish.

He dropped the letter to save himself from ripping it up, and took a drink. He was angry, because it destroyed his last hope that Grandfather had known what he was doing. The poor old sod, labouring for hours over that rambling stupidity, never realising how gaga he was. There was no reason for the trip to Scotland, only senility.

He picked it up again, went over the first page. All those foreign words. He could identify about five. All the years of having to talk Polish at home – part of Grandfather's effort to make sure the homeland and the past were not forgotten – had come to nothing. He had given up speaking it at the age of twelve, when he began to assert himself a little. The odd phrase struck memory: *bać sie* – 'to be afraid'. And the Hatik-vah, which was – could he recall? – the Hebrew song of undying hope. The rest had a faint odour of familiarity, as if he might understand if only he tried a little harder, but that was all.

He searched for more English phrases. Even some of these meant next to nothing – stumbles into mental side-streets: one about the colour of the flowers on his mother's dress. Then something made him sit up. A recurrence of the word *źli*. The sentence containing it was English.

I must find this *źli*, this monster, you understand?

Another sentence touched the same ground.

Yitzhak says I am crazy to try, but I tell him – as I tell you – if no one else does it, I must.

More Polish, breaking suddenly into a section which began:

Listen to me, Benjamin . . .

David frowned. Benjamin again. How could you trust anything the letter said, when half the time Grandfather thought he was writing to a son who had been dead forty years? And who was Yitzhak, another ghost?

He put the letter away, sat for a while, struggling with his certainty that it was a waste of time. But the repetition of 'evil' bothered him. He wanted to know what was in the rest of the letter. He was already behind in the work he had wanted to complete. It would not hurt to make sure. He got the car out and went up to the University of East Anglia bookshop, bought a good Polish–English dictionary and a couple of teach-yourself books.

Just to be sure.

Sarah knew he was keeping things from her. When she got home that evening, he was working on something in Josef's room. He covered it as she entered. She did not ask what it was. It bothered her, because she had never caught him hiding a solid fact from her before, but she did not pry. When she first moved in with him, she had made sure he understood that their lives were not suddenly wound together. They were adults, and they were to live by rules she had made to protect herself a long time ago.

He put an arm round her as she came to his side, rested his head on her hip.

"No news?" she said.

"No. He's still hanging on."

"Are you going back?"

"In the morning, early. You can't come, of course?"

She thought it had the faintest tone of an order.

"Not with Nick on the sicklist." She gazed at the rough sketches on the desk. She saw textbooks of some kind underneath. "I wish I could get away."

"Grandfather's not taking much notice, anyway." He got up. She knew he wanted to leave the room. "Come on, I'll make us a drink, then we'll go down to Hobbs. I can't face the kitchen tonight."

They had an early dinner in Hobbs, which was gorgeous as always, but it was really a waste. He tried too hard to be bright, and she kept thinking of his secrets. Going back to the almost hysterical way she had declared her independence in the early days, she could not blame him. There were so many pieces of his life that he did not let her into. It only happened sometimes, like tonight, but then she could not get away from the notion that he was acting for her, as for everyone else.

61

Consequently, they both drank too much, and went straight to bed when they got home.

An hour or so after falling into uneasy sleep, she woke. He was not beside her. She slipped out of bed and moved to the top of the stairs. A light shone up the hallway from Josef's room.

She thought: If we were married, I'd go down and see what's wrong. She stayed where she was, because they were not married. At such times, she felt her unofficial status in the house very much.

She returned to bed, skull thumping from drink.

Whatever he was doing, it was none of her business.

She wished it were.

He stopped when the first page was roughed out; partly because he had come to some Yiddish which he could do nothing about, partly because translation did not make things clearer.

More had come back to him as he worked: grammar and construction; odd words arriving in his brain before he turned to the appropriate page. Yet the translated stuff was just as disordered. A few words about how sorry Grandfather was for making trouble, a mention of hiding in an attic or cupboard, more confusion.

He put down his pencil and sat back from the desk. It was half-past one in the morning. He was wearing himself to a frazzle with sleeplessness, but he could not shake the hope that somewhere in the letter there might be a plain and simple explanation.

There is, he thought. Senility. Plain enough for you?

He ran back over the page of notes he had made, read the cogent sentences.

It is a long time ago, but time makes no distance in this. What happened a lifetime ago is what happened today, this hour, this minute. I know you do not understand. Perhaps you cannot. It is not your fault, my son.

Then:

Oh, that creature. How could you know?

He wandered about the room. The chess set was still arranged for a game they had been playing six weeks ago. He had to go to bed. He was booked on the 7.20 flight to Edinburgh. He had heard Sarah creeping about upstairs. She was worried, he knew that well enough, but he did not want to trouble her with the letter. His shame in still hoping made it impossible to share.

The desk covered with notes reproached him for his lack of understanding, like a stupid old man who thinks it is everyone else's fault.

He went to the chest of drawers by the bed and took out the belongings Grandfather had carried with him when he was knocked down.

A wallet, some money, a notebook and a rail ticket. The little map – if that was what it was – in the notebook told him nothing. It was too rudimentary. He opened the wallet, took out the folding money, looked in the pockets. It was old, the silk lining coming away from the corners in one pocket. He turned it towards the light and noticed a tag of white paper lodged in the corner. He stuck a finger in and prised it out. It fluttered to the carpet. He picked it up and unfolded the creases. A cigarette paper. But Grandfather did not smoke. Across it, in a hand he did not recognise, was an address:

> Cedar House,
> Stinton.

10

"How is he?"

The Sister smiled fondly down at the bed. "Stable," she said. "He must've been an amazing man."

"He is," David said.

Mid-morning. A tea trolley rattled down the corridor.

"Stay as long as you like," the Sister said. "Someone'll be here to clean him up in a bit."

"Can I help at all?" David said.

"You just talk to him."

He nodded. He had forgotten to shave.

"I don't suppose you'll mind, will you?" he said to Grandfather. There was no movement.

He stayed with him into the afternoon, talking to him, asking about the letter, about the address in the wallet. He tried a few words in Polish. They felt strange in his mouth. He thought Grandfather's hand twitched once in his; it could have been wishful thinking.

Lymon came in on his way elsewhere. They discussed the possibility of moving the old man down south.

"Not advisable," Lymon said. "Much as you'd like to have him nearer home, the journey would kill him."

"D'you think he could pull through after all?"

"Stranger things, Mr Kalska, stranger things." They exchanged a look of perfect understanding. Lymon pulled at his tie. "Found out what he was doing up here?"

"No." He had not told the police about the address yet. He wanted to be sure it meant something.

"He really wants to live, doesn't he?" Lymon said.

"Always has," David said, thinking vaguely of the past.

Then he and Grandfather were alone again. David leaned close to the old man and kissed his forehead. "I'm going out for a while," he whispered, longing for some reaction. "To find out if this was where you were heading."

The sound of the heart monitor followed him down the corridor.

A thin gruel of rain scoured his face as he crossed the road to the taxi rank opposite the hospital.

The driver of the first car in the rank gave him a bleak smile. "Afternoon, sir. Where'll it be?"

David took out the address. "Whereabouts is Stinton?"

"Away to Dunbar. Fair distance."

"Will you take me there?"

"If that's where you want to go."

The driver started the engine, happy at the notion of a large fare. David sat back and closed his eyes.

"My name's Arnold," the driver said, and asked what line he was in. David said boatbuilding, which was a mistake, because Arnold had ambitions to be a seafaring man himself.

Piloting the taxi through the city, he launched into a monologue on the subject. David wondered silently whether there was any taxi driver in the world who did not want to be something else.

He opened his eyes again to keep track of where they were going. The city had fallen away. They were going out along a dual carriageway. The country was low and sweeping, the sky huge and brightening towards the east. Over to the left, he could see the blue-grey sheet of the Firth of Forth.

"Stinton," Arnold murmured. "Now which way would be best?"

"Is it so hard to find?"

"It's a small place. Have business there?"

"I don't know yet."

They passed Haddington. A long stretch of quarry workings, then dark green hills rising in the distance on the right. Had Grandfather come here? Was anyone checking that? He wished he had a better idea of where the accident had occurred.

Arnold warbled on about sailing magazines, and decided that he might as well try the next right. They sped through wet fields bordered with stone. Far away in the Firth an island sailed against the weather. Forested hills were before them.

"You sure you know where you're going?" David said.

"Of course." Arnold squinted at a map on the passenger seat.

They dithered at a couple of turns. Arnold pulled up at the signs and stared hard before going on.

"What would be the best boat, then?" he said. "In your opinion."

A sign zipped by, announcing Stinton. A moment later they were passing through a small village of red stone backed by blue hills.

"In the eight to ten-ton class, naturally," Arnold said. "Which is the place you want?"

"Cedar House," David said, looking for cedars.

A pub, a church, then they were out of it. The road falling away into trees.

"Sure it's Stinton?"

He looked at the address again. "Just carry on a little farther." Ahead, the road dropped steeply into a valley. "Maybe we missed it."

65

"Ah, hang on there." Arnold hauled on the brakes. They had passed an opening in the trees. He backed twenty feet. "This the place?"

An old bay-windowed house stood away from the road behind a low wall. It was strongly built, imposing. High cedars flanked it.

"Why were you looking for this place?" he asked Grandfather.

"Pardon?" Arnold said.

"Nothing. Wait for me here, will you?"

Arnold checked the meter and was a cheerful man.

David got out and crossed the road. He went through a heavy wooden gate and up a path between ornamental flower-beds. Smoke feathered from one chimney. As he reached the front porch, dogs began to bark. Big ones by the sound of it, to go with the house and the Range-Rover that must be parked round the back somewhere. He rang the bell.

A cold wind shuffled through the trees and pressed at his back. He zipped up his jacket and stuck his hands in the pockets. He fingered the cigarette paper. No one was coming.

He pulled the bell one more time. The dogs, who had started out some rooms away, were at the door. They yelped and scraped their claws on the wood.

Maybe that was why he did not hear the approaching footsteps. One minute he was alone on the step, shivering. The next, chains were pulled, bolts drawn. The door opened like a trap.

The dogs poised on the threshold. Two German shepherds, growling low in their throats, held back only by a softly spoken command of "Stay." Then, to him: "Yes?"

He swallowed hard. Words stuck in his throat.

"Can I help you?"

David stared at the stocky, handsome old man. He could not unfreeze.

Miller waited for him to reply.

"Was there something you wanted?" the old man said. His smile was uncertain. His eyes were cool green. The full head of white hair and the wrinkles under a healthy tan aged but did not weaken him.

In his shock, David referred to the scrap of paper again. He felt stupid. Being taken by surprise was something he hated. His defences were down. "This is Cedar House?" he said.

"Do you see any others?" Miller asked, half-amused. His Scots burr had a clear, formal note. One of the dogs nosed close to David's hand, sniffing the paper. "Come back, Egil." The dog retreated.

"Mr Miller," David said, "your son-in-law was killed the other day?"

"Are you some kind of journalist?" Miller said. The dogs sensed a change from polite enquiry. They strained the barriers of obedience. David was sweating. He had not been so nervous – so scared – since he was a boy. It was the dogs.

"I'm not a reporter. My grandfather was . . . he was involved in the accident."

The white brows contracted. Miller's expression was obscure. His hand tightened on the door frame.

"Your grandfather?" he said, digesting the information. Then he asked: "Has he died?"

"No. He's still critical."

"I see. So what brings you here, Mr – ?"

"Kalska, David Kalska. I'm not quite sure, to tell you the truth. You didn't know my grandfather, did you?"

"What?" Confused, beginning to be a little tetchy. A man who disliked wasting time. "Of course I didn't know him. And I knew nothing of him. What is this about, please?"

David wished the dogs would go away. It was like conducting a conversation with a sword swinging over his head. "I was going through my grandfather's belongings last night. I found this address."

The green eyes flickered over him. "Mine?"

"It seems as if he was coming to see you. At least, he had this address in his pocket. He was knocked down near here, wasn't he?"

"At the bottom of the hill behind the house."

Taking in that surprise, he struggled to keep his voice steady. "I don't know whether the police gave me all the details. Did he actually get here?"

Miller leaned forward. He shook his head slowly. "Mr Kalska, do you understand that we are in mourning here? My daughter's husband is dead."

He felt he was wading deeper into a bad dream, found

67

himself imploring the old man. "I'm trying to find out why he had your address."

The compact features hardened. "I've never seen your grandfather, I know nothing of this."

One of the sons – the red-haired one with the meaty face – appeared at the end of the hall. "Dad, what's going on?" He started towards them.

"Look," David said, "I don't understand either. Can't you see – "

The son was with them now. His eyes were suspicious and superior. "What is it, Dad? Is he giving you trouble?"

David tried to control the situation, but it was out of his hands. He noticed a photograph on a table behind them. The daughter, a few years younger, laughing and pointing at a neat young man who was probably her husband.

"My grandfather had the name of this house on him when he was knocked down. I want to know why."

"The old man?" the son said. "The one who killed Richard?" He bristled dangerously. "What d'you want here?"

Miller stopped him as he had stopped the dogs. "Alex, please. I'm sure there's some mistake."

"Oh, there's a mistake, all right," the son muttered. "What's your game, anyway?"

"Alex, that's enough." Miller was in charge of them both. "Mr Kalska, I'm sorry. I know nothing of why your grandfather should have this address. All I can tell you is that he did not get here. I'm sorry he is hurt, but perhaps if you had taken better care of him."

Anger finally broke through. "Who the hell d'you think you are?"

The son pushed towards him. "Let me deal with him."

Miller still held him back. "You'd best leave now, please."

David saw it was hopeless. The doorway was crammed with silent hostility. Frustration balled in his stomach, but there was nothing he could do. "I'll find out," he said. "Believe me, I'll find out."

Then he was stuck on the end of a limb with nothing to do but leave. He turned on his heel and stalked away.

All the way back to Edinburgh, Arnold talked boats. David did not even pretend to listen. He was furious and sick at heart.

68

He was experiencing something no longer familiar to him: shame. The shame of the bullied, the inferior. A throwback to early schooldays, listening to taunts about his mother, his race, his stupid grandfather who could not speak proper English. Miller and his son had the same assurance as the kids who used to torment him. The certainty of being better than him, of having the right to behave like that. It was common enough. Every class he had ever dealt with, from the peasants in Witherley Heath to the higher-toned clients he sometimes designed houses for, possessed it when they were in their little groups. That was one reason why he worked alone, in charge of every aspect of his affairs. He could deal with people and keep them off.

By the time he was dropped off at the hospital and paid Arnold his sizeable fare, he felt ill with it. He could not face anyone yet. He wandered over to The Doctors. It was full of medical students blasted by tiredness. He fought his way to the bar and ordered a double Dewar's and soda with a pint of thin bitter as a chaser. He wedged himself onto a seat by a smoky brown window and tried to banish the shame. His performance had been pathetic. It was so out of character for him, he was only glad no one else had seen it. He took the cigarette paper from his pocket and smoothed it on the table between two beer puddles. It had to mean something.

He drank, and thought about Miller. The green eyes and the straight, handsome lines of his face. He looked like some great conductor; von Karajan in his prime. Fine hands and features attached to a still-powerful body. A surgeon. Certainly a man to inspire confidence, leavened with a little fear. The son, Alexander, was a coarse-grained variation on the father. Strength running to fat and blood pressure. The full, spoilt mouth of a properly brought-up son.

He sipped the beer as the juke box changed to something old by Level 42. The memory of the daughter, the widow, rose up. First the photograph in the hall, then the way she had stood at the window that evening, gazing without seeing. The way she held herself alone as the sons clung round the father. The darkness of her hair and the loneliness in her eyes set her apart from them.

But there were resemblances. The innate pride of her profile.

69

She was probably just like the sons: full of her own superiority.

Except, of course, she was mourning a dead husband.

He returned to Grandfather and sat with him for two hours, talking about what had happened. Grandfather showed no signs of hearing. Frustration kept biting at him. The explanation – if there was any – was locked in the fragile body on the bed, just behind the sunken eyelids.

A nurse came in to clean Grandfather up. David helped for a while, but handling the poor, broken body made him feel worse.

"You let me finish." she said. "I'll bet you didn't have lunch, did you?"

He had not.

"Och, and it's nearly six. Why don't you get yourself something to eat while I see to him? Don't you worry now."

He went out, but not to eat. He took a taxi to a car hire firm and arranged to hire a three-month-old Montego with unlimited mileage. He was abrupt with the girl behind the desk, and knew it was because of Miller. He was re-asserting himself like some offended nobody. He apologised.

At six-thirty he was on the Dunbar road, trusting memory to take him back to Stinton.

He drove through slowly, passed Miller's house and went down the hill. At the bottom the road curved and climbed steeply again. In gathering gloom, he pulled over to the roadside and saw immediately where the accident had happened. Below the curve tall trees dropped away to a stream in a gully. Above it were the woods surrounding Cedar House. A dry stone wall bordered the grounds. A wide gateway led up a rough drive. Everything was obscured by the undergrowth.

He left his car and walked over the road. Black smears stretched from the entrance, stopped suddenly on the other side. Scrapes and paint-marks flecked the wall there. Slivers of headlamp glass littered the grass.

A light came on above. That was the rear of the house. He went back to the car and made a quick turn in the driveway, then headed into the village. The pub was open. He parked in the yard and entered the bar.

It was defiantly unmodern. Light music came bopping out

70

of concealed speakers, and the paintwork had a nicotine shade. A lady of uncertain age and hair colour leaned across the bar, looking as if her weight had been carefully assembled above her elbows. A couple of young men in overalls supped pints by the dartboard. Another sat at the end of the bar. He was fair-haired, bearded, wizened by alcohol at forty-five. He was the regular. Every pub has one, and you tell him by the boiled yellow eyes and the sleepy determination of his drinking.

David ordered a pint and a sandwich. He sat up to the bar, two stools down from the regular, and opened his paper. The regular noted him, gauged his possibilities as a source of further refreshment, decided in his favour.

"Evening," he murmured.

David looked up with a preoccupied smile, also a touch of gladness at the welcome. "Hello there," he said, and returned to his paper and his makeshift meal.

The pub filled. David was noticed, then ignored. He wondered about the chances of Miller or his children coming in, but it did not seem their sort of place. He ate and read and waited for the regular to engage him in conversation.

"Anything in yon paper?" the regular said at last.

"Not much," David said, making himself appear eager to be interrupted. "Usual bad news."

"Aye, it's always the way. I don't bother any more with it myself. Too depressing, wouldn't you say?"

David finished his pint. "I think I'll have another of those." He signalled to the landlady, pretended to notice for the first time the regular's empty glass. "Can I get you one?"

"Well," the regular said, gracious in bestowing a favour, "that'd be very kind of you, sir. Very kind. I'll have the same as yourself, if you would nae mind."

David got them in, and shuffled his barstool a little closer. They drank each other's health.

"Of course, you're not from these parts," the regular said.

"No. Way down south."

"Funny time for a holiday, if you'll pardon me."

"I'm not here for pleasure," David said. "I'm touring a bit. Start work for an electronics firm in Edinburgh tomorrow."

"Electrics?" The regular nodded sagely. "Would that be for poor Mr Colvin's company?"

"Who did you say?"

71

"Mr Colvin. Him from the big house. He died, you know. They put him in the ground yesterday."

"No, I don't think that's anyone to do with my people. In electronics, was he?"

"Computers, and so forth."

"That's a coincidence. But you say he died?"

It cost another pint of bitter and a Macallan with a splash of water, but in the next half-hour David received a potted history of the family in the big house on the hill. Mr Miller had come over from Switzerland after the war and made a very successful career at the Royal Infirmary. He also had seats on various boards, which kept him occupied now he was retired. He held a good stretch of the hills beyond the village, where he and his friends did their shooting.

The regular's vein-threaded nose wrinkled at the mention of it.

"You don't care for them?" David asked.

"Oh, no, not at all. I was only thinking that the Lord doesn't always give his riches to the nicest people."

"Are they not liked?"

"Oh, they're liked," the regular said. "Well enough." The addition spoke volumes.

He went on to say that the family was close, especially after Mrs Miller died fifteen years ago. When you married into it, you tended to move in with it. So there was Mr Miller and the two sons – Alex with wife and child, Paul with wife; and – just recently – the daughter and her husband again. Very close family. It was the father, of course. Or so his Missus always reckoned, and so he thought himself, for what his opinion was worth, and – thank you, sir, he would have another one, yes. As he was saying, there they all were. Until last week, and the accident.

David listened, conscious of the lies he had told the regular. He was hiding things from Sarah, from the police.

"It caused quite a stir," the regular remarked. "As you might imagine in a wee place like this. Two of the morning, ambulances and police cars all over the road. That poor old man and Mr Colvin, it was terrible. They say the old chap was off his head. Must've been, out on a night like that."

"What was this Colvin doing out so late?"

"Oh, they come and go."

"Did anyone see the old man before it happened?"

"Ah, now that's an interesting thing. I got it from Hugh Puttram, who heard it from Mrs Beales up in the woods. She thought she saw him late afternoon of that day. But she's such an old woman, you see – confined – the police never asked her. And she reckons that the old chap stopped by at Cedar House. She says she saw him turn in at the gate."

He steadied his hands on the bar. "When was that?"

"Oh, late Wednesday afternoon. Mind, she's not so far from loopy herself, and her window's a fair long way from the gate. I only say what I'm told she said."

David sipped his drink and stared hard at the shelf of bottles opposite.

"It's funny," the regular said, "'cause I read in the paper that he was just wandering down the road. That's what the Millers said, anyway."

11

The brothers did not look happy. They sat together on one side of the interview room table. David and Inspector Gilston were on the other. The room had no windows. It reeked of anxiety.

He had tried to contact Gilston the previous night, as soon as the regular told him what he wanted to know. But it had taken most of the next day to find him, persuade him to organise this, and to get the brothers to come in. He pretended to ignore the way they looked at him, but waves of contempt were surging across the table.

Gilston coughed on the back of his hand. "Thank you for coming in, gentlemen."

"Thanks for inviting us." The younger brother smiled. This was Paul. He was smaller than Alex, dark like the sister. Exquisitely suited and polished. He had the mouth-only smile of a respectable hatchet man. His voice was dry and insolent. David guessed he was a solicitor. "Your invitation was irresistible."

"Police cars at the house again," Alex muttered. He was still

73

smouldering from the afternoon. "Whole bloody village gawping."

"Yes, sorry about that," Gilston said. "But it was your father I really wanted a word with."

"He's busy this evening," Paul said. "At a dinner, which I believe your Chief Constable's also attending."

"That so?" Gilston nodded. "I'll ask him how the food was when I see him."

"Look, Inspector," Alex burst out, "the only reason we came in at all was to settle this nonsense. Let's get on with it."

"Well, now . . ." Gilston paused as Humbie returned with a tray of coffees. Only Gilston took a cup. He sniffed it carefully as Humbie sat down and took up pencil and notebook. "At the moment, we want to clarify things on account of what Mr Kalska here's been telling us."

"I don't know what he's been telling you," Alex said. "All I know is he turned up on our doorstep yesterday afternoon, harassing Dad. He's lucky we didn't call you ourselves."

David sat forward. They were referring to him in the third person, trying to ignore his presence.

"You could have told me what I wanted to know without the bullshit."

"You watch your mouth."

Paul raised a hand for peace. "Let's not forget that my father is still in mourning for Richard. As we all are. Perhaps Mr Kalska could think of that before he starts throwing accusations."

"I'm not making accusations," David said.

"Sounds like it to me," Alex countered.

"I was after the answer to one simple question."

"Richard's dead because of that old man."

"Now then, sir," Gilston said. "I know this is a time of great strain for your family, but let's not forget Mr Kalska's grandfather's still in intensive care."

"At least he's alive," Alex said, like a child who must have the last word.

Paul picked up where he had left off. His politeness was like a knife. "I want to make it clear right now that we won't be harried in this fashion. Naturally we're . . . very sorry about Mr Kalska's grandfather, but we don't see that we have to put

74

up with his interrogation in our own home. Or here, for that matter."

Gilston squeezed his coffee cup. The plastic squeaked. "Let's go over this, shall we, then we can all go home." He fingered a few sheets of carbon copy on the table. "This is a report of the accident. Now, according to this, no one residing at Cedar House had ever seen the old gentleman before. Yet Mr Kalska tells us his grandfather had your father's address on him when he died. Also that he was seen at the house on the evening of the accident."

"I'd like to know who said so," Alex said.

"Did you find this address?" Paul asked.

"No," Gilston said.

"But Mr Kalska did. After the police made a very careful check for themselves."

"Not that careful, sir."

"It was tucked away in his wallet," David said.

"I see." The smile again. David wanted to hit him.

Gilston tapped the report. "What I'd like to clear up is the matter of whether Mr Kalska senior – if you'll pardon me for a moment – did or did not visit your father's house on the Wednesday evening."

David watched them. For what? Evidence of subterfuge? What did he think they had done? They stared back: Paul blandly, Alex hot and heavy breathing. Finally Paul said:

"It seems he did."

Humbie expressed surprise and scribbled faster. Even Gilston raised an eyebrow.

"How is it, then, that you all said he didn't?"

"I'm sure we said nothing either way," Paul replied. "If you'll check the report, you'll notice that my wife and I weren't home. As for Father, Alex and his wife, and Jenny, they were never specifically asked."

"That's right," Alex said.

"They couldn't have mentioned it, I suppose?" Gilston asked.

"I think they had other things on their minds, Inspector. Whether or not an old man – who appeared to be a crazed tramp – had been to the front door or not was the least of them."

75

David wanted to knock the cool bastard off his chair, but Gilston kept him out of it. He turned to Alex.

"Since you *were* at home, Mr Miller, could you tell me exactly what did happen on Wednesday?" He had his own quiet edge of sarcasm. "I'd be very grateful."

Alex sat twisting his hands on his lap. "Nothing to tell. About five, six o'clock in the afternoon. Mrs Hawbee – "

"Your housekeeper?"

"She answered the door. There was this old man outside, saying he wanted to come in, asking to see someone."

"Who?" David said.

Alex ignored him. "First of all, Barbara, my wife, went to see what the fuss was about. Then they called me, because the old man was getting a bit nasty. I came down from my room and found him trying to force his way in. Tell you the truth, I thought he was drunk. I couldn't make head nor tail of what he was raving about. But he was strong. I had to manhandle him a bit to get him out."

David scowled. "Who did he want to see?"

"He was making no sense. Kept gabbling off in a foreign language."

"Then what happened?" Gilston urged.

"There wasn't a lot we could do. I told Mrs Hawbee to lock the door and call the police if he came back. He stood out in the garden for a while, talking to himself in Russian or whatever. Then he went round the house and tried to get in at the back, but we'd already locked up there. He groaned a bit, then he stumbled off down the drive. That's all."

"That was the last you saw of him?" Gilston said.

"First and last."

"You sent away a sick old man." David glared at him. "You're a good samaritan, aren't you?"

"I wasn't to know," Alex exploded, actually talking to him. "What would you do if some mud-spattered old loony came raving at your door?"

"You could've phoned the police or something. It was a frosty evening in March, for God's sake."

"Don't fret yourself. He got his own back, didn't he?"

"You stupid bastard."

Alex rose sharply. "I'll break your neck, you – "

Humbie was out of his seat too. Without any fuss, he was

ready to intervene. Gilston stretched out an arm and barred David from getting up.

Paul picked a fleck of ash from his knee and glanced at them as if the sight pained him. "It's all right, Alex. Sit down." He waited until Alex subsided, then said: "This is very difficult for all of us, and we must try to understand each other in our separate griefs. But I have to warn Mr Kalska that we're getting very close to the point where this situation will end up before the courts. He really can't go around making wild statements."

"If one of your family had made a phone call," David said, "none of this would've happened."

"It's easy to be wise when you know how the story turns out."

Alex looked as if he would burst a blood vessel any minute. Humbie picked up his notebook again.

"Are we calm now?" Gilston said. No one replied, so he went on. "If Mr Miller could fill in the details for us, we can get this over with. You say only you, your wife and the housekeeper spoke to Mr Kalska senior?"

"That's right," Alex fumed. "Father was in town."

"And Mr Kalska never asked for anyone known to you."

"Most of it was gibberish."

"And none of you knew him?"

"Of course not."

Gilston turned the pages of the report, studying the fuzz of carboned words. "That just leaves us with the one question. What was the address doing in his pocket?"

"*If* it was." Alex said.

"Let's assume it was for the moment."

Paul chipped in again. "Has it occurred to you that my father is very well-known?"

"He's on every front page," David sneered.

"They tell me Mr Kalska was suffering from senility."

"He wasn't senile."

"He was ill, I think we can agree. And my father has been one of the most respected surgeons in the neurological field for many years. Is it not possible that Mr Kalska senior got his name from some medical journal or through talking to another patient at his residential home, and came up here looking for a cure to his problems?"

David gaped. "What?"

Paul spread his hands in a gesture of reason. "I offer it as theory, that's all. Perhaps the poor old gentleman, in his confusion, got the idea that my father could perform some miracle for him. Unfortunately, he was too far gone by the time he reached the house to make himself understood."

"This is ridiculous," David protested, weakly. But it sounded as likely as anything else. More likely, in fact. Grandfather had talked to him once about an experimental operation that was supposed to reverse the effects of Parkinson's disease. "Maybe they have an operation to make me think straight again," he had said, smiling crookedly.

"Is this what your father thinks?" Gilston asked.

Paul shrugged. "I discussed it with him this afternoon. There's no record of Mr Kalska corresponding with him, so it's no more than a guess. But it could fit with the little we know."

David began to rub either side of his eyes. His head throbbed.

Gilston nodded. His bald head shone through a fine skein of hair. "I can't think of anything else just now." He closed the report. "It's all a very sad business."

"We're allowed to go now, are we?" Alex said. "Now that Mr Bloody Kalska's finished pointing the finger."

"Now then, sir . . ."

"He's only lucky Jenny wasn't home when he gave his little performance."

"Mrs Colvin," Gilston said, putting the brakes on violence again. "How is she now?"

"About as you'd expect," Paul said.

"And if we wanted to interview her about Mr Kalska senior's visit?"

"You'd have a bloody long way to go," Alex said.

"She's staying with friends in Cornwall," Paul explained. "Silcombe. We thought it best for her to get away for a while."

"Probably true, sir." Gilston stood. The interview was ended.

Paul got up, put his hand on Alex's shoulder as if to give permission to follow. "I hope this is the last of it, Inspector. We've had enough grief from this mess as it is."

Gilston escorted them to the door, pausing to get the address in Cornwall where the widow was staying.

David stayed where he was, chewing over his anger.

At the door, Alex glowered at him. "Don't bother us any more. Understand?"

Gilston ushered them out. The room was quiet. An odour of unpleasantness remained. Gilston sat down, put the scribbled address on top of the report. David tilted his head to read it: something like "Caradoc, Old Cottage." Gilston noticed his curiosity and covered the address with his hand.

"Is that it?" David said.

"For the moment. Unless you have anything to add."

"No. No, I don't." He rose. "They seem to have a lot of pull around here."

"Not with me, sir."

"The old man's very well-connected," Humbie said.

Gilston frowned. "We'll keep an eye on it. But you know they could be right with that idea."

He refused to agree.

"Is he any better?"

"He chugs along in neutral. That's about it."

"I'm sorry."

"So am I." He pulled himself together and put on his coat. "I have to go back tomorrow morning, but I'll be up again soon. If there's anything – "

"There's very little, sir. Perhaps we'll never know why."

"Maybe," David said.

But as he left the police station and headed back to the hospital, his anger was telling him that he would find out the important and stupid thing. He hated Miller and his sons as he had not hated anyone for years. Through no wish of his own, he had been thrown up against their confidence and superiority, and they had treated him like some animal. He could not say whether they were lying, or why they should need to. But he would know.

12

Yitzhak was talking with Charlie Bennet on Saturday morning, when he saw Josef's grandson pass through the hall. He stopped in the middle of a sentence, and Bennet – who was extremely deaf – raised a hand to his ear and squawked: "Eh?"

"Shut up a minute," Yitzhak snapped. The boy was going across the hall, Mrs Hawkes at his side. He had to talk with the boy this time. He waved at them. Bennet grew more petulant.

"What? What're you playing at?"

They did not see him. He would have to go after them. But when he tried to move, the pain almost sliced him in half. He crumpled in his chair, making a high, whining sound between his teeth.

"What the devil's the matter with you?" Bennet grumbled.

"Oh, shut up, you stupid old fool."

"We're keeping his room exactly as he likes it," Mrs Hawkes explained, as they climbed the stairs. "We hope very much that he'll be back with us soon."

"Thank you, I'll tell him," David said. He had come home on Thursday morning, but every time he had tried to get away for a while, a new problem arose.

Mrs Hawkes unlocked the door to Grandfather's room. "Here we are." She switched on the light to take away the morning gloom. "Nothing's been touched. What exactly was it you were looking for, if you don't mind my asking?"

He did mind. He sat on the edge of the desk and lifted the cover of a book called *The Struggle for Poland*. "As you suggested earlier, a few bits and pieces. Familiar things to have around him if he wakes up." He knew that loyalty should have made the "if" a "when", but Mrs Hawkes was too busy prying to notice. "Incidentally, in the weeks before he disappeared, what was he doing?"

She mused. "He was always happy to be up here in his room with his books and papers."

"Was he receiving any medical magazines?"

"Why, no, not that I'm aware of. But I could find a list of publications he received. It's quite extensive."

"That's okay. I'll probably find them here."

She squinted at the chess board. Beneath it were more paperbacks. "Most amazing," she said. She realised he was waiting for her to go. "I'll leave you alone then. If you should want anything . . ."

"Thank you, I'll be fine."

She dithered out, left the door ajar. When her footsteps faded, he closed it.

He turned and surveyed the room. It was a long space, made to look smaller by all the books and magazines. Grandfather had not been able to continue his trade when he came to England, of course; there were few opportunities in England for a bookseller who spoke only Polish. But he only ever felt safe in a room once it was lined with books; perhaps they reminded him of happier times in his former life.

The trouble with that idea was the nature of the volumes. Some were old, Polish or Yiddish, things he had ordered or picked up in second-hand shops. Most, though, were post-war: histories of the rise of the Nazis; the war; Poland after 1939; writings by people like Primo Levi and Bruno Bettelheim; fat volumes containing transcripts of war crimes trials. David knew many of them by sight. They had crammed the shelves at home when he was a boy. He used to ask: "Why go over it and over it? How can you sleep at night with this stuff hanging over your head?" At first, Grandfather would argue; later he settled into tolerant silence. That was in David's teens. They never talked about it much after that.

Looking around now, he sensed again Grandfather's silent reproach, as if the books themselves whispered: "Read me, you have to read me." He shook his head. Grandfather might have done better in the last forty years if he had spent fewer of them in the past.

He started with the bookshelves, looking first for medical journals, perhaps Miller's name on some textbook. There were titles like *Warsaw Death Ring*, *A History of the Jews*, *And We Are Not Saved*, names like Wola, Kaplan, Kermish, Falstein. He made himself go along each shelf until he was certain Miller's name was not there.

81

Next he went to the desk. He pulled out the drawers one by one, found several filled with stationery. Another held carbons of letters typed on the old portable beside the desk. The top one was to 'The Archivist, *Jerusalem Post*', asking for information on some trial. Another was to the librarian of the *Jewish Chronicle*, requesting the same. Others had gone to various publications and official bodies. Grandfather had been writing to some faraway places in the last six months. The letters were mostly in English, and David flushed with embarrassment at some of the mistakes. To think that the old man had been making a fool of himself in front of all these people.

He pulled another drawer. It was stuffed with notebooks. Grandfather's handwriting, very small and tight and in Polish, covered the pages. Some were rough books, where he had taken notes from his reading. One was something like a diary. It had an entry in English:

David and his young lady come today. The young lady is very pretty. Maybe at last he thinks of marrying.

He smiled. It was dated April last year, just after he had started seeing Sarah. She was at home now, perhaps wondering what he was doing at Brackford House. He had told her nothing. He felt guilty, and dug into the drawer.

There were two Denbeigh commercial books, green boards and red spines, older than the rest. The prices on the backs were in shillings and pence. They were numbered *I* and *II*. He looked at the first. Polish again, but the writing much steadier, younger. His eye went down the page, picking out words familiar from the translating he had done: *rozumieć*, to understand; *pamietać*, to remember; *pytonie*, question. In trying to make sense of it, though, he came up against the same problem as before. Most Polish words change slightly to indicate their function in a sentence. It took a lot of remembering to deal with that.

He started to put it down, then saw his own name. He ran over the paragraph around it again.

On to powinniście wiedzieć.

What was it? Something like: "You ought to know it."

He put both notebooks aside.

Nothing else of interest. He closed the drawer and reached

for a pile of magazines. Somewhere close by a quavering voice began to sing 'If You Were the Only Girl in the World'. He could not tell whether it was male or female.

Depression settled more heavily. The magazines were a mixed batch: Sunday supplements, copies of *Time*, *Newsweek*, *Stern*, *Paris Match*. Lots he had not seen before. They had one thing in common, and he already knew what it was. In each, either as a cover story or inside, there was something concerning the war and what was done in the war.

He grew angry again. There seemed to be no emotions left him but grief, anger and depression. It was the thought that, even in his dotage, Grandfather would not leave it alone. The famous and infamous photographs flashed in front of him, pinched faces gazed from the grain of black and white. They were always there.

He finished the pile and put them back. Then came a stack of assorted documents. Magazines, broadsheets, photocopies; the kind of things sent out by libraries and small societies. He scarcely glanced at them. At one time Grandfather used to leave such things lying about for him to find, but he always failed to show interest.

He turned to a final stack of newspapers. They were recent, none more than two years old. He chuckled ruefully. Grandfather's taste was certainly varied these days. All the quality dailies, some copies of the tabloids. He studied a few front pages. Sometimes it was difficult to find the reason for their being saved, but here and there, names jumped out of the print: Klaus Barbie was there; and many columns devoted to the investigations into Kurt Waldheim's war career. He read fragments of the stories, thinking how ridiculous it was to prosecute frail old men for things they might not have done almost half a century ago. Not that he denied the seriousness of it. But the actual process of hauling some toothless idiot into court and having other dodderers pretend they recalled in detail horrors forty years old struck him as pointless. As he used to say to Grandfather – when they still talked of such things: "Yes, it was the right thing to do back in the fifties and sixties, but not now. It's too far gone."

"Tell your family that," Josef would cry. "Tell your mother."

And he would shake his head, because he did not know his family, or even his mother, and could tell them nothing.

83

He turned up a copy of *The Times*. Top of the page was the headline:

WAR CRIMINALS IN BRITAIN.

His eye ran over the story.

Nazi-hunters from the Simon Wiesenthal Centre yesterday called on the British Government to investigate the cases of thirteen suspected Nazi War Criminals who have been living in Britain since the war.

There was plenty more. He half-remembered the fuss. It had been fairly big news in a dull week, when someone claimed that nearly seventy Nazis had been let loose in Britain after the war. Then the Wiesenthal Centre provided the names of thirteen men whom they said were still alive. Another wave of shock-horror reports followed.

The next paper was the *Independent*.

Allegations that a Middlesbrough man accused of war crimes lied to officials when he applied for British Citizenship are being investigated, the Government confirmed yesterday. Mr Katas, 71, is accused of being a member of the 13th Lithuanian Police Battalion which was responsible for the deaths of thousands of Lithuanian Jews.

An edition from a few days later featured the story on page two, pushed out of the limelight by a wrangle over education.

A Home Office spokeswoman denied that the British Government was 'soft' on war criminals. They were studying a thousand-page dossier on Mr Katas, and if anything could be proved, they would take the appropriate action.

The story revived once more when some MP threatened to use Parliamentary privilege to read out the twelve other names, but it came to nothing. Reading the collection of newspapers was like having a fast-forward view of the news process. Front page splash to begin with: outrage from the tabloids – although it could hardly compete in the outrage stakes with the loves and hates of a soap star who had just deserted his family for a teenage blonde; editorials in the quality press going over the issues of morality in war and out of it. Then the reaction: the question of whether it is right to continue dredging up the terrible memories; letters from public figures and private fools; the story itself moving to page two or three. A day is a long time in newspapers. When the Sundays had got their column inches out of it, the whole matter began to slip away into the spaces between local government and international news. The last mention he could find was a short press release from the Home Office. It stated that investigations of the thirteen were continuing, but no hard evidence had so far been found. End of story.

He had avoided news programmes and papers at the height of the shouting. He recalled people arguing in The Brewers. Someone who knew his family background had asked his opinion. He said he was too busy to notice. And he had been. He made sure of that.

He looked back through the pile. He felt cold, although the heating was full on. There was a little voice in the back of his head, telling him to leave it alone. He found a copy of the *Star*. A big-breasted model posed down the left-hand side of the front page, holding a fistful of bingo cards. "WIN, WIN, WIN!" said the caption. "NAZI KILLERS IN BRITAIN." said the headline next to it.

Someone knocked at the door.

He jumped, then called: "Come in." Nothing happened. Only a faint, rasping noise.

He went to the door.

A little old man on crutches leaned against the wall outside. His face was blue.

"For God's sake, get me inside," he gasped, "before I fall off these things."

13

David put his arms round the old man and helped him inside. He was feather-light, the bones of his shoulders sticking through his clothes. He kept grunting as David steered him to an armchair by the window.

"Is this all right?"

"Fine, fine," the old man whispered. "Just let me down gentle."

They had an awkward time with the crutches. One clattered on the floor and the voice next door stopped singing. It resumed with 'Violets for your Furs'. The old man grasped the arms of the chair and David lowered him slowly. He grunted all the way down, and pain was written in the lines of what had once been a chubby face.

"I'll get someone," David said.

"No!" the old man cried. "Listen, young man, you stay here, please." He settled into the chair, sighing. "I'm fine now, believe me."

David hesitated. The old man looked very ill. "I think I should get one of the nurses."

"Nurses," he cackled and coughed. "You keep them off me, boy. They like to practise injections on me. A pin cushion, that's what I am."

"Someone should know you're here."

"Will you listen? I tell you I'm okay. Don't go running. It's you I came to see."

"Me?"

"Across the lounge, into that lift – a death-trap, that's what – and all the way along the corridor to here. Not bad, considering."

"I'm sorry, I don't think we've met, have we?"

"You're right. Better be sure who's talking to who. Yitzhak. Yitzhak Zuckerman." They shook hands. "Friend of your grandfather's. How is he, anyway? They give us news three days old here."

"Still serious, but stable."

"At our age that means: 'Pardon me, sir, we have a little delay in processing your papers.' They think he'll pull through?"

"They don't know."

"That old fool. I told him not to."

"Not to what?"

"Go, escape, leave, disappear like a thief in the night. I said: 'Josef, you're an old, old man, gone weak in the head parts. You don't run off on crusades.'"

David sat down. "What do you know?" he said.

"I know, I know." Yitzhak's fevered eyes turned to the desk.

86

"You've been going through his files. Come to any conclusions?"

"I see one I don't like."

Yitzhak smiled, gestured at the room. "Look at this place. Three years this man is in hell. He's lucky, he gets out. And what does he spend the twilight of his life doing? He lives it over again every day. What kind of mind is that? I said to him: 'You're missing some screws, it's past.' And he'd say: 'No, no, no. It's not the past. It's now, this minute, all the time.'"

David watched the way his long, delicate hands flicked and swooped as he spoke. Sometimes pain would hit him, but he could not stop it. A lifetime of talking with his hands had made them as necessary as his mouth.

"You know, I came here six months ago. Is it six? My loving son and his wife shuffled me out here. After I bought them their house, you understand? Anyhow, this is when I meet Josef. Being the only couple of Jews in a place full of rich goys gives you something in common. I get to know him pretty well, pretty well. And of course he's chopping away at this 'work' of his. Always books delivered or letters coming. And that I don't understand. He bucks the trend, if you understand me."

"I'm sorry," David said. "I don't."

"Well, I've lived a long time. Not so long as Josef, but long enough for me. I was in Holland when the Germans came – never think so to hear me now, would you? – and I didn't get out in time, so I saw my wife go away one day and never come back. We didn't have children, anyhow. So I know what it's all about. And I realized something years ago." His gaze danced restlessly over the books on the desk. "It's this. You take a look at the people who do this Nazi-hunting – who eat, sleep and breathe it, nine times out of ten they were never there. The ones who make big with the outrage, they're the ones who got out, or come from safe countries, or weren't even born yet. Josef was the only man I ever meet was in the concentration camps and wanted to make a fuss about it."

David's face must have shown something. Yitzhak said:

"He told me you don't like to talk about it."

"I don't see the point."

"Yes, yes, he told me that. Talked a lot about you, wanted for you to understand." He winced, clenched his teeth suddenly. He held himself very straight as it passed.

87

"Please," David said. "Let me fetch someone."

"They can't make it go away, boy. It's better now . . . Yes, he wanted you to know, just to listen to him. Looks like he don't get the chance now."

"All I want to know is what he was after. It wasn't just sickness, was it? There was a purpose."

"You could doubt it? Look at this place. Missing on some cylinders he may be, but he had plenty of reasons."

The voice next door lost its thread. It stuttered twice over the first couple of bars of 'Night and Day', then launched into 'Without a Song'.

"He was already into this when I arrived," Yitzhak explained, indicating the newspapers. "First he doesn't talk to me about it. He's keeping secrets. But then we play a couple of games of chess. You play, don't you? Anyway, we play some games, and he sees I'm not a total schmo, and he starts to tell me. Even allows me into his inner sanctum here to see the files. And at this time, he's particularly steamed because of these 'Nazis in Britain' stories."

"He never told me."

"Why expect to be told things you don't want to hear? Your message got through to him, so he didn't bother you with it. But me, I got everything there was. What really annoyed him was how it all died down and nothing else got done. He's writing to all kinds of people, demanding they take action. He wants those bastards named. Had quite a pile of correspondence about it, too. Phone calls, even. I wouldn't want Josef on my back, I tell you. Persistent, that's what.

"He tried to bring me in, you know, writing letters, cutting his newspapers. But I say: 'Josef, I got better things to do with my dying days than play with scissors and paste. Besides, I don't know a thing about it. I don't want to waste my time.' But I used to have some contacts, so I give him a couple of names I think might be of use.

"I guess he was a little loose in the springs sometimes, but I tell you, he was a man with a purpose. Every day I get progress reports. He's in contact with someone – very secret – who can give him a list of the names. I figure this is not bad for an old man in the middle of nowhere. Either that or he's dreaming. I just play him the odd game when he's free and worry if I should say something to someone.

"So it goes along. Then one morning – this'd be six, seven weeks back, when we had that big snow – this particular morning, we have breakfast with all the other zombies, and he's looking very serious. Absolutely. I know something's wrong, but he won't tell me, just stares at the morning's correspondence, a big heap, and don't eat a thing.

"Later, I find him walking around the hall. One of the kind girls who looks after us, she's trying to stop him going out in the snow, and he's kicking up a fuss, saying he has to go. I help calm him down before they call someone with the needles, but he's really worked up, and still he doesn't tell me.

"In fact, I have to wait three days before he talks. One afternoon, I'm watching some trash on the box, and he comes to me and says: 'Yitzhak, I must talk to you.' I say: 'Sure.' What am I but his audience? So, he sits us down in a corner and tells me. First I think it's about the list. See, it turns out he's got the list, from someone connected with the war crimes investigators, and it's more than a dozen or whatever. But it's not the list. None of these guys he knows. What's got him so steamed up is something else he's come across, not connected at all. A picture in the paper."

"What of?" David said. "A trial?"

"Nah, nah," Yitzhak raised his hands. "He brings it down. It's from *The Times*, or one of those, one of the feature supplements they do these days. All about the pharmaceutical industry. There's just this photograph of three distinguished looking types at a conference table."

David rubbed his eyes.

Yitzhak said: "I look at this picture, and nothing's about Nazis. It's these three surgeons. I look at Josef, and I ask him what's it about? He gets flustered, expects me to know what he means by telepathy or something. He points to the one on the left and says: "This one.""

"Miller?" David said.

Yitzhak was surprised. "That's him. He says: 'This one I know. He's not Miller. He's Gelzer. He was a medical officer in Auschwitz when we were there. No one else knows.'"

David got up and went to the window. The old man watched him closely. He felt like a slide under a microscope. He felt sick. The voice sang, 'I'll Never Smile Again.'

"Did he have any proof?"

89

"About Miller/Gelzer, whichever? No, I don't remember so. He just knew. That's what he said, anyway. This Gelzer, he's meant to have died in Yugoslavia somewhere in forty-six. But Josef said he couldn't be wrong."

"From one photograph, after forty years?" David leaned his forehead on the cold glass. "Tell me something. Do you think he was . . . in control?"

"Who's to say? He looked mad-angry not mad-mad. He tries to get something done – writes to all kinds of people. Nothing much happens. He gets very broody then, tells me he'll go and confront this Miller himself if he has to."

"And you let him do it?"

Yitzhak's eyes blazed. "Did I say that? On the one hand I think he's just talking. I mean, neither of us is young stuff any more. The idea of him getting out of this place and making it all the way to Scotland, I don't think it's a possibility."

"And on the other hand?"

Yitzhak fell silent. His expression changed, grew cold. "We shared something. You couldn't understand it, haven't tried. The truth is, if he really wanted to do it, I wasn't going to stop him. We had everything stolen from us once before. I'm not going to take away his chance to do what he thought was right."

14

A fiery haze of morning sunlight burned over the distant marsh as David and Tony walked down to Haverley Dyke. A few cars were parked outside the church, and the sound of scattered voices singing 'Onward Christian Soldiers' threaded into the clear air. The lane was frozen hard, but the sun had broken through. Sal leapt in front of them, nosing the broken puddles. Grandfather's condition lay over the day like a shadow, but Tony had suggested the visit to the boats as a way to get David's mind off things for a while.

"Feels like the first day of spring at last," he said, ostentatiously beating his chest. "Only one thing mars the perfection."

"What would that be?" David asked.

"The mess the boats'll be in."

David yawned. He had been up late last night, reading in detail the newspaper reports on the Nazis in Britain. He now knew as much as it was possible for the general public to know, which was little enough.

The dyke was deserted. It was early in the year to be thinking of repairing the slow attrition of winter. They climbed on to the waterside path and went to inspect the boats. The *Marie* was exactly as he had seen her when he looked for Grandfather. *Calliope* was a little further up the dyke, between an old motor cruiser and a dinghy. They elected to look her over first.

She swung gently against the bank as they approached. The tarpaulin covering her cockpit was stained with bird lime and heavy in the centre with accumulated rain.

"Oh, God," Tony said gloomily, stepping aboard. "Let's retire to the pub."

"They're not open yet," David said. "Come on. We can get that water out before she gives way."

They unfastened the tarpaulin and spilled the water over the stern. David dumped a rucksack full of tools on the cockpit sole and helped to haul the canvas back. Underneath she was fine. A bird had got in somehow and died. The skeleton lay on the floor. Apart from that it just looked worn and sad, as boats do after a winter on the water.

"Every year," Tony said, while he found the keys for the cabin door, "I swear I'll put her on the hard for the winter and let old Matthews in Lotton worry over her. And every year – " he broke a fingernail getting the hatch open " – I let it pass, and have to endure this."

They clambered inside, the boat moving under their weight as they explored. It was cold and damp, but they warmed as they started the work of cleaning out and seeing what would need scraping down and re-painting. About eleven-thirty, when both were sweating to put up the sails and check them, Tony grinned at him and said: "This is more like it." David was grateful to have him for a friend.

At twelve-thirty they made themselves as comfortable as they could in the cockpit and took out sandwiches and Thermos flasks of coffee. Julia had made them, and she knew how much they could eat, so there was plenty. The taste of food and hot coffee after exercise gave David a fleeting sense of

91

well-being, but it passed. The little sleep he had managed last night had been like staying awake in the middle of a lonely place of hills and sky. When he closed his eyes he saw Miller and Alex and Paul and the daughter, Jenny. Could this be the man Grandfather thought? Gelzer. The face and the bearing, and the trace of accent. Someone had said he came from Switzerland.

"Have a look at your hulk after this, shall we?" Tony's mouth was full. He was pleased with everything because he lived always in the present. His openness was genuine, David knew, and had not been blunted yet by the job he did. He sorted through his remaining sandwiches. "Bloody peanut butter here. Hate peanut butter."

"Swap you an egg mayonnaise," David said.

The exchange was made, and Tony tucked in ravenously.

David gazed at the water out at the mouth of the dyke. It was alive, black and silver where it reflected sky. The banks were dry and yellow, but the worst of winter was done.

"Tony?"

"Mmm?"

"How much do you get to hear about – down in London, I mean?"

"You're speaking of London in general, or my little patch of it?" He spoke indistinctly through his lunch.

"Specifically your patch. I mean, do you get to hear the news behind the news?"

"Tell you some choice tales about shady business deals. Not just the Conservative benches, either. You'd be surprised what some of the Brothers get up to once they find themselves in the House. Or is it the naughty stuff you're after? The lads who harp on about old-fashioned family values while they're knocking off everything in sight, the number of my honourable colleagues who spend their evenings in public lavatories." He grimaced. "Must say I'm shocked and horrified. This is the first time you've shown any of these tendencies."

"I don't care if the Prime Minister's sleeping with the Leader of the Opposition," David said, too emphatically. Tony's playful glint died away, replaced by concern.

"It's about Josef," he said.

David shrugged. "I don't want to abuse a privilege."

"Oh, for God's sake. How long have we known each other?"

92

"It's something . . . It's important."

Tony half-closed his eyes. Then he said: "Well, tell me."

David told him. Tony stopped eating. He filled his cup and drank steadily as he listened, growing incredulous then irate.

"And this chap was helping out at Auschwitz when Josef was there?" he said.

"That's what he told Mr Zuckerman."

"Good God."

"I don't know whether there's any truth in it or not. No one seems to. Miller isn't mentioned anywhere, not even in the list of possibles. I don't know who to go to about it."

Tony drew a notebook and pencil from his jacket. "All that damned hue and cry." He drew his spectacles from a pocket and put them on as if this was a move from pleasure to business. "It was before I got into the House, but I remember it. Thirteen names that couldn't be divulged and a lorryload more too obscure to be bothered with. That's our wonderful system for you: a crowd of evil buggers like that can sit tight and ride it out. What name you say this chap goes by?"

"Miller, or Gelzer."

Tony wrote the names down. "Damn it! Poor old Josef. Gets himself buggered up because some swine who should've been strung up in '45 spent the post-war years getting fat over here."

"If it's true," David said.

"I'll see whether I can find out. I know a few people who ought to be some use. I'm going down on Tuesday for some bloody farming debate, but I'll start ringing round straight away."

The day had lost its brightness. Both of them were simmering with anger.

"You've thought about what it could mean," Tony said at last, "if Josef was right?"

David nodded.

"He was knocked flat outside the man's back door. Very convenient for Mr Gelzer-Miller if he wants to keep his identity secret."

"I've thought about it," David said.

He was thinking of little else.

15

At home that night, David began to read his Grandfather's notebooks. Using the phrase books, dictionaries and memories of speaking, he began, slowly and painfully, to translate.

It began: "My son." For a while, he thought the books were written to Benjamin or Aron. But further down the page was his name.

> *David, when you read this, I will be gone. You will think perhaps at last you have peace. But I am here to trouble you again.*
>
> *All the years you have lived, you have been an orphan. No family but me, no country to call your own. Later you made this so yourself, because you did not wish to hear. Perhaps you were right: to live in a past which is lost might be very bad for a boy growing up in a changed world. Perhaps you had to be free of the past so you could grow into the fine man you have become.*

He could not remember Grandfather ever saying he was proud of him. Love, yes, but not pride. Everything had to be guessed.

> *You might read this soon, or many years after I am gone. But I believe no one exists only in the present. Where is a building without foundations? Even if everything you would know if the world had gone differently has been destroyed, I think you will reach a day when you do want to know.*
>
> *All my life I had the knowledge of a past – familiar places and people, family and history. This is what you lost, and maybe it is worse than anything else you have lost. That is what I want to tell you. Not so far back, not generations. Just about your mother and where she was born, what happened to her, and to us, before and after the changes came.*

He almost stopped then.

But his eye ran over the next sentence, and was caught by words he understood. It was like trying not to look at a car accident. Laboriously, he translated the rest.

> *Your mother was born on a Sunday afternoon. July 17th, 1928. In Bodstan.*

94

It was then, he would think later, that it really began; the descent into the pit where he lost all contact with what he had been, so that he hardly knew the days any more. The ground tilted gradually, so he did not notice at first, but it went out from under him all right.

16

No word from Tony until Tuesday. He called from London to say that he would be meeting a chap on some committee who might provide information.

"Don't worry,' he said. "If there's a grain of truth in it, we'll get the bastard."

He went back to Brackford House and spent most of a dull afternoon going through Grandfather's mini-library again. He dragged down each book that concerned itself with the fate of the Jews between 1939 and 1945, checking each for references to a Gelzer. He ran down each index in turn, finding some unmarked, others scored and asterisked in varying colours. He tossed aside nearly a hundred volumes, and found nothing.

He began to think: What if it's all bullshit? What if Gelzer never existed? Auschwitz was mentioned again and again, whole columns given over to it. But under G he found only headings like 'Gas', 'Ghetto', 'Grese, Irma', and 'Grabner, SS Lieutenant'.

He went downstairs to ask one of the staff whether he could have a cup of coffee, wandered into the lounge searching for Yitzhak Zuckerman. Yitzhak was not there. His 'illness' had taken a turn for the worse, so he had been moved into Norwich, where proper care could be taken of him.

Carrying a mug of instant, he returned to Grandfather's room and went on with the search. Three books later, he finally saw the name. It was in a fat brown volume called *Testimony of Survivors*. 'Gelzer, Ernst Eduard': one reference on page 542, a few paragraphs in the memories of a woman called Anna Bruskin who had been sent to Auschwitz from Lublin in 1943.

And there was another doctor there, who helped Mengele with his 'chores'. We would hear the cry: 'Lagersperre! Lagersperre!' and have to strip off and line up for selection. This selection might mean they needed more bodies for Mengele's experiments, or it might be just another winnowing of the sick from the relatively healthy. Mengele would come with Lagerführer Hossler and Rapportführer Taube, sometimes Dr Rohde, sometimes Gelzer.

Mengele wore white gloves. Going along the lines, he would occasionally order us to run. Those who could not summon the strength were sent to the left. Mengele would point them out. Left was death, right meant a little more life.

And this Gelzer, he was young. I remember he watched Mengele work with admiration. He was just like the rest of them. As a civilian, he had been in some good position at a hospital in the Reich; saving lives, I suppose. He had come to assist one of his professors from student days in experiments. Using living flesh for bacteria culture, performing operations without anaesthetics, making poisonous injections into healthy wombs in attempts at sterilization.

And sometimes he came to the barracks late at night, and took away whoever he wanted. For 'further work'.

That was all. No physical description, no real history of the man. Certainly no photograph. David worked through the remaining books without coming across the name again. Whoever Gelzer was, he had not been a huge cog in the machine.

Except to the people whose sexual organs he hacked about on the operating tables. Except for the ones he burned with concentrated doses of X-rays. Except for the ones who woke in the night to see him beckoning.

Was it possible that a man could do those things, then escape, and turn himself into a highly respected surgeon? Wouldn't he give himself away?

He remembered like a fuzzy newsreel the reports of Mengele's death in South America, not so long ago. Mengele had done all right for himself, and he was far more infamous than this Ernst Eduard Gelzer.

"Kate, ask Barry Ockley to pop over, will you."

While he waited, David resumed studying plans for the Wensum Mall. It looked very good on paper, but then it always had. When it went through, his part of it would probably make him a rich man. He had never cared much for money on its own terms, only the security it gave to please himself. At the moment, though, it was difficult to believe in the mall or any of it.

The intercom buzzed. Kate announced the visitor.

Ockley came in, as long, thin and pale as ever. David stood up to greet him, marvelling as always at the man's droopy, Norfolk air of being half-asleep, and none too bright even wide awake. He offered him a chair and a drink. Ockley accepted a lager. Sipping it as he arranged his awkward limbs in a swivel chair, he wrinkled his high forehead and said:

"Terribly sorry to hear about your grandfather. Wonderful old gentleman."

"I'll give him your best wishes," David said. "Listen Barry, you working on anything major just now?"

"Some divorce cases, bit of writ serving. We're ticking over." He always said 'we' when he meant 'I'. "But if there's anything you want done, I reckon we could fit it in as a priority."

"Good. How are you with investigations going back a few years?"

"Depends how far."

"Wartime."

"Wartime?"

"If you can't deal with it, I'll probably have to go to a London firm."

Ockley stirred. "Tell me what it is exactly."

"I want you to look into a feller called Miller. George Miller. He's an Edinburgh surgeon with lots of important letters after his name. Semi-retired now. Supposed to come from Switzerland."

"Surveillance at all?"

"I'm not interested in what he's doing now. Just get some documentation from wherever you get stuff like that, about when he was born, where, what he did in the war, that sort of thing. I want to know whether he is what he says he is."

"I can do that." Ockley said. "Might mean some pretty extensive travel, though. Scotland, at least, if not Switzerland."

"Just send me the bill."

"All right. It's a bit different to my usual stuff. Make a change, anyway." They talked the details into Ockley's micro-cassette, then he rose and shambled towards the door. His hand went suddenly to his straw-coloured hair and he turned. "Oh, one thing."

"Yes?"

"There any risk involved?"

"Shouldn't think so. Not unless a filing cabinet falls on you."

"Okey doke." He nodded and was gone.

David resumed work. Ockley sounded like a bit of a joke – the only Private Eye with a Norfolk accent – but he was good at his work. Tony had said he would do what he could, but there was no harm having a little insurance of his own.

Luba was a pretty child. You might not believe it from the pictures you have seen, but it is true.

She was a very good swimmer, she could ride a bicycle at three years old. From very early, she loved to go on the walks we used to have on Sunday afternoons. We would set off after lunch, all the family, and climb into the hills.

We were not rich, but we did well enough. I had the bookshop on Gorsky Street, and we lived in comfortable apartments. There was a nanny for the children, a gentile girl. Later this girl spat on the children she had helped to raise, but that was later. Four children: Benjamin, the eldest; Aron and Luba, and little Janka, who came late, in the June before the war.

We had been in Bodstan for five generations. Longer than many gentile families. My great-great-grandfather came to the place after the pogroms in Podborodz in the nineteenth century. We had a position in the town. A Jew is never truly safe anywhere, but we had been there so long, and I trusted that this was life. I ran my shop and did very well. I collected old editions, and in those days I knew a great deal about the literature of our people.

We were never a strict religious family. Your grandmother – my wife, Feigele – made sure no Hoshana Rabba or Succoth was ever forgotten, but I was relaxed about these matters. We lived in a Christian community, our children went to school with Christian children. We integrated, to use a modern catchphrase. It was the best way, so I thought; to remember the Day of Atonement and the night of Simchat Torah, but to keep it in its proper place in the modern world. I was very enthusiastic about the modern world then. I believed the twentieth century would solve all the old problems. The result of nineteenth-century ideas of rationality in my education. I did not know then how irrational the world could become.

She was a bright child. Quick, learned fast. Sometimes bad. She could be a ringleader, and she knew how to get whatever she wanted from her brothers. She could outswim them, outskate them. But for all that, she liked to be alone. I think we understood each other well because of this similarity. Fathers should not have favourites, but it is impossible not to. All my children were dear to me but, in my heart, Luba was my special one.

I do not think she knew about the hatred of Jews until she was quite old. There were sometimes incidents in town, none major, hardly noticeable. But there was that time when she went to an inter-schools gymnastics competition in Lodz. She came home and told me how some of the children in the audience – Polish children – shouted and jeered at Jewish members of the teams. She asked what it meant. I tried to explain as much as a child should know, but I was not good at it. Uncle Mavro was the man for that. He knew every crime ever committed against the Jews. I think she did not understand what I was telling her. The idea of people like her schoolfellows nursing hatred of us because we followed a different creed, it was beyond her understanding.

Who really can pretend to understand it? I always knew. It was so much a part of every day – the little snubs and whispered words, the occasional roughing-up on a street corner. I accepted it, like the rest of my family and friends, as some kind of natural phenomenon, like earthquakes or storms.

Perhaps you must know this before all else. People read the history books. Disbelieving, they say: "Why did you not see what was happening? Why did you not try to stop it before it went so far?" We had no history books to tell us that things would suddenly get much worse than we ever imagined. We did not have it ordered on the page. Everything happened slowly at first, and so scattered that no one knew it all. Even after everything speeded up, you listened and did not know what to believe.

But this is not a history. I will not tell you what you can find for yourself in any library. This is only my story. And your mother's.

At the time when the life we had known came to an end, Luba was ten years old. The news had been growing worse for some time. Everyone seemed to know it was coming, but could do nothing about it. One day the war had not begun, next day it was there. They came into the country on trains. It is said that the carriages they travelled in were daubed with slogans the good German boys had thought of. 'We're going to Poland to thrash the Jews.' That was 1 September.

Bodstan was less than a hundred kilometres from the border. That night we went to the Synagogue. We had not been for some time before that. It was crowded with people praying, welcoming the Sabbath. We took the children and they knelt between Feigele and I, and we joined the prayer. I had been thinking we should go to Lodz – Feigele's sister, Esther, lived there, but now the whole town was in uproar. The railway station was crowded, buses all gone. We could not hire a car. We decided to sit tight, hoping we could ride out whatever storm was coming.

But it began even before they arrived. Gangs of youths roamed the streets, burning shops, beating up any Jew they found. Bodstan was a place of many bloods: Germans, Poles, Jews. All three languages you could hear in the streets. For so many years everyone lived together as best they could. Polish forces were fighting. Poles side by side with Jews. But consider: many German heroes of the First World War were Jews. It did not stop Hitler – an old soldier himself, from having them destroyed.

The first we saw of the official enemy were the planes. I was in my shop in the afternoon, discussing the price of some rare volumes with an old collector friend. He was getting out and needed to sell the books for travelling cash. I was still doing business. Can you believe it? But so were my neighbours. Look at any war, and it is the things that continue that will surprise you. Suddenly, there was the drumming of engines far away. My friend gathered up his books. I said: "Wait, they are probably our planes." And just then the first explosion came. They were bombing the city.

Friday came and he climbed on board the plane at Norwich airport. As it climbed steeply away from the city into a cold blue sky, he worked steadily on the first notebook. The businessman next to him kept glancing at the pages and the way David's lips moved as he spoke the words silently. When coffee was served, he said: "That Russian?"

"Polish," David muttered.

"Look alike, don't they, those Communist languages?"

At the hospital, the nurses several times caught him pronouncing a sentence to Grandfather, asking what it meant.

Lymon told him there was an improvement, but Grandfather appeared further from life than ever.

The temptation to drive out to Miller's house was very strong. He spent a useless evening at the hotel, drinking too much and developing intricate fantasies about confronting him. Supposing Grandfather had already done this, and that was why he lay in hospital now? It raised interesting questions. Say Miller was Gelzer: would his children know? His wife was dead, but he had married her after coming to Britain anyway.

Every time he went into the streets of the city, he expected to meet one of them. He was not certain whether this pleased or frightened him. Even in the hospital, he never felt completely free of Miller's presence. The man had spent a long, distinguished career in this place, performed thousands of operations, saved many lives. Some of the older nurses remembered his formidable presence. Without being too obvious, he pumped them for information. That was how he found out about the new techniques he had developed to decrease the

100

risks involved in cranial surgery, about his continuing contact with the hospital.

"Why, you'll still see him on the wards from time to time," a Sister told him, "striking fear into everyone he passes." She smoothed her uniform approvingly. "If the consultant gets a problem he can't see his way round, he'll call in Mr Miller for an opinion. Retired he may be, but he still takes an interest."

"What part of Switzerland does he come from?"

"Why, I don't know. He's not the sort of man you ask personal questions. One of the old school, Mr Miller. Still it'd be a lie to say he's cold. People think that, but he cares, right enough. Why, he's keeping an eye on your grandfather."

"Is he, by God?"

"Oh, yes. And when you think that it's because of Mr Kalska – if you'll excuse me – that his son-in-law died, well it just shows, doesn't it?"

David said: "Yes it does." It definitely does.

It took only a little while. They came like a whirlwind. Tanks, armoured vehicles, lorryloads of troops, all on the way to greater glory. There were people in the streets to welcome them, cheer them as if they were saviours.

Luba came to me and said: "I see men on the houses." We went to look from her bedroom window. Machine-guns were being mounted on the roofs of German-owned houses across the street.

The fighting forces passed on soon enough. But they left 'special units', operational groups of the SS. The first day, they gathered a number of Jews in the market place, a few important citizens. Our next door neighbour was in the crowd. I was there, with Aron and Benjamin, but they did not take us. They surrounded this crowd – women, children, old people – with machine-guns. The rest, the Poles, Germans and Jews who were not taken, had to watch. Rain was falling in a light mist. I remember the rooftops gleamed with it, and the machine-gun crews on the roofs, their helmets like black slate.

No one was sure what this was. Perhaps the invaders needed working parties to clear the mess they had made. Nothing was clear except the feeling of terror. I wanted to get out, but I could not go. Aron and Benjamin cried, and I told them they must be quiet. I was afraid we would be noticed. The people around us, many looked like the crowd at a football match. Their faces were eager, waiting for the game to begin.

And then the first shootings, there in the market place. The shots rang round the square. It was difficult to tell where they came from, until the screaming started. I tried to see over the crowd, saw people inside the ring moving like iron filings away from a repelling electrical field. They were trying to get out of the way, but there was nowhere to go.

Dragging the boys with me, I fought through the spectators. The officers in command spoke quiet orders, the soldiers herded more people into a line against a wall. I saw the soldiers take a man perhaps my age. They threw him across the cobbles then forced him up and into line. A girl, thirteen maybe, screamed and ran after him, shouting for her father. She was stopped by one of the soldiers. A tall, well turned out young man perhaps ten years older than her. She pleaded with this man to spare her father. She spoke in German and in Polish, a babble of words. She actually wrung her hands before him. She begged him to let her father go.

The soldier smiled at her. He looked very reasonable. His face suggested that her pleas touched his heart. He said – his voice was soft, but I heard it clearly, because everyone nearby was silent and waiting, only the women and children in the line sobbing gently – he said to her: "You are very impudent, child." It was like gentle scolding. The girl must have thought she was succeeding. Her eyes lost a little of the fear. He said: "Open your mouth." Confused, she did as he told her.

He raised his pistol and fired into her mouth.

Before he left Edinburgh on Sunday, he phoned Tony's home number.

Julia answered. She sounded distracted, but they exchanged the usual greetings and enquiries after Grandfather's health. Then David asked if Tony was in.

"He's not, I'm afraid," Julia said, in her fruity, well-educated voice.

"We're supposed to be messing about in boats again on Wednesday."

"Ah," she said. "I don't think he can make that after all. He's not back from London, you see."

"What's up? I didn't notice the Government tottering on the news last night."

"Oh, it's something to do with Brussels. He said he'd probably have to hang on until the end of the week."

"That's a pity." He was doodling eyes on the pad by the phone. Wide, scared eyes, netted with wrinkles. "Did he say anything about some information he was digging out for me?"

"I don't think so . . . No, definitely."

On the flight home, he thought about the conversation. He had a vague, queasy notion that Tony was being evasive.

Paranoia, he thought. You're getting crazed with this. A

seventy-year-old surgeon's a retired Nazi, one of my best friends is avoiding me, and Sarah's giving me a hard time.

Sarah, Sarah, Sarah. He wished things were better between them, but he knew they were not. He was stuck head first in the whole rotten mess. All he wanted was for it to be over, however it ended; yet he could not back away from it. Grandfather was speaking to him through the notebooks.

At home, there was no one, just a note from Sarah. She had gone to visit her parents in Leicester for a long weekend. Another drop in the bucket: she'd mentioned nothing about it before he left. Everyone was keeping secrets.

It was eight-thirty on Sunday evening. There were a dozen people he could see. The Brewers across the bridge was full of people who would do to pass the evening.

He locked the door, slammed a pizza in the microwave, and slotted a Suzanne Vega album in the CD. He left his post on the hall table and got back to work on the notebooks.

That evening they provided another taste of what was to come. Two hundred Jews were herded into the synagogue, the doors locked, and the building set on fire. Uncle Mavro saw it. He had gone there to pray, but arrived too late to be included in the crowd. He had such a knowledge of the things that had been done to our people over the centuries, but had never seen it himself. Not until this night. Weeping hysterically, he told us how the flames caught, how the people inside realized what was happening and tried to get out. He said those few who found a way, through a window or a back door, were shot as they escaped. The fire burned for hours, and the smell drifted across the city like the smell of cooking.

And this was hardly more than a week after it began. One week for the world to change so completely. I remember the children talking in their rooms, where we sent them so they shouldn't see or hear Uncle Mavro crying and retching as Feigele forced him to drink.

The Germans issued a decree. A five o'clock curfew. Anyone found in the streets after that would be shot. Everything was in chaos. Feigele and I agreed that we should keep the children in safety, and perhaps as the Germans advanced, we would have a chance to escape. But I had to venture out, to get food. In secret I met with friends and tried to discover what was happening from them. I heard, at second or third hand, the stories told by those who had reached the city from towns and villages nearby.

One was about the Rabbi of Widawa. The Germans ordered him to burn the Holy books. He refused to do it, so they set him alight, and burned him with the Scrolls of the Law in his hands.

103

A report from Ockley arrived at the office. It had been typed on a portable machine in London, where Ockley was staying while he delved in records offices. He had found papers relating to Miller's entry into England in 1947. They seemed to be in order. He would be back in Norwich at the end of the week and would report in person then.

David was disappointed. What had he been hoping for? A written statement, brown with years in some official file, that said: 'George Miller is actually Gelzer, the war criminal'?

An itemised list of expenditure followed, right down to a mention of 40p for photocopying.

David threw the report in a drawer and hoped Tony would finally come up with something.

He was going through the box of papers he had brought back from Brackford House when he came upon a glossy page torn from a book. It contained six small photographs, black and white, very old. Under each was a name and a rank, written in German.

Some were clearly from identification papers. One had the round black mark of an official stamp in the corner. Others were copies of copies, so fuzzy that he could hardly make out the features.

One of these showed a man in the black uniform of the SS. He was turning away from the camera, arm raised.

Underneath, it said: 'Dr Ernst Gelzer'.

Sickness rose in his throat. He gulped it back and forced himself to remain still. He studied the photograph as closely as he could.

What it portrayed was an indistinct grey face partly shaded by a tilted cap. It seemed he was passing a remark to the uniformed figures at his shoulders. Possibly he was smiling. The background was a dim suggestion of coniferous trees and sky. It looked as if it had been taken secretly. The grain made it almost abstract.

The caption said it was Gelzer. The photograph said it could be anyone.

He strained hard to persuade himself that there was a distant echo of the old man he had seen in Scotland, but even the desire to see could not convince him. The man in uniform was perhaps tall, perhaps dark-haired. His nose might have been prominent, or it might simply be the angle of the shot. No one was going to haul Miller in for questioning on such evidence.

He turned the page over. It was blank on the other side, as illustration pages were in older books. On it was Josef's handwriting. Blue ballpoint, years old.

"This was one of the devils."

One day, he rang Trevor Games' office to confirm lunch. Trevor's secretary said Mr Games had been forced to cancel. He was in Essex on urgent business.

David resumed drawing. Unease worked at the pit of his stomach. It wasn't like Trevor to cry off a lunch date. Especially when the mall development was coming up for consideration at a council meeting in a couple of weeks. There were all kinds of details he had been desperate to discuss last week.

Mid-morning a call came in from his solicitor. He waited for Kate to put it through, tapping a pencil against the cover of Grandfather's first notebook.

"Ah, David?" Laurie Hollaston's voice oozed out of the phone like rum. "Can I trot round?"

"Now?"

"If it's not inconvenient."

David said it was not. He changed Mahler for Mozart on the office stereo, poured himself coffee from the machine by the window and looked down on the traffic pounding Prince of Wales Road.

Laurie arrived ten minutes later. He came into the office with his usual long-legged stride, expensively tailored and clean as a well-polished piece of maple. They shook hands and Laurie folded himself neatly into a chair. David sat at his drawing board, hand on the notebook.

"Well," Laurie said, one eyebrow hoisting itself into its usual quizzical position. "And how is your grandfather?"

"Getting by. You're not carrying an armful of files, Laurie. What's the game?"

Laurie coughed genteelly. He seemed relaxed. He always did. "As your solicitor, David, it behoves me occasionally to ask difficult questions. In this case, I thought I'd better come straight to you for my information."

David's eyes narrowed. "What's up?"

"Are you presently under investigation by the Inland Revenue?"

A bus roared away from its stop below the windows, shuddering the glass. David frowned. Surprise made him slow.

"No," he said at last.

"Any government body?"

"Not that I'm aware of. Why?"

"Forgive me. But there's no reason why you *should* be of interest to anyone like that?"

David's temper was already short. The fuse was burning very close now. "Laurie, what's the problem?"

Another polite cough. All chaps together. "I have to tell you that there are nasty little rumours flying about. Trevor Games was on the phone to me yesterday, demanding to hear what I knew. Of course, I know nothing at all. Trevor was in quite a lather, though."

"He's always sweating. He should lose some of that weight."

"Well, of course I tried to calm his fevered brow, but it was difficult when I had nothing concrete to offer."

David returned to the coffee pot and refilled his cup. "Where the hell did he get an idea like that?"

"One of those grapevine things, apparently. Trevor got it from a friend, who heard it from some other unidentified face at a Saturday night party."

"You find out who it was," David said, "and we'll sue him."

"Exactly." Laurie studied his elegantly crossed trouser leg. "Considering the timing – with the Wensum Mall business getting so close to finalisation, I immediately assumed it was an attempt at a spoiling operation. Discrediting you at this point could be quite ruinous to the entire venture."

"Not to mention letting quite a few envious people in on the deal. We've got to nail this one fast," David said. "And the bastard who's spreading it. Anyone else contacted you?"

"No one. But if Trevor knows, I expect everyone else will by now."

"Okay. I'll start repairing the damage." He picked up the phone and asked Kate to get hold of the other members of the consortium. Laurie was already up and ready to go. David showed him out.

"I hope you understand," Laurie said. "As your solicitor, it's necessary for me to ask. I've had clients who kept quiet right up till the moment I received a call from the gaol."

"That's all right," David said. He paused, not releasing him. "Laurie, what do you know about – " he searched for a word, but had to resort to the known term " – the Holocaust?"

The solicitor blinked rapidly. His face took on a guarded look as he tried to connect it with the previous conversation. "The Holocaust. Don't think I'm with you, David."

"What do you know about it?"

"The same as everyone else, I suppose. Terrible things. The films they show occasionally to remind us of what happened, so it won't happen again. I don't quite see . . ."

David shook himself out of it. He was embarrassing Laurie, and worrying Kate, who had stuck in mid-word at the type-writer. "Never mind. Just go back to the office and get the writs drawn up."

He returned to his desk, cursing loudly. As much for his behaviour as for the news of rumours.

"Hello, is that Anthony Chandor's office?"

A modulated Hampstead voice said: "This is his secretary. Can I help you?"

"I'm trying to get in touch with him."

"I see. Is it constituency business?"

"Personal."

"Could you give me your name?"

"I'm a friend of Mr Chandor's. David Kalska."

"Mr Kalska." No recognition. "I'm afraid Mr Chandor's not in the House at the moment. He's fulfilling a speaking engagement in the City."

Pause to control the urge to shout. "Could you take a message for me?"

"Certainly, Mr Kolska." The faraway clatter of other lines and tones as she reached for a pen.

"I'd like him to call me as soon as possible. Even if he has no news for me."

"Right. I'll give him that message for you."

"Thanks."

"But I can't guarantee when that'll be. Mr Chandor may not be back in the House today. He's very busy at the moment."

"Yes. I've noticed."

They organised things very well, and then we could not hide at home. We were forced to work for them. The boys and I were taken in work parties to clear rubble and carry their equipment. I saw men cleaning toilets with their prayer shawls, women stripped and forced to dance for their tormentors. But we were lucky. Some were taken in trucks and never returned. One morning the baker on the corner was there, the next gone.

Our New Year in 1939 was 14 September. By then, the conquerors were passing laws to transfer all Jewish owned business to Aryan hands. I saved as much valuable stock as I could, but books are cumbersome things. How I prayed for diamonds and gold and good hard cash in those days. But the Germans had already taken that.

They took other things that mattered more. The brilliant psychology of the ignorant. On the Day of Atonement, when we are supposed to repent and pray with hope for the year to come, they broke into the halls where the people were gathered and shouted down the prayers with their own drunken songs. It was the holiest day in our calendar, and they broke it in pieces with obscenities and gunfire. They were good, too, at the smaller indignities. The same day, they ordered several hundred Jews into the hall of the Religious School on Zegarow Street. They kept them there all day without food or water or access to lavatories. They made them shit on the floor. Then they gave them the curtains of the Holy Ark, prayer shawls, Holy books, and told them to clean up the mess.

The next day, I found the children gathered at a window, watching silently. I followed their gaze. Down in the street, old Mr Feferman was kneeling on the ground. They had cut off his beard, and his white hair hung about his face. Three young soldiers were making him pick up dirt off the middle of the street. Cars were passing, the people in them jeered and waved.

Aron and Ben were pale with fear and anger. They understood. But Luba's face was merely curious. We had kept her from these scenes until now. She said: "Daddy, why are they doing that?" The soldiers, laughing and staggering, kept prodding the old man with their fixed bayonets. He could hardly stay on his knees, but they kept 'encouraging' him with kicks and stabs.

I bundled her away from the window, took her to where Feigele was nursing the baby. I wanted to go help Mr Feferman. Feigele cried at me not to go, upsetting Luba and the baby. Soon all were wailing. Feigele told me I must not go down there. What would it accomplish? I would be shot, and she and the children would be left alone.

I allowed myself to be persuaded. God alone knows whether it would have been better to go to the old man then, to end it quickly with a bullet. At least that way I would not have seen what happened to my loved ones afterwards.

A couple of days later, David and Sarah went across the bridge to the Brewers. Both were tired; Sarah from work, David from trying to lay the rumours to rest. They said little as they left the house, walking several paces apart. A cool blush of sunset hovered over the city, and the pub was busy. David opened the door for her and they went inside.

The chat did not actually stop, no one stared outright, but his arrival was noted differently. It used to be that people smiled or waved as he came in. He had a lot of friends in this pub. Neighbours and associates. Now they nodded curtly and pretended to be deep in conversation.

Sarah caught it too. She glanced at him, her pale blue eyes making a question. He had not told her about the rumours, but everyone else seemed to have heard. He offered her a barstool. She perched on it uncomfortably, looking at the other customers.

"What's wrong?" she whispered, as he bent close to her.

"Tell you later," he said.

All the while he was fighting rage. No one in business had ever talked dirty about him like this. For one crazy moment, he wanted to hammer on the bar, call everyone to attention, tell them that the entire story was a lie. He did not do it. He had been self-contained all his life. Now was not the time to go public.

Sarah's face was in her hand. She did not understand what was going on, and was too tired to shrug it off.

"You all right?" he said, leaving his pint of bitter untouched.

She lifted her face to his, and it was almost as if she had joined with the rest of them, all his other 'friends'.

Later on, she told him she had been followed back from the studios by a man.

He was sitting at the desk in Grandfather's room when she told him. She stood in the doorway as if the threshold were a checkpoint beyond which she could not pass. He stopped reading, but his hands continued turning the dictionary's pages.

"You sure you're not imagining things?" he suggested. It was the wrong thing to say.

"He was hanging around over the bridge the other day."

"Maybe he's a fan."

She contained her irritation. "I'm not worried about me,"

she said, coolly. "I wondered if he might be sizing this place up for a burglary."

"Oh, no one'd do that." He bent to the task again.

"He was following me, David."

"I'll call Willie Roach. He'll throw a scare into whoever it is."

She stayed in the doorway, until he looked up again.

"What?" he said, irritation colouring the question.

Her lips were pressed tight together. "Thanks for your concern," she said, and slammed out.

It snapped a wire in his head. He threw the dictionary after her, watched in sick amazement as it struck the door and fell to the carpet.

He caught up with her in the bedroom. She was on the phone, waiting for an answer. She ignored him when he came in, but he sat next to her on the bed.

"I'm sorry," he said.

She replaced the receiver and turned to him. She was close to tears with the anger.

"What're you doing down there?" Her voice was tight with strain. "Someone's following me around, I get phone calls all the time from people you're supposed to see, you won't talk to me. Everything's falling to pieces. I want to know why."

"I can't let you in on something until I know what it is," he said. Irritation was still there. He did not want to explain himself at all. He knew he should but he kept thinking that it was none of her business.

She said: "You've been sitting in Josef's room for days. Either that, or you're working. I might as well be at my place for all the contact we have. I'm scared to say anything in case you get angry. What's going on?"

"I'm trying to read Grandfather's notebooks," he said. "That's all. He left a lot of stuff around, but it's mostly in Polish. I have to translate them, and my Polish is about as good as your Swahili." He took her hand. She flinched for a moment, but yielded.

"What's in them?"

"I've only managed a few pages so far."

"Something else is happening. I can feel it."

"Nothing's wrong. Apart from Grandfather's dying."

"You're not telling me the truth."

He contained the anger. "I'm telling what I can. I don't

110

know what's going on myself. But I have these notebooks, and he wrote them to me. I just want to find out what he wanted to tell me."

"I get such a bad feeling," she said, returning the pressure of his fingers.

So do I, he thought, but tried to make her – and himself – believe otherwise.

"It's nothing," he said, sliding his arms round her. She let him, but her voice came muffled in his ear, as if someone else was speaking:

"It's not working."

It was the end of September. The weather was turning. We heard on the radio that the Polish army was defeated. East of Warsaw, the Russians and Germans met and partitioned the country. The fighting stopped, but the borders were not closed yet. So hundreds of thousands of Jews set out to reach the Russian side, believing they were the lesser of two evils. In Bodstan the tide had started almost immediately. People arrived daily from the west. They were hungry and ragged. They went on, and more of our people went with them, leaving their homes and their possessions.

I did not know what to do. We had the children to think of. Because of the food shortages, the baby was sick. I was afraid to stay, afraid to go in case I took them all to their death on a strange road somewhere.

It continued. By now, the daily bread was a matter of hunting and bartering. I gave away rare manuscripts and old volumes for a few loaves and a jug of milk. Aron and Ben went into the streets also. I wanted to stop them, but knew they must help to find food. My two boys; one scarcely sixteen, the other still a child of thirteen. Ben had already been caught in the market place by a gang of soldiers and beaten half-senseless before they let him go. The bruises were still yellow on his dark face.

One afternoon I came home with my paltry gains hidden in my coat. It was half-past four. Feigele had been at the pawn shop, selling off the silver toilet set her grandmother gave her when we were married. It had come from Paris in the 1890s. The brush was in the shape of a girl's head. The hair hung down and made the curling handle. Luba and the baby were there, also Ben. Aron was not at home.

I asked where Aron was. Ben said they had separated in the town to double their efforts. Looking at the clock, I berated Ben for letting Aron out of his sight. Did he not know what would happen if the boy was not home by five o'clock? Luba sensed the worry in my anger. She sat at the parlour table, drawing with pencil crayons a bright picture of summer hills, dripping tears on the paper. The baby cried.

Feigele said: "Stay a minute longer. He may be home any moment."

111

The clock crept towards the hour. Light was failing in the streets. Ben kept watch at the window, but there was no sign of the boy.

Finally, when ten minutes were left, I put on my coat and went out again. Feigele was white-faced but silent. I told her to look after the children, not to let Ben follow me, even if I did not return.

It is strange how you remember such moments with more clarity than the good, calm days of ordinary life. I still recall the prickle of chill air on my face, the wet scent of the street as I stepped out of our doorway. The threat of a rifle shot between the shoulder blades makes all life vivid.

In a fever I went down the street, asking at every friendly door, had they seen my son? At the Krzepickis, the eldest daughter said she had noticed Aron by the old trading hall in the town at three o'clock. She did not know what became of him afterwards.

Past shops where people tried to run their business as if all was normal. The yellow lights inside dimming, the shutters coming down. No one had seen him.

By the little fountain in Kazimiera Square, I saw the old coffee shop where I used to sit and play chess with Uncle Mavro. Luba used to come with me sometimes, and eat ice-cream with chocolate sauce. The café was dark. I breathed as if I had run a race, my chest hurt. I sat down on the edge of the silent fountain and heard a clock strike the hour. A voice from a window above hissed: "Go home, Josef. You want to leave your family without a man?"

I skulked back to our apartments through empty streets, hiding in doorways when traffic passed. I prayed that Aron would be home, laughing at some narrow escape as if it were a great game, producing hoards of food from his pockets.

When I knocked at our door, the bolts and chains were drawn back, and Feigele stared at me, the children behind her. He was not there.

We waited all that night for him to come. German patrols passed under our windows like black slugs in the shadows. We put Luba and the baby to bed, where they would not sleep. Ben refused to leave the window. Feigele sewed something for the baby. I counted our money over and over again, as if repeating the operation enough would make it increase.

And we never saw him again. We heard later that he had been rounded up with a group of older boys that afternoon, taken on some work detail. No idea where. None returned. It took some time for the 'authorities' to tell what happened. They finally explained that the working party had 'been shot while trying to escape'. They often said that in those days. They liked to pretend that the slaughter had good official reasons. My son – your uncle, boy – died, and we do not know where or when. Perhaps he was already dead when I was searching the streets for him. They never returned his body.

He would have been twenty-nine when you were born. You would have known him well. He was your uncle.

We decided we must try to reach Lodz. Our relatives there could take us in. We would be safer in a larger city. From there, we could plot escape.

112

He closed the notebook. His eyes ached with it. To imagine himself with a young uncle, with an aunt who would have been even younger: it was hard, because one thing led on to another. Before he knew it, he was trying to place himself in streets Grandfather mentioned. If things had been different, he would not be an Englishman reading laboriously through a strange language. He would have been a child drinking hot chocolate at a café table, while his grandfather played chess with some friend. He would have known that square with the fountain, and that family of uncles and aunts and all their kin. His mother, the ten-year-old girl drawing pictures through her tears, would have been there as a grown woman.

But of course, if things had been different, he would not exist at all. He was the result of things occurring long after. In that land, there would have been another child of another father.

Ockley called. He sounded tired and weak.

"Where are you?" David said. "Scotland?"

Ockley was hesitant, almost ashamed. "No, sir. Truth is, I'm at home. Been in a bit of a rumpus."

He called round to Ockley's flat, above the little shop off Ber Street where he had his office. He stepped over a cat licking its backside in the alley and pressed the doorbell. There was a lot of shuffling movement as someone came down the stairs, then a number of locks and bolts being drawn.

Ockley looked out from behind the chain. His left eye was deep purple and swollen almost shut. Another bruise discoloured his chin. He undid the chain and stepped back. David saw the sling on his left arm and the painful way he held himself.

"I'm one big contusion from shoulder to thigh on me left side," Ockley said, as David helped him back up the stairs. They went into an unloved living room where the television screen shone bright emerald with a bowls tournament. Beer cans lay on the settee, some full, some empty. "Right leg's still swollen. Doctor reckons I'm lucky it weren't broken. Want a cup of tea?"

David shook his head. He was still taking in the extent of

the injuries. Ockley eased himself down on the settee. He had been badly scared.

"How did it happen?"

Ockley tilted a can to his lips. His throat moved, swallowing. "Buggers caught me out the back. Should've remembered it was Friday night, shouldn't I?"

"How so?"

"Friday night's piss-up night. We get all sorts of trouble round here. It's the pubs. Black Fox up the road, Gun and Pheasant round the corner. All the bloody hooligans you care to name. Should've remembered."

David picked up an empty and gazed at the printing on the side. "So you think it was an accident?"

"Accident? What're you talking about? They jumped me, three of 'em."

"I meant it wasn't anything to do with work?"

Ockley scowled. "Why should it be? I was down in London all week. Got beaten up here. I just called you to let you know why I didn't get in touch."

"Know who did it?"

"If I did, they'd be in clink already. They were three yobs. Skinhead types, you know, all 'Paki Go Home' tee-shirts and National Front badges. London accents, but half the kids in the city have them. Police reckoned they might be from out of town. They know all the violent buggers. But it was dark anyway. I got out of the car, started walking up to me own door, and they came down the passage, singing and yelling. Next thing I knew, me paperwork was all over the yard and they were kicking hell out of me. Then I'm in Casualty with a constable asking me dippy questions."

"I'm sorry you got hurt," David said.

"Not your fault. They let me out this morning, but you can see I won't be much use for a while. Sorry."

"Did you get anything?"

He reached across to a coffee table and fingered out several mud-spattered photocopies. "Just these," he said, handing them over. They were of applications for entry to the United Kingdom for George Miller, and papers relating to the exams he had to pass to practise medicine in England.

"Sorry about the muck," Ockley said. "That was when they jumped on me."

114

David folded the documents and put them in his pocket.

"When you were digging out this stuff for me," he said, carefully, "did you notice anyone taking an interest?"

"There was me and some old geezer researching his family tree most of the time. And a lot of dust. It was all so long ago, that's the trouble."

David looked at Ockley's battered face. He said: "Yeah. It was, wasn't it?"

Sarah was in the bath. He picked up the phone and punched in Tony's number.

Julia answered. This time he *knew* that she was uncomfortable. As she heard him say hello, the ease went out of her voice. She said: "Hello, David. Is your grandfather any better?"

"Julia, is Tony there?"

"No," she said. "He's . . . having dinner with his father in Ely tonight."

"I see." He was quite polite. He did not lose his temper. "I'll see you, Julia."

He put the phone down. Just for a second he stayed where he was, as if everything were normal. Then he leapt up, grabbed his coat, and headed for the door.

Sarah was coming downstairs, her hair wrapped in a towel. She cried out: "David?"

"Back in a while." He slammed out of the house, jumped in the car. An old woman walking her dog in the evening street gawped curiously as he roared away

The Hall was lit for a party, every window blazing against the dark trees of the covert. He skidded down the muddy lane and pulled up between expensive cars in the yard. The dogs howled and scraped at the back garden entrance.

He crossed the puddled gravel, hammered on the kitchen door. The middle-aged woman who cooked for them when there was a party answered.

"Mr Chandor in Ely, is he?" he said, and went by her towards the dining room. Haydn's 'Trauer' Symphony played softly through the house, complementing the sound of laughter and polite conversation. He pushed the door open, and there they were: Tony at the head of the table, in evening dress; Julia opposite, gorgeous in red silk; and a selection of important guests ranged about a table full of food, fine wines and candlelight.

Everything paused. No one particularly disconcerted; they were too well-bred, too monied to feel in the wrong. Only Julia, who had once got drunk and made a pass at him while Tony was absent, glanced at him with a mixture of fear and . . . yes, it was annoyance, or whatever people feel when they've been lying for someone else.

Tony stood up. "David." He nodded curtly. "Everyone, this is David Kalska, a friend of mine."

Muffled 'Good evenings' from the guests. They were so polite he could have upended the table.

He looked at Tony. "You're in Ely, Julia tells me."

"Some mistake, I think."

"Looks that way. I'd like a word."

"Certainly." He dabbed his lips with a napkin and gave a very good politician's smile to the company. "Carry on, everyone, I'll be back shortly." He left the table, pleasant expression fading rapidly. He closed the door, sealing the gracious living off from unpleasantness, and passed David by without looking at him. "In the study," he said.

Sal got off her favourite chair and slunk away as they entered. The fire was burning low. Tony swung towards him suddenly.

"What the hell do you mean by bursting in like that? I've got the Minister of Agriculture in there." This was the side David had only ever seen used on others: the disdain and righteous wrath of an 'important man' for troublesome inferiors. It was like a low blow, and – coming from Tony – it hurt more than he would have believed.

Control, he thought, and tried for calm which emerged as sarcasm: "Well, you've been so difficult to get hold of ever since you said you'd help me out."

"That was a favour I said I might be able to do for you. It didn't give you any rights over my time."

"One word would've been nice."

"You've been pestering Julia for weeks. It's getting on her nerves and annoying me. Who on earth do you think you are? You try to exploit a connection, then nag when you don't hear what you want to hear in a couple of days. I put it down to

116

worry about your grandfather. But this is the limit. You're getting a bit above yourself."

David blinked. He almost laughed. "I don't believe you said that." Tony could not hold his gaze. "A while ago you were up in arms on my behalf, you remember? My good friend, my boating buddy. Now someone's told you to leave things alone, and I'm an uppity little peasant. You know what comes next, don't you? 'That Kalska. He's nothing but a troublesome little Jew'."

Tony protested: "I never – "

"Forget it, I knew this was happening. I just didn't want to believe it of you." He turned. "Night, Tony."

He was out of the door and heading down the passage to the kitchen. A voice at the back of the mind was saying: This is the last time you'll ever see this house or that man, and he could not believe it. He passed through the rich smells in the kitchen, out into the yard, working on automatic, because something had to get him through this.

As he reached the car, Tony's voice called him from the door.

"David, wait a minute."

He stopped and waited. Tony came out of the house, the light over the yard throwing him into deep shadow. His face was changed again. The hard surface had gone, and everything seemed to be working for expression at once. He pulled up some paces away, arms hanging at his side, palms spread, as if he were about to beseech God.

"Will you understand?" he said. "Please. I can't stand for you to think I didn't want to help." He looked away, into the trees where owls were calling. "By Christ, can't you see I'm ashamed?"

He saw it. Tony had been strong all his life. Now he was facing weakness in himself, and suffering agonies with it.

"I went down to the House after that weekend intent on finding out anything I could. I mean, my old man fought in the last war. If there're ex-Nazis banging about in this country, I wanted to know as much as you." He bit his lip. "But when I started asking questions, all I got was: 'Oh, there's a commission looking into that.' And when I pushed and prodded a little more, I began to get the cold shoulder from people I thought could help." He reached up and pulled uncomfortably at his tie, as if it were cutting off his air.

"You see, it's not a very popular thing to ask about. For every Nazi butcher who was allowed to go free, there's a signature on a piece of paper in a secret file somewhere that gave the order. Some of those signatures belong to very venerable names." He managed to look David in the eye again. "I mean *very* venerable. The truth is, there was a lot of it going on immediately after the fighting stopped. The Americans saved some, we had some more. For intelligence purposes."

"Intelligence," David said. The word was stone in his mouth.

"I know, I know. It sounds terrible. It *is* terrible. But it was made crystal clear to me that I wouldn't increase my popularity with anyone if I continued making waves on the subject. Nothing was said outright, but the hints were strong enough." He shook his head miserably. "I'm in politics, David. It's what I do. I want to change things for the better. I can't do that if I help to bring down a government."

"Tell me something," David said. "If your father had been caught and tortured by the SS, and you found out the man who did it was living the good life just up the road from here, would you feel the same?"

Tony burst out: "Why do you think I couldn't face you? First of all I was so angry I wanted to contact the papers. But it's still under the Official Secrets Act. I couldn't produce any evidence if I had it. It's not clean, I know that. I must have been as green as grass to believe I could be in this game without the muck rubbing off, but I can't do anything. It's not that it's really dangerous any more. It's simply that no one who knows is interested enough to do anything. It's a dead issue."

"Six million dead," David said.

Julia appeared at the door, peering short-sightedly into the night. She looked scared. "Anthony?"

"I know this won't make any difference," Tony said. "It couldn't now. But I didn't want you to think I never tried."

David saw what he must have been going through, but it could not change anything. He got into the car. Tony was still standing there. They had been friends for years.

"See you, Tony," David said. "Have good luck."

In the mirror as he drove away, he saw the Hall and the covert, and his best friend, dwindling into the dark.

He sat in his armchair in the corner of the sitting room watching sightlessly the blank television screen.

Control. He picked up a big crystal paperweight that held down odd papers on the side table. His hand was trembling. He wanted to throw the crystal through the television screen.

Sarah came in. She saw him sitting there, coiled. She said nothing, but her eyes were asking questions.

He had to fight his breathing down to normal pace. He looked helplessly at her, clutching the paperweight until his hand was white. She was so beautiful, and he wanted to smash the crystal in her face.

Maybe she sensed it, recognized his hurt, anyway. She whispered his name in a dry, sorrowing way. She moved towards him. Knelt, forcing her body between his knees, put her arms around him, pressed his head to her shoulder.

He released the crystal. It hit the table and rolled on to the carpet with a soft thump. He needed to cry, but could not do it. He held her tentatively, like a form of fragile glass, and murmured: "I'm sorry, I'm sorry."

The feeling of someone having died was very strong. For a moment, he thought it was Grandfather. But it wasn't.

17

"Mr Kalska?"

"Speaking."

"Lymon here."

A sense of the bedroom whirling away, of Sarah, half-asleep at his side being too far to touch. An inability to say anything for a moment, for fear of the reply.

Lymon said. "Look, I know it's two in the morning, but the ward sister at the Royal just called me. He just spoke."

"He's awake?"

"Not that good yet. But he's showing signs. I wasn't there

119

myself, but the Sister assures me he mumbled something in a foreign tongue."

"What did he say?"

"She tried to write it down, but of course no one here know any Polish, if that's what it was. She said it was something like 'simnee' or 'zimnee'."

"Cold. *Zimny* means cold."

"If he carries on like this, he may well wake up."

"I'll be there as soon as I can. If he speaks again, get someone to try and take it down."

"Is it important?"

"Could be."

"I'll see if there's anyone on the premises who knows the language."

"Thanks. Oh, Mr Lymon."

"Yes."

"Is Mr Miller still taking an interest?"

"I didn't know he was. Be like him, though."

"Don't let him near my grandfather."

"Pardon me?"

"Just don't, all right?"

This time he could not put Sarah off. She was climbing into her clothes before he could think of the reasons why she should stay.

"For Christ's sake, David, there's no way you can get a train or a plane at this time of night. If I come we can share the driving."

He saw the sense in that.

Twenty-five minutes after Lymon's call, they were in the car, David at the wheel, heading along the empty A47. The night was black. No moon or stars, only solitary lights gleaming out of invisible countryside.

Sarah said, "If he wakes up, he might be able to tell you something, mightn't he?"

"I'll settle for having him awake. Can you put some music on?"

She hunted for cassettes in the glove compartment. "That's what this is about, isn't it? Something to do with who knocked him over."

"It might be. I still don't know anything."

120

Her smile flickered wanly out of the gloom in the corner of his eye. "Neither do I."

The road drew them onwards into darkness.

Some travelled with their belongings in handcarts. Some caught the last uncancelled passenger trains and by a miracle got away. We finally discovered a friend who was going to attempt the journey by car. He was a dentist. He had spent the last weeks filling people's teeth with diamonds and other small stones. His own children were walking deposit boxes. We made an arrangement whereby he would take us with him when he left.

Understand how dangerous this was. If anyone were caught trying to go from one city to another without the necessary permits, they were likely to be shot on the roadside. We hoped to get by with the big car, which the dentist had hidden in a garage, and the fact that he could pass for a non-Jew. The plan was to reach Lodz, where we had family, then to strike eastward in whatever way possible and cross the River Bug to Russian territory. Thousands were attempting the same, but we had no idea what was going on. All we had was one big black car for nine adults and children.

God must still have been smiling then. We made the journey packed in that car like faggots of firewood, smothered in blankets to keep out the cold. We had only our clothes and the smallest personal belongings, and whatever food we had bargained for. Luba carried her rag doll. The journey began in the early hours of a Monday morning, and took us over narrow, winding roads through countryside dead with early frost. Most of it we drove blind, fearing to light the headlamps.

The dentist drove; I could not. Everyone else tried to sleep. But Luba and I stayed awake. I held her tight in my arms and I could tell that part of her was excited by it all. When she had first seen the German soldiers, she thought they were very impressive in their black uniforms. You could not blame a child for this; millions of adults felt the same.

We saw people on the roads, carrying their belongings on their backs. They scuttled into the trees or behind walls when we passed, thinking we were Germans. Once we stopped on a bridge over a little river, and watched as veiled lights rumbled by a hundred metres away. The dentist smoked incessantly, dragging at his strong cigarettes as if they contained oxygen to help him breathe. The car was full of the smoke, until he stubbed out the last one and said "No more. What shall I do now?"

Crossing over the M62, Sarah driving, David said: "How long's that Jag been there?"

"Couple of minutes. Came out of a side road to Darrington. Why?"

He looked back cautiously. The car was keeping pace with

121

them. It could have overtaken if it wanted, but it was hanging back about fifty yards.

"You don't think it's the police?" Sarah said.

"Slow up and see what they do."

She came down from eighty-five to seventy. The Jaguar slowed too.

"Damn it!" she said. "I'm sorry. I shouldn't be going so fast."

He glanced back again. The Jaguar made no moves. It covered road smoothly, as if it were tied to their rear bumper.

"Shit," he said. "Step on it again."

They pulled away. The Jaguar stayed back for a moment, then reeled itself up to their tail lights once more.

He was thinking: What if they don't want me to get there? This time of night, an accident would be easy.

The Jaguar was close. Both cars were topping ninety-five.

"I don't like this," Sarah said. Her foot pressed down a few more degrees and the engine whined as they accelerated.

David wished he were driving. He started to say: "Don't let him get up beside you."

Then blue lights burst from within the Jag's radiator grille and the siren began to scream.

I'm going crazy, he thought, as the police car swept to a halt in front of them. Sarah was tense and pale, clutching the wheel as the car ticked and cooled in the stillness.

Two officers got out and walked slowly up the hard shoulder toward them.

David wound his window down. He saw the policemen flinch then come on. Headlamps flared behind. A red-and-white appeared. It parked close up to their rear, blocking them in. The first two officers stopped some distance away.

"Both step out of the car, please," one of them called.

Sarah looked at him. She was scared. "This isn't how they do it."

"Come on," the policeman said. Two more got out of the red-and-white. "Just get out and step away from the car."

David began swearing quietly. He patted her hand and opened the passenger door. They got out of the car.

The four policemen boxed them in at the front of the bonnet. The one who had done the talking – a professional boozer, by

122

the look of his cheeks and eyes – studied David with a half-sneer. David glared at all of them. Not long ago, he would have waded in confidently. Now he smouldered.

"This your car?" the policeman asked, his voice a flat-vowelled Yorkshire drawl.

"Oh, yeah," David said.

"Your lady friend were pushing it a bit, wouldn't you say?"

"We're trying to get to Scotland," Sarah started, too loud with anxiety. "David's grandfather's in hospital there."

The policeman nodded. "I see." He switched back to David. "Name?"

"Kalska."

"Funny sort of name."

"It's the one they gave me."

"Well, you wouldn't choose it, would you?" The others smiled a bit at that. "You say this is your car? What's the licence number?"

David gave it.

Sarah could not keep silent. "Please, officer. You don't understand. If we don't get to the hospital, it might be too late."

"Oh, there's plenty of time. Let's see your licences, and the car paperwork."

Four o'clock in the morning on a ghost-lit highway. David had mixed with the police often enough, but never on the receiving end. It *was* frightening. One of them breathed down his neck as he reached into the car for the papers.

The policeman studied the documents by a torch beam, frowning. His tongue searched up between top lip and teeth. "Mmm," he said again. "Well, I'll tell you our problem, and you tell me what you think. We've had a report that this car's been stolen. What would you reckon to that?"

David spoke slowly, with effort. "This is my car. I bought it from Trident Motors in Norwich in July last year. Who told you it was stolen?"

"I don't know about that. We get the call on the old squawk box, man and woman driving stolen car, in possession of personal belongings of a Mr Kalska. Ours not to reason why. We just come and get you. Someone's not telling the truth, are they?"

"Listen, officer, the lady's correct. My grandfather's lying in the Royal Infirmary right this minute, and if he dies while you keep us standing around here, you will never hear the end of it."

The policeman pursed his lips, unimpressed. He was in charge.

"I think what we'd better do is take you and the car back to the station and get it sorted there."

"You son of a bitch."

One of the others laid a hand on his shoulder.

"Now, now," said the policeman.

"You're enjoying yourself," David said. "You really are."

The policeman nodded to the other two. "You take him in the car. Steve, you go with the lady and make sure she doesn't get lost. We'll all meet back at the station for a little chat."

They had to apply some force to make David get in the red-and-white. Not much, but some.

They were taken to Castleford station. David sat in the back seat, nursing a hatred of the uniforms so strong that he felt ill with it.

They were escorted inside with sarcastic politeness. A desk sergeant with long, pitted cheeks grunted at them as he took details.

Then the pieces began to fall in place.

The story went that a Mr Kalska had rung the police from the 24-hour garage at the Blythe Abbey junction, saying that his car and all his belongings had been stolen by a man and woman in their late twenties, early thirties. A car was sent down to pick him up. David and Sarah were being questioned just as the message came through that he wasn't there, that no one had seen him or the car.

The policemen were still suspicious. Having battened on the idea that he and Sarah were felons, they did not like to let it go. He finally convinced them by getting in touch with Willie Roach. The desk sergeant checked that the telephone number really was Norwich Police, then had words. Fortunately, Willie was on duty. After several minutes of description and conversation, even the officer who had done all the talking realized it must be true.

Then, while Sarah went away to be sick, there was a rigmarole of questions. Who would waste police time with such a thing? Did he have any idea who would play such a joke on him? He said that it wasn't a joke, and the sergeant agreed.

All the while time was burning away like the fluorescents in the ceiling. Sarah returned, still looking ill.

There were apologies, some given with ill grace. The impression remained that they thought he was guilty of something, if only they could see what it was. However, in view of the facts and the matter of his grandfather, they would let him off the speeding ticket he should have received and were releasing him right away. David said nothing about taking action against them; he was too concerned with other things. He demanded the use of a phone and called the Royal Infirmary, was put through to the ward. He sat holding Sarah's hand as he listened to the ringing tone, telling her it was all right. It rang for almost a minute but no one answered. He put it down, saying: "We haven't got time now," and they walked out of the station into the first grey rumour of dawn.

It all took a couple of hours, which was a very long time.

"Who'd do it?" Sarah asked, as he drove them back to the A1. She dabbed her eyes with a tissue. The strain had broken through into tears. "I don't see who could've done it. No one knew we were driving up here."

"Those bastards," he said.

"Who?"

He did not reply. His mind was working over the campaign they had been running since he started looking into Miller. First the lies, then Ockley beaten up. Now they did this. He pushed the speedometer needle up to ninety and let it hover there, daring anyone else to stop him. He would nail Miller. Grandfather would give him the proof and he would nail the old bastard to the wall.

Down a long corridor of diagonal tiles, morning light leaking through the windows. Sarah ran behind him, wishing he would slow down. A long way off a nurse came out of a room, walked away round a corner out of sight. Something metallic crashed to the floor in a distant ward.

"Be awake," David was muttering, prayerlike. "Be awake."

He dodged left suddenly, went through a door on the left.

125

She followed without thinking, and stumbled into him, because he had stopped just inside the room.

Beyond him, two nurses worked at a solitary bed. A sheet was drawn over a shrunken figure. She could not see the face because of the nurses. There were no machines round the bed, no tubes or wires or lights.

The nurses looked up in surprise. One of them recognised David. She started toward him. Her eyes were shiny.

"Oh, Mr Kalska . . ." she said. "We couldn't reach you."

David sagged. Though his back was to her, Sarah heard him choke as if he had been struck. She was afraid.

He moved past the nurses, feet shuffling like an old man's. The other nurse looked frightened and stepped aside. Sarah had a glimpse of Josef's proud face before David moved in front of it. He sank down at the bedside, head resting on the sheet where it rose over Josef's chest. The bed was too high. He slipped and fell on his knees. She started towards him, then he began to cry. Great, dry sobs of anguish that tried to tear him apart.

She stood frozen to the spot, chilled by the sound. She had never heard him cry before.

18

Lymon said: "I'm so very sorry."

The sound of lunch trolleys being trundled down the corridors came through the office door. Lymon faced them across a desk littered with photocopied forms and pencils. "When I called you last night, it really seemed as if there was a chance."

David sat forward on his chair, head hanging down. Sarah wanted to touch him, but he was a few inches too distant.

Lymon referred to the notes in front of him. "The trouble is, when someone is as old as your grandfather was, there's no certainty."

"You said he was getting better." David's voice was low.

"Perhaps I should've been more guarded. It's often true that the old perk up a jot just before the end. It's like one last bit of juice left in a battery. The real miracle was that your grand-father lived for so long after the accident. We got too used to that, began to take it for granted."

"You said he was trying to talk." It was like a child trying to find an explanation for the unthinkable.

"He was. But that was at midnight. At five twenty-one this morning, his heart just stopped. Everything that could be done was done. His heart was tired and it gave up."

"We might have made it," Sarah said. "If it hadn't been for those policemen, we might have been with him."

David raised his head. His eyes were bloodshot. "Was anyone there?"

Lymon frowned.

"Was anyone with him when he died?"

"I don't believe so. You understand he was attached to machines that set off an alarm at the nurses' station if anything went wrong."

"You said you'd keep someone at the bedside in case he said anything more."

"We did that. But another patient developed a critical aneu-rysm. The nurse had to attend him."

"How long was he alone before it happened?"

"I don't quite see what you're getting at."

"It's very simple." David smiled. "I think Grandfather was killed by your Mr Miller. When the post mortem's carried out, we'll know."

The stillness in the room was like glass about to shatter. Lymon stared, first at David, then at Sarah. He considered for a moment. Then he spread his fingers unsteadily on the notes again. "In a case like this, it's not . . . usual to have a post mortem."

David's head tilted. He eyed the surgeon suspiciously.

"Your grandfather was with us for too long, you see, and a heart attack is what we'd expect. There's nothing suspicious about it."

"No post mortem?" David murmured.

"Not in a case like this . . . Mr Kalska, you're obviously under a great strain."

David stood up. "There'll be a post mortem," he said, explaining carefully. "You get that, Mr Lymon. I want the police here, and I want your people to find out how my

127

grandfather was killed. Because that's what's happened. Miller, or someone connected with him, they killed him."

Lymon was unnerved, but he succeeded in sounding reasonable. "I think if you were to go and rest for a while, you'll see that we just can't take that accusation seriously."

Sarah stood, reaching for David's arm.

Lymon continued. "Mr Miller is a very respected man. I've worked with him myself. You can't honestly believe – "

David exploded, jumping away from Sarah. "All right! Don't worry about Mr Fucking Respectable Miller. I'll do it myself."

He stalked out of the room. The door crashed shut.

Lymon remained in his chair. Sarah covered her eyes.

"Has he been harbouring these ideas long?" Lymon asked, striving for detachment.

Sarah swallowed a sob. "I don't know."

Lymon reached for the phone. "He may need sedation."

He found himself walking in the park behind the Infirmary. A scabby black dog was keeping pace with him. The trees that stretched away to the fine tall houses of Meadow Drive were showing bud. What was the date? He did not know. What was the day?

A man about his own age – a bit unkempt, probably unemployed – strolled past. He listened indulgently to a little boy who kept saying: "Dad, can we – " The man nodded and smiled, nodded and smiled.

David cut off across the wet grass, battling to keep himself in one piece. He repeated: "You are a man, you are a man." Something Josef used to tell him when he was hurt. He glanced up at the net of branches above, then around at the distant figures walking in the park.

He was alone. Truly alone for the first time.

Later, at the hotel, Sarah found him on the telephone. He was waiting for an answer.

"Who're you calling?" she said.

He waved a hand to quiet her. He had been drinking most of the day. He no longer looked like himself. He breathed in sharply, then spoke in a gruff, aged form of his voice.

"Ah, is that the Miller residence? . . . Could I speak with George?"

Sarah recognized the name. She tried to take the phone from him. He shook her off.

"This is Dr Taggart at the Royal Infirmary."

"David," she hissed, "for Christ's sake . . ." She struggled to get the phone away from him. He held her off, all the while talking in a friendly, ordinary way.

"I see. Not there. Could you tell me where I might possibly get hold of him this evening?"

"David!"

"The Royal Scottish Hotel? Oh, the National Medical Awards dinner, yes, I should have realised. Thank you."

He threw the phone down and she almost fell across him. All the breath went out of her.

"Get out of my way, damn you!" He lifted her off and dumped her on the bed. "What're you trying to do?"

She sat up, panting for breath. "Stop you from making a fool of yourself, of course."

"Well don't, all right?" He crossed the room and pulled a cardboard wallet from his case.

"What's that?"

"Some of Grandfather's material on Gelzer."

She pushed her disarranged hair off her face. "I don't understand all this. Who is Miller, who's Gelzer?"

"Gelzer is Miller, Miller's Gelzer. If Grandfather was right, nice old Mr Miller spent the early years of the forties gassing Jews. Do you get it now?"

She got up and moved towards the door. She had it in the back of her mind to stop him leaving the room somehow.

"You can't go to that place."

"The Royal Scottish? It's a short walk from here."

"David, you *can't*. Will you listen?"

He lifted his hand, speaking clearly. "You listen. I want you to go home. There should be time for you to get out to the airport and catch the last flight back. I want you to get on it and go home. I'll be back as soon as they give me Grandfather's body. Now get out of my way and keep out of my business."

She moved aside without thinking. She searched his face for some sign of the old David. "What're you going to do?"

"Well, I don't have a gun, do I?" He opened the door. "It's quite simple. I'm going to see Mr Miller. I'm going to show

129

him the stuff in this file, and I'm going to ask him who he is. That's all."

She shook her head disbelievingly. "What's happening to you?"

He tapped the file. "I'm finding things out."

We entered Lodz in full daylight. It was the only way, because of the curfew. Communications between cities had been so disrupted that we did not know what to expect. The dentist drove his car to a side street near the home of his relatives, and we piled out into the crisp sunshine of the late autumn day. There was no time for thanks. We had to get away before we were noticed. There were Germans everywhere.

From there to the house of Feigele's cousin Esther was two miles. We had no choice but to walk through the streets, praying no one would pick us out.

We tried to go quickly, but not so fast that we were conspicuous. I wanted to keep all of them, Feigele and the baby, Luba and Ben, wrapped in my arms, but I had to let them walk free so we should be ordinary. Ben stared at the soldiers each time they appeared, until I warned him to stop. So many Jews with bruised faces.

I was not familiar with the city then. I cannot recall the name of the street we were on when two soldiers came out of a bar and started towards us. Instinctively, Feigele stepped off the pavement. Ben and I followed her example. We had seen in Bodstan that Germans expected Jews to step into the road for them. But Luba, though she moved beside me, remained on the pavement, only averting her head from them.

There was a sick cracking sound, and Luba stumbled against me. She fell to the ground, blood pouring from her head. I looked up. One of the Germans was wiping the butt of his pistol clean with a rag. The other found it amusing, but the one who had struck her was quite furious. As she staggered up, crying with pain and shock, he screamed in her face: "That will teach you to make way for your betters, Jew."

Ben started towards him. The soldier turned the pistol on him. "Oh yes?" he said. I grabbed Ben's arm and held him. I apologized to the soldier. I bowed my head and apologized to the animal. It seemed to mollify him. He grinned at the other. "Well, at least some of the scum have manners."

We were allowed to pick up Luba and go on our way. I carried her, while Feigele lamented at my side and Ben cursed the soldiers and the Germans and the Poles who were helping them. Luba gazed at her mother with unfocused eyes.

"Don't worry, Mama," she said. "I'll stay out of the way from now on."

The Royal Scottish Hotel stood near the North Bridge end of Princes Street. In the electric glow of evening, it towered like a dirty church organ above the noise and smell of traffic.

David walked quickly through the thin crowd. The rasp of traffic beat at his ears. Seedy, damp-smelling people waited for buses, more were being thrown up from the Waverley Steps. Outside the store across the road, an old man in a kilt played a set of bagpipes, nodding rhythmically each time a coin was thrown in his suitcase. It was impossible to hear a tune.

He went up the steps and into the hotel. The lobby was warm and yellow-lit, a scene from a Victorian novel, except for the casually dressed Americans and Japanese who lounged on comfortable chairs and waited for their keys.

A uniformed doorman glanced at him with curiosity, but he drew breath so no whiff of booze should reach the flunky and pretended he knew where he was going. His eyes searched the lobby until they came upon a sign by the lifts: 'National Medical Awards Dinner'. An arrow pointed through a set of double doors.

He headed for them, conscious of the doorman following with his eyes. He went through into an empty dining room. At the opposite end, light spilled round the edges of another set of doors. The sound of cutlery and conversation floated across. When he reached them, he could hear one amplified voice above the rest, a dainty Edinburgh drawl recounting some story.

He edged the door open. It was a wide, spacious hall, with the same air of leftover Victoriana as the rest of the hotel. Round tables filled most of the floor, with a five-piece band and space for dancing on the right. The audience was in evening dress. To the left was a long table, backed by flunkies, where the VIPs sat. Dinner was over, and the scent of wine and cigars diffused over the scene like goodwill.

One of the flunkies, a young Asian boy, stared at him as he slipped into the room. He waved the file as if it were an official pass, and it seemed to work. A photographer from the *Evening News* was hanging about, looking despairingly for picture opportunities. David moved up beside him, glancing around for Miller.

"Dull as buggery," the photographer muttered. A thin priest-like gentleman stood at the microphone, talking about advances in the field of heart surgery speeding up every year. "Soon," he was saying, "we might find a way of doing without

131

the heart altogether, and then where will we be?" The audience chuckled politely.

David looked along the top table. Three seats from the end, Miller was watching him.

David froze. The old man's green eyes burned palely over his wine glass. He had no particular expression. He sat back a little, inclining his head, studying.

David swallowed at a spasm of alcohol-flavoured acid. The whole room glowed with self-satisfaction. He had been to plenty of dinners like this himself. Could he just gallop through the tables and slap his documents and photographs down in front of everyone?

Miller sipped his wine. He seemed quite calm. His eyes flicked over the audience as it laughed at the speaker again. His mouth moved, as if forming a word. Then he returned to contemplation of David.

The flat stare finally began to anger him. Now was his chance, he had to take it. He gripped the file and started away from the wall.

Miller rose from the table. Not in a hurry at all. He whispered to his companion, who smiled, nodded. He left his napkin on the table and walked away towards a side door.

David thought quickly. He backed out the way he had come in, went through the dining room to another door. Beyond it was a corridor that went round the hall. He walked down it swiftly, looking for Miller. A trolley with piles of glasses stood by the door where Miller must have come out. He passed on, looking for signs. An entrance to a stairway was empty. He saw the lavatories at the end of the corridor, broke into a run as the audience applauded loudly beyond the wall.

He went into the toilet, searched each stall. Miller was not there. He saw himself in the long mirror over the sinks, hardly recognized the desperate face he saw there. He hurried out, cursing. Back at the entrance to the hall, two dinner-suited figures waited with a pair of security guards.

"That's him!" the red-faced one said, pointing.

Alex and Paul. He had not noticed them in the hall. That was who Miller had glanced at. The security guards came after him. They were big, ex-army types. He tried to get past them to the brothers.

132

"I want to see your father," he called. "I just want to see him, that's all."

The guards grabbed him by the arms, one either side.

"Just let me talk to him," David yelled.

The guards half-carried him up the corridor until he was facing Paul.

"Shall we call the police, sir?" one asked.

Paul showed concern. "Oh, no. He's rather unbalanced, I'm afraid. Keeps following my father around. Just show him out, will you."

The guards were happy to oblige. David began to struggle. There was still no sign of Miller. He threw his head back and shouted at the brothers. "Let me see him, that's all."

"Give it a rest, sir," one of the guards soothed.

David struggled harder. "You evil bastards, your old man's a fucking Nazi, you hear me?"

"Now then, son," the guard said, and applied more pressure. It was too late. David was raving as the brothers went out of his sight, back to the hall.

"You get the news? He's a Nazi. He killed my grandfather, you bastards. He killed my grandfather."

"Better call the police, Jim," the guard said. "We can't have this."

They held him, screaming and fighting, all the way down to the kitchens.

The police came. They took him to the High Street station, and made the mistake of trying to take his file away. He fought to keep it, so one of the officers twisted his arm until he dropped it. Then they put him in a holding cell, where he sat on the edge of a hard bed until Gilston arrived. When Gilston saw him, he called Lymon. The surgeon came away from dinner with his family, still angry at the accusations David had been making. The two professionals discussed him as if he were a dangerous mental case.

"Of course, the officers had to bring him in," Gilston said. "They thought he was drunk – which he is, at least partly – and out of his mind – which I'm not too sure about myself."

"He's been under a great deal of pressure today," Lymon said. "That goes a long way to excusing things. Still, I'm not

133

sure we shouldn't have him in overnight, keep him sedated. He's all in."

David watched them from the end of the cool little room. He was in prison. That fact had been working on him for a couple of hours now. He arranged his face into a semblance of calm. He thought: This is what calm looks like, I think. All I have to do is hold it for a while. He said:

"I'm all right now."

The policeman and the surgeon glanced at him, surprised. These were the first words he had spoken since they arrived.

"I'm . . . calm," he said.

Lymon approached, looked at his eyes. "You know what you've been up to tonight?"

David nodded. "It's all very memorable. But I'm okay."

Gilston wrinkled up his freckled eyelids. "You understand if you're caught playing about like this again, we'll have to bring charges?"

"Oh, yes. Haven't the terrible twins tried to get me for harassment or something?"

"We haven't involved them so far. No need, if you're going to see sense."

David got up. His body felt like a length of weatherbeaten timber. He began to laugh quietly, then stopped because it did not look good. "I'm sorry, it's been one of those days."

"For all of us," Gilston said. He held the file up and tapped it with a bony finger. "As for this . . ."

"I'd like that back, please." So humble. Please and thank you. The calm mask wanted to crumble. He wanted to grab the file and hammer Gilston to the ground.

"You have to realise, this is just a pack of nonsense," Gilston said. "A few quotes from books, a couple of blurry photographs. Don't you see you're building a case on grief?"

"Yes, I see that now." He savoured the words like a foul taste. He could lie so easily. They were right; the file did not amount to much. But he had more than that: there was Grandfather's certainty, and his own feeling when Miller looked at him across the crowded hall. Something *was* wrong about the old man. However, what he wanted now was to get out of this place. He kept the mask in place. "I want to apologise for being so much trouble to you, both of you. Things have been getting on top of me a bit."

134

"I'll give you something to help you sleep," Lymon said, happier now that the discussion was on firm ground.

"Will I be allowed out of here?" David asked Gilston.

"I expect so. You're not actually guilty of very much. Perhaps disturbing the peace, but we'll let it pass. If you promise to go to your hotel, and not indulge in any more of this amateur detective stuff. When do you go home?"

"As soon as they give me the body."

"Tomorrow, I expect," Lymon muttered.

"There we are, then." Gilston knocked for someone to let them out. He handed the file to David. "If I were you, though, I'd get rid of this stuff."

"I will," David said.

As he waited for them to arrange his release, he huddled secretively over the file and went through each piece of it. He held the photograph of Gelzer, and saw Miller's green eyes piercing out of the blob of a face. He could even see how the young Gelzer resembled Paul. There was a family resemblance.

He stared at it harder, until his eyes began to water and the picture blurred.

Who am I kidding? Who do I really think I'm fooling here? What if Gilston's right? I don't have any evidence, I don't have a single thing.

His tears dropped slowly on to the picture. The knowledge of Grandfather's being dead got mixed up in the hopelessness of it. He slid over on to the bed, buried his face in the blanket, and sobbed quietly so no one should hear him.

There must be a way, he thought, as his head seemed to burst with it. There must be some way I can get to him.

There had to be a way.

Feigele's cousin Esther lived with her husband and three children in apartments on Kosciuszko Street. When we arrived, they were all well, but their home looked as though they had already moved. Esther's husband, Jacob the lawyer, sported a long, ragged scar down the left side of his face, where three soldiers had set about him outside his office. They had not been able to leave the city because of Jacob's mother, who was old and sick. After we had cleaned and dressed Luba's wound, both families sat round a bare table and they told us how things had gone since the Nazis arrived. There had been the shootings and beatings and the looting of shops which were familiar to us. The children were not allowed to go to school, and no Jew in the city was allowed to practise his profession. Some young people had tried to escape, to join the Partisans still fighting the Germans. Jacob was past forty, but he still yearned to do the same. His duty, though, was to stay with his family, to get them all to safety if he could.

We sat up long into the night, discussing our situation, making plans, separately or together. Of course, there was Jacob's mother, but he worked around her, saying she might be well enough to go with them soon, keeping in the back of his thoughts the notion that she might die before long. I asked what were our chances of getting to the River Bug. He told me the city was already swollen with Jews in transit. The entire country seemed to be on the move from west to east.

Finally we went to bed. Two families crowded together in three rooms.

As we tried to sleep, there was a great noise in the street below. We peered through the shutters, caught slatted glimpses of a German car and motorbike drawn up outside a house opposite. There was much yelling, then lights in a first floor apartment. Shapes moved against the windows, there was screaming. A machine-gun rattled once, then more shouting and the lights went out. Down in the street, soldiers appeared, pushing an old man and woman ahead of them. They punched and kicked this couple into the car and within seconds they were gone, the sound of their engines dwindling away in the night.

Jacob shook his head. I dared say nothing. There was no sleep for me after that. I had thought in some stupid way that we could feel secure there until we had devised a way to escape.

There was no security any more.

19

The morning of the funeral was fresh with coming spring. The grass in Bowthorpe Road Cemetery was dry and faded, but sunlit with dew. David recalled what Grandfather used to say when he saw such a ceremony taking place in fine conditions: "Ah, this is being-born weather, not dying weather." As if people could time their dying to a nicety.

Few people had attended the service at the synagogue, few were there to see the coffin put in the ground. Willie Roach turned up, and one of the staff from Brackford House. Yitzhak was fighting his last battle in the Norfolk and Norwich. None of David's business colleagues were there, which was hardly surprising. There were wreaths from some of them, and one in particular from Anthony Chandor. Sarah was at David's side, although they hardly spoke or touched throughout the entire ordeal.

He knew he had pushed her too far, left her out once too often. She was still living at his place, doing her best to help him through, but they were strange to each other. He kept wanting to take her hand, to say something that would make it all right, but then his glance would fall on the coffin again, and he would be overwhelmed once more with the knowledge of Grandfather not being there any longer. It blanked out everything but the desire to find out about Miller.

He had forbade the Rabbi to mention the war in his address. "He's dead," he told the man, "and there's no one left to mourn that, so let's leave it."

When it was all completed, and the gravediggers were moving in to tidy up, Willie Roach came over. He looked as neat and spare as ever. He shook hands, his fingers cold in a pair of thin leather gloves.

"David."

"Thanks for coming."

"He was a great old man."

"Yes."

Willie inspected him carefully. "You went a bit wild up there."

Sarah caught that. She hovered nearby.

"I don't remember much about it."

"Everything's all right now, though?"

The morning of his return with Grandfather's coffin, he had been informed that the Wensum Mall venture was under further review by the council. The rumours about 'business troubles' had given the authorities the jitters. It meant that he would be forced to back out; the others would see to it. He took it placidly, though. He had other things to worry about.

"Everything's okay, isn't it?" Willie insisted.

David nodded. "Fine."

Willie was satisfied. They turned and watched the men at the grave.

"You decided to go for burial," Willie said.

"It was in his will."

"Must say, when my time comes, I want to be cremated."

David smiled unsteadily. "He didn't want to be burned.

137

Always made me swear to that. You see, the rest of the family went that way."

The baby fell ill. We were all beginning to suffer from the lack of decent food, but the baby was weakest, despite Feigele refusing to eat her share so the children might have more. It was an infection. The doctor – who could no longer practise at his surgery but saw patients in a spare room of his house – feared it might turn to pneumonia.

We could not travel. Just when speed might have made some difference, we dared not move. It would not have been a comfortable car ride or a jaunt on a train this time. More likely two or three hundred kilometres on foot, praying each night to find Jewish communities to give us shelter, while thousands of others were attempting the same thing.

So we stayed, and saw exactly what happened, until it was too late to go.

I remember the yellow star. A decree came from the Central Government – that is what they called themselves by then. Every Jew was to wear a white armband with the star of Zion marked on it. Both the inner and outer clothing.

We discovered that the Germans themselves were deporting all Jews from the western regions. It was part of their plan to make the country free of us. Daily more and more travellers filled the streets, their clothes dirty, faces haggard with the walking and starvation.

Despite the horror of losing another child, we had to let Ben and Luba go out in search of food. There was no choice. Life gradually became a simple matter of finding enough to survive on. Most days, there were only Esther and Feigele and the youngest of the children at the apartment. The rest of us were out foraging, bargaining, stealing what we could.

The large atrocities went on as the grip on us became surer. In November, they burned the synagogue on Kosciuszka Alley to the ground. I remember I had to go out and fetch the children, who stood among the lamenting crowd, transfixed by the blaze, warming themselves at the flames.

And the more personal indignities continued. We discovered why Esther and Jacob's apartment was so bare. At any time of day, there might be a knock on the door and German neighbours would 'ask' for things. Anything they wanted, be it an ornament or bedclothes, a picture or an item of furniture. There was no refusing. You meekly gave them what they wanted, or you found other, more dangerous faces at the door.

There were so many things they did to break our spirit: girls were made to clean shit from latrines, then had the scarves they had used wrapped about their faces; a rabbi was forced to spit on the Scrolls of the Law until his mouth was dry, then a German spat into his mouth so he could continue, while a crowd enjoyed the spectacle. If soldiers were bored, they would enter a house and force the family to strip naked and dance with each other. With luck, that was all that might happen. Without it, brothers and sisters, fathers and daughters, every combination warped minds could create, would be forced to do vile things with each other. Then the luck was just to survive. This happened to a family down the street. The youngest daughter was fifteen. She went out of her mind. When I heard of it, I looked at Luba and Ben, and I wondered what I would do if — But it was unthinkable. Many things were unthinkable then, which later became part of the fabric of everyday life. We kept telling ourselves, and one another, "This is as bad as it can get." Yet somehow, it always got worse.

David went to Brackford House to supervise the removal of Grandfather's belongings. His main concern was to pick up the bulk of the documents he had only skimmed before.

The van was already there. Two kids in overalls were loading the first crate of books.

He went upstairs. A couple of ancients leaned on their sticks in the corridor, watching proceedings. Mrs Hawkes stood at the door, gazing over half-spectacles at a clipboard on which a list was neatly typed.

"Ah, Mr Kalska." She took his hand. It was a dry, swift expression of sympathy. "We were so sad to hear the news. We all feel for you."

Beyond her, the room was boxed and parcelled. He wondered if she already had a new 'guest' lined up. Brackford, after all, had a lengthy waiting list.

"Thank you for taking care of the packing," he said.

"It was the least we could do. Your grandfather will be very much missed."

The urge to weep pricked the back of his eyes again. He turned to business at hand. They went into the room.

"All his books," Mrs Hawkes said, shaking her head fractionally. "Will you keep them?"

"I expect so."

The removal men came in and hefted a tea chest between them. David stopped them to check what it contained.

"Don't worry yourself about that," Mrs Hawkes said. "I had every box numbered, and the contents listed here." She showed him the clipboard.

"There were a few things I wanted to take now," he said, and began touching each box as if it would reveal itself in his mind. The ancients at the door peered suspiciously.

139

Mrs Hawkes talked in her quick, precise sentences. "I wanted to be sure everything was in order. But there was such a great deal of material. I never realised just how large a collection of books Mr Kalska had here. Amazing, really, that he found space for everything."

David read the titles facing him on top of another chest. *The Destruction of the Jewish Community at Piotrkow, Documents of Crime and Martyrdom, Roads to Extinction*. He would have plenty of time to read them now.

"And all the magazines and papers he stored away," Mrs Hawkes continued, as the men returned for another load. "A really incredible quantity. They almost choked the boiler."

David was examining the old typewriter on which all the letters had been typed. He glanced back. "Beg your pardon?"

"People in the village must have thought the house was on fire. It kept Mr Rogers busy for hours."

With a dead, sunk feeling in the middle of his body, he turned to her. "What papers?"

She sensed danger, raised the clipboard slightly like a shield. "Why, all the loose magazines and newspapers and carbons of old letters that you told me to dispose of."

He breathed out slowly and found the edge of the desk to rest on. He looked at her. "We discussed this on the phone two days ago," he said. "Everything was to be saved."

The sharp little eyes focused certainly on him. "But your secretary rang yesterday morning and gave me your instructions to destroy all loose papers."

"Everything's gone?" he asked.

"Mr Rogers saw to it. Everything went into the boiler."

The men came in, wanting to remove the desk. David stood up and watched them go.

Mrs Hawkes stared at him. "There hasn't been a mix-up, has there?"

He would not even bother asking Kate; she would know nothing about any call on his behalf. In his mind, he was already down in the boiler room, tearing through the dust and litter for any last shred of Grandfather's papers. In his mind, he was screaming at this further interference. He conserved the rage. It was almost all he had left.

"No," he said to Mrs Hawkes' perplexed face. "There's no mix-up."

140

They set up the ghetto on 8 February 1940. We were given a day to move from the Kosciuszko Street apartments to one of the most run-down areas of the city.

You would scarcely believe the chaos of that day. Thousands of people thronging the streets, trying to carry all their belongings with them, the congestion becoming worse as we converged on the allocated areas. Onlookers had great fun with us, leaping in to steal things or turn pushcarts over. A great joke. Then blind panic as the dilapidated buildings filled to bursting and late-comers searched for places, pushing their barrows along the streets, knocking on doors, asking.

The two families could not stay together. We were split up in the search. Jacob and his family ended up sharing a two-room apartment down a back street. We finally came to a similar place in a tall, grey tenement building off Wiosny Street. One bedroom for all of us, and the rest shared with the family of a fishmonger called Peltel. You fetched water from a standpipe in the gloomy courtyard. It was filthy, damp, infested. When we put down our few belongings at the threshold and saw what we had come to, Feigele bowed her head over the baby and cried like a little girl. Ben stood holding Luba's hand, and he said: "I can't stand any more of this. I want to join the partisans." That only made his mother weep the more, and I begged him to stop such talk.

Walking about the cramped rooms, seeing the peeling walls and dirt-smeared windows, I realised how thin and ghostlike my family were becoming. We had come through the winter somehow, freezing, always hungry, but starvation had started its work. The old and the very young had been dying through December and January. No one helped —

That is not true. There were a few who tried to do something. Priests, a number of Polish citizens. But they were few. The penalties for helping Jews were too severe.

When they had crowded us into the two districts, the ghetto was closed. This was the end of April or May. Spring blossom was on the trees, anyway. They erected barbed wire and wooden fences round us and gave orders that anyone seen trying to get out would be shot.

Just so. We were now caged. Only the animals were on the outside, and we were inside, with old Chaim Rumkowski, the 'Eldest of the Jews', as the leader of the Jewish Council.

Yes, we had a form of self government. Rumkowski was quite the King of it. We had policemen, gaols, ministries. We were supposed to do as the Council told us. And the Council did what the Germans ordered. I suppose they had no choice, and perhaps they did save us worse suffering at first. But many of us came to hate the Council, and that old man Rumkowski particularly, as much as the Nazis themselves.

Sitting in Grandfather's room at home, surrounded by the chests and boxes from Brackford House, he read and re-read the documents in the file, carried on translating the notebooks, speeding up gradually as it came easier. That was all he did for

141

several days. He ate whatever he found in the kitchen; drank until there was nothing left in the bottles, then stopped completely; forgot to shave or wash very much.

Sarah was working very hard at the station. She came in late every night, and avoided entering that room. He knew she would not go, she was concerned for what he might do if left alone. It was his fault, this he also knew. He had dealt with his withdrawal from the Wensum Mall project, then given Kate a week off. He refused to answer the phone. Business was falling apart round him. Everything was falling apart.

But, beyond all the reading and the blank hours when he dozed on the bed, he was trying to see a way of getting at the truth. Miller seemed to be able to reach out and touch his life like God, while he was powerless. Nothing more had occurred since the burning of the documents, so perhaps it was thought he had learned his lesson. But he could not go near Miller, not now. They would have the police on him in five minutes and, in his present state of mind, he half-suspected he might end up in some mental ward. He thought and thought, but nothing came, except self-doubt, the notion that he was creating a monster from coincidence and grief. Supposing he was wrong? What was the point of getting in touch with all those organisations Grandfather had gone to? If there was any hard evidence, surely Miller would already be behind bars.

He had to prove Miller was Gelzer by some other method. And it *was* a matter of that. He no longer wanted to be told "No, you're quite wrong." He wanted Miller to be Gelzer so much he could not sleep for thinking of it. His stomach rolled and sickened him with thinking of it.

His mother as a young girl looked at him from old family photographs. The last was a studio shot, taken a few months before the war. There was Grandfather as a stooping man in his late thirties, his expression showing quiet pride. Feigele, his grandmother, shorter and rounder, a solemn dark face and pretty hands holding the swaddled baby, whose glazed little eyes held no knowledge of the future. Ben and Aron, his two uncles, very alike apart from their size, smiling crookedly in neat best suits. And Luba, a shock of black hair half-covering a big silly grin, her arms and legs poking from her clothes as if she wanted even then to be up and playing.

There was another picture of her. A cracked snapshot, taken

in the back garden of the house in Witherley Heath. It was the same person, because it had to be. She was holding a baby, and the baby was him. She smiled into bright sunshine, looking down at the laughing child. He felt he should remember that, the laughing with her. She did not look thin or ill, like the little official picture that had been saved from her entry papers for the United Kingdom. On that you could see the bones of her face, the skull within. In Witherley Heath, she appeared to be a reasonably robust woman of twenty-five or so, not apparently unhappy. But the eyes gave it away, or seemed to. Maybe he saw what his knowledge wanted him to see, like Miller in the pictures of Gelzer. Yet the eyes were empty. The smile was a good attempt, dredged up from memory. He felt as if you could have removed her from the photograph, and it would have made no difference to the feeling of the picture, which was sadness. He must have seen this many times, years ago when he had to do as Grandfather told him. He remembered sitting with the huge old man as work-roughened hands turned the album pages and the gruff voice identified each picture. None of the faces meant anything then. Only now were they coming into focus. Which was why he felt so terrible when he stared at his mother holding him in her arms on a summer day long gone. He felt he had missed grabbing hold of something, though in fact it was never there for him to reach.

What can I tell you of the time in the ghetto? When your loved ones are hungry, all your thoughts are for getting enough bread to stifle the gnaw of it in their bellies. If it goes on long enough, you begin to think more of yourself than of anything else. Dozens of families lived packed together in that tenement, yet for all the spirit of togetherness we tried to foster, you could only really care for yourself and your own.

At this time we were more like prisoners in solitary confinement than before. We knew almost nothing. The Germans gave occasional reports on the progress of the war, and many lies about what they intended for us. Those with secret radios, who could pick up British transmissions, kept us informed of the battles. But they told nothing of our own people. We could not be sure of what was happening in Warsaw, let alone the rest of Europe. Rumours flew of mass deportations, killings, all manner of horrors. We believed everything and nothing, depending on how empty our bellies were.

And yet, some moments of relative peace, a kind of happiness. The baby celebrating her second birthday, the little cake Feigele managed to *make. Luba singing in a concert organized by teachers from the Jewish school, a red paper flower in her hair.*

Ben still ached to leave. Several young men of his acquaintance had already attempted escape. Some were killed before they got ten yards, others did not come back, and the optimists said they were in the forests somewhere, fighting the Germans. Ben hated to remain, but he saw his family duty. He knew it would kill his mother if he left. Besides, he was an important breadwinner for us. So he stayed, despising himself for what he thought was his lack of courage. He was almost seventeen now, and Luba was growing up, leaving behind the traces of childhood. Her first romance was then. A shy young lad from across the stairway. It was very beautiful, and more terrible because of the situation it took place in. I used to see them sitting on the steps of the top floor, holding hands secretively. It made me boil with anger, because she should have been entering upon womanhood in happiness and safety.

At least the summer meant we could keep warm, and try to use any spare patch of ground to raise vegetables or grain. When autumn came round again, the death rate began to rise once more, and the enemy called for workers.

One morning, Luba came running home, frantic with terror. Feigele tried to calm her, but the strain which she hardly ever showed was breaking out all at once. I shook her and demanded to know what was wrong.

She squirmed in my hands, then cried out: "They've taken men for work. They've taken Ben."

He was half-asleep, head resting amongst the scatter of books and papers on the desk when Sarah came in. He became aware of her and sat up, pulling at the flesh round his eyes and yawning. She regarding him coldly.

"Christ, David, you should see yourself."

He could do that. There was a mirror by the bed, it gave him a sideways view of his unshaven face. He smiled crookedly at her.

"I've let myself go," he said, licking his lips slowly. "Well, that's a first, anyway."

She compressed her lips in a thin line. She had just returned from work. She wore a grey suit, shadowy stockings and black court shoes. She looked very desirable, and he felt as if his balls had been cut off. He could find no more than a detached appreciation.

"Have you seen my playlist?" she said, staying back by the door.

He did not hear. He rubbed his eyes and blinked at the pile of books. "Found something useful at last," he said. "This one –" He picked up a gaudy paperback called *Demons of Auschwitz*. "This one's really sick. Specially written for the chaps who love atrocity stories. But it does have an account of Gelzer's death."

Her face closed up, but he was not looking at her. He read from the tattered pages. "Ernst Eduard Gelzer, like many SS men, tried to escape justice. Adopting the identity and papers of a dead soldier, he fled from Auschwitz-Birkenau and attempted to reach Yugoslavia. He was captured by forces of the Russian army early in 1945, and killed in the bombing of a troop convoy of which he was part two weeks later. So ended the terrible career of one minor but infamous cog in Auschwitz's machine of death!" He laughed. "That's what it says here, anyway."

"So, he's dead after all?" she said.

He threw the book on the pile. "It means someone's dead. But dear old Mr Gelzer, or Miller, as he much prefers to be known, he's enjoying all the good things in life up in the Highlands. Lovely world, isn't it?"

She closed her eyes. "Why can't you accept what it says? If he's dead, he's dead."

"Bullshit!" He got up and moved toward her. She backed slightly. He thrust a book at her. Photographs of the camps after liberation. Pits full of sticks and parchment, mounds of bones in the charnel house. "Look at that," he said. "Makes you proud to sleep at nights, knowing there're still people out there who helped to do this."

She smacked the book away. "Oh, you've just realised, have you? Finally, David Kalska catches up with the rest of the world." She stabbed at his chest with her finger. "Don't involve me with your guilt because you only just started taking notice."

He smiled savagely. There was a reek of violence in the air. "You're such a help, you know that?"

"I could've been. You wouldn't let me."

"Oh, listen everyone," he wheedled, "not only is he in trouble with the taxman and going round the bend, he also neglects his girlfriend."

"I'm not a girl, David. For Christ's sake – "

"For God's sake!" he corrected.

She screamed in his face: "Shut up! Shut up, will you. For

145

God's sake, for my sake, for any bloody sake, just stop talking."

Silence. Their faces were inches apart. He sagged visibly, realising what was happening. He shuffled away. She moved to the window, shaking with the reaction. He sat on the bed, turning the pages of the book. He said:

"I have to get to him, don't you see? You think Grandfather was really so gaga he'd traipse halfway round the country in search of a ghost?"

"I don't know. But you're sick, David. You're not thinking any more."

"That's not true. I think all the time. I think as hard as I can, but I can't see how to do it. He's blocked everything I've tried to do."

"He hasn't done anything." She touched the cold glass and the night beyond. "Can't you even see that now? You say all these things have been done to you, but there's no proof. You just want them to be his fault."

"I *know* they are. I know he's Gelzer." He closed the book, and he was too pathetically insistent to convince even himself. "I'm sure of it."

She came closer, but did not sit on the bed. Her long blond hair gleamed. Her mouth and eyes were set carefully. He thought: Now we get to it.

She had strength. He had not known it before. "You have to get this off your mind," she said. "You're letting it ruin you."

"Maybe I needed a little ruining." He gazed up at her. "Always had the sneaky feeling that things went a little too smoothly. There's a Jewish notion for you. If things are going well, there must be something wrong."

"Let go, before there's nothing left of you. You can't do anything about this Gelzer, even if it were true. Don't you think someone would have exposed him by now if it were?"

He saw the sense in that. Hated himself for it, but saw it nonetheless.

"Josef wouldn't want to see you like this. He loved you too much."

Finally she sat down next to him. Her arm went around him and he slipped over until his head was in her lap. He felt so tired. Her hand stroked him. He wanted to sleep and leave it all behind.

"If you just give yourself a chance," she said. She sounded as she used to. He thought back to the time before all the trouble started, and he wanted it to be that way again.

"You think I'm crazy?" he said.

"No. Only hurt." The hand stroked. He saw that she was right, that he could go on battering himself against the walls until he ended up like one of those pathetic cases who wandered about the streets of the city, all their grievances in a carrier bag and a cheap bottle of sherry.

He had never had much chance to be a child. Now he heard himself asking: "What should I do?"

Her lips brushed the back of his head. "I think you should get away."

"Away?"

The words struck and held in the back of his mind. He stopped breathing for a moment. Of course!

"Let me up."

She stiffened. "What?"

"Quick, let me up. I've got it."

He broke away from her and lunged at the desk. She sat there, stunned by the change. He yanked open a drawer and started tossing the contents out.

"It's in here somewhere."

"What is? David, I don't – "

"The address. The daughter's address." He was alive again, and did not have time to see hope die in her. He rooted through the drawers, talking to himself.

"The night Gilston pulled in the brothers, they said she'd gone away to get over her husband's death. I took a note of the address, just in case it might turn out handy. It's in here somewhere."

She tried one last time. "David, don't. I can't bear it."

"It was somewhere in Cornwall, I think. Don't you see, if she's still there, I might be able to get something out of her. She's never seen me. I could get to know her and she might tell me things without realising it. This is the way I can do it."

Sarah said nothing more. She watched him throwing aside papers and books, his excitement close to hysteria, and she rose, straightened her skirt and walked towards the door. At the threshold, she looked back one last time.

"It's here somewhere," he was muttering, to no one but himself. He did not seem to realise she was going.

"I care about you so much," she whispered, so that not even she heard it above the row he was making.

She closed the door and made her way unsteadily down the passage to the front door. All the way out, she could hear him searching for that piece of paper.

Outside the wind began to blow from the west. She leaned over the railing of the bridge, staring straight down at the water. Music and talk drifted from the windows of the Brewers. So much for her. She had finally learned to say "I love you," and it was too late.

She glanced over her shoulder and saw the man who had followed her. He was coming up the street, carrying a McDonald's takeaway.

She moved on quickly.

She wondered if she would ever see David again.

PART TWO

In the Birch Wood

20

Joseph Halborough stopped the car at the brow of the hill. He got out and walked to the edge of the road.

It was a fine spring afternoon, the last day of April. The ocean was a dazzle of sunlight stretching west, south and east. The road dipped between verges of brilliant green, winding down through woods to the town. Grey roofs glittered steeply round the end of the sheltered bay, a straggle of bigger houses perched on rocky slopes to the west.

He took out a pair of binoculars and scanned the houses, whistling quietly in the blustering air.

He drove into town. Many of the houses showed signs of upgrading for the holiday market. But it was early in the season, there was little activity. He found the offices of the Endellion Estate Agency in one of the streets leading off the harbour. The girl there handed over the keys to the flat he was renting.

The flat was in a narrow street behind the harbour, on the top floor of what had once been a small hotel. Only one other flat was occupied ("By a lady writer," the girl had said. "Not that I've read anything of hers.") It was new and clean inside. The latch on the door was faulty, but locked when he shut it hard. He opened windows to air the rooms and leaned out. The sea front was largely obscured by rooftops, but he could see the two piers that made a horseshoe of the harbour and the craft at rest there. A fishing boat was in, smoke churning from her stack. A dog ran along the west pier, the sound of its barking out of synchronisation with its mouth.

151

He breathed the salt air and studied the houses on the hill to the west.

He threw his luggage on the bed to unpack. A file and two notebooks came first. He put them on the bedside table. Then Joseph Halborough took the driving licence, credit cards and other identifying possessions of David Kalska and put them in a drawer, covering them with his clothes.

In the evening, he took a look round Silcombe. It was a pleasant, village-like place, all ups and downs and little alley-ways leading off to steps that took you back to places you had already been. He did not find 'Old Cottage', but suspected it was up on the hills to the west. People said hello when he passed, and he nodded back with a smile. He wanted to be accepted as part of the scenery. Nothing suspicious.

Most of the business was concentrated in the sandy-coloured houses on the front. One classy pub called the Harbourmaster, two others of more dubious appearance, a chandler's, an art gallery, a café, one decent-looking restaurant and one Sea-man's Mission. At the far end was the corrugated monstrosity of a shipwright's, and other buildings housing marine services. A car park, with the harbourmaster's office and public toilets in the middle, filled the space between. A couple of slipways went down to the water. He entered one of the dubious pubs, and sat by the smoky window, watching the harbour for a familiar face. She did not appear.

That night, he turned in his bed and heard rain spattering the half-open window. He listened harder, until the wash of the sea came to him, thought of *Marie Celeste II*, slumbering at her moorings in Haverley Dyke. It would have been good to sail her down, but a broads boat does not make good sea-going, and he did not have the time. For all he knew, Miller's daughter might already be gone; he had not dared to check, in case it alerted them to what he was doing. So far as anyone knew, David Kalska had closed up his office and gone to Morocco for a month's holiday. He had sold his car at a garage in Northampton, part-exchanging.for a two-year-old BMW, then opened an account at the local branch of his bank under the new name. He had thought of calling himself Joseph

Benjamin, or even Joseph Aron Benjamin, but did not push his luck.

The rain strengthened. He was fanned by wet draughts that smelt of the harbour. Sleep would not come for hours, so he slotted a disc of Terzi's lute music into the portable stereo and let it play to him in the thinking dark.

The Chronicle of Events *tells well enough how it was in Lodz in the winter of 1940–41. They began compiling a list of deaths in January, and it records that 5,000 were dead by June. Before that, no one can be sure. The bodies were buried in mass graves inside the ghetto, often separated one from the other by nothing more than boards. Even in the cold weather, you could smell them everywhere.*

We stayed alive somehow. Froze and starved, yet did not die.

Luba always trying to be cheerful, to keep her mother from despair. Janka – who was growing somehow – crying too much at the lack of food. Even Ben, weakened by his time with the work party in Ruchocki Mlyn, pulled through the winter. But the nights were always bad for him after he returned. He would wake from dreams and pace the floors until neighbours thumped the ceiling. He could not banish from his mind the lice which crawled on them when they lay down in a barn to sleep at nights. "Handfuls of the things," he would cry, "and boys dying all round me from the cold and the filth."

Still, the Council had been negotiating with the Germans to set up workshops in the ghetto. It was Chaim Rumkowski's theory, you see, that if we became necessary to them, we would be saved. Anyone who spread the stories of mass murder which occasionally reached us was considered by Rumkowski to be an enemy of the ghetto.

In February, all of us, including Feigele, got jobs producing clothing for the Reich. We thought now, finally, things would improve. Later that year, they even gave us a postal service so we could tell family and friends we were well. I do not suppose many of these cards ever reached their destination. It was just another way of keeping us quiet. But at the time we hoped. Just as we hoped the stories of what was happening in Chelmno were not true, just as we hoped that the Red Army would come to save us. In those days, it was what we mainly lived on.

David rubbed his eyes. From the reading he had done, he knew that the first experiment in mass killing with Cyclon B had been carried out early in September of that year at Auschwitz Main Camp. Six hundred Russian prisoners of war. Until then, it had been a matter of shooting, or using exhaust gases from diesel engines. Sealed lorries at Chelmno: pack your Jews as tight as possible in the back of a specially adapted truck, drive off and ignore the screams from inside, and when you reach your destination, they might all be dead. Although they carried on using the lorries for a long time, they were not efficient enough. Cyclon B was prussic acid. In those days, it came in crystal form. It was very efficient.

They demanded work battalions. Rumkowski complied. Then they demanded 10,000 people for deportation. Finally, the refugees who had come from Wlockawek the previous October were chosen. Seven hundred a day. Then gypsies. Then more Jews. They were all going to be 'resettled', we were told. Some even volunteered, thinking resettlement was a good alternative to the ghetto. They were taken to Chelmno and gassed.

We carried on. We were all working, we were eating enough to stay alive, though no more than that. I was beaten up twice in three months, Ben narrowly escaped shooting. Poor Janka was constantly ill, there was not the treatment to cure her. Feigele became more and more depressed, until she seemed to do no more than walk through each day, caring only for the children. I began to see that she might die, and it was like Kiddush Ha-Shem.

Knowledge comes slowly to those who do not want to know. A huge train carrying three hundred cars of underclothes for cleaning gave rise to talk. Where did they come from? Perhaps we knew, but the sheer scale of the idea made it somehow too nebulous when compared to things that happened close by.

A family who tried to hide from one deportation were discovered and taken to a nearby cemetery. Father, mother, grandmother and two girls. The father managed to bring a bottle of vodka. When the Germans got them among the graves, they all drank from the bottle, Lekhayim. The soldiers became angry. They shot the wife and daughters right away, then slit the bellies of the father and the old woman, and trampled on their stomachs till the bowels burst from them.

This in a cemetery in a town where people had lived and worked and gone about everyday business. I did not believe it when I heard, but later I saw blood on the ground where they had died. Other things were happening in the world, great battles, but this was what was happening to us.

He drove out along the coast road, looking for 'Old Cottage'. It turned out to be grander than the name suggested: a sprawling house of mellow stone, distanced from its neighbours by woods and farmland; a garden bounded by drystone walls overlooking the road and the field that sloped to the sea; and a big converted stable at the back that was all windows and roof. He did not slow down, for fear of being noticed, but stopped further up the road where he could pretend to be taking in the view.

He wondered whether she was in there now, and tried to conjure her face from memory. It had stayed with him well.

The idea of how Miller would feel when he found out gave him a queasy feeling, like looking over the edge of a high drop. Something hard and unpleasant.

But he had not reached her yet. He might not.

Thoughts of his mother, a young girl with old eyes, replaced her.

This is most difficult to tell. This more than any other. It was the first day of September. A week before, Feigele had finally taken Janka to the hospital. Her sickness had reached such a point that we could no longer look after her. The hospital was understaffed and crammed with people, because it was thought that you could avoid deportation by being sick, but they found space for Janka, and we had all given thanks for that. Thanks.

I was at work, lined up with a hundred others in a dark workshop. We were sewing new buttons on to clothes from which the originals had been ripped. A man no older than me had just fainted where he stood. Two others were trying to revive him when a child burst in, yelling that the Germans were surrounding the hospital. The others hurried out to see what was occurring. A moment later, Luba appeared. She was employed in a workshop close to the place. She grabbed my hand and started to pull me with her. "They won't let anyone in," she said. "I tried to see Janka, but they wouldn't let me."

We rushed to the hospital. The Germans had cordoned it off, the streets were filling with those who had relatives or friends inside. We saw trucks, soldiers leading the medical staff away. Just as we reached the edge of the crowd a man appeared in a high window, screaming and struggling. He wore a white gown, there were soldiers behind him, pushing his legs over the sill. The other soldiers stopped and looked up, while the crowd shouted and cried. Then the man at the window lost his grip. He fell three floors to the ground. I tried to cover Luba's face, but she struggled out of my grasp. She screamed for her little sister.

More people were thrust from the windows, the soldiers leaning out to see them fall. One woman struck some railings and was transfixed on them, limbs jerking until she died.

That was terrible enough. But then someone threw out a child. A toddler of perhaps two years. It turned as it fell, and Luba screamed: "Janka!" But I knew it was not Janka.

I thought: "Is Feigele here? She must not see this." It was impossible to locate her in the crowd. Another baby was pitched out. I heard it strike the ground, a dull, liquid sound. A young SS man went to his officer and asked something of him. The officer nodded, and there were shouts of approval and laughter from his fellows. He yelled up to the men in the windows. "Throw me one," he called to them.

155

We waited, hushed for a moment. Luba realised what was happening.
I told her not to look, but she ignored me.

A soldier appeared on the second floor. He grinned at us, then
stretched out his arms with a bawling child in them. It could not have
been more than six weeks old. He leaned out as far as he could, then
rolled the child off his hands.

It continued to cry as it fell. I saw a white arm reaching. The one on
the ground raised his rifle. He caught the child on the point of his
bayonet.

Luba fell against me. Her hands gripped at my coat, her nails dug
through the clothes into my flesh.

"Pray for your sister," was all I could think to say.

The SS man tried again, and missed, at which his comrades jeered.
But he got the third one, and a fourth, until he proclaimed that blood
was running down the barrel of his rifle and making him dirty, so he
gave up.

"Papa!"

Luba gripped my arm. The crowd were lamenting, weeping, and I
looked where she pointed. Up on the second floor, a soldier held a girl
child by the back of her gown, dangling her over the drop.

Luba cried: "It's her, Papa, it's her."

I told her she was wrong. I insisted upon it. I pulled at her to make
her turn from the scene. She would not do as I ordered. She strained
against me and I held her, otherwise she would have fought her way out
of the crowd and tried to stop them, and been shot.

I did not see it. She saw it. I only heard the crowd gasp and Luba
scream, and a long, horrible cry from Feigele, who was there after all.
Then Luba's body drooped and she fell at my feet, and I tried to pick her
up, but the crowd were milling, almost stepping on her, and I finally
reached her and drew her up, by which time the soldier at the window
was gone, and she blinked up at me with eyes not seeing, and I knew
she would not be who she had been any more.

He had pills to help him sleep, but he woke in the night to
find his eyes full of tears. Drugged, on the edge between past
and present, he concentrated confusedly on the day he had
just lived through in Silcombe.

The finding of the house, then the waiting to see if anyone
came out. Lunch in a pleasant pub on the harbour which he
thought she might go to. Nothing happening. He was quite
calm and ready to bide his time then. Not now, though.

He clambered out of bed, stumbled to the window and held
the cold sill. He stared at the sea shining black beyond the bay.
This is real, he told himself through the fuzz of the pills.
You're here and now.

Back in bed, the past began to push against him once more,

and Luba was there, silent and withdrawn, huddled in a corner of the room which was suddenly rotted and peeling.

Here and now.

He put on old clothes and made his way up to the west road. In the half-light of dawn it took a while to find a good place. He settled on a spot at the bottom of the field below the house, made himself comfortable behind a wall, and set in to wait. If anyone asked what he was doing there, he had a handbook of British birds and a camera to show.

Surveying the sleeping house through binoculars, he thought: She's probably one of those snotty rich bitches who stays in bed all morning.

But he was wrong. She left the house in the bright hour before seven, wearing an old tweed coat, faded brown cords and good walking shoes. There was no mistaking the way she walked. Her long black hair blew loose in the sea wind. He listened. She was singing to herself, a sad tune without composer. She climbed over a stile and started across the field. He put the binoculars away as she passed close to him. A sketchbook stuck out of one pocket, a paintbox and water bottle bagged the other. She descended the field, watching gulls fly and rags of cloud drifting beyond them.

She stopped singing, paused. He thought she had seen him. She looked back at the house, biting her lip. Her forehead was lined with thought, the eyes half-closed. He shivered. Then she continued, though not singing, disappearing finally through a gateway by an old stone shed.

He skulked towards the road, following the wall so no one in the house should see him. There was only one place she could be going, so there was no need to track her like an animal. He got back on the road to town, like a man out for a morning stroll. His heart was racing. He had expected contempt at the sight of her careful beauty, not fear.

Old Cottage reared up on the roadside. He glanced over it with tourist curiosity. The stable windows flashed in the sun. It was a studio, full of canvasses and benches.

Boats were putting out from the harbour. He remembered sailing up the Yare with Grandfather on one side of him, Sarah on the other. It was so long ago.

Hating her, he strode down to the town.

*

A kid on a moped buzzed out of the lane up to his flat. He stepped on to the pavement and walked along the front. There was no sign of Miller's daughter.

He wandered out along the east pier, taking a look at the craft still at their moorings. Two fat men with City accents were wheezing around on a big motor cruiser, complaining about the fishing.

At the pier's end, he stopped and looked at gulls fighting over scraps of bread. Looking back, the harbour was complete in his view. He searched it, and found her at last not a hundred yards away, on the other tip of the horseshoe. He tasted bitterness again. She was leaning against the sea wall gazing out over the bay. So thoughtful. Now she moved away. An old man with a scraggy mongrel dog nodded hello. She wandered along, pulling at her hair to keep it off her face. Stopped beside a worn-out old fishing boat, where a boy of eleven or twelve was cleaning up. She said something, the boy replied, then they both laughed. She walked back down the pier, tapping a pencil against her lips. He followed as she left the harbour, going up the lane behind the shipwright's. He let her stay well ahead.

A milk van clashed down the narrow gap. He stepped aside to let it pass, and climbed the slope between close-stacked and shuffled houses. At the top was a slice of bright blue-grey sky. He came out between the houses, above the water. A church stood in a graveyard of lichened stones.

She was there, at the edge of the yard where a flaking rail guarded the drop to the shore. She sat on an old bench, sketchbook on her knee, drawing the church door.

He approached no farther. She was on her own. He did not want to scare her. Not at this point anyway.

21

Feigele died when Janka died. Not in her body, but behind her eyes. She stayed in our squalid room for weeks, not speaking, hardly hearing. Only Luba could persuade her to eat and drink. But Luba was not the same after the hospital. Gradually, in the days after, she seemed to come back, to smile sometimes. But I knew she had gone inside herself. I could not tell her comforting stories any more. That was all gone. While Ben grew more angry in his weakness, and Feigele simply gave up, and I cried when I could, she seemed to grow another skin.

The ghetto was a place of frail ghosts, bodies in rags that were too large, faces protruding on sticks from threadbare collars. You thought, when you were outside in the streets, that everyone was moving very slowly and carefully, and you wondered why. Then you realised that you too were doing this, because you had no energy to do more. A whole huge community ran on low voltage, while the conquerors dipped into us and took as many as they wanted, whenever they wanted. Even to the 'Children's Action' of March 1944, when they took all the children up to the age of thirteen. The only blessing then was that Luba was past that barrier.

A proclamation in June 1944 asked for volunteers for labour outside the ghetto; Rumkowski said they would be clearing debris in bombed cities. Three thousand every week.

The first batch went on 28 June. Rumkowski assured them that they would only have to travel in goods wagons for a little way, because of the shortage of passenger carriages. They left. The train returned next day. The news went round the ghetto like fire. There was a story of a note found in one wagon. It said that they had gone only thirty miles or so to Kutno, then been transferred. Another tale was that one wagon had written on it: 'You are going in the carriages of death.'

When we were finally taken in the deportations of August, there was no drama. Drama is for people with full bellies. There was no talk of work; only that we were being taken to safety in Germany, far from the advancing front. For all that we were exhausted by five years of deprivation, we did try to escape. Like starved animals who remember vaguely how they should behave. We barricaded ourselves in a tiny cupboard in that dreadful apartment, and listened as the soldiers went through the rest of the block. As they came closer the screams of those they took echoed up the stairwell. Ben, poor broken child, was crying behind me, Luba comforting him as if she were his mother, Feigele only sat and murmured to the darkness. I wonder if she knew what was happening.

We were found, beaten, and taken to the railway yards where thousands waited. Several hours later, in the warm sunshine of that August day, we were loaded on to a train. Dozens in each wagon, until there was scarcely room to breathe. A little old man near us winked and said: "At least we don't walk to our deaths, eh?" The others shouted him down for such scaremongering.

More waiting, while the sun beat down on the carriages. Officers strolled by, smiling and assuring us that we would soon be on our way to a better place. Someone asked for water, and the request was politely refused. "Soon," they said, "soon."

It was six hours before the train moved, by which time at least the

cool of evening had fallen. They shut the doors on us, and the train
jerked into motion, throwing everyone against his neighbour.
Luba said: "Do you think this is the end, Papa?"
I prayed that it was.

Next day, he sat at a table in the Harbourmaster, drinking a pint of mild, and watching her across the lounge.

She was with friends. Probably the Baxter Caradocs, given their age. A man and woman in their early sixties, the man whippy and grey, the woman with deeply hennaed hair and heavy eye make-up that belonged on a version of herself fifteen years younger. The man wore a sweater and loose fitting trousers, the woman a paint-spattered fishing smock and jeans. The Caradocs were artists. He had seen their work in the art gallery on the harbour.

She sat opposite them in a window seat, the light from outside throwing her into sharp focus. She wore a cord skirt, a jacket several sizes too large for her, and a check shirt like a man's. She was drinking orange juice, laughing at some story the old man was telling. She did not look much like a bereaved widow.

The pub was busy with the lunchtime crowd, a cross-section of Silcombe itself. Business suits from the estate agents and offices off the harbour, a few early tourists done up in sailing holiday chic, and a number of salty dogs who appeared to be auditioning for a pirate film.

An old boy came in and stood at the bar, blocking his view of her. He shifted his chair to keep her in sight. She seemed healthy and happy, more relaxed in dress than the night he saw her at the hospital. Her make-up was light. She needed very little to set off the fine bones of her cheeks and the dark eyes. He kept hearing snatches of her voice through the bubble of talk and the faint drone of the radio. It was a low, tuneful sound, like her singing the morning he first saw her. She was animated, but made no wild gestures. She was in control of herself, fitting exactly with her company and surroundings.

Part of the upbringing, he thought. Like father and the brothers. Complete self-confidence, because you know that everyone else is less than you.

He sipped his pint and toyed with the remains of a sandwich.

160

Mr Baxter Caradoc was into another story. Mrs Caradoc gazed at him sideways, thick lashes trembling over her slightly bulging eyes. She seemed to adore him. Miller's daughter listened, close attention turning to amusement, then a full-throated laugh. She would be the perfect guest. No matter who you put her next to, she would appear interested and be good company.

Daddy's girl, he thought. A new surge of contempt. It fitted. There she was, a married woman of, say, thirty, and where had she and her husband lived? With Daddy in his big house. These people, the Caradocs, would be family friends.

She was looking at him. He had been thinking too much and she had caught him staring. For half a second he stuck like that, while she held him. Then he switched to the bar, to a calendar with a lifeboat pictured on it. He blushed like a boy.

It was some time before he glanced at her again. The old man rose to get the next round. She leaned towards Mrs Caradoc and began a murmured conversation. He thought: She's telling her about me. But, of course, she was not. She had forgotten him the moment she looked away. It was only what he knew that gave the moment significance. To her, he was a stranger, and that was his advantage, as long as he could play his part and not let the importance of meeting her ruin his composure.

Still he was angry. If he could not stifle the nervous turmoil in an exchange of looks, how could he get close enough to ask her the questions he had in mind? He finished his pint, pushed the sandwich aside, and left the pub.

The intolerable heat of that goods wagon. We travelled for only a few hours, then stopped and were left for the night. We did not know where we were. A boy stood on his father's shoulders and spied through a crack in the side of the car, saw a goods yard and some buildings. I think four people – all old ones, very weak – died during that time. There was hardly room for them to fall, but when they were gone, somehow we managed to lay them down and tried to avoid stepping on them. The floor of the car was strawed. After a time, it became matted with shit. The dead lay in it. There was very little urine, though. We had to drink that, for lack of any other fluid. Farther down the train, we heard occasional shots, and that made us quiet.

As the heat of the next afternoon began to build, the doors were opened and we spilled out, blinking in the fresh air, begging for water.

An officer, very neat and clean, told us kindly that it had all been a
terrible mistake, and apologised profusely.

We were given a little water, a taste to remind us what it was like,
then herded away. I was carrying Ben, who had fallen into a fever by
then. Luba led her mother by the hand as we were escorted across a
network of rails going off towards the spires of a town. Some people fell,
and if no one was there to pick them up, we heard the shots a minute
later. A German stopped me and pointed to Ben. "He's sick," he said.
"He can't go." I begged him to believe that the boy was only in a faint.
He would be well soon enough.

Maybe you wonder why I begged, why we were not angry. After that
first part of the journey, could we really believe their intentions towards
us were other than murderous? I tell you: to turn and fight, empty-
handed and starved, against well-fed men with machine-guns, it takes
more courage than I possessed. A man alone can make a martyr of
himself, except that no one would ever know of the martyrdom, but not
one who had the remains of his family to think of. If I had attacked that
soldier they would have shot us all. The important thing for any animal
is to survive. You stop thinking of the rights and wrongs, the long
term. You just say: I must stay alive now.

We were put aboard another train, real passenger coaches, except that
the windows were barred and painted over, and there were no seats.
The coaches were divided into small cages, with a central aisle down the
middle. A single bulb burned in the centre. We managed to stay
together, four of us and two strangers crammed into a cage meant for
four. Every space was filled to overflowing. The train moved. Feigele
and Ben were too weary to stand. The others who shared the space
complained bitterly, but finally we found a way of letting them sit on
the floor. Luba knelt between them, holding their hands. She talked to
them about how it had been when we lived in Bodstan so long ago, how
it would be when we returned, where the light had been so bright in the
windows, and the piano had rung gently to the sound of Feigele's
playing. It brought tears to my eyes, because it was almost lost, even to
memory. The strange thing was, Luba herself never appeared to believe
it. Perhaps she had been too young then, so that what remained was to
her like a story she had heard of a better life.

He saw her kneeling there, a sticklike girl of fifteen, holding
their wasted hands in her own, wondering why she had not
been allowed to grow up properly, to concern herself with the
things that were really important: the strange, exciting changes
in her body; the sweet hint and fear of sex; the worry over
what dress to wear; how to do better at school and still enjoy
herself. Where was all that?

Ben died, eaten up with fever. Feigele did not notice. She slept with
eyes open. We had to leave him there next to her. A man in the next

*cage, who still had a son, told the boy to sing. He was weak from
hunger himself, but began in a frail voice to sing the Kaddish. Others
joined in, even me as I cried. It was all the funeral there could be. The
train halted again, and we were there almost a day. Locked in the
carriages the whole time with the bodies and the smell of our own
excrement. We sang the Kaddish and the Hatikvah several more times,
until they seemed as empty as our bellies.*

He watched her again the following morning. She kept to
much the same routine; leaving the house after seven, going
down to the village, wandering round the harbour. This time,
though, she went to the Seaman's Mission, where there was a
museum devoted to the local lifeboat. He did not follow her
inside. He sat in a café three doors down, drinking sweet
milky coffee and charming Mrs Wembury, the old woman who
ran the place, into telling him things. Eventually, he expressed
an interest in the work of the Caradocs, and Mrs Wembury
said: Yes, they were a lovely couple, came from Wales, of
course. Mr Caradoc, in his day, had been hung in the Royal
Academy Summer Exhibition, and he did lovely sea pictures.
Mrs Caradoc – Isobel – sculpted interesting things out of
driftwood. They were local celebrities, really, even been on the
telly, but they weren't snooty at all.

David thought: I bet old Baxter's got a scar somewhere
where Miller saved his life. He smiled at Mrs Wembury and
got up. Miller's daughter went past the window.

He let her go, having other things to do. He stopped at the
art gallery and took a long look round, talked with the tall,
bejewelled woman who ran the place, made notes on the
paintings of Baxter Caradoc and the driftwood sculptures of
Mrs Caradoc. Personally, he thought the canvasses too self-
conscious in their attempt at elemental simplicity, and the
sculptures obvious as woodwork exercises. However, he
enthused for the jewelled lady, assured her that he would be
buying some before he left. He was even surprised when she
informed him that the artists lived only half a mile away. He
asked whether they minded people calling on them. Oh, no,
the jewels swayed and chinked together, they were a very
friendly couple. And they were always willing to show the
works that had not come down to the shop.

He returned to the flat, wanting to get his story straight

163

before doing any more. There was a way in now, and he did not want to ruin it by lack of preparation.

Another change of train, another strange place. We were forced to leave Ben. "We will give him a decent burial," they said. "It is the confusion," they said. "You are going to safety." Goods wagons again. They bolted us in and we were once more on our way. Psalms were recited. A voice cried: "What's the point, you think He hears you now? Only a miracle will save us." Someone recalled the old Yiddish saying: "Don't rely on miracles, recite psalms." Hear us, O Israel, the eternal one is our God, the eternal one is unique.

A boy worked a hole through the wall and peeped out. He said we were travelling through flat country. Others fought for a view, hoping they might recognise it. Some were certain we were in Germany, others that we were heading away from Germany towards the Russian lines. I did not look. I would not have known either way.

Night fell. The train slowed, jolted, went on again. "Any moment now," someone said. The wheels began to grind over points. Prayers again.

We came to a halt. "Alle Herunter! Everyone out. Come on!" The doors were pulled back and a great draught of cold night air rushed in. In the glare of floodlights, we scrambled down and tried to get our bearings. Hundreds milled about on the uneven ground, the train shunted and the soldiers ordered people here and there. I saw men in rough striped uniforms and caps: Jews, but they were with the guards and the officers. The new arrivals tried to get near them, to ask where on earth we were and what would happen. They spoke gently, calming the nervous. Luba and I held Feigele between us, trying not to be noticed. Guards moved in and screamed more commands. "Get into columns," they said. "Men one side, women the other." I determined to stay with my wife and child, but Luba saw what happened to others who tried the same. They were beaten and shoved into the proper column. "Go, Papa," she said. "Before you get your skull caved in."

I moved over to the left, still dazzled by the lights. A group of SS officers stood on a ramp above us, surveying the scene with interest. When we were finally organised, one stepped forward and spoke to us. He said: "We must apologise for the terrible time you've had getting here, but now you are safe. You are in Auschwitz." A low buzz of talk went round. Those who had heard of it at all knew it by its Polish name: Oswiecim, a little town in the lowlands, not two hundred kilometres from Lodz. Why were we here? The officer went on to explain. "Here you will work and be fed and be kept safe. Do not worry yourselves. If some of our guards are a little rough, that is only because of the great number of people we have dealt with today. We are tired too." His brother officers smiled agreement. "Soon you will be able to eat and rest," he said. "But first we must have our doctors examine you, to make sure who is well and who is sick."

The officers and other men came down the ramp, and we were lined up for examination. I called out to Luba: "Try to stay close to me." A guard dug his gun barrel in my ribs. "No talking!" I lost sight of them in the crowd.

Feigele was lost to me from that moment, and I was not to see Luba again for a long time. All that I tell you now is what I learned months later, from a woman who was her friend there. These things were told me when Luba was fighting for her life in Belsen. This was after the British soldiers came and saved us, when three hundred a day were still dying from what had been done to them before.

He threw the notebook down. It was long past midnight and his head was pounding. He went out into the silent street and walked towards the harbour.

Polish into English, sketchy notes into images that his reading gave colour, sound, smell. What was happening to him? In a few months, he had taken in huge amounts of information, all the books Grandfather wanted him to read. Now he could almost sense what came in each line of the notebook, as if it were buried in his memory, in the part of him which was his mother.

He went out to the end of the west pier. The sea brushed and drove against the stones of the wall. He sat down and closed his eyes, seeing it all.

The doctors sorted sick from healthy at phenomenal speed. Luba feared every moment that her mother would fall, and tried to whisper encouragement to her. She took her hand, looking for some flicker of love, or just recognition. Nothing.

The doctor dispatched an old woman to his right with a nod to the guards. He turned on them with a bright, confident smile. "Now, then," he said.

He was ready next day. Shaving carefully, he recited the facts which he would use later on the Caradocs and – he hoped – Miller's daughter. He had to feel, when he drove up to their door, that he was exactly who he said he was. So after he dressed, he stood looking at his reflection; at the new clothes he had bought, the old pair of Grandfather's spectacles which he pretended to use for reading. After a while, though, he stopped seeing Joseph Halborough. He studied his face, searching for resemblances to the photographs of his mother. Was she there? He had never much asked, Do I look Jewish?

165

Now he thought about it. Would Miller's daughter see a Jew behind his features, would it be something she would care about? Did she know anything of her father?

Of course she did. How could anyone not know what their father was?

I don't know about mine. Except he was a lorry driver.

He put the glasses on. They fitted well enough: they were too old-fashioned, but they blurred his image in the mirror, which was what he wanted just then.

It was nearly ten o'clock. He needed to cash a cheque at the bank. After that, Old Cottage.

"Now then . . ."

He came out of the bank, folding a wad of cash into his back pocket. It was another brilliant morning. The harbourmaster's office was open; the two fat holidaymakers were discussing something at the door. The harbour was smooth and clean, men in parkas and caps were fishing off the east pier. A Fourtrak with a trailer full of pocket cruiser behind was manoeuvring to back down the west slipway.

He crossed the road and walked towards it. The driver was having all sorts of trouble getting straight. It reminded him of those wonderful times trying to haul the *Marie Celeste II* up on the hard for repairs. Swearing and cursing were part of the equipment for such operations.

He started to cross in front of the Fourtrak. It jumped forward suddenly, gears grinding. He dodged sideways, and the bonnet reared up within a foot of him before the driver got his foot on the brakes.

"Apologies," Baxter Caradoc called, rolling down the window.

Mrs Caradoc struggled out of the passenger seat. "Honestly, Bax, you nearly killed the man."

"Well, get out and give me some directions, woman. You're all right, are you?" he asked, sticking his head out.

Shaking free of surprise, David nodded.

"There, what did I tell you? Now get out, woman, for God's sake, and let's have a little supervision here."

Mrs Caradoc slammed her door. David peered through the windscreen. There was no one else in the car.

166

"Now then," the old man snapped, plunging the gears into further torture.

David went on. He could not deal with them yet.

Five paces later, a crunch of metal on stone, and Mrs Caradoc cried: "Oh, Bax!"

He looked over his shoulder. The trailer was skew to the slipway, its offside tail light in fragments. Caradoc was out of the car, standing over the point of impact and shaking his long white-haired head as if the whole mess were an act of God.

David made a decision. A few men nearby were showing interest. He turned on his heel and approached.

"Can I be of any help?"

Mrs Caradoc looked up gratefully. "I think you very well could."

Caradoc was equally relieved. "Anything to rid me of this monstrous regiment of one," he said. "If you'd be so kind as to tell me when I'm about to hit something. My lady wife seems unable to grasp the nature of the task."

"Give me a man who can drive," Mrs Caradoc said.

"Okay, then." David went round the back and checked the state of the boat. "She's still safe," he called.

"Good enough." Mr Caradoc climbed into the driver's seat and slapped the gear in.

"I expect he'll run over that cyclist next," Mrs Caradoc sniped.

"Woman!" Caradoc bellowed.

"Go forward about ten feet, and put her over to port a bit," David said, keeping his hand on the rear of the trailer as Caradoc let the clutch in.

They got the trailer straightened up. Caradoc craned his thin neck out of the window. "Just the way I wanted it," he said, and ducked back inside.

David directed the backing up, stopping the old man a couple of times when it seemed all he cared about was wrecking the boat before it ever touched water. Finally they slotted the trailer down the slipway. Then it was a matter of keeping car from following boat into the waves. Caradoc joined the work party at the rear.

"You wouldn't care to assist us a little further?" he said, almost shyly.

"Be glad to. If you don't mind my interfering."

167

"We'd adore it," Mrs Caradoc said quickly.

Caradoc glanced at his wife, and a smile broke out on his lined face. "She thinks I'm getting long in the tooth for this," he said, getting back in the driving seat. He reversed gently until the trailer was all but submerged. David let the winch go a little. The *Cader Idris*, its name swooping down one side, gained buoyancy. Mrs Caradoc stopped her from scraping the wall.

"That's it," Caradoc said, coming round to take over on the winch. David leapt aboard as she slid away.

"Where do you want her, sir?"

"Fourth mooring on the west pier. Key's in the engine."

David put the plate down, yanked the outboard into life, and steered for the mooring. The boat was only sixteen feet, light and easy. He looked back and saw Caradoc pulling the trailer from the slipway. Mrs Caradoc was hurrying across the car park.

Gulls shrieked as he ploughed through their patch of water. The well and the fittings of the boat were dusty and cobwebbed. It must have wintered in their garage. He switched the engine to neutral and put the tiller hard over, changed sides of the cockpit and stretched out his hand. The smooth stone met him perfectly. The hull nudged tyres like a kiss. He reached for the mooring ropes, found the old iron rings and made her fast. Then he bent over the engine again, fiddling with the idle control. He had it running about the right speed when Mrs Caradoc's voice reached him.

"Oh, well done . . . This gentleman's been giving us a hand, Jenny."

Two sets of footsteps approaching. He looked up sharply. Mrs Caradoc was hurrying towards him, talking in her nervous, birdlike way to Miller's daughter.

He stood up mechanically.

Mrs Caradoc, eyelashes beating like birds' wings, beamed first at him, then at the other woman.

"Here he is," she said.

Miller's daughter smiled down at him.

22

"Now then." The doctor smiled at them under the shining black peak of his cap. He was very young, handsome. Luba noted this; the way he stood so proud and healthy. She thought he might be kind.

He asked where they came from. Luba told him, explaining that her mother was a little sick from the train. The doctor agreed that she did not look well. He signalled to a man behind him. They conferred, glancing now and then at Feigele. A guard roared close by and struck a woman with his stick. The doctor was rather upset. He told the guard to stop it.

Luba waited. She wanted to go to the toilet very badly.

The doctor enquired whether she had any brothers or sisters, if she were a twin. She shook her head, unable to understand. He was irritated. She was dumb before his rightness. In the midst of the erratic hiss of lights, the shouting and the atmosphere of barely-suppressed panic, he was sure of himself.

He said: "Pity." He told her to go to the group on the right. Feigele he pointed to the left.

Luba hesitated. Her mother gazed blankly at the doctor. A guard appeared and butted her forward. Luba reached for her as she stumbled. She looked to the doctor, asking where her mother was going.

He smiled at her again. "You can see for yourself that your poor mother is ill," he said. "We just want to take her to the hospital to make her well again. Meanwhile, you will go with all your healthy friends and be processed. There's nothing wrong with that, is there?"

She did not believe him. Something was wrong. It was not just sick ones in the group on the left. There were old people and children. Their eyes were deep and frightened in the shadows thrown by the lights.

She pleaded to go with her mother, though she was afraid. He told her that the hospital was crowded already. There was no room for the healthy. Again the smile. Her stomach turned over. "Besides," he said. "You don't really want to go with them, do you?"

Her bowels spasmed horribly. She felt that any moment she would lose control and mess herself in front of him. She could not speak.

"Now go along," he said, "and have no fear. Your mother will be well looked after." A flick of his hand again, and the guards moved in. She was pushed roughly towards the group on the right. When she was there, she looked for her mother in the other group, saw her standing alone on the edge of the throng, staring at the ground. She called out that she would see her soon. A guard sniggered. She looked for me but I was gone. All she could see now was the doctor, legs slightly apart,

169

He stretched his hand up. She shook it firmly. "You saved them from disaster, then?" Her voice was Edinburgh without the prissy quality it sometimes has. A light, throaty sound, as if she had a slight cold. She wore a waterproof jacket; her hair was captured by a band.

"Well, they almost ran me down, what could I do?"

She kept hold of his hand as she stepped down into the boat. "Every year we get the same letter about how Bax nearly ruined the *Cader* getting her back in the water."

"He's getting worse," Mrs Caradoc said.

Miller's daughter looked around the cockpit, trying the hatch.

"Do you know about boats, Mr – ?"

He could not slow his pulse, was sure his hands were trembling.

"Halborough," he said. "Joe Halborough. Little bit."

"Have you got one here?"

"No, but I'm looking around."

She gave him a quick smile. "You should persuade Bax to rent you this one. One of these days he'll sail off round the bay and disappear forever."

"Jenny!" Mrs Caradoc hissed. "Don't say such things."

"Local artist lost at sea," she quoted from imaginary headlines. "Coastguards and helicopters search through night, find pipe bowl and a tube of Flake White."

"Jenny!"

Caradoc himself was advancing down the pier. "That was work well done," he declared. "Thanks to our friend here." He raised spiky eyebrows at David. "Is she well?"

"Idling a little fast. I've slowed her down."

"Whole engine needs dismantling. You don't do that as well, I suppose?"

"I can manage a Mercury."

"A practical man," Mrs Caradoc said. "Oh, how we need one of those."

Caradoc checked his watch. "Time for a little lunch, I think."

"It's not twelve o'clock yet," Miller's daughter said.

"Then we'll extemporise with a little aperitif until the kitchen opens. Mr – ?"

"Halborough," she told him.

"Joe," David said.

"Mr Joseph Halborough, would you allow us to buy you a snifter by way of thanks?"

They retired to the Harbourmaster. The Caradocs sat together in the window, David found himself next to Miller's daughter. The old man appointed himself master of ceremonies and chief speaker, something the ladies were clearly used to. They let him forge ahead, smiling as if he were a boisterous but charming child. All drank hot whisky and ginger, and introductions were made. David expressed proper surprise. Weren't they the artists responsible for the works he had admired so much in the gallery? This got him very warm looks from both Caradocs. He even went so far as to say he had been meaning to pop up and visit their studio.

"Is it a collector you are, then?" Caradoc asked.

"A little bit."

"You're full of little bits," Mrs Caradoc giggled.

"I can't lift a brush to whitewash a wall," he said, "but I admire people who can really do it."

"Ah, but you can take an outboard to pieces and launch boats," Miller's daughter said. She was slightly outside the conversation.

"And you're on holiday?" Caradoc said.

"Sort of. Work was getting on my nerves, so I thought I'd come down and be at one with nature until the clouds cleared."

"What work is it that shreds your senses, then?"

"Plastics."

"Really?" said Mrs Caradoc, and he could tell he had hit on a good job. They were not interested in plastics of any kind, and he knew just enough to get by.

"You're not a polluter, are you?" Caradoc growled.

"We have awards from Lincoln city council for our cleanliness."

"What did you really want to be?" Miller's daughter said.

It was not an ordinary question. But he knew what to say without knowing how.

"Engineer," he said. "I wanted to build bridges. But most of the big rivers have them now."

They ordered food from the bar. He fetched another round of drinks, non-alcoholic for Miller's daughter. He could not

171

believe his luck. He kept saying he should leave them to their own business, but Caradoc and his lady waved aside his attempts to leave.

Miller's daughter spoke little during the meal, but was not unfriendly. At times she appeared to be concentrating on something no one else could see. How long had she been widowed? A couple of months? It seemed distant. Occasionally he caught a trace of her perfume. It was subtle, unflowery. He found himself wanting to look at her properly. Glimpses as he turned in her direction showed him the same good profile, strength under smooth flesh. Her jacket was off; he could see the curve of her breasts under a deep red cashmere sweater.

A foul thought trailed through his mind as he talked of sailing in the Lake District. Wouldn't it be something to screw Miller's daughter? Wouldn't it have a nice tang of revenge when the old fascist found out a Jew-boy had been fucking his sweet child?

Shaken by the heat of desire that went through him, he fell silent, picking at his food.

Caradoc was telling the story of a painting expedition in the Lakes just after the war. Mrs Caradoc played her part by correcting him when he strayed too far from fact. Their voices danced like birds against the background hubbub.

David lifted his head and glanced at her. She was examining his hands. Her eyes shifted, and they looked at each other, as they had in the pub the first time. Again the feeling of being upended. It lasted a fraction of a second, then both looked away.

"So you see," Caradoc sniffed at a piece of carrot on the end of his fork. "Ransome wasn't the only chap to get some inspiration out of the place. Mind, he made more money out of it than I ever did."

David shifted on his chair. He was rigid with desire, afraid she would see. Her expression had been surprised, disturbed. He had suddenly imagined her rocking beneath him, screaming at the top of her voice. He pushed his plate away.

"Not hungry?" Mrs Caradoc said.

"I eat breakfast in the café," he said. "It sets you up for today, tomorrow and the next day."

"Mrs Wembury believes in the health-giving properties of a

172

full English breakfast." Caradoc rose abruptly. "I must go and open the floodgates."

"Me too," Mrs Caradoc said, fluttering as she shuffled out from the table. "Back in a minute."

The smooth flow of things while the Caradocs were running the show ground to a halt. The radio behind the bar ticked out the Greenwich time signal and a doomy voice began reading the headlines.

David said: "They're interesting people."

She swivelled round to face him better. No eye contact now. "They're great fun."

He had to make a real effort to keep his gaze from straying all over her, but the simplicity of desire made it easier for him to be confident. "Have you known them long?"

"Oh, years. Isobel was at school with my mother. They're my godparents. Not that I ever got much religious instruction from Bax." She drew a face out of a puddle on the table. "How long're you staying in town?"

"It's a kind of open-ended arrangement," he said. "I left my partner in charge. If anything desperate happens, he'll call me."

"Are you so tired of it, then?"

"I'm appreciating the change. What about you?"

"Me?" She sipped her drink.

"You on holiday?"

"Sort of. At least, I'm not working, so this must count as some kind of holiday."

They fell silent again.

"Which painters do you like?" she asked.

"Graham Sutherland, Andrew Wyeth."

She grimaced. "Ugh! Corpses."

"He does have a hard style," he agreed.

"Bloody Helga," she said. "I mean, if you're going to spend fifteen years painting the same woman, you could at least make her pretty. Still, I'm just a weekend dauber. All my opinions are based on jealousy."

He wished the Caradocs would come back.

"You paint too?" he said.

"I do all sorts of things. None of them with any great success." She frowned, then smiled again. "Pardon me. It's those two with their painting and sculpting and never stopping

173

to think for a minute. They get it so easily: I spend my time worrying how."

The Caradocs returned, Caradoc opening a packet of cigarettes from the machine.

"And what do you have planned for the afternoon, Mr Halborough?"

"Thought I'd drive into Falmouth and take a look round. There's a few things I need."

"Ah. Never mind. I'd have invited you to participate in the sea trials of our old tub. Maybe another day."

"I'd like that very much," David said, as they got ready to leave.

Outside the wind was picking up. They stood on the pavement as the local bus careered by.

"Fine weather," Caradoc said. "Oh, don't forget, if you want to have a look round the studio, pop up when you feel like it. No obligation, of course."

David put on his jacket. "Good luck with the boat."

"We always have good luck with her."

He looked at Miller's daughter. She nodded to him. He wanted to say something, but settled for a similar gesture.

Then they were going away from him across the car park, Caradoc explaining something to his wife with sweeping motions of the arms. Miller's daughter followed a pace or two behind, obviously thinking her own thoughts.

He set off to fetch his car.

23

They marched beside the railway line. A gate with words of iron stood out against the black sky:
ARBEIT MACHT FREI
Work Brings Freedom
She stumbled. Another girl picked her up. "Come," she hissed. "You want to be shot." Grey faces stared from watchtowers, training machine-guns on them. All around was noise. They left the railway line behind, came to another gate, passed through. A roll-call was in progress, hundreds of women lined up outside long huts like chicken sheds.

174

The guards drove them into a narrow, brightly-lit building. Short-haired women in striped clothes waited for them. They had green triangles sewn on their left breasts. Some carried whips.

The new arrivals were told to strip. They stood shivering as their clothes were thrown in vats of steaming grey water. They were sent under icy showers, then into baths of blue-green antiseptic. They were shaved: head, armpits, between the legs. New clothes were handed out. There was little attempt to fit clothes to bodies. Luba came away with a pair of men's trousers, a woollen shirt with odd buttons, and a pair of scuffed wooden clogs. She stood, feeling her head through the spiky remnants of hair.

They were lined up again. Girls with longer hair sat behind desks and wrote down details of the new arrivals. More girls waited farther on. They tattooed numbers on the forearms of each woman. Luba was shoved towards them. The needle stabbed her skin. She wondered out loud if it would come off. The girl told her of course it wouldn't. She dotted the digits in place, asking if Luba was alone. Luba told her where her mother was. The girl looked away. Another paused in her work. "Hospital." She sneered.

"Perhaps you'll see her again after your quarantine," the girl said.

"Quarantine?" Luba said. "For how long?"

One of the uniformed women smacked her between the shoulders with the butt of her whip. "Six weeks, brat," she said. "Don't worry. I don't expect you'll last that long."

Miller's daughter tossed a palette knife aside and threw herself on an old horsehair sofa in a corner of the studio. All without a sound.

David squinted painfully through binoculars. He rested against a wall at the top of the hill behind Old Cottage. Three hundred yards distant the lights in the studio made warm squares on the dark.

He had gone to Falmouth, because he did not want to be caught lying. On return, he had been too restless to stay in the flat. He had come out here because watching the house, hoping for a glimpse of her, renewed his sense of purpose.

An owl left its haunt in a subsiding barn to his left. It beat out over his head with a soft rush.

Miller's daughter stretched her legs out. Her head was back, eyes closed. She sat up again, retrieved the knife and returned to a big canvas whose back was to him. She gazed at what was there with dissatisfaction. One hand rose and wiped at her breast. He saw how her body moved in the sweater and the old jeans. She pushed hair out of her eyes and leaned towards the canvas. She looked as if she hated the whole thing. She raised the knife.

Most of that day they stood on a baked piece of ground behind the huts. She saw the daily routine: breakfast – which they did not have; work parties going out to the music of a brass band; lunch of foul kohlrabi soup; more standing; work parties returning, carrying their dead in makeshift stretchers. Then a well-fed woman in decent clothes came and announced herself as the boss of their hut, the Blockalteste. *They were given evening rations – a chunk of stale bread and a dab of margarine, which was breakfast also – and allowed in to a long, stone-built hut which had once been a stable. A brick channel ran down the centre, rows of three-tiered bunks either side. Slogans were painted on the walls: Respect Your Superiors; Work Hard and Obey.*

She took out a piece of the bread she had saved and nibbled at it, retching. A scrawny woman leapt at her and snatched the crust, thrusting it into her mouth. Luba watched her limp away, tears springing into her eyes.

A small woman with cheeks ludicrously red against her pale skin took her hand, comforting her. She said her name was Helena. As the new arrivals explored their surroundings, they talked. Helena had been in the camp for six months, she had lost her daughter not long before, but she had a new 'family' now, girls who were alone. She knew how things ran. She told Luba that she and her family would look after her.

The new prisoners were fighting to find sleeping places. Each bunk made for one person held three or four. If you did not get space on a bunk, you slept in the dirt, but she would see that Luba had somewhere to go.

"Is this where we have to stay?" Luba said.

"This is it. Get used to it, child, and maybe you'll survive."

He was breakfasting in the café half a week later when they met again. She came in to escape a sudden shower. Mrs Wembury glanced up from the pages of her *Daily Mirror*, murmuring in time with the music on the radio. A couple of boys up from the harbour were devouring plates of fry-up. Miller's daughter nodded hello to them, then saw him sitting in the window. He rose.

"Can I get you something?"

"It's all right," she said, shaking the rain off her coat. She went over to the counter for a cup of tea.

"Mind if I join you?"

"Please do."

She sat down opposite, ladled three spoons of sugar into the tea. "Builds energy," she explained, as rain fretted the glass.

"Also replaces lost body heat." She drank, her throat moving softly. Then she began to empty her pockets, grimacing at the state of the contents.

"Look at that," she said, unsticking the pages of her sketchbook. "This is what Bax means by wet on wet."

"Were you sketching?" he said.

She gazed at the book, paintbox and water bottle. "Water ski-ing."

"Sorry. Obvious sort of question."

"Never mind." She left the things to dry. "I forgot you had breakfast here."

"And if you'd remembered, you'd never have come in."

"Oh, I had to go somewhere to get out of the rain. Besides, there's nothing wrong with intelligent conversation. Do you have any?"

"I'm taking a holiday from that too."

"You have to come up to the house, you know. Bax has a lot of old stuff he wants to unload on a rich art lover."

"I'm not rich."

"Well, he still likes to show people round. The gallery only takes the smaller stuff. He's a muralist at heart."

"What about you?"

"I told you, I'm a dauber."

"You have all the equipment."

"Anyone can buy the trappings."

"You're not an artist, then?"

"Me?" She laughed. "Niver, Sirr."

He lifted the sketchbook cover on a fine pencil sketch of the church. "You're being modest."

She pressed the book shut, laying her hand over his to do it, then snatching her fingers away. "You should never look at people's private notebooks," she said.

"Sorry."

"Don't fret. If I were prouder of what I'd done, I'd most likely be shoving it under your nose."

"The church is very good."

"All the lines in the right place, but there's more to it than that, as my father always says."

He kept his expression neutral.

"What makes him an expert in the field?" he asked. "He an artist too?"

"Oh, my father's an expert in everything," she said. She tapped the sketchbook. "He's right about this, anyhow. When I was a little girl, Mother used to bring us down here to stay, and I thought: This is the life, up to your eyes in oil and turpentine. So I went to art college and all the rest of it. But all it did was teach me the difference between competent and good. You either have that or you don't. So I went into the commercial side."

"What branch?"

"Textiles mainly."

"Fabrics?"

"And wallpapers and rugs. Not now, though."

"What do you do now?"

"Not much." She sipped the tea, staring out of the window. Eyes almost emerald, the skin around them crinkled in thought. Her wedding band plain thin gold, the engagement ring an expensive affair of diamonds.

"We have something in common, then," he said. "We're both involved in the serious business of doing not very much."

"Hooray for us."

The conversation faltered. He had said the wrong thing by mentioning their having something in common.

"Has Mr Caradoc taken the boat out yet?"

"He always dawdles over the first trip. I told him he should hire her out to you, but he likes to have her ready when the urge strikes."

The rain was slackening. She finished her tea and scraped her chair back.

He stood too. "Time I was moving on as well."

She seemed to race him for the door, as if she wanted to get away. He caught up with her going towards the east pier. Her shoes splashed in the puddles.

"More sketching?" he said.

"Perhaps. It's really oils weather now."

"Or oilskins."

She shook her head at him, at the feeble joke. He grinned as if to say: "I can't help it," and saw the life like electricity in her face.

They walked along, side by side for a moment. The harbour was picked out in hard patches of brilliant light. Over at the shipwright's, three men clambered high on the raised and scaffolded hull of a fishing boat, hammering, building.

"That's a real job," she said. "Do you make things?"

"Personally, you mean? Not any more. I just create the conditions for other people to do it."

"Well, that's something."

They paused at the entrance to the car park. He wanted to hurt her. He said:

"What does your husband do?"

She watched the men working. "Computers." Gulls circling, screeching. She coughed. "Not now, though." She dug her hands in her pockets and turned away. "Cheerio, then."

He stayed where he was, watching her walk towards the gallery.

He thought: The bitch is unbalanced.

That's the other thing we have in common.

Six weeks of being locked out every day. A reserve for anyone who needed work parties. Perhaps half of the women she had come in with died then. Dysentery, typhus. Mainly it was shock. When quarantine was over, they were transferred to another camp and assigned to outside work.

She learned many things: to work her way towards the middle of the crowd at roll-call so as not to be noticed; to stay with the other girls who made up Helena's 'family'; to 'organise' everything with the one aim of staying alive; to accept that it was largely Jews themselves who ran the camp day to day, and that you could expect little help from them. Often someone you knew, once she was chosen for special duties and given little privileges, became more brutal than the Germans.

She learned that I was still alive, but that her mother was dead. And she learned what had happened to her mother, what the smell of roasting meat that drifted over the camp meant. And she learned that you did not talk about it. The official phrase the Germans used, when they made the rounds of the sick, was 'Selection for special treatment'.

She came to recognise Mengele, Taube, Hossler and some of the other doctors. They always looked as if they were going on a round of the wards in a hospital, except for the armed guards who went with them.

She learned also to think of the lice that swarmed on her almost with affection. Her lice. They burrowed into her skin and she tried not to scratch, but had to. And every time she squeezed one out, the hole it made would get bigger and more infected. She became a mass of scabs, and like some of the others, she washed in the tea they were given in the mornings, because there was no water. The important thing was not to look too unhealthy. Otherwise, when Mengele came round, she might end up on the right.

Next afternoon he drove out to Old Cottage. The windows flashed sunlight as he approached the front door. He knocked, no one answered. He saw a car in the open garage, strolled round the side of the house, peering through the windows. At the back, he tapped on the kitchen door. A tortoiseshell cat wound itself round his legs, but no one came. Then the studio door opened.

"Hello, again." She wore a paint-streaked smock, a dab of vermilion on her forehead.

"Caradocs out?" he said.

"Correct. Over at Shrampton."

"I came to see the paintings."

"Come in, then. Bax'd never forgive me if I turned a customer away."

He crossed the lawn and went in. It was strange to be where the binoculars had already taken him. There were the couch and the easel, there was Miller's daughter. The difference was detail and the spring daylight from many windows.

"Would you like a drink? Bax usually offers people a large one before he tells them the prices."

"I'll pass, thanks."

She slung a dirty sheet over the canvas she had been working on, wiped her hands on a rag. He indicated her forehead. She rubbed the mark away.

"Most of the finished stuff's in that lot over in the corner. Mind you, there's some he's not done with yet." She started setting the canvasses side by side against the wall. He watched her until she turned to see what he thought. The paintings revealed themselves. Seascapes, a few landscapes, a still life or two, a portrait of an old character from the town. "I don't know what kind of thing you're after," she said. "Anyway, this is just the viewing. You'd have to see Bax to make him an offer. He'll only blame me if I get the price wrong."

"That's a good one," he said, pointing out a half-completed study of the bay from the eastern hills.

"He *is* good," she said. "I mean, he'd be the first to tell you his limitations, but he's very good at what he does."

"That's the best way to be, isn't it?"

"I used to think accepting your limitations meant you'd never try to step beyond them."

"What do you think now?"

180

She chuckled faintly.

"Still trying to overcome yours?" He indicated the canvas on the easel.

"Just slapping the paint on to see what comes of it." Her eyes were deep. "You're always asking questions, Mr Halborough."

"Joe, please."

"I think I prefer Joseph. Joe sounds like a boy in short trousers."

She pulled the largest canvas from the stack. He took the other end and they stood it in front of the rest.

"That's very fine," he said, and meant it. It showed a flat expanse of calm water fringed with reeds, a narrow wipe of riverbank, a single figure cut into a huge evening sky. The whole thing textured in blues and purples and deep greens. It captured perfectly the feeling of world's end which Haverley gave him.

She was standing close. He smelt her perfume again, the scent of her behind it. Maybe she sensed what was happening to him. She darted forward suddenly.

"It's one of the Essex ones, I think." She tilted it to look on the back. "Yes. One of his favourites. He's not really so desperate to sell it."

"I'm sorry if I come across as nosey," he said. "I don't mean to be."

She looked past him. "I'll see if I can find Bax's price book. He keeps it in the house somewhere. But I wouldn't go getting your hopes up about this one."

She went out. He watched her through the window, the smock flicking in the wind and holding tight round her body. Then he wandered over to the easel. The palette on the sofa contained the vermilion, French ultramarine and lemon yellow. He lifted the sheet and sneaked a look at the canvas. It was a mass of unmixed colours, vaguely suggestive of a familiar shape.

"As you were saying . . ." She came back in, snatched the sheet and yanked it down again. "You don't mean to be nosey, it just comes across that way."

He smiled, unflustered. Be charming, he thought. "Pardon me. Can't help looking at work in progress. Bad habit."

181

She ignored him, flicking through an old hardcovered exercise book.

"You like the church, don't you?" he said.

She glanced up, surprised.

"I didn't think it was recognisable."

"I'd like to see it when it's finished."

"No one'll see it." She tapped the book. "Like to see some prices instead?"

As he went through them, she moved restlessly about, rearranging things.

"Bax wanted to hunt you out the other night," she said.

"How so?"

"I think he's taken a shine to you." She gave him a sidelong glance. "They don't know what a snooper you are, of course. He thought you might appreciate some company, being here on your own."

"He's right."

"What *do* you do in the evenings?"

"Catch up on my reading. Be glad to be interrupted though." He wondered if he might risk inviting her out now, but let it be.

"He and Isobel do a lot of their boozing in the Harbourmaster. You can find them in there in the evenings, if you want to talk prices."

"And what d'you do?"

"I've been watching an awful lot of television. It's very good for numbing the brain."

"You want it numbed?"

She shook her head. "You really do snoop, Mr Halborough."

"That's because I'm interested, Mrs Colvin."

Her lips pursed for a moment. They glistened. "Jenny, I think."

"Thank you."

They went out again. A tractor was dragging across the field behind the house. He got in his car.

"See you down the Harbourmaster then."

"Stranger things have been known," she said. Her manner was almost flirtatious.

"I hope you *will* let me look at your painting when it's done."

"You can use the canvas to repair a sail," she said.

No sense of weeks or months. She knew it was August when she entered the camp, some time late in September when quarantine ended. After that, the days were marked only by 4 am roll calls and the killing work outside, the selections, the random brutalities of Blockalteste or camp police.

Sometimes there were rumours about the war. She did not believe them. Occasionally, she would look out across the flat, misty countryside and think: It ends where the horizon ends. How could anyone believe in armies or victory? There was nothing but this camp. One of the girls in her 'family' heard that her last brother had died in the men's camp. In no time at all she changed from a brave little fighter into a sickly, disorientated figure: a Mussulman, without the inclination even to avoid a kick or the bite of a guard dog. She died because she no longer cared to live.

Typhus struck Luba down when the first snows came. One day she was coughing and light-headed, the next, delirious. She realised she was being picked up and taken somewhere. She screamed, begging them not to put her in the ovens.

She regained consciousness in the hospital block, sharing a bunk with three other women who also had the typhus. Two were dead.

Helena, who worked in the hospital, had kept her safe. She had been trying to get her onto the staff. Now she promised it would happen if only she got well.

Luba fought. Helena told me that she seemed to survive despite her pock-marked, flea-ridden body.

When finally she could stand by herself, she found that she was to be a cleaner in the hospital. Nothing fixed, though. There were no permanent jobs. After a time she was 'promoted' to 'Nursing'. This was another name for carrying out the dead. It became clear to others that she had a knowledge of German, and that gave her another advantage. She could take messages – not like the girls who were allowed to grow their hair and wear better clothes, secretaries in the administration blocks, but within and around the hospital.

One day there was a selection. The young doctor who had sent her mother to the gas chamber passed through the block, accompanied by Taube, Haase and others. Those who could not leave their bunks were marked down. Luba and another girl had to pick up the sick and dying, carry them to the lorries, and throw them aboard. A young woman with huge eyes tried tying herself to the bunk, but they cut her loose. All the way out of the block, she struggled feebly, crying out that she had babies to look after. It was not true, of course. Any children she had were long since dead. But she believed it, and Luba could not bear the look in her pleading eyes as they struggled outside with her.

Those being hefted onto the lorries were sobbing and yelling, those forced to do the throwing were in a similiar state. An SS man ordered them to shut up.

The young woman with her pleading eyes begged one more time to be spared. The guns pointed at them.

183

Luba and the other girl, blind with tears, swung her up on the truck.
A sack of potatoes.

24

The Harbourmaster was the venue for impromptu jam sessions by local folk music buffs. When David entered that night, five of them were by the big fire in the bar; a twelve-string guitar, mandolin, accordion, violin and flute working their way busily through 'Soldier's Joy'. The place was packed, the audience appreciative, banging out the quickening rhythm on the tables.

He wound a tortuous way to the bar. The music kept speeding up and speeding up, but the players stayed together, eyeing each other with the wordless satisfaction musicians have when they are working well. As David got his pint, they brought the whole thing to a thrashing conclusion that had the audience applauding with the joy of it. The musicians, flushed with effort and pleasure, had a drink, then settled down to a quiet rendition of 'All to the Fair'.

"Ah, you're here." Caradoc appeared at his side. "Glorious stuff, wouldn't you say?" He thrust a note at the landlord and barked: "Same again, John."

"You alone tonight?" David asked, watching the musicians take turns at solos.

"What, on a music night? Isobel never misses a chance to hear catgut scraped. Come and join us, boy."

Caradoc led him to a table in a corner near the music. Mrs Caradoc was there, fingers drumming on the table, eyes closed in extravagant enjoyment of the music. And Miller's daughter – Jenny, he forced himself to think – was at her side, watching the musicians with close attention.

Mrs Caradoc opened her eyes delightedly. "You decided to join us?" she said.

David bowed and kissed her hand. She loved the gesture. He did not try the same with Jenny, just nodded to her, receiving the same in reply.

They talked about boats and the weekend weather. The musicians let rip with 'Paddy McGinty's Goat'. There was little conversation through that. Caradoc shouted odd words and sank his pint like a man dying of thirst. David pretended to pay attention to the music, watching Jenny as much as he could. She was drinking halves of mild. Good. A little alcohol might loosen her up. She glanced at him. He smiled, and tapped the beat on the edge of his glass.

There was a lull while the musicians let their instruments cool down.

"Jenny tells me you had a private view," Caradoc said.

David put down his drink. "I was very impressed."

"That's the truth," she said. "He did look impressed."

"Especially the big canvas of the marshes."

"Beautiful, isn't it?" Caradoc grinned.

"No false modesty, please," Jenny said.

"I was on a good hot streak with that one."

"That makes it sound as if you'd rather not sell," David said.

"Ah, Mr Halborough – Joseph, I can't afford to be so picky. Mind you. I've always hoped it would go to a good home."

"He means a well-off one."

Mrs Caradoc gave her an old-fashioned look. "You're very cruel, child."

"Must be the booze." She lifted her glass and drained it. "They don't have mild in Scotland, you know."

Caradoc growled a laugh. "That's more like the Jenny of old. None of this teetotal rubbish."

David fetched another round, by which time the music was on again; a gentle tune called 'Portmeirion'.

Talk continued in low voices, Caradoc giving details of when and where the painting was done. "Mostly executed right on the spot," he said. "A bit of studio work later, but what you see is largely what was there. Had to work fast two evenings in a row to get it."

"I wish I had your touch," Jenny said, leaning her chin in her hand.

"You have a touch of your own, girl. Leave mine alone."

"He's very jealous of his craft," she said to David. "I'm surprised he lets me muck about in the studio."

"It's on sufferance," Caradoc declared. "*I* can't work there any more. Women messing about with bits of wood and canvas. That's why I'm cleaning up my fishing gear."

185

Isobel turned from the music. "The truth is, he sees Jenny's work and knows he can't compete."

Jenny grimaced. "That'll be the day." She drank again. "Mind, I think I could dash off an Andrew Wyeth or two now. Maybe I should drink mild all the time."

There was another singalong to 'John Barleycorn'. David joined in lustily. All the time, as the Caradocs rocked together and Jenny stumbled through the words, he was thinking. He drank at the same rate as them, but they were ahead by two rounds, and he had a good head for beer. He noticed Jenny missing words. He started shouting them to her and conducting the table in the choruses.

"Sing up," he said. "We're not drowning out the band yet."

"My voice wasn't made for singing," she answered.

"I noticed."

She mocked a threatening fist at him, then plunged into the last chorus. David saw an exchange of looks between the Caradocs.

The song came to a bawling conclusion. Jenny sat back, sweeping hair out of her eyes and laughing as if there had been a great joke.

"I don't know which of us sounds more like a tortured hedgehog," she said.

"Thank you, ma'am."

The ladies retired to the toilets while Caradoc bought the next round. He placed a pint in front of David and sat down, fingering a beer mat.

"She's having a good time tonight," he said.

"Who?" David said, knowing all that was coming.

"Jenny. Haven't seen her relax so much for ages."

"That's good, I take it?"

"Oh, that's very good. It's what she came here for."

The guitarist struck all twelve strings and made a deep drumming sound.

"See, she's not long been widowed."

David assumed the proper air. "Widowed? But she's so young."

"Twenty-eight. Her husband was killed in a car accident two months ago. She came down to us to get over it."

"I'm sorry."

"Isobel thought you ought to know. Jenny can be a bit up

186

and down at the moment. We thought you'd understand better if you were told the state of play."

"That's very . . . trusting of you." A little humility.

Caradoc sighed. "Well, she's a bit of an honorary daughter to us. It's been hard to see her hurt like this." There was an extra note there. It meant that Caradoc, or his wife, could see the possibilities in Jenny spending time with him, and he was being asked to behave like a gentleman. The very way it was hinted at made it clear that they believed he could be trusted; he was the sort of man who would have respect for her pain, not take advantage of vulnerability.

(*up on the truck. A sack of potatoes.*)

The band were into 'Wild Rover' when the ladies returned. Again he saw the quick looks between Caradoc and Isobel. He was fortunate, in a way. Knowing the tragic secret already, it did not affect his behaviour towards the widow, and the Caradocs obviously thought he was being subtle and considerate. Mustn't look too damn gentlemanly, though. Trying too hard might blow it.

They ordered sandwiches because drinking had made them hungry. They got back to boats, and Isobel told good stories of Bax's incompetence when first he put out to sea. That led to reminiscences of holidays Jenny had spent with them as a child, and near-fatal adventures in the *Cader Idris*.

"In those days," she said, "he liked to impress us – me and Paul and Alex – that he knew everything. The truth was, he didn't even know the names of all the parts of the boat."

"There's a lot of parts to your average yacht," Caradoc defended.

"He nearly drowned Alex once."

"Alex couldn't drown. That boy has cork for brains."

"Don't be so bitter and twisted," she giggled, almost swiping her glass over.

"I had enough bother being a father to my own boys. No wonder yours never came with you."

"Why was that?" David asked.

Jenny regarded a sandwich with interest. "Oh, Dad's a surgeon. Was, I mean. He took a holiday with us three times when we were growing up – One of those he was called back to perform an operation."

"He's a cutter," Caradoc said. "A butcher, in fact."

187

"I thought you came from an artistic family," David said.

"Not so." She decided to take the sandwich. "I have one brother who thinks the height of culture is shooting anything with fur or feathers, and another who only knows about the art of making money. Why d'you think I adopted these wonderful people here?"

"Jenny's mother was a very fine watercolourist," Isobel said.

She surprised them by joining in suddenly with 'Shotover River'. He wondered what was behind those pretty eyes, what she knew about her father. There was something of the old man's cool appraisal in her, and a little of brother Paul's straightforward condescension. They flitted like bats behind the clear beauty of her face. Like unpleasant truths.

She said: "Don't you know the words to this one?"

He had stopped singing. He took up the chorus again, switching his attention to the musicians and the frantic mess they were making of 'Over the Waterfall'.

The evening rounded off with a stint of *a cappella* singing on 'Hanging Johnny'. Then the landlord rang the bell and shouted Time.

The Caradocs made their exit as well-known local characters do, waving and shouting to old friends as they made their way to the door. David went with them, taking Jenny's arm to steady her through the scrum.

Then they were out in the chill night air, and the sea was scouring the harbour near the height of its flow. They walked along the front. Isobel sang 'Shotover River' in a fragile soprano, Caradoc joining in with occasional grating bass notes between puffs on his pipe.

"That was a good evening," David said, releasing Jenny's arm.

"It's not what I usually do." She was not very drunk, but her words were soft round the edges. "Fun, though." She stuck her hands in her pockets and shivered.

"Borrow my coat?" he asked.

"It's just the night air." Caradoc and Isobel strolled ahead. "Look at them," she said. "I admire them like hell."

"I see why."

"They've been together forty-something years, and it still works."

He made no reply to that.

"They're good people," she said. "They help you through trouble without interfering."

They left the village behind, climbing the hill towards the scattered string of lights on the headland. A tawny owl cried in the fields nearby.

"Bax told you about Richard, didn't he?"

"Your husband?" he said. "Yes, he did."

"I thought so. Isobel's terrible at pretending."

"He just thought I ought to know. So I wouldn't put my foot in it, I suppose."

"He was killed in March. A stupid accident not a hundred yards from home."

They ambled on up the road, occasionally blinded by headlamps.

She said: "Shouldn't you have turned off somewhere back there?"

"I need a walk to clear the head after all the beer and pipe smoke."

"A bracing hike."

"Something like that."

"Were you raised in the country?"

"Boothby Pagnall."

"Bless you."

"It's a little place near Grantham. Where do you come from?"

"Racially mixed parentage."

"Which means?"

"One Celt – that was Mummy – and one Swiss. I don't know what Swiss people are, racially. Not Nordic, not Latin. What would they be?"

"I don't know. Bit of French, bit of German?"

"I'll have to ask Dad. He only ever took us there once."

"Have any relatives there?"

"Just a couple of distant ones that we never see. He was an only child, his parents died before the war."

"So he came to Scotland to be a famous surgeon?"

"That's about it."

If you tell a lie often enough, it sounds like truth. She seemed quite open. But if she knew, she would hardly go around looking guilty.

"But *where* do you come from, as opposed to who?"

189

"Scotland?"

"I sort of guessed that."

"Stinton, to be precise. Little place near Edinburgh."

"Nice country?"

"Very, if you like it. And when you're raised with it you tend to. But I'm a wee bit tired of it just now."

"How long you staying?"

"Until Bax and Isobel throw me out, probably." She threw her head back and breathed deeply. He put out a hand to steady her.

"I'm all right," she said. "It's just I haven't been squiffed for a while."

Lamps were going off in the village. South the faint lights of a ship blinked in and out on the edge of the sea. The Caradocs were serenading each other with 'There Are Such Things'.

"That's not folk," Jenny called.

"It has great sentimental value to certain people," Caradoc told her.

"He means we used to sing it when we were courting," Isobel said.

"Courting!" Jenny got another fit of giggles. She stumbled against him. "Aren't they wonderful? Courting."

He let her regain balance. Only the glimmer of starlight gave them sight. Anger gnawed his guts. Was she flirting? Husband dead less than three months and she was flirting with him? These people, what were they? Was it the money, or the breeding? Anthony dropping him without a word because of possible damage to his career, the Miller boys threatening to set the police on him, and this woman with her accidental touching. He remembered one of the girls he went out with at college. She had told him: "I never touch any man accidentally. If I do it, it's because I want to."

So what was the widow's game? He felt disgust with her even as he saw how useful it could be.

"You know, I really think I could do something good tonight."

"In what way?" he asked.

"Palette knife and a few tubes of colour. I think I could go in the studio and do something good."

"Common mistake amongst the drinking classes," he said.

190

"Drinking glasses?" She broke into giggles again. He had been wrong; she was drunker than he thought.

They arrived at the gate of Old Cottage.

"You still here?" Bax said.

"Thought I'd escort you home. Didn't want to wake up in the morning and find you got lost."

"Come in for a final snifter, then."

He demurred, they insisted. He gave in with good grace, supporting Jenny up the path to the front door.

The interior of the house was what he expected. Old dark wood, paintings everywhere, shelves groaning with art and nature books, a pleasant smell of woodsmoke and pipe tobacco. Isobel switched on low lights and drew back the curtains to reveal a picture window of the bay and the town, Bax put on a Charlie Webb record.

They sat round until half-past one, and it was all very jolly, very friendly. He had no trouble with the drink, and remembered that he was Joseph Halborough throughout.

It ended with a round of jokes. Jenny told one about a doctor and a patient, and her enthusiasm began to fly close to quiet hysteria. After that she dozed off.

"She'll hate herself in the morning," Bax chuckled. "Showing herself up in a drunken frenzy."

"You hush," Isobel said. "She's been through a lot."

Whispered farewells were taken as Isobel woke Jenny and suggested it was time for bed. David was standing in the doorway by then. She looked up at him, waved a hand.

"Goodnight, Mr Halborough."

"Goodnight, Mrs Colvin."

Outside, Bax clapped him on the shoulder. "I shall be fishing tomorrow, I think. You brought any tackle? No? Well, if you fancy hooking a few down on the harbour, we can probably knock a rod together for you."

"I might do that," he said, starting down the path.

Bax stood in the doorway, pipe fuming darkly. He waved. "Watch your step, boy."

"I will."

He reached the road, head swirling with drink, and cut off over the field. Released from being someone else, the reaction came like a wave of nausea. He stopped by the wall at the bottom of the field, leaned against it, shivering.

Miller's daughter, the widow, Mrs Colvin, Jenny.

25

One day she was cleaning the floor where a typhus patient had lost control of her bowels. She heard noises farther down the corridor. Looking up, she saw a burly soldier pressing one of the nurses back into a cupboard. The girl was lifting her dress and the soldier was fumbling with his breeches. Luba glanced about. No one else was in sight. The girl, half-concealed by the cupboard door, lifted herself against a shelf. The soldier's body moved between her legs. Then he began stabbing at her with his hips, lunging. Luba looked at the girl's stick-thin legs and the bristled back of the soldier's head.

When it was over, he was brusque again. He handed something to the girl. A scrap of sausage and a piece of bread. The girl tucked it away in her dress.

Luba only felt her mouth water at the sight of food.

Two days later: iron-bright sky and a brisk north wind; a clear spark in the air, galvanic charge. He was driving along the front. She came out of the post office, carrying a rucksack over one shoulder. He tooted the horn and pulled up across the road.

"Morning. Recovered from the other night?"

He thought for a second that she was going to retreat, but she smiled.

"I have to confess I spent next morning in bed."

"Lucky you. I roamed the countryside, holding my skull between cotton wool pads. Give you a lift?"

"Oh, no, I've got shopping to do."

"I can wait."

She hesitated. He tried to make her say yes.

"Well, if you don't mind."

"Mind nothing. I'm desperate for employment."

"Okay. Won't be a minute." She ducked into the shop on the corner.

He sat there, beating the steering wheel to the rhythm of the Pretenders' 'Don't Get Me Wrong'. Vibrating. She emerged after five minutes, ran across and got in the car.

"Would it be home, milady?"

"Well, you could give me a lift to Falmouth, if you're feeling unkind, but I'd only have to get a bus back."

"I shouldn't have asked."

They drove out of the narrow streets and up the hill.

"Did you get down to that masterpiece the other night?"

"You're joking. I could hardly find my room."

"All that on a few pints of mild."

"I'm not a drinker. Was I embarrassing?"

"You were fine. Just relaxed."

They arrived at the cottage. He let her get out before he said: "You don't know of any good deserted beaches, do you?" Her hand was on the door. "With caves, preferably. I fancy playing pirates."

"Oh, there are great ones round here. Really difficult to get to."

"Not on my map."

"Och, that's no good. You need a guide who knows the area."

"You volunteering?"

Hesitation again. He had pushed too far.

"I pay well," he said.

She brightened. "All right. I haven't been down to them myself yet." She closed the door. "Start after lunch? You'll need decent boots."

"I'll hire a mule and some coolies in town."

"Right, see you about half-past twelve."

He turned the car in the drive and accelerated away down the hill. He began to laugh, violence worming in him. The feeling was bad.

She was waiting by the gate when he drove up.

"You can park the car," she said. "They're walking distance." The moment she spoke, he knew she had thought better of the expedition. But she would not go back on it. Her character allowed no mistakes.

He put the car under an apple tree snowbound with blossom. Caradoc and Isobel peered out of the studio windows. He raised a hand. What were they thinking?

She was walking briskly up the road ahead, trying to leave him behind. He ran to catch her. Clouds dazzled in whiteness.

The sea was specked with yachts. Over on the other side of the bay, a microlight rasped slowly towards town.

"Beautiful," he said, stealing some of Anthony's old enthusiasm and one of his fragments of verse.

> " 'The wind blew hard for Plymouth Rock,
> The Captain called for calm.
> 'Lads,' cried he, 'trust Neptune's grace,
> And we'll be safe from harm.' "

"You do talk some rubbish," she muttered.

"I could tell you about injection moulding."

"Oh, recite some more poetry." She was resigning herself, easing up a little. He admired the view, tasting her danger in his mouth.

"You and your brothers used to come here a lot?"

"Not so much them." She kicked a soft drink can into the verge. "Usually, it was me and Mummy. Once in a while she'd call Dad, Paul and Alex to a meeting and say: 'I've had enough of looking after you lot. Jenny and I need a holiday.' And we'd come down here for a week or two."

"Didn't they mind being left alone?"

"Paul and Alex sometimes complained, but Dad never cared. I don't think he feels comfortable with Bax. Besides, he's a workaholic. Doesn't know the word 'retired'."

"Does he still operate?" Occasional practice with the knives, to bring back the old nostalgic thrill.

"He advises, he writes pamphlets and books, he has investments, and he looks after the shooting in the hills outside Stinton. *And* he sits on several boards and committees." She drew breath. "He's not a relaxer."

They went along a mile or so, following the dips and rises of the road. All the while, he asked innocuous questions about her family, partly on the grounds that the best way to ingratiate yourself with anyone is to make her talk about herself, partly so that her family would become a familiar subject. Hearing their names stung his hatred too. He nursed the clawing darkness in his chest. They left the road, skirting a ploughed field, tangling in thorns and long grass. It ran out in a series of curves where the tractor had turned. Beyond was rough grass, then the drop to the sea.

"This is the climbing," she said. They went down a narrow, slippery path overgrown with bracken and wild flowers. He watched her moving ahead, precise and quick. Taking herself farther and farther away from help.

"Don't worry," she said. "We went up and down here hundreds of times. Never had more than a broken leg."

They picked their way down to the beach.

Pencil scratching across a clean white page.

They sat on rocks at the eastern end of a shelf of clean sand. He watched her work, head bent close to the book. She talked constantly, almost as if it were an unconscious part of the drawing.

"Mummy used to talk about staying here, living in a cave. She was a dreamer. How she and Dad ever got together I don't know. It's not the sort of thing you ask, is it? . . . It's funny: you want to understand someone, but you never get round to it. Then something happens to take them away, and it's too late . . ." A pause to cut off something she did not want to say. The pencil outlined rocks and sand. "She could really draw, she could do oils or watercolours. We still have some on the walls at home. Not because they're hers, understand. She had talent."

He imagined grabbing her, shaking until truth fell from her mouth. "Did she . . . 'give it all up' to marry your father?"

"Oh, no."

"How did they meet?"

She rubbed with her finger at the outline of the rocks, blurring them and giving them shade. "How *do* parents meet? What about yours?"

"Oh, the ordinary thing." He picked up a shell to examine it closely. It disintegrated between finger and thumb.

"Mine came together at a party. Dad hadn't been in Edinburgh very long then. He was taking the exams so he could practise in Britain. His English was a little eccentric. They arrived at the buffet table at the same moment, and he asked whether he could pass her the 'canopies'. She had a fit of the giggles, he took umbrage. It all started from there." She put clouds into the sketch. "Which, I suppose, is just as well for me . . . There." She flipped the book shut. "Sorry to keep you. You should've gone on."

They rose and continued along the beach. Rage beat at the inside of his skull. Mummy, funny old Dad. "Did you speak two languages when you were a kid? I knew someone born of English parents in Germany, she had a hell of a time sorting out one from the other."

"I'm not bilingual, if that's what you mean. My French is better than the German. Besides, Swiss Germans aren't the same as real ones."

"I thought you said he was German?"

"You were drunker than I was. Swiss."

Protesting too much? They were quite alone. Rules could be broken.

They clambered up the rocks, gaining a twisted path that was more vertical than horizontal. She pulled herself up, finding familiar handholds. He followed, thinking about Germany and Swiss bank accounts. She edged round an outcrop that left only a precarious ledge for the feet.

"Mind here. It feels as if you're hanging off the side of a house."

He eased carefully along the ledge. Seventy feet below the sea dashed with steady beats at the cliff. He looked down. It was no yawning precipice, but one slip could kill him. One foot wrong, no more existence. One bullet in the skull, no more thought. One more bag of bones in the gas chamber, nothing left of his grandmother. Strange how easy it was.

"Want a hand?" she said.

He grasped her outstretched fingers. He imagined jumping, dragging her with him.

"Thank you."

"I forgot to ask if you're afraid of heights," she said, as they went along the clifftop single-file. "Paul nearly killed himself there once."

Blood and bone on grey rock. The sweet idea of the brother ceasing to be.

"Not because it's dangerous," she added. "He was acting the goat, as usual."

"It must've been hard, growing up with two brothers."

"Did I say that?" She paused to put her escaping hair back into its pony tail. He gazed at the back of her neck with a pulsating sensation in his belly. "They're all right. I mean, Alex is a bit stupid, to be honest, and Paul can be a bastard.

But they left me alone. Boarding school helps. What about you?"

"Big family," he said. "Two brothers, two sisters." Unwished for, there came a noisy, bulging house, a Polish city which never saw war, a teeming family who might have existed if the past had been other.

He asked again about her family.

A wedge of sand and rock, a pocket beach. They climbed down, hanging on to every tuft of grass. As they reached it, the breeze freshened. A squall of rain came in over the sea. They took cover in a shallow cave.

"I was a lot younger last time I did that," she panted.

"Should've brought ropes and crampons." He ran his fingertips over the damp wall, let the silence go on. A pair of birds slewed close to the water, swooping up again in a long, graceful curve. Jenny glanced up from her sketchbook.

"You've shut up," she said.

He tried to keep his voice normal. "Nothing to say."

"That's a change."

He took a silver hip flask from his pocket and offered it to her.

"What is it?"

"Lemonade."

She sipped from the flask, let the brandy lie on her tongue. "That's good."

He drank more than he should have, but he was in a state of tension and needed it. She accepted the flask when he offered it again, drank without wiping the neck. She was beautiful, healthy.

She had been attending a woman who died. In the daily struggle, searching the deceased for food or valuables was a crime only to the authorities. Taking from the sick or sleeping was nothing short of murder; but the dead were dead, and if she did not organise whatever remained, someone else would. This woman had somehow kept a little piece of potato for herself, even to death. It was stuck away in the grime of a pocket. As she and another girl removed the body, Luba took it.

A big, butch cow of an SS woman caught her. Her name was Gerda. Her green uniform was always starched and neat. She demanded to see what was in Luba's hand.

Luba tried to stuff the piece of potato in her dress.

"You steal some food?" Gerda asked. She was well-fed and strong. She liked to beat male prisoners, saying it proved how superior her race was to ours.

"No," Luba said.

The butt end of the whip came down. She staggered.

"Liar!" Gerda screamed. "Liar, liar, liar!" With each word, another blow, on Luba's head and shoulders and back.

The other women began to whimper and cry. Helena tried to intercede. Gerda spat at her to keep off, or she would go up the chimney too. She turned again to Luba and demanded the scrap.

Luba fumbled in her dress, found the miserable bit of grubby food. Gerda snatched it, stared at it.

"You risk your life for this?" she said. "You're crazy, you Jews."

Starving, we were starving.

Gerda tossed the potato out of the door. Luba and the other women followed it with their eyes, saw it land in the icy mud outside.

The whip handle came down again and drove her to her knees. "You never learn, do you, you filthy animals? You make me sick." She struck once more, then walked out.

The others gathered round, sobbing and whispering words of comfort. Luba raised herself, tried to see out of the door, wanting to keep track of the potato.

Gerda paused, lifted her boot, and drove the little fragment of food into the mud.

He thought: I could force it out of you now. Pin you down and clobber you till you tell me what I want. Beat your pretty face out of shape like a Kapo beating the life out of a prisoner.

He heard a choking sound above the patter of rain, turned to stare at her. She was crying.

He was shocked, even though he knew she was near the edge. The sight of her tears pulled at his own grief. He saw the page on which her hand rested, a sketch of a castle, reminding her of something. He passed a handkerchief.

"It's worst when you remember they're gone," he said, his voice unsteady.

She dabbed her eyes. "I go for hours, almost whole days sometimes, without thinking about it, then suddenly I remember and it hits me again. I feel guilty when I don't think of him, and guilty when I do."

He thought of Grandfather.

"I'm sorry," she said.

"It's okay. Don't worry."

She was quieter already. "You lost someone, didn't you?"

198

His voice failed. He nodded, pieces of his insides tearing away.

She closed the sketchbook. "When my mother died, I was seventeen. She didn't go easily. We had a lot of time to get used to the idea, even to wish for it, so she'd be out of her pain. When it happens suddenly, you don't have that. What was it with you?"

"Leukaemia."

"I wish everyone died slowly."

"Quick is better."

"No. You can't settle things." Tears re-formed, glistened on her cheek. "One minute everything's normal and you think: I'll deal with it tomorrow. Next it's changed and you can't – " He waited. Finally she took the handkerchief from her face and began scratching circles in the sand where tears had fallen. "I keep thinking: If only we could've talked one more time, we might've . . ."

"There're always things you don't get to say." The words he had spoken to Grandfather, when he could not know whether they were being heard. "That's part of it. You can't blame yourself."

"But if what you didn't say was part of the reason for it?"

He was confused. "He was killed in a car accident."

"Oh, yes. A hundred yards from where I was sitting. But it was my fault. I'm to blame."

"You don't mean that," he said.

"Don't tell me." She drew her knees up and rested her forehead against them. "I'm the grieving widow, full stop. Even Bax and Isobel think that. But it's not so bloody easy."

"Stop doing this to yourself."

"I was living in my father's house." Her body shook with a fresh onslaught.

He wanted to run, get away. He concentrated on his mother, but Jenny's words broke through.

"I wasn't really living there," she muttered. "I'd . . . I was doing what Mum used to do, taking a break. Only I went home. Things weren't so wonderful between us. We were still 'together', you know, officially speaking, but it was awful. We argued all the time, all the usual subjects. He was . . . a cool man, my husband. Admired that when I met him. I was twenty-three then, not very mature." She looked to him, and the calculating part of his mind saw how he could use even her grief. Calculate, calculate. He moved closer to her. She drew circles within circles. "Going home was wrong. It's hard enough to sort things out, but it makes it twice as difficult if one of you uses the family for armour. Maybe that was the biggest problem in the end: we were having these conversations about staying together, having kids, but he had to come to my father's house to do it. Maybe they should have a rule: No going home to Mummy and Daddy after you tie the knot." Rain danced on the sea. "I listened to him talking about why we should keep going, and in the back of my mind I was thinking: If it's a choice between going with you or staying without you, I don't believe I want to go."

She groaned. "This sounds terrible. I'm sorry."

He touched cold stone. "Why didn't you divorce him?"

She pressed her head into her knees. "Maybe I'd have thought of it if I'd got away like this. But it's not that easy. Not in my family." Moisture ran down the cave walls. He sat before her, an expression of understanding tacked to his face.

"That night was awful. Dad was in a foul temper, we'd had that fuss with the old man who came to the door, and I had to go with Richard to some dinner party. We argued all the way there and all the way back." Her voice came wet and muffled. "I can't even remember what about. It gets so ordinary that everything sounds the same. But we both drank too much. We got home, and he came in with me. We hung fire until we were upstairs – no fighting in public – then went at it hammer and tongs . . . No, that's wrong. It wasn't vicious, just dreary, you know? Five years gives you that kind of familiarity, anyway. I kept telling him to keep his voice down, and he got angrier and angrier. Snipe, snipe, snipe. Then he said something, and I must have said something worse than usual back. I knew he was going to do his Stalking Off Into the Night routine then. He'd done it before. Maybe that's a sign of my staying power. I could always drive him from the field. Suppose it helps if the house is your father's.

"Kind of a judgement, wouldn't you say? Poetic justice. I heard the car drive away, then the crash."

She was no longer crying. She was still. The rain dripped from the cave roof onto her shoes.

"I keep telling myself it was coincidence. It didn't happen

that way to provide a Victorian melodrama end to things. Still feels like my fault."

The doubled view of the crash split him neatly down the centre. He felt as if the halves of his brain were tearing away from each other. He wanted to reach out and hold her hand, wanted to take her by the throat and tell her what her old man had been up to.

Get proof, for God's sake. One little shred of evidence.

To gain someone's trust, then to discover the sneaking need to deserve that trust. It clicked in his head like a geiger counter, roaring when he was close to her. In the following days, they sailed in the *Cader Idris*, first with Bax, then alone. He sat with her as she painted the church. The mess of red, blue and green was gone. She painted with the light, touching the canvas with certainty. And she talked. The need to carry on was more powerful than any doubts she might have had about being with him in her widow's weeds. Their conversations were long, playful, serious by turns. The ease of it almost lulled him into wanting to tell her the truth. He invented a past for himself, a family to complement hers, built from the scattered or demolished pieces of reality. Joseph Halborough came to be more real than the self he had left behind in Norwich, with the Wensum Mall and Sarah and Grandfather's grave.

And at nights, penitential, alone in the flat, he made notes of anything she told him. The pitifully little things: a family friend called Hossman; her father came from Glarus, not far from Switzerland's Austrian border. She had been there once, with Richard. She said it was not worth the visit. She said, she said . . .

He knew he was not pressing hard enough. Watching her as she gained some kind of strength from his presence, it grew less and less easy to hate her, to believe that she knew anything, to wish her unhappy.

He cursed himself for weakness, returned to the notebooks, driving himself through them again and again. Alone with the books and the pictures, he would stun himself with liquor, only to dream of an electric fence sizzling in the cold December rain, the red glow of fire leaping from the chimney of Crematorium Three, his mother lying awake in the night, listening to screams.

26

They were passing the headland when the sky darkened and the sea grew choppy.

"Trouble?" Jenny asked, putting down her beer.

"It wasn't in the Marineline forecast this morning," he said. "No problem. We'd better head back though." He put the *Cader* about and began the run for home.

The wind got up to three or four. A slight sea was running. The main was reefed right in and he rolled the genoa a little more to balance the helm. She ran before the wind like a knife. Faint rumbles of thunder rolled across the open sea.

"Have you noticed," she said, above the splash of the hull and the clatter of sails, "how the boat gets smaller as the weather gets rougher?"

Rain dropped like a curtain. She pulled up the hood of her jacket and leaned towards him.

"Anything I can do?"

"It's okay. This is inconvenient, but we're in no danger."

"Of course not." She began to laugh, and he caught her amusement. The *Cader* was showing how small she really was now, but they kept looking at each other and breaking up again. It felt good.

On towards the headland, wind beating past their ears, the boat forging ahead to catch it. They rounded the low cliffs below Old Cottage and saw the town misting in and out of view in the rain. David pulled the outboard into blue-smoking life and got the sails down. They went into the harbour under bare poles, rain drumming on the cabin top. "You did say you were experienced?" She grinned.

"On rivers," he said, as they caught their mooring and made everything fast.

They bustled about the confined space, clearing up the beer cans, covering the engine.

"God, I'm freezing," Jenny said.

"Too late for the pub. Come up to my place. I've got towels and dry clothes."

The speed of action carried them through what might have been awkward. As the rain drove in on the emptied front, they ran along the harbour and up the alley by the bank.

He turned up the heating in the flat. Shivering, she stripped her coat off and went into the kitchen, while he fetched towels and dry sweaters. He had a moment's fear as he tried to remember whether there was anything in the kitchen to give him away. But everything that made him David Kalska lay in a drawer in the bedroom.

She was sitting on the floor in front of the gas fire when he returned. He tossed her a towel and began to dry himself off. She got up on her knees and hung her long hair before the orange flames.

"Not too wet?"

"Just the hair." She rubbed viciously, and her head steamed faintly in the iron light of the storm.

He made coffee and found some biscuits, brought them in with the flask of brandy. She hummed quietly, rocking from knee to knee, her slim body arched over the fire. He put on a dry sweater and left another on the chair for her. Drank a scalding cup of coffee, pretending to look out at swords of sunlight breaking through the rain.

"Do you have a brush?" she said.

He found one, gave it to her with the little mirror from the bedroom, resumed the window-watching.

"That's better," he heard her say, and turned to look. She was examining her reflection, hair pushed behind her ears. She let it fall. "Same old mess," she said.

"Not quite the phrase anyone else'd use." He smiled. "At the moment, you could pose for a ship's figurehead."

"I always thought you needed thrusting bosoms for that." She leaned close to the mirror, tutting. "A mess."

"If you say so."

She looked away, remained before the fire, kneeling at the coffee table while he sat and poured a cup for her. They drank, and she glanced round the flat.

"Not bad. You haven't personalised it, though."

"In what way?"

"It looks as if it's still waiting for you to arrive."

"Have some more."

She poured, opened the biscuits and began to eat with her

usual appetite. He wondered how she kept her figure. Wondered what she was thinking, sitting in the flat of a comparative stranger, her husband not long dead. What did it mean about her? Maybe only that she badly needed a friend.

"Did you think we were going to have trouble out there?" she said.

"No . . . Well, maybe a little. Rivers are kinder."

"Bax and Isobel – "

"They probably saw us coming back across the bay." The calculator in his skull decided to try an experiment. His tone lightened and he gave her an old-fashioned look. "They're probably more concerned about what you're doing now."

"Mmm?"

"Alone, unchaperoned in the apartments of a gentleman."

She started to laugh, inhaled some biscuit crumbs, and coughed ferociously. "I'm an adult, you know. I've been partaking of coffee for quite a few years now. Besides, where's the gentleman?"

"I wouldn't want Bax to hear evil gossip in the pub and come after me with a shotgun."

"He doesn't have one. Will you shut up."

"It's easy for you. I've got my reputation to think of. Perhaps you should drink it outside."

She was in the happy mood of things. "Oh, well, if that's the case . . ." She started for the door, but only went as far as the window. She was looking at him with an amused, tolerant expression. Outside he was part of it, smiling and shrugging at her. Inside he saw the chimney of Crematorium Three pumping greasy smoke into the misty air. Jenny started talking about her university days, about a boy who had tried to get her drunk without her knowing. He shut her off for a minute, feeling as if his insides were being pulled two ways at once.

After a time it got easier, and he came back to the room, to her voice talking softly and the afternoon light deepening into blues and greys. He focused on her, sitting on the floor, resting against the armchair with her legs folded under her. She still held a mug of cold coffee. He noticed she had stopped being jokey. What was she telling him?

"Maybe I've always had a little-girl view of him. You know, all the hero-worship stuff. 'No one's as good as my daddy.' I never thought about it before. He was just *there*, like the Forth Bridge and Edinburgh Castle are there. You don't question things like that. It's only since things started to go bad."

He thought of how she kept talking about the old man. He received a fatter share of her time than the husband.

"Once, when Alex was in the third year at big school, he came home with a terrible report. English rotten, Maths worse, you know the sort of thing. Well, we were having dinner that night and everything was absolutely as usual. We were getting excited about going to France for the holidays. Then Dad took out the report and put it on the table. Alex looked pretty sick. Everyone else stopped talking. Dad looked at Alex and he said: 'As Alex hasn't seen fit to work this year at school, he won't be going on holiday with the rest of you.'

"We were flabbergasted. I mean, he could be like that, but the way he came out with it. And he wouldn't change. Mum tried to talk to him, even I had a go. He just kept reading his newspaper. 'I'm not pleased with Alex,' he said. 'I dislike failure in my children.' And I could see by his face he meant it." She tipped a little more brandy in her coffee. "I remembered it when I told him Richard and I were having problems." She drank, eyes drooping. "I mean, he got the same look. It was that first, before any questions or concern. I stood in front of him, like a naughty girl in front of the headmaster, and I felt ashamed. Not worried or upset because my marriage was skidding. Ashamed, because I'd had to bother him with it."

The calculator threw in a judicious remark to spur her on: "It's difficult for parents to accept their kids' faults sometimes."

She was drunk enough to say what she might not have when sober.

"Listen, I was having enough trouble trying to work out how to hold my marriage together. I didn't want it to happen, didn't want to get divorced, but he acted as if I was doing it all on a whim. My own father."

"Perhaps he saw more clearly from the outside what was wrong."

"I'll tell you what it was. He's more interested in my failure to live up to his idea of perfection than anything I might be going through." She drank again, coughing over the brandy. "Must be a sign of my immaturity. Being so upset by what he thinks. Wouldn't you say that? Do you worry what your parents think?"

"It hasn't been the same for me," he said.

"You should try it. It hardens the arteries." She swung her mug up in a mock-toast. "Here's to marriage and families and all attendant agonies."

He rose half off the settee to take the mug before she spilt any. "Take it easy."

She kept hold of the mug, fingertips brushing his until he got it away from her. He stepped back, feeling his throat tighten.

"Sorry." Her head dropped and she made a chuckling sound in the back of her throat. "I'm a mess. I'm painting better than I ever have, but I'm a mess."

"You're three parts cut," he corrected.

"And whose fault is that?" She lifted the empty flask.

"Maybe we'd better have something to eat," he said, and went into the kitchen.

He stood at the sink, the calculator screaming for action. Outside it was dark. He heard her routing among the CDs, slotting one into the player. The 'Valse Triste' began to weep from the room. He looked back. She was kneeling over the machine, head almost touching the speakers.

She turned her face to him, the eyes clear and sad. "Why are we so lonely?" she said.

He went to her, sank down and took the outstretched hand which seemed to have been left there for him to take. A small shock went through her, she started to look away, then her head swung back and she gazed at him, biting her lip. Her other hand came up as she shifted to face him, and touched his cheek, and rested there for a moment. He could not move at first. He had hoped for this, but now that it was happening he could not bear it. The lies he was telling her, the betrayal of Grandfather and his mother. She searched his face for a long time, breath trembling, and he thought she must see what was in his mind. But that was not what she looked for. She wanted him to make the final move, to remove responsibility from her.

Reason said: Do it. Heart said: Do it. But he no longer wanted to cause her pain.

He reached up and took her hand, put it gently away from him.

She turned back towards the music with a faint groan of disappointment. Her fingers closed on the hand she still held. They knelt on the floor together, like two people still praying when belief was gone.

When he took her back to Old Cottage she was very tired. She rested half-asleep against his shoulder in the car. She kept saying: "A mess," like an echo of herself.

He saw her to the door, where she was met and taken upstairs by Isobel. Bax hovered at the door of the sitting room, a whisky glass in his knotty hand. David watched the women going up the stairs. At the top, Jenny turned.

"Tomorrow?" she said.

He nodded. Isobel took her arm and led her away, and despite the fact that he wanted to crawl into a dark corner, he knew he had better say something. If the Caradocs got too uneasy they might contact Miller, get him discovered. It doesn't matter, he thought, then saw his mother fading and tried to tell himself it did.

Bax said: "Have a drink?"

They went into the sitting room. Isobel returned as Bax handed him a glass.

"She's dead to the world," she said, looking sharply at David. "What've you been letting her do, Mr Halborough?"

"Talk, Mrs Caradoc." He put his drink aside and sat forward intently in his chair. Full sincerity switched on, the force of what had brought him to this little town took over at the moment when he felt it was at its lowest ebb. He proceeded to tell them he was no psychiatrist, but was doing his best to help Jenny through her grief. Since she had seen fit to talk to him about it, he would not be insensitive enough to refuse. But he did not want them to worry. He would do nothing to . . . betray her trust. He realised as it was said that he meant it somehow.

Then the Caradocs began to tell him things. About Jenny's family, about her father. He nodded and looked understanding, listening half-heartedly for any clues they might drop. But it was chiefly what he already knew: that Miller was an authoritarian, a perfectionist who tended to run his children's lives as he used to run his professional subordinates. "Tell you the truth," Bax said, choosing his words with care, "we've never had a great deal in common with the male side of the family. Just Jenny and her mother, see?"

"Not that they're not very nice," Isobel interrupted.

"But that old bugger," Bax insisted. "To listen to her sometimes, you'd think she was still in her teens. Can you believe a father who cares more for the family reputation than his daughter's happiness? In this day and age!" He almost spat on the floor.

"Now, Bax, I'm sure it's not that bad."

"You look at her and tell me."

Reassured as to his intentions, they were friends again. They sat up for another hour, talking. He asked all kinds of questions, listening with studied interest. And all the while, he was thinking of her, lying in bed upstairs. He wanted to be there, watching over her.

The white hours, Grandfather used to call them. The hours of the long night when sleep was a bad joke. He paced the carpet in his flat, then threw himself on the bed and forced his eyes to look again at the pictures, the pits in the woods where they used to burn the bodies, his mother as a young girl in another country, his mother holding a child with his eyes.

"You did not come here for this," he said, listening to his own voice in the silence. Then it failed him and he was left with the memories of touch and smell and the way her fingers clutched at his when he knelt beside her. She knew nothing about her father. She was wrecked by grief, as he was.

He turned up the photograph of Grandfather. He had never known he would miss him so much. Yet he was involved with this woman he was meant to be interrogating. Already he was reaching a stage where he would not want her father to be Gelzer.

Which was real life? The hours of sunlight with her, or stumbling around with your bones sticking through your skin, wondering whether you would survive the day? Both had happened, but he was no longer certain which was more important.

He filled his glass, concentrated on Miller, whose eyes sometimes burned disconcertingly from Jenny's face. The blurry images of Gelzer lay on the bed with everything else; all the notes he had made, all the suspicions. Miller was Gelzer and Gelzer was Miller and Jenny was Gelzer and Luba was lying in a filthy, stinking hut full of the dying, forty-five years ago. He thought he knew what had finally done for her there. Reading what Grandfather had written, he was sure he knew the point at which she had given up.

It would not leave him alone.

She was not allowed into the special barracks. These were the ones set aside by Doctor Mengele for certain experiments. Every time a train arrived and selection was made, there would be a small number who did not go with either of the usual groups. She had seen them on occasions. They made one think Mengele was interested in building a freak show or a carnival. Usually those saved were children, twins. Sometimes she would see them at the windows of the barracks, a strange sight because no other children were allowed to survive. Once there had been a pair of dwarves. They had come waddling across the compound, flanked by a doctor and a guard. A ridiculous sight, so small and funny-looking. They seemed to be father and son. They were neatly dressed in clothes that must have been made especially for them. They gazed in terror from under their hats, while the doctor talked quite kindly and showed them the way. They went into the special barracks, and some hours later she chanced to see Mengele and one of the young doctors stroll in.

There were rumours all the time about the end of the war. There had been some orders and evacuations to indicate truth in the rumours. But Mengele continued with his experiments.

She had heard a little of these. He was most interested, it was said, in 'genetic' theories. She did not know what this meant, but they had had a gypsy girl in the hospital early in November who had been in the special barracks. Her eyes were swollen and discoloured, she was blind, delirious. She kept crying at the pain, saying that They had put needles in her eyes. She died after a few days.

The other stories were too horrible to be true, she used to believe. Things with wombs and babies. Post-mortems on people who were still alive. Sometimes she would be cleaning out the bunks, and there would be a long scream from the special barracks. "They're examining another corpse," the women would say, only to be silenced by Helena.

The good-looking one who had separated her from Mother when they arrived, Luba saw him often. He always behaved as if he were walking the wards of an ordinary hospital. His enthusiasm for research was almost catching. He spent a great deal of time in the special barracks.

Luba was not usually allowed into the special barracks.

He checked the bottle. He did not want to get drunk again. If he must be sleepless, let it be sober. He put on his coat and went down the echoing stairs to the street.

*

209

Time passed and Jenny was still awake. She switched on the light and tried to read, took up a pencil and scrawled hundreds of little faces on the flyleaf of a book of Magritte paintings. The faces all became Joseph.

She listened to the sounds of the house as it contracted in the night. The clock in the hall downstairs chimed the second hour.

She got out of bed, pulled some clothes from the dresser.

"You girl, over here."

She turned from the bed where she was cleaning a girl who had recently died. The doctor, a weak-chinned German with an astigmatism in one eye, beckoned her. He was examining a woman blown up like a grey and purple balloon. "Go and find my colleague for me."

Luba's head tilted on one side. She was so hungry. There had been problems with food because the fighting was closer. This morning she had drunk foul herb tea. That was all they had been given since the dishes of kohlrabi soup for lunch the previous day. She blinked uncertainly at the doctor.

"You speak German, don't you?" he snapped. The woman's shallow breathing rasped from her swollen throat.

Luba nodded.

"Then don't be insolent." The doctor smacked her alongside the ear. Red and black dots swam in her eyes, but she kept her balance. "Go and find him," the doctor said, "and ask him if he would be so kind as to step over here and see me for a moment. I'd like his opinion on something."

She nodded. Her head felt so heavy that she could hardly keep it erect on her neck.

"And hurry," he said.

She started towards the door, clenching her fists as dizziness swept over her.

"Hurry, I said!"

She stumbled out of the door, into the freezing sleet that was October's gift to the camp. Under her rag of a coat, she wore only a rough smock open at the neck, a pair of threadbare socks and some shoes she had organised in exchange for a hat. Her underwear did not deserve the name. Shivering uncontrollably, she trudged across the stiff frozen ground, hoping to avoid any guard who felt in need of exercise.

David found himself a place out of the wind on the west pier. No one about, no one to see him in the shadows. He sat on cold stone, hunched over to keep warm. The Caradocs' boat weaved faintly near the wall. Other craft slopped and creaked in the quiet. The sea moving against the outside of the harbour calmed him a little. He touched the stone with his hands and prayed to have rest from the images that circled lazily in his mind. Still they returned in grainy detail: faces peering bleakly from the pit; a gas chamber where corpses did not fall because there was no space; the stainless steel tables where operations were performed without anaesthetics, without need, without mercy. Through it all, his mother walking, dragging her wasted body, looking for the doctor.

Over in the gypsy camp, hundreds of people were gathering. She thought a selection was being made. She saw green uniforms passing between rows and rows of scarecrow figures. But there were no doctors among them. It was another deportation. When she first arrived, work parties had been constructing huts beyond the fence for a new camp, to be called 'Mexico'. She had wondered since whether there were that many Jews left to kill, but the Germans must have thought so. 'Mexico' was to have been bigger than all the present men's camps put together. Lately, though, work had slackened. Instead of building, they were sending people away.

A green triangle yelled: "Get a move on, you."

She hurried away. Hurried? What a joke. She was barely limping. She asked at the offices. A Jewish girl who had been given secretarial work, with all the attendant privileges, wrinkled her nose and crouched behind a desk.

"He's not here," she said. Her hair had been allowed to grow long again. She wore decent clothes, even a proper coat. "Try the special barracks."

She left the office. A staff car with a well-fed officer in the passenger seat splashed by.

The special barracks? Why did he have to be there? She thought about going back, saying she could not find him. That would gain her a beating, though, something she could not afford in her state of health. Perhaps the Russians were going to save them. Better than that, the English or the Americans. They might be a hundred miles away, or ten. So you did as you were told, and maybe there would be a pale shadow of the being which used to be you to greet them when they arrived.

But the special barracks. She had a horror of the place, which she knew was stupid. After all, she accepted the gas chambers, the crematoria, people jerking as they burned on the fence. She could think of them now without a tremor. Why this special horror of one little part of the camp?

The sleet drove more steadily. She shut her eyes against it and trudged towards the special barracks.

Jenny saw his windows were lit as she came round the corner. She paced at the foot of the steps to the house, grinning stupidly at a grey cat on a garden wall. Then she said: "Damn it!" in a low whisper, and went up them two at a time. In the gloom of the doorway, she fumbled for the buzzers, scared that she might press the wrong one. As her fingers went up the wall, she felt a draught on the back of her hand. The door was open. She went through and up the stairs.

They were standing at a gap in the screens surrounding a bed when she found them. Two doctors involved in conversation. The young, handsome one made swooping, stabbing motions with a pen, as a conductor gestures with the baton. Both ignored her, and they ignored the cries of a baby nearby.

"It's an interesting case," the young one was saying. "Really, I see what he's getting at, but I think he's trying for the impossible."

She waited, knowing better than to interrupt.

The screams of the baby were terrible. They beat against her ears. They came from behind the screens.

The other suggested something. The young one laughed.

She reached the top landing, paused to pull her hair back in some kind of order. She approached the door, knocked softly.

Nothing stirred inside. She raised her fist to knock again, let it hover uncertainly before the wood. The fist uncurled and she placed her palm against the door, pressing tentatively. The latch that was only half engaged slipped with a click and the door opened.

"Joseph?"

"Oh, come now," the young one said, glancing up the corridor confidentially. "We're talking about a very large problem. The combination of two separate living organisms into what is effectively one. Even with twins there will be all kinds of troubles." He did not seem to hear the cries at all.

Luba thought: How can they ignore it? She shuffled from foot to foot, hands behind her back. She could see a little piece of the screened area to the young one's left. A fragment of floor, the leg of a bed, a patch of blanket. Something else. She closed her eyes and swayed.

"Connecting a few veins is all well and good," he was saying. "Admirable idea, but too little thinking. Now I would have said — "

Eyes open to stop herself from falling down, she moved back so that his body was between her and the bed.

I have seen everything, she thought. Nothing can shock me any more. I have seen everything.

" — Septic, you see. The whole site of the operation — "

He leaned forward, making a point. She closed her eyes again. That

*did not stop the screams. Nothing stopped them. She squirmed,
desperate to give the message and run. But to interrupt would be to
invite a blow. She felt she would pass out in a moment.*

She ventured further inside, tensed for him to appear.
"Joseph?"
She sat on the arm of a chair, punching the fabric in her
frustration. But she could not sit still. She jumped up and
wandered towards the bedroom. The door was ajar, the bed
rumpled, covered with papers. She noticed the file and the
paperwork, the photographs. At first she thought they were
something to do with his work. She went in, leaned over the
bed, reaching to shift the papers.

> "Yes, I agree. Two infants are best to try it with. But who knows,
> perhaps two adults would fight infection better. This is what comes of
> working in primitive conditions."
> Only one baby cried. She only heard one.
> "I suppose it would be kinder to put her out of her misery too, but
> you know what he's like."
> One child screaming.
> He turned sharply, staring down at her. "Yes?"
> She swallowed hard, found a voice to give the message.
> He swivelled his head toward her, frowning. Did he remember their
> first meeting, when he sent her mother to the chambers? "Speak up,
> girl." He could not hear her whisper above the child's crying.
> She repeated the words.
> He nodded. "Very well. Run along."
> He took his companion by the shoulder and walked away, leaving her
> with a clear view of what was on the bed, and why it screamed.
> She looked at the bed.

The papers on the bed.

And then . . .

Then nothing more. He knew it in his heart. Everything that
occurred afterwards – the last gassings at the end of October,
the dismantling of chambers and crematoria, the planting of
grass seed where thousands of bodies were burned and buried,
the evacuation and the marches in which thousands more died
– they were a sleepwalk. She had long suspected that there
was no longer a real world left outside the camps. No matter

213

what happened after the special barracks, she could never be convinced that she was wrong.

He knew the details of Bergen-Belsen when the Allied tanks arrived. The condition of the prisoners who were left; cannibalism, filth, bushels of lice living on the bodies, the half-dead asleep beside the dead. Even then it was not over. Incredible as it seemed, the tanks went on, and the camp was left under the nominal control of Hungarian SS guards. More than eighty Jews were shot – for stealing potato peelings – before the British arrived in force.

By that time, Grandfather had found her again. He had been transported there in a sealed cattle truck, while she and Helena were marched across the frigid miles of Europe in late February. He saw her one day through the wire, as men and women lined up to wash in the thin trickle of water from a pipe. He recognised her, though there was only a pock-marked, ulcerated skeleton where his daughter had been. He was a bag of bones himself, but he called out to her, and she seemed to recognise him.

The medical teams came, were overwhelmed by what they had to deal with. Eventually, they marked red crosses on the foreheads of those they thought stood a chance of survival. Josef and Helena begged a doctor to mark Luba, though no one believed she would recover but him.

And hundreds died every day for weeks afterwards, because help had come too late. Many gorged themselves on rich foods the soldiers brought, and that was enough to kill them, because their systems could no longer tolerate such stuff. Rich foods like milk powder and oatmeal, biscuits and chocolate.

None of which she knew as her body continued struggling for a life she no longer wanted. After a time she left her bed, walked around in the slow motion of the starving, wondered why the British soldiers were so shocked by the sight of her. She came to understand that her father was with her, that for most people it was 'over'. Then there were the months of regaining strength, the trip that ended at last with England. These were all after the end for her. The end was that day in the special barracks; only it was delayed for years, until she had made one last attempt to regain life. She had reached out to a man who perhaps saw the bright, alive girl she had once been, and she gave birth to her bastard son, and she cried over him like a child herself, and died at last with the words of the Kaddish on her lips.

Nothing more.

He dragged his sleeve across his eyes. The local police car purred along the harbour, making its nightly round. He waited by the *Cader Idris* until the car was gone, then turned for home.

He entered the flat, cursing the loose catch on the door, went into the bedroom. The draught must have caught his papers; some lay on the floor. He gathered them back into their file. Stupid of him to leave them out like that. He put them in the drawer with the other pieces of his life.

He had to leave this place.

27

He half-expected her to arrive at the flat next morning. He breakfasted on coffee after a sleepless night, and kept looking at his watch.

At half-nine, he went down to the café, and sat there for an hour. She did not come. He wanted to see her, if only to say goodbye. He circled the harbour, watching for her on the street. He imagined her painting in the studio.

Anxiety began to work at him. The last few days, she had seemed so dependent. She had said: Tomorrow.

Old Cottage gleamed high and bright beneath a clean blue sky. He would go up and see her himself.

Walking up the field, he noticed her car parked by the side of the house. The Fourtrak was not in the garage. Willing himself to look wide-awake and healthy, he climbed over the stile, crossed the road and went up the path.

No one answered. He stepped back, looking up at the windows. Unease growing, he stepped round the side of the house.

Baxter Caradoc stood at the studio door.

"You young bastard," he said.

He knew immediately that he was discovered, but some-thing made him carry on the act. "I beg your pardon?"

"You clear off."

"Mr Caradoc . . . I don't understand. Where is she?"

"Gone where you can't get at her, you heartless sod. Isobel had to go with her, she was in that much of a state."

"What's happened?"

"Don't give me any of your flannel. We know all about you now."

He moved towards the old man. Caradoc lifted a shotgun he had been holding loose at his side. He held it lazily on David's belly.

"I don't know what your nasty little game is," he said. "But you should be ashamed of what you've done to her."

David backed off.

"Now get away from here, before I give way to the great temptation of letting go with both barrels."

He found that he wanted to explain his side of the story, but it was no use. There were tears in Caradoc's eyes. He had been betrayed just as much as Jenny. His fury was for himself and Isobel, as much as for her.

"I'm sorry," David said, before he turned to go.

"Don't you dare," Caradoc snarled.

He headed for the flat. Only last night he had been wondering if he should continue duping her; now it was out of his hands. How he had been found out did not matter. He only knew he must pick up his belongings and get away.

The street was quiet as he raced up to the house. He noticed the lady novelist at her sea-facing window, tapping away on her typewriter. He went into the entrance hall, up the six flights, and barged through the door before remembering that he had locked it tight when he went out.

Someone hit him in the stomach, and he went down on his knees. Another blow caught the back of his neck, driving his head to the floor, and he felt daylight slipping out of his eyes. The door slammed. Hands grabbed him under the armpits and yanked him upright. He fought for breath, but the centre of his body was paralysed. For a moment he thought he would black out, but someone slapped his face, and the paralysis passed. He drew in wheezing lungfuls of air.

Two men held him. They were under thirty, well-built, casually dressed. Their faces were pale and clean. The only thing to differentiate them was that one cropped head was dyed blond, the other mousey. Blond kicked him in the small of the back, and he ceased fighting. His breath came in short bursts. Mouse gripped his hair and pulled his head back. A big slab of a hand clamped his jaw shut.

Paul Miller sat in an armchair facing the door, one leg crossed elegantly over the other. He looked like a lawyer who had been waiting for a client. On his lap was the file. He was examining Grandfather's notebook. David jerked towards him, wanting to take the book away. The grip tightened; Blond drove the point of his shoe into David's back again. He saw the faint raising of Paul's eyebrows.

"Mr Kalska," he said.

David tried to curse him, but the hand on his face stopped anything but a muffled grunt.

"You *have* been causing us some trouble." Paul put the file aside and stood up. Hands in trouser pockets, he sidled closer. "I mean, you were asked to desist from bothering my father, and this is what you do instead." He gazed at David in a sorrowful manner. "As you've probably guessed, we're more than a little tired of it. I had enough of you in Edinburgh, but I thought I'd better come down and sort things out myself. I brought these lads along to help. Of course, we're not actually here," he explained carefully. "As you'll discover if you try to make anything out of it. We're more figments of your diseased imagination, if you want to think of it that way." A car went by in the street below. "I don't know precisely what you think you have in that collection of rubbish – " He indicated the file " – which you'd doubtless call evidence, but you do have to realise that it doesn't amount to very much with the unbiased reader. Which is to say, Mr Kalska, that you're going to stop now."

David tried to speak again. Paul nodded and the hand was removed from his face.

"Your old man's a Nazi," he said. "He played doctor in a death camp. He killed thousands of people – " Another nod. Blond delivered a kidney punch. The hand returned, shutting off his yell, and he sagged in their grip.

"You *are* crazed, aren't you?" Paul said. "That's why I

217

brought the lads; thought it might be difficult getting you to listen to reason. But believe me, they're being gentle compared to what Alex would do to you. He's much angrier than I am, can't control himself the way I do. I had to insist that he didn't come, because he might well have killed you. I can quite easily agree with the sentiment, but I don't want him going to gaol for scum like you." His voice turned even colder. "You see, the one thing you shouldn't have done was come bothering Jenny. That's something . . . Well, imagine how you'd feel if it were your sister."

He bobbed down on his haunches so that his smooth, dark face was inches away.

"Now, I'll just ask you one question," he said. "She hasn't said a lot about what's been happening here. She's too upset, but the Caradocs told us something. All I want to know is, have you laid a finger on her?"

David felt as if his eyes were bursting. He tried to prepare himself for what he knew must be coming, stared hard into Paul's eyes, looking for evidence of knowledge. What if there was none? What if this really was just a man trying to protect his family from a lunatic?

The lads dug their fingers into his shoulders. One of them began to grind the joint of his first finger insistently at the base of David's skull.

"Have you?" Paul asked.

He gagged on his own vomit, made no gesture either way. It was the only small triumph he could take from this situation, dirty as it was. He stared.

Paul sprang up, shaking his head disgustedly. "Oh, go ahead," he told the lads.

They dragged him up. He was pulled round and a hand closed over his mouth again. They pushed him backwards to the wall. Between the knife-edge expression on their pink faces, he saw Paul go to the door. He was guarding the premises while the lads did their job, watching the proceedings with a proprietorial air, as if he'd paid for the labour, and was hanging around to make sure it was properly carried out.

Then he was slammed up against the wall, and he thrust his hands down in an attempt to protect himself. But the lads knew their business, and they went to work anyway.

*

The lady novelist found him a couple of hours later. He had managed to crawl and fall down two flights of stairs, but he was not looking for help. When she opened the door and saw his bloody figure on the landing, he was clawing the banister rail, trying to get up.

She overcame the shock as if she saw badly mauled strangers every day. She went to him and tried to hold him down.

He was muttering through a split lip: "You wait, you bastard, you wait and see."

"Hang on," the lady novelist soothed. "You mustn't try to move."

He was half out of it, talking not to her, but to the phantom of Gelzer in his mind. She hefted him up and somehow they staggered into her flat. He groaned incessantly from the pain of moving, but she got him to the couch and lowered him gently down.

"I'm going to call a doctor," she said, wiping her bloodied hands on her slacks. "And the police."

He sat up sharply, hurting himself again. "No," he said. "No bloody police." He sounded like a punch drunk boxer.

The violence of his refusal frightened her. She went into the kitchen to fetch warm water and towels. He lay back on the couch, nursing the ruin of his face and body.

Whimpering faintly, he swivelled his head and spat a mouthful of blood on his shirt. They had done a good job. There was not a single part of him that did not hurt. More than that, they had not even bothered to take the evidence. They were that sure of its worthlessness.

He drifted in and out. The lady was cleaning his face with a towel, getting blood everywhere. She was telling him he must see a doctor, asking what had happened. He must have replied occasionally, but when she suggested the police again, he denied her even more furiously.

The police must not be involved. He knew what had happened before with the police. He could not trust them, he could trust no one. He was a Jew.

The only thing he had now was the incredible pain throbbing in his body, and the certainty that he must not mess around with Gelzer and his boys any more. He had made things too complicated in his desire to be fair. He had let the daughter lead him off the path, got lost in a stew of conflicting moral viewpoints. Moral viewpoints. He would have laughed, but his ribs seemed to be grinding in his lungs. There could be no more confusion about rights and wrongs. He must simplify.

The lady novelist grimaced as he winced at her dabbing hand. "Sorry," she said.

He was not listening to her. He was holding his bruised ribs and the solid ache of his stomach. Holding, too, the simplicity of pure hate. Every resentment – against Paul and Alex and Jenny; the police; the rumourmongers who had taken his business to pieces; the kids who had made his life a misery at school – all fused together in one cold and perfect idea. He thought only about Gelzer.

How he was going to kill Gelzer.

PART THREE

Kaddish

28

The receptionist's voice came through from the lobby. Sarah hunched the phone between ear and shoulder as she searched her desk for the details of a bestselling author's itinerary.

"What is it, Ros? I'm busy."

"There's someone calling you."

"Unless it's the publishers' PR with reasons why her author hasn't turned up, I don't want to know."

"It's a man. He won't give a name."

Mike Proctor, just finished with his show, passed by the office door with a cheery wave.

"Well, tell him I'm not here," Sarah said. A wad of advertising handbills slithered to the floor. "Damn."

"He says it's urgent."

A suspicion fluttered in the back of her mind. She stopped what she was doing, feeling sick suddenly. "All right. Put him through."

The line clicked. A fuzz of background noise came through the earpiece. Traffic, a suspicion of breathing.

"Yes?" she said. Her voice was tight.

"Sarah?"

She swallowed hard and took the phone in her hand. "David? Is that you?"

The traffic surged. She heard horns tooting. A long time seemed to pass.

"Where are you?" she said. "Are you all right?"

Hesitation again. "I'm fine," he murmured. He sounded weak, tired.

"Are you back in the city? Are you home?"

"Not yet. Will be soon . . . How are you?"

Tears pricked behind her eyes. She wished the door were closed. "I'm . . . okay. Run off my feet, as usual, you know." Platitudes.

The traffic roared. "That's good," he said.

Silence beat like her heart in the earpiece.

"I don't know how many units this card's got left," he said. "Better not waste your time."

She sat forward, holding her arm tight across her stomach. She hurt. She had thought she was getting over it, but her entire body hurt. "David, for Christ's sake . . ."

"I'm sorry. I shouldn't be calling."

"Shouldn't be – I've been worried sick about you."

"I know." He sounded as if he were struggling to hold panic down. "I don't deserve it. I wasn't ever good enough to you."

A secretary went past the door. She swivelled her chair to hide herself.

"Couldn't be," he said. "I wasn't right to myself."

"David, don't."

"I'm a Jew, Sarah. Half by birth, half by what Grandfather tried to make me. If I deny it, I betray them again."

"I don't understand. I want to see you." She could say it now.

"No, that – wouldn't be right, not now. I have to do something, and I don't want to risk you getting hurt."

How much more hurt was there? The careful structure of her days since he had gone lay in rubble.

"Why are you calling me?" she cried.

"There's something I – I need. You're the only one I can trust."

Heat tracked down her face, drops splashed on her skirt. "Oh, God, David . . ."

"Please. I know I haven't the right to ask, and I won't bother you again – " she wondered if he knew what she was going through " – but I can't turn to anyone else."

"Just let me see you."

"I can't. Not now. It's too dangerous. Afterwards, maybe, if you still want to."

Afterwards. She did not know for sure what she wanted, but at least he was talking about an afterwards. "What're you doing?"

"Please. It's nothing illegal. I just need you to do this one thing."

She heard the word 'illegal' and it hardly registered. A bright summer pop hit jangled through the building from the p.a. She heard the pain in his voice and knew it matched her own. There was no such thing as better judgement.

"What is it?" she said.

When he had finished talking to her, he got up, hobbled across the room, and closed the window of Grandfather's room. The row of a boat passing on the river beneath was shut out. Sitting among the crates and boxes, he pulled himself together. Since his return to Norwich, someone had been coming to the door most days. He never answered, and left the phone to deflect callers with its taped message. He thought of Sarah, how she had sounded on the phone. But it was right that he did not give in to the desire to see her, to explain. It was putting her in enough danger asking her to help him. She was better free of him, even if he wanted to be with her.

He was healing. The yellow memory of a bruise under his left eye was all that showed. His stomach still twinged occasionally, and breathing too deeply tended to remind him of his ribs. Apart from that, three weeks after the beating, he was almost back to full strength. Physically, anyway.

He turned the pages of Grandfather's notebook. Familiar phrases now, words he understood. His favourite was a quote from his mother. One word from 1939, when the entire Jewish community had been assembled for a lecture by some SS chief. He went on, Grandfather wrote, about how the Jews would be safe under the German rule, so long as they did as they were told and had respect for their superiors. Luba, listening with a disbelieving face, muttered: "Spadaj!" under her breath. "Drop dead!" in other words. A few people around her, though scared, stifled laughter at her pugnacious courage.

Of course, that was before they broke her.

He was at home because that was where they would expect him to be. They would expect him to crawl home, a defeated wreck, so that was what he had done, leaving Silcombe the moment he was able to drive. He did not know for sure that they were watching him, but he assumed they were. Everything he did was meant to convince them that he was finished.

There were other reasons for being in Norwich. He had spent the past week and a half selling shares and securities, taking losses where necessary, because he needed ready cash for the purchase he wanted Sarah to make for him.

He was prepared to stay another week in the city before he started the next stage of his plan. Nothing must be done in haste. He would have them think he was taking longer to get over his injuries, that his nerve was shot. He wanted them to be sure he was done with, so a sense of security would return.

He got up and looked out of the window. The river flowed gently by below. It was a beautiful June evening. People were sitting at tables outside the Brewers. That was ordinary life. The television news and the people walking home from work. All of it going on as usual. Except for him.

29

Dinner was over. She heard Alex come from the dining room into the hall, still telling some story. She missed the words, but knew the joke was finished when Dad's laughter started, the deep bass notes of it overshadowing everyone else.

She pushed her plate aside and reached forward to touch the glass of the conservatory wall. When she first came home, she dined in her bedroom, spent most of her time there. The same four walls had begun to get on her nerves, but she still could not face the others *en masse*.

The conservatory faced west. There had been few plants since mother died. It was just a pleasant room to sit in. She wanted to see where the sun touched fire on the clouds and the hills reaching south, but she disliked being unprotected. Glass walls are no more safety than pulling the bedclothes round your neck when you are a child, but they served their purpose. She got up and walked the length of the conservatory, watching a blackbird on the lawn.

The night she had discovered what Joseph – not Joseph; David, or something – was up to, was the worst she could remember. Worse somehow than the night Richard died. That had been comprehensible, such things happened to people all the time. But in the fragile condition she had been in afterwards, to find out that a man she had come to trust was not what he pretended, that had gone beyond the limits she could deal with.

She had returned to Old Cottage, quietly hysterical. She did not rave or cry. She walked in as if it were broad daylight, not bothering about the noise she made, went to the studio, picked out all the canvasses she had worked on since getting to know Joseph/David/whatever he was, and dragged them onto the lawn to burn them. When Bax appeared in his dressing gown, hair awry, eyes frightened, she was standing over the flames, kicking the pieces together to make sure everything was consumed. Then she did break down, and it took Isobel a couple of hours to get the truth out of her. After that it was out of her hands. Isobel rang home, spoke to Paul, told him what had happened. Bax plied her with whisky because she was uncontrollable by then. And finally Isobel packed her things, put her in the Fourtrak, and drove her to Falmouth, where it was thought she would be safe to wait for her brothers to come and take her home.

A wonderful performance, she thought now, opening the conservatory door and letting the cool evening breeze fan her. What she should have done was wait for him with a breadknife.

Just thinking about him made her want to drive her hand through the glass. He had really made an idiot of her, and she had been all too ready to go along with it.

"Taking the air?" her father said.

She turned and her mouth twitched in a half-smile. She could not look him in the eye, feeling obscurely as if she had let him down.

"You should get out and walk," he said. He was carrying some textbook, and his little ivory-framed spectacles hung on the end of his nose. He looked grandfatherly in cardigan and baggy corduroys.

She nodded, lowering her head on one side so that she would not be as tall as him. An unconscious gesture. "I will," she said.

"It's beautiful with summer coming." He settled on the edge of the table and rested the book on his lap. He observed her kindly over the spectacles, then they both fell to watching the evening again, because there was always this slight problem of what to say to each other. Especially now.

"Are you feeling . . . well?" he asked, after a minute. She noticed the precision in his use of English. Forty years in Britain had not entirely removed the traces of his original tongue. Generally, she thought nothing of it. Only since that night with the notebooks and photographs.

"I'm fine." She sat down in one of the big overstuffed armchairs they kept in the conservatory. "I feel much better."

"That's good . . . I hope you'll soon feel able to join the rest of us at dinner again."

"I keep meaning to. Only I feel such an idiot."

"Ah, you're your father's daughter." He smiled indulgently. "Never eager to admit a mistake. But you mustn't worry what we think. We're your family, darling. We simply want you back with us."

"I know, Dad. You've been kind about everything."

"What else should I be with my only daughter? The one thing I wish were different is that this – this man had not preyed on you in such a way. God knows what he might have done if you hadn't found him out in time. As it is, it's enough to make me wish I were younger, so I could thrash him myself. It's rather unnerving to have my sons tell me: 'Leave it to us, Dad. Don't worry yourself'." He chuckled, then looked at her more seriously. "You haven't talked to me about it."

She shifted uncomfortably. "It's not the kind of thing you want to discuss."

"I know. All the same, we've all been shaken by this. A madman having such free access to you. When you decided to visit the Caradocs, I did wonder whether it was the right thing. You were in such a delicate state after Richard died."

"Well, it's too late to change it now."

"Yes." He put the book down. She recalled the pictures on Joseph's table. Looking at her father, could she see any resemblance to the young man in the SS uniform? He was studying his hands, as he always did when thinking. Strong, well-made hands. "Perhaps, if you still feel the need of escape, you might go further afield. Somewhere abroad. You could stay with old friends, be safe from harm."

"You think he'd try anything again?"

"I imagine not."

"I don't understand why you didn't just call in the police. Surely he'd done enough to warrant it?"

"The boys and I talked it over. Whatever this man did to you," a fall in the tone, as if to skirt round a matter whilst posing the question, "you didn't actually come to any physical harm. I decided that it would be better not to involve the authorities, for your sake. After all, such a matter would bring publicity, and you can imagine what the tabloid press would do to the story of your time in Silcombe. I thought you'd been hurt enough, and we should limit any further damage to the man himself. I hope I was right?"

She agreed that he was.

"It still makes me angry. If he had attacked me personally it would have been less painful."

"Oh, I'm all right," she said, and stood up again, too restless to keep talking face to face. With her back to him, watching the blackbird still on the lawn, she heard him say:

"Something still troubles you." It was not an enquiry. More a statement.

She shook her head too emphatically.

"You've not been the same to me since you came home. I don't like that. You know I care too much for you to let anything come between us this way."

She was embarrassed now, also ashamed, because of what she was thinking.

"You want to ask me a question, don't you?" His voice went on. Very deep, soothing.

She spun round. He was sitting, arms at his sides, gazing honestly at her. Her father, her dad.

"It's too bloody awful," she said. "I don't really think – "

"You must ask, anyway."

She hesitated, actually blushing with the awkwardness of it. "It's just – this man, if he's taken all this trouble, he must really believe he's got something."

"Unless he is mentally disturbed. It's quite possible."

"He had all these photographs and papers."

"Yes?" He was forcing her to speak it out loud. He never made anything easy.

"You know I don't believe it."

The expectant expression again. "You must be strong," he

229

used to say, "even when it is difficult." She steeled herself, then it came out of her mouth as if escaping.

"It isn't true, is it?"

He did not reply immediately. The green eyes fixed her. She began to feel nervous again. Then his head shook slowly from side to side, and quietly he said: "No."

"I knew it couldn't be. It's too stupid to believe. All those fuzzy pictures could be anyone. I didn't believe it, you know that."

"It's all right, darling." He put up his arms for her, and she went to him, and laid her head on his shoulder. It was the first time they had embraced since she returned.

"That's better," he said, stroking her hair. "I don't like it when we're estranged."

"We weren't, not really. I just had to ask you. You're not hurt, are you?"

"Only that anyone could think me capable of such things. This poor lunatic included."

"How did he get the idea, though? Where did it come from?"

"As far as I've been able to see, the old gentleman who caused Richard's death had the notion first. He was quite senile. But perhaps this was the grandson's way of getting over the old man's being killed as he was. Or perhaps he wished to blackmail us. There are some very bad people in the world. The only protection you have in the end is your loved ones."

She slipped out of his arms and looked down into his face. "I'm sorry I had to ask."

"I understand. You're confused and hurt. Anyone would be, after all you've been through. Never mind." He pulled her head down and kissed her brow. "Now put on your coat and come for a walk with me. I want to see how the game's shaping over the hill."

He went back into the house, and she stood there for a moment before following him. She felt better for having asked. And he was telling the truth. He could not lie to her. She knew him too well.

But her mind kept returning to that much-reproduced photograph of a German officer, and she thought of how there were no pictures of her father from before the war. Only snapshots taken since he came to Scotland. He always said that orphans do not have family albums, and, anyway, he was too ugly to keep pictures of himself. She had never given it any thought beyond mild curiosity before. Parents do not become real human beings to their children, usually, until it is too late. She had accepted him all her life as a given fact, like day and night.

He called from the hall. She snapped out of the reverie, told herself that such things did not happen in ordinary families. Dad was just Dad, and he had married her mother – would Mum have got involved with a former Nazi? Could he possibly have hidden something like that all these years? It *was* too ridiculous to believe.

"Jenny? Are you coming?"

"Just a minute." She went inside, and despite herself, she took the handsome young officer of the picture with her.

30

David allowed himself to be seen in the city a couple of times. Once when he went to visit his Grandfather's grave, once when he looked in at his old offices to pick up some worthless pieces of paper. On both occasions, he made sure to appear weaker than in fact he was. He improved on the limp which the lads had given him, walking slowly and with a slight stoop at all times. He behaved in a nervous manner and paused occasionally, as if he were gathering low energies just to move around.

In fact, he was almost back to full strength. He exercised at home, lifting large string-bound packages of books as replacements for weights, and had cut his drinking to a minimum again. He still slept little, but it seemed to matter less and less. He hated sleeping, anyway; the dreams kept coming. Sometimes he was Ben, passing away like a ghost on the train taking them to Auschwitz; sometimes Grandfather near the end in Belsen, fighting the temptation to eat the flesh of a dead prisoner, which happened before the British arrived. And sometimes he became his mother, throwing the living bodies up on a truck that was to go to the gas chambers. Sleep was

231

not worth having with dreams like that. He wondered how Grandfather had lived so long with the first-hand knowledge of it, how he had remained such a good man with all of it racketing around in his head.

At the end of June, he wrote letters to his accountant and bank manager, stating that he would be out of the country for some months. He had been overworking, he said, and needed an extended holiday. He enquired at the travel agents in St Stephen's Street about *pensions* and small family hotels in France and Spain. He wrote letters to several in the Toulouse and Saragossa areas, establishments where he had stayed before, reserving rooms for mid-July. With great care, he prepared his fishing gear, went out and bought new lines and flies. As an added touch, he threw out many volumes of Grandfather's library. If they were watching him, and taking any trouble over it, he wanted them to have plenty to look at. He even arranged through an estate agent to let the house for three or four months while he was gone, suggesting at the same time that he might well wish to sell at the end of that period, because he would be moving on.

He was a beaten man. He tried to be sure never to overstep the line. If he played the part too well, they would immediately suspect he was up to something. But he took pains to look and act the role at all times.

And when the curtains were drawn at night, he fetched his small collection of guns down from their strongbox in the loft, cleaned and oiled them, and decided which one he might make the best use of.

In the days when he and Tony used to spend a lot of time together, he had taken up shooting in a desultory fashion. A beautifully tooled Purdey shotgun and a BSA rifle were the results of the initial enthusiasm. He had not touched them for some time though, having discovered that he did not much care for blasting away at anything alive.

That might be a problem later, he thought, as he weighed the rifle in his hand.

No it won't, said the gun, and all his family – known and unknown – seemed to repeat it for him.

232

31

That summer was a quiet one for the Millers. George Miller was invited to join the board of a new AIDS hospice in Glasgow, and he threw himself into fund-raising for it with his customary vigour. Paul and Alex went about their business as usual, never referring to the incidents in Cornwall. Once Jenny asked Paul what he had done when he came down. Paul only smiled and said: "I did exactly what Father told me."

Jenny remained in her father's house, although after Richard's affairs were settled she was considerably wealthy. She did not wish to venture far. The world felt dangerous in a way it had not before. For the first month or so, she expected to come across David Kalska every time she went out. Sometimes she could not believe that anyone who had seemed so honest could have been hiding all that he did. Other times she wished him dead.

When she grew less fearful of stepping outside, she spent a lot of time on the hills around Stinton, walking in the long plantations of fir and pine, climbing the steep slopes to the scrubby moorland where the sky seemed to come down within touching distance, and the Firth of Forth was a bright blue line to the north.

She also began, tentatively, to draw again. She took up position in the conservatory, where the light was good, and fetched out her paints and brushes. When she was several hours into a study of the stream at the bottom of the hill, she thought: "It's still coming out right." She had expected to have reverted to the pinched, careful execution of her early days in Silcombe, but whatever else those experiences had done, they seemed to have released her to do better work.

One morning, alone in the house but for the dogs, she began a picture out of her head. It formed up as a portrait, an imaginary face. She worked on it for three hours before allowing herself to realise that it was Joseph. She kept on with it for a little while afterwards, blocking in the colours and making suggestions of detail, and she saw that it was a good likeness. She bent close, staring at the whirls of paint where his eyes nestled. Then she stepped back, dug her brush into Prussian blue, and started painting into the face.

When it was covered, though, he still looked out at her.

At the beginning of July, Father celebrated his seventy-fifth birthday. The house was filled with cards from old friends and patients who remembered what he had done for them in the past. There was a quiet family celebration at the Denzler in town; Father at the head of the table, his children, in-laws and grandchildren around him. Jenny sat at his right hand, taking the place she had been given since her mother died. Throughout the evening, she watched him talking and laughing, thought of all those cards he had received. Could any man who had done the things this Gelzer was supposed to have done command such love and respect?

A pang of guilt went through her. Here she was, his loyal daughter. And in the last week, she had been up to the Central Library, hunting for books on the Holocaust.

She glanced up from her wine, and found him watching her with his knowing smile. She flushed and looked away, as if he had caught her speaking the thoughts out loud.

David left England on July the fifteenth, travelling with his car on the Folkestone–Boulogne ferry. Unbroken sunshine lay on the sea like silver and blue steel. He sat on deck throughout the crossing, watching the families and young couples who were crowding over to the Continent for their summer holidays. He flicked through his passport and wondered whether some sharp pair of eyes in the customs office had noticed it and made a telephone call to inform interested parties. No telling where it started or finished. The millions made out of gold and jewels that were ripped from the Jews when they went to the camps had disappeared into numbered Swiss Bank accounts throughout the war. The good old boys of the SS who actually got out of the mess when peace came had all that to help them with their post-war careers. After all, Gelzer could not have disappeared in Yugoslavia in 1945, and turned up in Switzerland in '46 with a whole new identity, without help. These things cost money and influence.

He was through the Boulogne customs by 2.30 that afternoon. He drove straight down to Sancerre, spending the night in a little guest house where half the view was of vine-covered hills. Next day he was in Carlat, taking his time, dining in a crêperie where the owner tested him on his French throughout the meal. He was tired all the time, but slept no better than usual.

It was only when he had been in France for a week and a half that he began to deviate from his supposed plans. By then he was staying in a tiny village in the mountains near Tarascon. In the morning, he breakfasted, paid his bill and set out for St Paul. He booked into a cheap hotel, paid two weeks in advance, then went out and rented a blue Citroën.

Two days later, he arrived in Carteret, on the Normandy coast. English students from a camp in town thronged the bars, talking about local cider and day trips to Jersey. He had been prepared to sleep in the car, but managed to get a room at the hotel on the town square. He went walking next morning when the tide was beginning to ebb, wandered about the Petit Port and the Port Abri, took a stroll past the slip and along the Prom de l'Abbé to the *quai*. The Atlantic seemed open and clear all the way to America.

In the afternoon, when the entire harbour was dry and people were walking across the sands to Barneville, he met Duhig, the agent's man who had brought Sarah's new purchase out from England.

They went to the Petit Port and checked the boat over. She was a simple RLM Entice, recently sandblasted, gelcoated and polished up to gleaming condition; equipped with a Navico auto-pilot and new Decca navigating computer. She was well stocked with food and the water tank was full.

Duhig left him with the papers and keys. He would return to England on the hovercraft.

David spent his last night in Carteret chatting with a bunch of students in the bar by the port. The evening ended in an impromptu concert of English folk songs, much to the chagrin of the French regulars. He thought of the night at the Harbourmaster, when he had first started to know Jenny. There had been happiness then. He remembered it guiltily, and after the last song was done, returned to his hotel with a raging headache.

And early in the morning of the following day, tide on the ebb and sky full of whirling gulls and portents of fine weather, he motored out of Carteret Harbour and set her course for the Channel.

Jenny was there the day Father had some friends round for a little practice with clay pigeons. Alex and Paul also attended. The cracking of the guns went on from late morning until lunchtime, resuming after sandwiches and beer. Standing in the garden behind the house, painting a study of roses under the wall, she could see them strung out across Low Field. Their laughter carried down from the hill between the reports of the guns. A perfectly respectable bunch of mainly old men, she thought. Mostly Scots, except for Laughton Bixby, the American stockbroker, and father's old friend, Maurice Gebhardt, the publisher, who was also Swiss by birth.

She had nodded hello to them as they arrived, taken a glass of sherry and talked about their children with them. They were an ordinary bunch of ageing high-achievers. She had known a number of them all her life. And Father fitted perfectly with them, tending to dominate in a good-natured way. Hard to imagine any of them as closet Nazis.

She had found the photograph of Gelzer in a book at the library, taken it to the Xerox machine and run off a copy, then carried it with her for three days. In that time, she stared at it long and hard, compared it to the oldest pictures of Father in the family album. Sometimes she saw no resemblance whatever. She would shake her head in disbelief that anyone could call it evidence. Then there were occasions when she saw his face under the neatly tilted cap, his fair hair and penetrating eyes, his quick smile.

When she tore it up, she did so in the woods, and made a little fire of it to be sure. The idea of his finding out what she had done was slightly terrifying.

In a small way, she had tried to speak of the accusation to her brothers, inviting them to agree how ridiculous the whole thing was. Alex always grew red in the face and walked about the room as he spluttered his indignation. Paul would just shake his head and say: "I think that chap addled your brains before we caught him."

Out on the field, having scored three out of five, Father turned and waved to her. She lifted her arm, the paintbrush in it, and waved back.

*

He put in at Lowestoft, notified the Customs Office and filled out a C1328. He would have preferred to get into England without any formalities which might be taken note of, but it was better to take that risk than to chance being picked up by the authorities for illegal entry. With luck – and he deserved some by now – his enemies were under the impression that he was somewhere in France or Spain. After this length of time, why should they continue to keep an eye on him?

A rented car took him up the summer countryside to Haverley.

The *Marie Celeste* lay at the overgrown bank. Many craft were absent, a few people were on their boats, preparing for trips. He went aboard the *Marie*, unlocked the cabin and retrieved the disassembled rifle he had placed in the forward locker on a visit in the small hours several weeks before. He was certain, anyway, that he had not been followed here. He put the rifle and the shells for it in a holdall full of laundry, and set off back to Lowestoft.

By the late hours of that evening, he was heading up the Norfolk coastline, Cross Sand light off to starboard. He had given his destination as Scarborough. However, that was not where he intended going.

He reached Anstruther on the afternoon of August 4th. Yachts and fishing boats punctuated the dark water, and the Isle of May was clear and shining in the Firth. Anstruther itself was set up on the coast in tiers of grey stone. He came in to the harbour, blearily watching the church over to the left and the square-built houses that straggled round it. The harbour entrance was a narrow opening between high piers, and he edged her gently in as he had seen another boat do a few minutes ahead of him.

He dealt with the harbourmaster, crossed the street to the village shop and bought fresh food, then went back to the boat, ate until he was full, and slept for eighteen hours straight. The journey up had allowed him little time for proper rest, and he needed to be rested.

Three days later, resting on his elbows under the trees a mile to the south of Stinton, he beheld Gelzer's house again. It hid in summer cover, showing a little of its roof and a few upstairs windows in the fading fires of evening light.

The ground about him ticked and burred with life. The warm, moist smell of it filled his nostrils. A couple of flies played tag around his face. He kept swiping at them as he lifted his binoculars.

He had recalled what the regular told him months ago, about shooting on the Glorious Twelfth. He had planned for it. He checked the time. A half-hour of daylight remained. He was here for one time only before the big day, to go over the ground.

"You must begin to go out again," Father said, sipping his glass of after-dinner cognac in the sitting room.

"I do go out," Jenny said.

"Think he means with people," Alex put in. He and Barbara were playing a game of doubles against Paul and his wife in the billiard room. He had come in to replenish his glass. "All you do is moon about on your own."

"I do not moon."

"Alex has the gist of my point," Father said.

The click of the balls came clearly through the half-open door.

"You are feeling better now, aren't you?"

"I haven't been ill," she said.

"A great loss, followed by a shock such as you had are like an illness. You're better now, but you haven't reached the point where you feel quite ready to get back into the world. Is that right?"

"I don't know, Dad. Can we not talk about it now?" She left her chair. He remained in the middle of the room, like a guard she had to pass. She swerved aside and ended up fingering the bookshelves as if there were something there she had lost.

"Why aren't we friends as we used to be?" Father asked.

"We are, Dad." She began to pick bits of non-existent fluff off her blouse.

His eyes were sad. "I feel as if you don't trust me any more."

A loud exclamation of disgust from Alex and cheers from Paul's wife told them the game had ended. A moment later, Paul stuck his head round the door.

"Care to play the winners?" he asked.

"In a minute," Jenny said. "I've got to pop upstairs."

She dodged round her father and went to her room. She actually wanted nothing, except to get away for a minute. Switching the light off so that moths would not gather, she opened the window wide and leaned over the sill, catching the scents of the garden on the night air. She reached for a brush and began to run it through her hair until static jumped in tiny blue flashes. Her sense of claustrophobia began to ebb, she breathed easier. No matter how she dealt with it, told herself that she believed only good of him, she could not rid herself of the tension she felt in his presence. His questions only made it worse.

A dog barked fitfully in the village, and she stopped brushing suddenly. Out on the hill, she thought something moved. Shading her eyes from the glow of the conservatory, she looked again. The scrub grass was a flat wash of blue-black in dim starlight. The dogs were not uneasy in the kitchen. Nothing else occurred. It had probably been a rabbit, perhaps a deer.

"Jenny, you playing or not?" Alex called from the bottom of the stairs.

She dropped the brush and went down to join them.

As he returned over the rough ground towards his hired car, the breeze eddied and changed, brushing through the trees. A coldness came blowing from the east. He lifted his head and saw the stars filming over. Rain on the way, chill coming. According to the weather reports it would get worse over the next week, driving August into autumn before its time.

He went down the hill, jumping rocks and trailing knots of root and branch. The car rested in a narrow lane off the Common Road, which was little more than a track itself, looping south from the highway at Stinton, into the hills, lochs and streams where no one lived. He stood on a ridge above the car for a minute, surveying the eight miles of shadowed countryside before him. He felt nothing much. Everywhere was the same to him now. But this was where they would be on August 12th. And he would also be here, waiting for his chance to set right all the crimes committed. The simple way.

Sitting in her room, Jenny heard Paul say: "Only one more day to go."

"Then, Bang, Bang!" Alex said.

"You shoot the way you drink," Paul said. "Without savouring."

"He's right, though, I think." Father again. Proposing a toast. "The shooting will be very good this year."

"The shooting." Everyone joined in, glasses clinked.

32

Birds began shifting and twittering a little before dawn. The wind slowed and the odour of the sea came damp and cold from the coast. The sky paled colourlessly, then was lit across the east by layers of gold. In the hollows where Stinton lay it was still dark.

A light came on in Cedar House. Curtains opened, a figure moved across a bedroom window.

The sun came over the hills, shadows slipping down the forest and the scrub towards Cedar House. Light broke over her like a slow wave.

Birdsong grew raucous. Finches and sparrows gathered on the lawn, a pair of house martins swung about the eaves. Far off the sound of tractors starting up, cars moving along the road towards Dunbar and Edinburgh.

And David arrived at the top of the plantation on Grannoch Hill. He checked the house and the countryside around, then descended, going down through shrouded avenues of firs to the Low Field. The rifle was slung on his shoulder. He carried nothing else but a detailed map of the area in his memory.

He came to the dry stone wall which separated plantation from field, saw dogs playing in the garden. He skirted the field, working along the edge to the corner of the plantation. He was four hundred yards from the house, and the ground was a gentle sweep down. Most of the cover was here. After that, nothing but odd rocks and the sort of ground sheep get stuck with. He debated whether to move in and find some depression from which he would have a better chance. But the rifle was good, and his aim was fair. There was even a chance, in this position, that he might get away. The car was half a mile distant in its hiding place off the loop road. With the shock and confusion – they might think Gelzer had been accidentally shot by one of his own party – he could run for safety, be back in Anstruther before the alarm went out.

He knelt on the needle-strewn floor, dragged a fallen branch across to the ferns at the edge of the woods.

The sun burned some of the chill from the air. It painted long strips of shadow on his arms. As he yanked the branch into place, one of the twigs cast a spiky print on his flesh. For a moment, he saw it as a number with a little triangle under it. He thought: It's coming through. It was in my mother's blood and it's coming through at last.

A car rumbled up the drive to the house. He resumed work.

The drive filled with Range-Rovers and old pickups. His scorn grew. The seven Guns were old or middle-aged; well-heeled professionals; senior medical men, presidents of thriving companies, JPs. He watched them climbing from their cars, bringing hordes of family, friends and dogs with them. What did they know about Miller? Plenty, he thought. He had seen enough 'pillars of the community' to know that they were careful who they called friends.

At any rate, he was prepared to lay odds that there was not a single Jew amongst them.

At least, not one they knew about.

The beaters – girls and boys from the village – were gathering down by Low Field gate. Mr Bairnsfather, the keeper, held forth on dos and don'ts. The guests stood about the garden, catching up on recent gossip and share prices. Jenny moved among them, nodding hello, watching for the slight change of expression that meant they were thinking of Richard's death. In previous years, Richard had been on the shoot.

She wandered into the house. In the kitchen, Mrs Hawbee was going frantic getting lunch ready. There would be something like thirty-two people to feed. Father was in his study, the French windows open. Gradually each Gun dawdled in, and was offered the numbered ivory counters from Father's old set. It had a civilised air, she thought, out of keeping with the actual business of plugging birds with shot.

He had asked her to go up to the shoot. She had said she

241

would prefer not to. But everyone seemed to expect her there. He expected her there.

He held the bag as another Gun fumbled for a counter. He seemed most British when indulging in the rituals.

David kept his head down as the keeper took the beaters over the field, going east round the hill towards the moor. A lot of them were kids. They might be witness to a man having his head splattered all over the landscape. A body shot would be less messy, but he wanted to be sure he killed the old man.

The beaters went out of sight. A tractor pulling a large bench trailer waited at the house. The air was a little warmer, midges swirling. The cars, loaded again, turned slowly off the drive and bumped across the field, going the way the beaters had gone. They passed within a hundred and fifty yards of him. He saw their grinning faces, heard the songs they sang to the glory of a good shoot.

Then the house again. He did not use his binoculars, for fear of reflection giving him away. Three men came out of the French windows: Paul, Alex and Gelzer. They spread out to talk with others as they crossed the garden. He flexed his hands, wiped them in the soft humus of needles and muck to dry them.

The tractor belched blue smoke as the eight Guns and five guest shooters mounted the trailer. Guns were passed up, cartridge bags slung over shoulders or tied round waists. He heard a burst of laughter, and one old man almost slipped as he clambered up.

He sank behind the rifle and adjusted his eye to the sight.

The dogs quartered in the garden set up a babble of howling as the tractor lurched up the long incline of the field.

He kept both eyes open, the proper way. It gave a double vision: the scene before him, coloured in washes of dark green, brown and grey; and a slightly magnified circle of more intense vision, where the heads on the trailer bobbed and shifted as he tracked them. They were coming up at a long angle to his position, heading diagonally over the field as the rest had done. Too close packed for him to try a shot. He watched it pass, the Guns crying: "Whoa!" as they bumped over a rock, then they were going on towards the moor.

He made sure he was unobserved, slung the rifle on his back, and turned into the trees.

The back of the Land-Rover brimmed with food and drink.

"That's the lot," Mrs Hawbee said, squeezing one more box of cheeses and cold meats in.

"Just need the glasses," Jenny said, "and we'll be off."

She went in to get them. The clock in the kitchen showed five past ten. The barometer under it pointed to fair. She saw a calm blue sea with the *Cader Idris* slicing across it like scissors.

That was no way to think. She collected a box full of plastic glasses and took them out to the car.

Over the hill and down the south side. He skirted the long stretch of iron-coloured water that flanked the hill, jumped where it narrowed to the burn that fed it. He cut away to the plantation's east side, reaching the edge as the tractor rumbled over the bridge across the burn. It climbed a rough track towards the high moor, looking as if it were going to the edge of the world. He went deeper in again, brushing the midges from his face, sweating profusely, the rifle heavy on his shoulder.

The plantation ended at the foot of the hill. He paused, searched the rising moor and found the shooting party just below the skyline. The tractor crawled towards it. He located the keeper, wanting some clue as to where the stands would be, then surveyed the country. At first glance it seemed too featureless to provide concealment, but he referred to the map in his head and looked to the right of the party. The ground rose slightly in a ridge of gorse and purple heather. He could get up on their flank using the ridge for cover.

The wind threw fragments of laughter to him. He picked a thorn from his trousers, scratched where it had penetrated skin. He saw Gelzer jump down from the trailer like a young man. They were five hundred yards off, a little green knot of people and cars on the dull moor, but Gelzer stood out. He was a different animal from the rest; stronger, more sure.

From far back a car was coming up from the house. Time to move, before people stopped chattering and started looking around. He gauged the lie of the ground between himself and the ridge, working out the safest way through the under-growth. He and the shooting party were alone in bleak country. He checked the rifle once more. It felt heavy and cold, except where his hands touched it and it grew hot. The dull black gleam of it contrasted sharply with the cartridges he had loaded in. Bright, clean brass with the smooth black nose of the round indicating direction and force. He imagined the bullet cleaving soft air, the forward-rushing metal tearing into the brain, exploding shrouded memories of cruelty, splashing years of secrecy into blood and pulp. Some kind of fitting end.

Except . . .

Except if he was not Gelzer.

He rubbed at his chest where the ribs were still tender; summoned the look in Paul's eyes as he watched the lads perform their duties; the two brothers watching triumphantly as he was carried yelling from the hall in Edinburgh. For a second he was unsure who he most wanted to kill.

He set off, carrying the rifle in front of his body, crouch-running across ground that would swallow foot or catch legs with claws of thorn. For fear of disturbing the wildlife, he dodged the thickest patches of gorse. He was on the lee side of the slope, the shooting party out of sight. As he went up the incline, the moor rose in sweeping layers until he could see miles across to Lothian Law and High Wood beyond.

Two hundred yards out he swerved left and slowed to walking pace, climbed the ridge, brushing yellow dust from the gorse. His throat was raw with it. He stopped and listened for them. A clink of bottles being unloaded. He got down on the ground and slithered forward on his elbows an inch or two at a time. Keeping the leaf-coloured cap well-pulled over his face, he edged over the rise. He was on their flank. They were setting up for the first drive, the Guns going out to positions marked by numbered pegs the keeper had placed earlier. A line of eight men carrying shotguns, spaced about forty yards apart across a smooth stretch of ground. In front of them was a shallow upturned bowl, islands of tall heather among seas of short grass. Beyond that were the beaters. He made sure he could not be spotted by the boys as they came forward, found a narrow opening between two clumps of gorse. He brought the rifle round and settled the barrel in among the tiny yellow flowers.

He rubbed either side of his eyes, aching from lack of sleep. The whistle blew twice. As the beaters began their slow walk towards the Guns, he put his eye to the sight and went searching along the line for Gelzer. The red, over-indulged faces wobbled into his circle and flew out again as he moved on to the next man. None of them was Gelzer. But Number Two in the line was Alex. He was taking first go on Daddy's stand.

He heard a flap of rising wings from the heather, and the first shot fired. Another followed almost immediately, then a lull. He was in among the spectators now, looking for his man. And there he was, standing with Paul and some old colleague. The whistle still raised to his mouth, he watched the sport with rapt attention. A woman moved in the way, making an extravagant gesture to a headscarved figure in tweeds. They turned and spoke to Gelzer, blocking a clear line of fire.

He raised his head, taking in the whole scene as the beaters moved on and the occasional covey erupted into the grey air. He watched one bird burst from cover and go skimming toward the nearest rise, never more than a couple of feet off the ground. The Number One Gun tried for it as it hurtled through his forty-five degrees, but it was gone.

Gelzer kept flicking in and out of view behind the ladies. He hunched farther down, let his finger curl round the trigger. All he could do was wait his moment.

The Guns fired on sporadically. Odd shouts from the beaters, then a flurry of activity in the heather, and the flat slam of both barrels letting fly.

The ladies bent forward to listen to Gelzer. His strong, angled face appeared, nodding, bottom lip thrust out. David swallowed hard. The stone in his throat would not move. Sweat began to ooze cold and sticky. He centred. Gelzer swivelled and spoke to the ladies. Something caught his attention. His eyes lit up.

"Ah, darling, you're here at last."

She came through the huddle of spectators, seeing him beckon. She paused ten feet from him, hands in pockets.

"Catering's all present and correct," she said, knowing to speak quietly while they were shooting.

"Come and join us," Father said, hand still raised.

*

245

David clenched his teeth to stop them chattering. The women were out of the way. They had stepped back a little as Gelzer called to someone behind him. He was a clear target, no one close, no one behind him who might take a bullet that passed through the old man's body.

A bullet in the skull to solve a problem, to take revenge in the way Gelzer himself might have done. How many times, in the fat histories and Grandfather's notebooks, had he read of an SS man wiping out 'a problem' with a single bullet in the brain? It was fair. If he did not do it now, no one would. The old man would die in his sleep one night, go peacefully to whatever heaven the Nazis had burned out for themselves.

He shifted his elbows in the muck, settling more firmly. He centred on Gelzer's big, rounded skull, just under the fore-and-aft. His stomach felt hot and liquid. The tractor was close, he could see the leathery wrinkles in the old man's neck as he turned his head. The muscles in his right shoulder pulled as he hunched lower. Gelzer beckoned, smiling. The image of the young surgeon, the handsome man in uniform bled into the eyepiece of the sight, and he looked a little like Paul, a little like Alex. Coldness crept into the centre of his body, and all the sick horror of it seemed to freeze. A piece of him was remembering everything at once, and it was calm, icy calm. He thought: Now you do it. And his finger began to draw on the trigger. It came back with a heaviness he had not noticed before. He heard the springs making tiny pops of sound as they tightened. Gelzer was exactly in the centre of the circle, dominating his eye as he had dominated his life since the night Grandfather was knocked down. His finger whitened as it pulled against the sliver of metal that would send a bullet into Gelzer's brain. He thought: It works, it works.

"Come," Father urged. "Come and contribute an insult on Alex's marksmanship."

She felt uncomfortable. He wanted her to be Daddy's little girl. Everyone was around them, closing them in. She had to go and stand with him.

The hand beckoned again. "Come tell me what we have for lunch." The same old smile, the reassurance of his authority.

"It's no lunch," she grinned. "It's a banquet on trestle tables."

"That's how it should be."

"You'll see." She started across the gap between them.

Now is the moment. Now before all the bullshit moral dilemmas get the better of you again. Now while he's alone in my circle, just me and him and the thousands he sent to the slaughterhouse and the special barracks. Pull the fucking trigger. Now.

His arm went around her, the other encircling Paul. He held them close, whispered: "You are my good children." She bowed her head, felt his lips on her hair, just below the crown. "Very good children."

His finger snatched off the trigger. He knew her face again as it had been in those long days of April and May.

And he saw the old man hugging his children tight to his sides, looking fondly on them. The tilt of Jenny's head as she smiled up at him. This man was her father.

The first drive was ending. The smack of the guns died away and smoke drifted gently across the heather.

He focused on Gelzer's head, but his finger was not on the trigger. He watched Jenny for a moment longer. To do what he had intended required splashing her with her father's blood and brains. He knew he could not do it. The moment was gone; and with it the certainty that Miller was Gelzer, that the rifle was his answer.

He rolled on his back, letting the weapon slide to the ground, stared at the unfocused sky. It was time to go. He lifted the rifle once more, to use the sight for a last glimpse of Jenny. She was standing at her father's side as they waited for Alex to come in. She looked beautiful.

"Bloody awful," Paul jeered.

Alex came toward them, pushing his cap back on his head. "What d'you mean? I got three."

"Two," Paul said.

Alex appealed to Jenny and their father. "How many?"

"I think it was two," Father replied.

"Two," Jenny said. "Sorry."

"You're a lot of help," Alex said, reaching for the beer she

247

handed him. With the first drive over, the spectators were busy discussing the sport. Old men rested precariously on shooting sticks while youngsters lounged about, making impolite comments on marksmanship. Slightly apart as usual, in unconscious imitation of his father, Paul gazed around at the blue distances of the countryside.

"Who's up next?" Alex asked.

"Paul, I think," Father said. "Unless Jenny cares for a turn."

"Not me, thank you."

He winked at her. "In that case, Paul will defend the family honour."

Paul glanced back at the hill.

"When's lunch, anyway?" Alex said.

"Not soon enough for you." Jenny tapped his swelling stomach.

"Here, now – "

Paul's eyes narrowed suddenly.

"What is it?" she said.

"Poacher, I think. Here, Alex, lend me your glasses."

Alex handed him the little green binoculars.

Father put his arm round her shoulders again. "A good day, with my children round me."

Paul opened his mouth a fraction. "Jesus Christ."

Father spoke quietly. "What is it?"

Binoculars removed, he stared at Father for a moment. Jenny noticed the exchange, turned to see what he had been looking at. She caught movement near the trees, nothing more.

The good humour of a second ago was gone. Even Alex stopped talking. He raised an eyebrow at Paul.

"We'd better go and have a word," Paul said. "Alex, come on."

They strode off, each carrying his gun. Jenny made a questioning face to her father.

"A poacher," he said. "Don't worry." He began to congratulate Laughton Bixby on his shooting.

The boys climbed into the Land-Rover. Someone burst out laughing nearby. His fat, red face got in her way.

"It seems I'll have to take their turns until they come back," Father said.

She watched the car racketing away down the track.

*

248

He only realised the Land-Rover was coming after him when it swerved off the track and came leaping over the broken ground.

At first he was so surprised that he did not move. He tried to make out who was at the wheel. Then the car slithered to a halt a hundred yards off and Alex jumped out. The car swung a tight circle and drove for the bridge. That snapped him out of it. He sprang up, catching his head on a low branch, and ducked into the undergrowth.

Something shot up in front of him; he saw a sleek feathered shape go screeching through branches to the light. Alex was crashing through the undergrowth, cutting off his path back to the open. Where had the car gone?

The ground rose sharply. He started up, slipping and scrabbling the earth, got onto what was clearly a path round the skirts of the hill. He took off along it, the rifle thumping against his back as he ran. Smell of wet earth.

The path dipped to bridge the tumbling ribbon of a gill. Below the thick-sodded planks the waterfall plunged down a deep gully. As his boots hit them a shape caught the tail of his eye. He sensed rather than saw Alex poised to fire on the lichened stones thirty feet below.

The explosion seemed like part of the stream's rush. He was caught by the outer edge of the shotgun's spread. Agony peppered his shoulder, but he was running too fast for it to bring him down. He hit the path on the other side of the bridge. The gun smacked again, booming in the gully, but he was ahead of it, and Alex did not lead his target far enough. Shot flickered through the branches and spent itself in the craggy trunks.

Down the hill again, feet hitting the angled ground with painful awkwardness. Branches slapped his face as he headed for the open. Alex was still with him, but slower now; he carried more weight than was good for a chase. He was almost there. Ten feet, five. A wash of pale sunlight broke over him and he smelt the odour of damp grass and the sea wind. He broke into open ground.

The Land-Rover was waiting.

He saw it start up a quarter-mile away in a narrow glen. It came thundering through the undergrowth, clearly running to cut him off. Despite the bloody fire in his lungs and arm, he speeded up. Farther up the hill, the coverage turned from short grass to clumped heather and gorse.

The crunch of gears changing and sudden acceleration made him dart a glance over his shoulder. He saw the Land-Rover hurtling at him. A flash of Paul's face, horrendously calm, and the car's engine screaming as it shot towards him.

He let it come on until it was ten feet from him, then stopped dead, jumped backwards and felt the hot wind as it shaved past. Its turning circle at high speed was wide. He spared a look for Alex, who had paused for a breather, and ran up the middle of the car's circle. That took him further up the hill again, while Paul wrestled the car round the steepening incline. It passed him coming down as he made it to a low crag ripped out of the green. Boots scraping, he got up on the first stage of the old black rock, dug his fingers in and heaved himself up the next. Alex's gun thumped, but it was nowhere near.

The angle of climb grew more acute. He spotted a gully which took some of the brute clambering out of the ascent, dodged toward it, warm blood running down his back. Paul could not bring the car up here, and Alex had no wind left for running. He would make it.

The sky was dull blue as he came up the gully. Transparent circles and strings danced in front of his eyes, beating with his pulse. Cresting the slope, it seemed as if the world ended a few feet ahead. He paced his breathing as he reached the top, prepared to throw himself onward.

. . . And skidded to a halt just in time to stop himself from flying straight into space.

He teetered over the drop, staring in disbelief. It was a long crescent of bare grey rock, a giant heelprint in the hill. Beneath him, it fell two hundred feet in jagged verticals to a pool of wind-brushed water. Beyond the crescent, the hill resumed a gentler glide to another valley and the deep green safety of woods.

He pulled back from the edge, starting to move left.

Paul was twenty yards away, gun ready at the shoulder. Breathing hard, triumphant.

David swivelled unsteadily on his heel and checked behind.

250

Alex, beet-red and heaving for air, glared over the sights of his gun.

He turned back to Paul, unslinging his rifle with slow deliberation. He heard his own breath like a steam train. His lips curled in a sneer.

Paul nodded to his brother.

Alex let off one barrel. A hammer falling on concrete. Some of the shot splashed off bare rock, burying itself in the back of his leg. He cried out, dropping the rifle. It clattered.

The brothers moved round, making sure he remained trapped on the brink. David watched Paul. Paul was the more dangerous, most like his father.

They halted. Not a word spoken. Paul raised his gun. David swallowed, stared at the black eyes. The sound of three animals at the culmination of a hunt.

Both barrels roared. Shot hissed past his face. He staggered toward the edge.

The gun was down again. Paul looked as if nothing had happened. He broke the gun, letting Alex keep guard.

The reloading complete, he shut the gun with a click. Another faint nod. Alex fired. Shot struck rock again, coating it with mirrored splatters of lead. The rest disappeared into air. Alex snorted.

Paul shot closer. One pellet caught David's scalp. He slewed round, clapping his hand to his head. Then Alex fired again, then Paul. Each time they waited until the other was reloaded. Paul's smile widened each time he pulled the trigger.

Trying not to give them the satisfaction of watching him flinch at each blast, David withdrew as far as he could. The noise of the guns was deafening, the smoke sickened him.

Something familiar. A picture in one of Grandfather's books. An old Jew surrounded by German soldiers. All young men, healthy and strong. They were kicking him, taking turns. The terrible thing was not the one who had his boot in the old man at the moment of the picture. It was the others, cheering him on, laughing as though it were a party. The picture had come back when he saw a television news report of Israeli soldiers beating Palestinian stone-throwers in the Gaza strip with axe-handles. A young Israeli had stepped into the foreground, smiling.

The shooting stopped. Down on one knee, David looked

251

from one to the other of them, hating again, understanding at last that he despised the sons every bit as much as the father. The two matters were no longer separable. Paul was gesturing to Alex to go ahead.

Aching and exhausted, he got on his feet, swaying but upright. He shuffled round to face the elder brother.

Alex already had his gun up. Piggy yellow eyes stared along the rib. David gazed into the barrels. They were unsteady, though with exertion or nerves he could not tell.

He thought: To come this far, and to discover it wasn't the answer, and then to finish this way. Grandfather would've given me a damn good hiding. What's the good of knowledge, he would have said, if you don't live to use it?

He was frightened, but angry too. He did not want to die. The breeze from the sea cooled him. He could smell heather and flowers. He had learnt what Grandfather wanted him to know, and now it was nothing.

Alex coughed. The barrels trembled. David felt like telling him to get on with it, but knew he would not be able to speak.

A footfall behind him. He started to turn. There was a glimpse of Paul's face, the stock of the gun swinging down. He tried to defend himself, felt his boots slipping on the incline. Then there was pain like a flash-fire, a nausea that vibrated through him. He lost balance, dimly knowing he must be on the edge. Another impact, more sickening than the first, and his mind was released from light. He vanished like a lamp going out.

33

First, there was smell. The odour of clean sheets. It wafted in and out of disconnected thinking. He was aware of someone nearby, thought it was his mother, because he was so small and the presence in the dark was so huge. Then there was a sensation of heat. When it died away, he was left with the throbbing ache of legs and shoulder and head. He thought he was strapped to a steel table.

A vertical line of light in gloom. A voice speaking, very soft and deep, asking a question. He struggled to move. The voice soothed him. A hand touched his brow, pressed him gently back.

One moment of glassy clarity: he was convulsed with a coughing fit, and a door opened far away across an angled room. A female face looked in. It said nothing, and after a time, withdrew. He sank again.

Birkenau returned. The walk in the abandoned camp, the drizzling sky. The wide enclosure with its grey earth rippling slowly towards him.

Finally he became conscious of the voice speaking again. He was muffled in a heavy, unnatural sleep, but forced his eyes to open. They picked out slabs of half-light: an expanse of ceiling; papered walls; a strange, mullioned window, narrow and arched. Someone had just moved out of his field of view. His head rolled on the pillow and found the shape again. A man leaned over him.

"David?"

He blinked, unable to see the face. "Yes," he said, his voice dry.

"Ah, good, you're awake. How are you feeling?"

The voice was familiar. He peered up. "I can't see you."

"Wait just a moment." The shape reached over. "Prepare yourself. It will seem very bright."

His eyelids drooped. He could hardly keep them open. When the light came on he flinched away from it.

"David, don't fall asleep again. Open your eyes a moment."

He did not want to. Another voice was trying to tell him something. He coughed.

"David."

The voice coaxed him. He wanted to help. He made a determined effort. He opened his eyes.

Gelzer.

He made a noise something like a scream, though it came out as a croak. He tried to squirm away.

"Now, David, now," the voice said. Strong hands gripped him by the shoulders, one of which burst into recalled pain. "Now, don't struggle. Don't. It's all right, it's all right, do you hear? Please, you'll hurt yourself."

He could not get away. His body reacted too sluggishly to the mind's instructions. But it did not prevent the terror. He

253

was at Gelzer's mercy, maybe strapped down, with the stink of disinfectant and the gleam of the scalpel. The hands held him, he was inches away from the old man's face. He stared wildly into it like a cornered animal.

Gelzer, on the other hand, was quite collected. He appeared concerned.

"I know," he said. "It's a shock for you. That's why I've given you something to blunt the edges a little."

David gulped on the dryness in his throat. "You bastard."

Gelzer pulled ruffled bedclothes straight. "I didn't wish you to face up to this moment without a degree of protection. Don't worry, though. It's only a sedative. You need to rest."

"What's going on?"

"You're in bed, recovering from various injuries. You'll be quite all right, but your body needs time to repair." He smiled. "You were something of a mess."

"Thank your boys."

"Yes. I'm sorry they were so rough with you. But you could hardly blame them, could you?"

"Like father, like sons."

"What I mean is, they were only protecting their family. Wouldn't you have done the same if someone had tried to kill your grandfather?"

"Someone did."

Gelzer glanced at his watch. "It's late, you're still very tired. I think we should talk again in the morning." He rose. A hand came down. David swiped weakly at it, but it still touched him, held his shoulder. "Please, try to rest. And accept that I mean you no harm."

"Like hell."

A needle went into his arm. He groaned. "Where is this?"

Gelzer left him. A door opened, letting in the low tones of a television. "Rest now," he said.

"Where?" David repeated, slipping. He wanted to move. Nothing answered commands. "Where?"

Sleep.

Again the slow surfacing. The only difference was that daylight showed at the window. He concentrated. The room was small, its ceiling sloped above the foot of the bed. The window was deep set. Outside was a suggestion of heathered hillside and sky. Nothing useful.

He was thirsty. Whatever drugs were being used, they made him dry. He put his hands flat on the mattress and pushed to get himself up.

"Now, then," Gelzer said, and placed a hand firmly on his chest.

David shivered. He had almost convinced himself that Gelzer had been a dream. But the man was with him again. In the daylight he was more real than before. Wrinkles on the face, little veins in the eyes, fine strands of white hair.

A glass touched his lips. He drank thirstily, while Gelzer held the glass.

"That's good, good. Those drugs do dehydrate you. It will be much better when you don't need them any more."

He spluttered on the last mouthful. "I don't need them now. Where the hell am I? This isn't a hospital."

"No, that's true. Relax a minute. You're weak as a child. Don't strain yourself."

He put his head back, wishing he could beat the effects of the drugs. "I should've plugged you when I had the chance."

"Of course," Gelzer said briskly. "I'm going to have a look at the damage now. Just assist me by doing as I ask." He rolled David on his right side and examined the dressings on his shoulder and legs. Confident fingers touched his head. "That's all fine."

"Who did this?"

"I did. I may be a surgeon, but I can apply a dressing and pick shot out as well as the next man. Mind you, you're lucky Paul didn't break your skull when he hit you."

"Should've plugged him too."

"He might say the same of you, David."

"Don't call me that."

"I'm sorry." He rolled the patient on his back again. "You'll mend well enough."

"You still haven't told me where I am."

"You're fifty miles north of Edinburgh. Perthshire, to be exact. We're roughly twelve miles from the nearest railway station and six miles from the nearest village. This is my shooting lodge. It's called Gallow."

David registered the information about their distance from other people. Gelzer, however, chatted amicably.

"It's very lovely countryside. Glens and lochs. The lodge sits in a cup of hills, a stream falls at the edge of the garden. I hope when you're up and about, you'll be able to see for yourself."

"Very kind of you. What the hell's going on?"

Gelzer's wiry eyebrows drew together. "I expect you remember little of what happened on Wednesday," he said. "Do you remember Trap Law? The crescent of cliff?"

"Vividly."

"Well, I suppose that Paul and Alex did have it in mind to throw you over Trap Law after the chase you led them, but common sense prevailed. Lucky Paul was there; Alex would still like to strangle you. He's a hot-headed boy, but you might agree he feels he has sufficient reason in this case. However, when you were lying unconscious, they cooled down very quickly. They looked around to see if anyone had witnessed all this. No one had, so they carried you back to the Land-Rover and brought you to the house. Then they came and found me. I made excuses to the guests about an urgent case requiring my opinion, and came back. It was interesting to see you after so long. The boys have been very protective since our first meeting." He spoke of them as an indulgent father would. "Obviously, you were bleeding from your various wounds, but nothing was very serious except for the head. That concerned me somewhat, but you seemed to have sustained no long-term harm. I employed my little skill to tend your wounds while the boys went out to locate your car. Then, of course, we had to decide what was to be done with you. We couldn't keep you in Stinton – small villages are so public. So we lighted on this scheme. Alex went back to the shoot to provide a family presence, while Paul and I packed you into the back seat of your car and drove you over the Forth Bridge and up the M90 to this place."

"If you're the innocent victim you say you are, why didn't you just call the police?"

Gelzer's gaze did not waver. "I have reasons, David. I think we need to talk."

David started to laugh, and then to cough. Gelzer brought the glass to his lips again. "Oh, you're a prince, you really are. What were you going to do if my head turned out to be bad?"

256

"Take you to a hospital. But I was confident I could look after you."

"Too kind." Words slipped out over numb lips. He did not sound angry enough.

Gelzer sighed. "Let me put it to you. As far as anyone knows, you're not even in Britain at the moment – "

"You *did* have me watched."

"In a small way, of course. David, you threatened my daughter. Wait until you have children of your own. You'll see how careful they make one. As I was saying, you are somewhere in deepest France, so far as anyone knows. Were I the beast you make out, this is a perfect opportunity to eliminate you. There are a thousand places to hide a body here, while the authorities would be searching for you on the Continent."

David gestured for the glass again. This time he curled the fingers of his right hand round it. Gelzer watched as he drank.

"So you see. Your notion of me is not quite at one with the facts of the situation."

"You're clever," David sneered.

Gelzer stood. "I think not. If I were, I don't believe you would still be alive. I'll leave you now. Breakfast will be in a little while."

"With my ration of knockout juice."

"No. I think you no longer need it. It was only to make you sleep better." He crossed to the window and glanced out. "Such a beautiful day." At the door, he turned. "I will confess something to you. With your mood as it is just now, I think you'll agree you're in need of protection. So, as you see, the window is too narrow to climb out of, even if you were up to the task. You could break the glass, but no one would hear you, even if you had a loud hailer. And I shall lock you in."

Thoroughly scared, David jeered: "You're so thoughtful."

"It's only because I don't want you running away before we can talk." Gelzer closed the door quietly. The key scraped in the lock, footsteps went away downstairs.

David tried to relax, but his body was thrumming under the blanket of drugs. "Before we can talk." Gelzer was kindness itself, the model of a reasonable man. He was right when he said they could have killed him. So why hadn't they?

House martins twittered under the eaves outside. He wished the window were open, that he could move. Despite what

Gelzer had said, he would have liked to try a few shouts for help.

His head ached, weariness was still on him. He drifted from fear and anger into a semi-doze.

He came awake with a jolt, heard a chink of crockery. His mind was a little clearer, but so was the sense of danger. He had plenty more questions for Gelzer now. He struggled up an inch or two as the key turned in the lock.

"Now, look – " he began, then shut up as if a switch had been flicked.

Jenny came in, carrying a tray with breakfast things on it. She did not speak, something had surprised her too much for that. She set the tray on the bedside table. He tried to make her look at him, but she was intent on everything else, anything else. Strain showed in the fixed expression of coldness on her face.

He flashed back to Silcombe and everything she had told him, all they had shared when he was someone else. Instead of being scared, he was now acutely uncomfortable. He felt as a confidence trickster might feel when confronted with a victim.

She left the tray, turned and went out. He almost spoke her name, but courage failed him. The door slammed and locked.

Going down the stairs, she speeded up abruptly, burst into the study, found no one there, went on through the dining room and out to the garden.

Her father was strolling on the lawn, taking in the bright morning air.

"Why did you make me do that?" she hissed, as he turned at her approach. "You said he'd be asleep."

"Now, Jenny – "

"Now, Jenny nothing." She was furious. "Don't you think we've been through enough, without you playing games?"

"No games." He observed the flashing stream and the steep hills to the north. "And don't be so horrified. I heard you look in on him the other night. If you had kept out of things on Wednesday, you would not have to know about this."

"It was pretty easy to guess something was going on."

"So you disobeyed me, and what you found out was not to

your liking. But you know about it now, and you must be part of it."

"I don't want to be here. I don't want to be anywhere near him, don't you understand?"

"I understand very well." His tone was less tolerant. "Mr Kalska was one of your larger mistakes, and you hate making mistakes. But this is one you're going to face."

"I won't go back in that room."

"You will. You will have to."

"I'm leaving."

"No, you're not."

"Why shouldn't I?"

"Because if you do, you won't hear what I have to say."

She backed away from him. "What does that mean?"

"You'll hear what I have to say when Mr Kalska does." He leaned against the garden wall, looking down on the steep lane that led away from the lodge and across the barren moorland to the hills. "Now go inside and occupy yourself, and in half an hour, fetch Mr Kalska's breakfast tray."

"You can't make me do anything. I'm not a kid any more."

"Jenny." He eyed her with cool authority. She felt about ten years old again. Then a hint of tenderness once more. "Please, darling, do as I ask. This is not easy for me either."

She wanted to ask him why not, what he had to say, why he could not tell her now. But he was closed against her as he had been to everyone since the boys brought David's body back to the house on Wednesday.

Biting her lip, she turned away.

He remained in the garden, inspecting the wild flowers that grew beneath the walls.

When she returned, David had finished breakfast. The resolve not to eat had died at the smell of toast and coffee. He had drunk the entire pot and still felt thirsty. He was shredding the last slice of toast and dropping the pieces on his plate when she entered.

The same silence as before. The strain seemed to have grown. He looked at her more closely. Her hair was drawn back off her face, increasing her severity. She wore jeans and a loose sweater. She appeared much the same as she had when he knew her. Only there was such disdain in her manner, a huge distance. Everything that had happened between them seemed a long time ago.

The tray was on his lap, he lifted it to give it to her. She hesitated, then leaned forward to take it.

"Jenny," he said.

No reply. She snatched the tray and hurried back to the door.

"I'm sorry," he said.

The door closed. He was locked in again.

He eased out of bed, taking his time because both legs and the shoulder were stiff as boards. He put his feet on the floor, used the bedside table for support until dizziness passed, then took a few steps. He checked the window first. As Gelzer had said, it was almost an arrow slit; not even a child could have wormed through it. He undid the latch and peered out. The garden below made a smooth handkerchief of green against surroundings of sparse beauty. The far-off hills were clean-cut in a fresh-blowing morning, the sky shone with good light. He drew breaths of scented air. Any use shouting? There was no house in sight. He glanced down. Gelzer paced across the lawn, raised a hand and nodded to him.

He retreated to the door, put on the blue dressing gown hanging there, and tried the handle. It was solid oak, the lock heavy and old. He would break every bone in his body before it gave way. The room itself was thick-walled, no trapdoor to the loft. Besides, he doubted he would be much use for climbing about in the roof. He returned to the bed, sat down hard while another twist of dizziness caught him. Where were his clothes? He got up again and looked in the old wardrobe in the corner. The clothes he had been wearing were there, still dirty. The rifle was not, of course. It was a strange situation. He had no idea what the old man's intentions were, but there seemed to be nothing he could do until Gelzer chose to tell him.

A car engine sounded. He could see nothing, but heard it approach and draw up somewhere round the front of the house. He went back to bed, picked up one of the books on the bedside table. *The Cricketer's Companion.* It was a relaxing sort of book. Calculated to calm him. He tried to read it, but all the time his mind was working on the problem: what was going to happen?

*

It was late afternoon when Gelzer looked in again.

"Are you quite wide awake?" he asked.

"Reasonably."

"Good." Gelzer stood back and ushered Jenny in.

"Very clever," David said, closing his book.

"I beg your pardon?"

"Bringing her. I suppose you figure I won't lay into you if she's here."

"Sit down, Jenny. The other side of the bed, on Mr Kalska's right."

She opened her mouth to protest. He silenced her with a shake of the head. Sullenly, she took a chair. David glanced at her, but she ignored him, shifted further away. Gelzer looked on solemnly.

"Don't attribute such psychological subtleties to me, Mr Kalska. Paul is a few feet along the landing. If he hears any scuffles from this room, he will come in." He drew up his own chair and sat down. For the first time, David noticed the tension in the old man. He was maintaining his self-control, but it was clear that he was extremely nervous.

"I might be able to kill you before he gets here," David said. "It might be worth it."

"You couldn't do it at the shoot. What makes you think you're willing to commit murder now?"

David averted his eyes. He almost told the truth: that he had spared Gelzer because of Jenny, but she glared fiercely at the window. She too was drawn tight. The atmosphere between father and daughter was like a cord stretched across the bed between them. She spoke quietly, but with force:

"Can we please get on with this?"

"Yes," Gelzer said. He looked at his watch, and it was clear that he was reluctant, wishing that something might interrupt him. Nothing did. He sat forward, hands curling slowly together on his lap. He began to speak.

"I know you would both prefer not to be in this situation. Believe me, I can sympathise with that. This has been a bad time – for all of us. It seems that the fates decided to strike each of us some terrible blows this year. David here lost his grandfather, Jenny, you lost your husband, and I lost a well-loved son-in-law. That was bad enough. But it would not end there. David, no doubt believing what he believes with the

261

deepest sincerity, set about exposing an evil old Nazi to the glare of day. Eventually, he even decided on murder. But before that, David, you drew my children into the whole messy business. My sons, in trying to protect the family from what appeared to be a madman or a crook, ended by acting like crooks themselves. And Jenny . . . Well, you two alone know what happened in Cornwall. All I am certain of is that because of this, I lost my daughter's trust."

She bowed her head, staring at the floor.

Gelzer carried on in the same unhurried tone. "The seed of it was planted, and despite herself, she wasn't sure. So she spent part of the summer looking in books and trying to see whether her father was in fact what you, David, said he was."

David said: "And are you?"

Gelzer gazed at him with very clear grey eyes.

"No," he said.

Jenny lifted her eyes to see his face.

Gelzer said: "I am George Alexander Miller. That is what I have been for more than forty years."

David clenched his fists. "Before that?"

"I was Ernst Gelzer."

34

Gelzer sat there, watching both of them for a moment. The confession had come so quietly that David could not persuade himself to do anything. Jenny began to cry, not hysterically, not loud. She brought a hand to her face and covered her mouth, but her eyes kept staring at her father like lamps that would not go out. All the while she sobbed quietly.

Gelzer faced her for a second more, but she would not stop. He stood up and left the room.

Without him there was emptiness. The sense of shock grew. David turned to Jenny. She was leaning over as if in great pain, the sobs breaking up in dry spasms. One hand now supported her against the bed. Without thinking, he reached for it.

She jumped away from him, knocking her chair over.

262

There was nothing to say. He reached for the glass on the table and drank a few mouthfuls, while she paced a tight circle over at the window. Now that what he had searched for was finally admitted, he felt as if the ground had been snatched from under his feet. He thought that at the moment of confession, he should have leapt on the old man, tried to hurt him as badly as he could before Paul reached them. Yet he had done nothing.

"You rotten, lousy bastard," Jenny said.

He put the glass down. She was holding onto herself, right arm crossed over her breast, right hand holding left arm. Looking at him for the first time. The tears were over, but her face was tracked with red where they had fallen.

"This is your doing," she muttered. "If only you'd stayed away."

"You heard what he said. That's nothing to do with me."

She came to the end of the bed, shaking with anger. "It's because of you. If it weren't for you, we'd never have found out."

"You'd prefer it that way, would you?"

"He's my father, you idiot. Who wants to know this about their father?"

"He helped to kill my mother and my grandfather. How does that score with you?"

She came at him with her fists. He got his hands up, but the bedclothes constricted him. She struck at his head and body, and some of the blows got through. They fought for a moment, until he finally managed to grab her wrists, at which she pulled away sharply and returned to the other side of the room.

Gelzer opened the door. He must have heard the disturbance. They were still breathing hard. He came in, resumed his seat. David straightened his bedclothes and thought about the unlocked door and his clothes in the wardrobe. Jenny moved suddenly towards the door.

"Sit down," Gelzer snapped. "I haven't finished yet."

She thought about it, then did it. Places taken again, the situation was much as before, except for the dead white pallor of Jenny's face and Gelzer's increased seriousness.

"Now I have told you," he said. "Both of you together, because I could not bear to say it twice."

"What about Paul and Alex?" Jenny said.

"They already know. They have done for several years."

I knew it, David thought. The way they had behaved from the start. It was clear.

Jenny said: "Mother didn't know, did she?"

Gelzer shook his head. "Not Sylvie. I would rather have died than have her find out."

"Why didn't you tell me?"

"For the same reason. Jenny, you think it is a thing to be proud of? Paul was only told because he had already discovered some things. He understands."

"Understands?" David said. "What's to understand?"

"Please, let me do this in my own time. You've spent six months on this. Surely you will give me a little while to explain."

"I don't want explanations from you."

"I know. You want vengeance for your poor grandfather. But you must realise, his death was exactly the accident it appeared to be. Richard knew nothing of my past, and he was not a man who would indulge in murder just to please his father-in-law. What happened was terrible, but it was not deliberate."

"Grandfather came to your house."

"And was turned away. Of course he was. What would you expect? After so many years, for one man to appear on the doorstep, calling for Gelzer. It was a shock. I thought after so long that no one would ever discover."

"Did you have him killed in the hospital?"

"No. He died finally of his injuries and old age. I am a surgeon, a medical man. I've spent my life trying to keep people alive."

"Except in Auschwitz."

"Auschwitz-Birkenau," Gelzer corrected softly. "Let me ask you something. Do you have any solid evidence of the 'crimes' of Ernst Gelzer? Any real proof?"

David remained silent.

"You have not," Gelzer said. "If you did, you would have taken it to the authorities, and they would not have been able to ignore it. The fact is that all you have ever had is an inner certainty that I am Gelzer, and that Gelzer did terrible things in the camps."

"You're mentioned in the books."

264

"I'm aware of that. But not very prominently. One version will say that I was a torturer, a murderer, another will merely list me as a member of the medical staff. The truth is that no one is sure. Except you."

"And my Grandfather."

"Yes." Gelzer took out a pack of cigarettes. "Do you mind if I smoke?"

"Your house," David said.

"Jenny?"

No answer. She sat bolt upright on her chair, watching intently.

Gelzer lit up, puffed, breathed a sigh of physical relief.

"David – Mr Kalska. I wish to ask you something. I . . . want to put a proposition to you."

David waited. His mind entertained a wild fancy of Gelzer offering him money to go away. It would have been funny, but there was nothing amusing in the room.

". . . And to you, Jenny, because you have been hurt by this as much as anyone. It is simply this: when you are quite well, you are free to go from here, and to do as you think right. But I ask first for the chance to tell you my story."

"You could tell it to a court in Poland."

"And I will, if that is what you decide. But is it too much to ask that you should hear me out first?"

"I'm your prisoner. I don't have much choice."

"Jenny, what do you say?"

She frowned. "Is he your prisoner?"

"Considering that he intended to kill me, I prefer to think of him as a guest."

"You talk a clever line," David said. "It won't work with me. I used to do plenty myself. I know bullshit when I hear it."

"Then you will soon see through me if I lie. Come, David, you are still weak from your experiences. Would it be so hard to listen to me, when you have heard all the other evidence?"

He thought about it. Jenny was there, and unless she was a great actress, her shock at her father's confession was genuine. If Gelzer was just putting up a smokescreen, would she stand by and allow him to be killed? The room was cosy and light, the bed and books evidence of a normal life going on. The normality he had known before any of this started and he

265

became submerged in the shadows. He looked to see what she was thinking, but her eyes were fixed on her father.

"I want to hear it," she said.

David nodded. "I'll listen. But no promises."

"I wish for none. If, when you have heard me, either of you still feel that I must face justice, I will not stop you. I am too old to run and hide."

From downstairs came the sound of Paul moving about. Gelzer stubbed his cigarette in the metal ashtray on the table, lit another, and closed his eyes as if to see the past for himself. "This is the way it was," he said.

35

"Ernst Gelzer was born in Stuttgart in the spring of 1913. He was the only son of – "

"Cut it out," David said. "You're not getting round anything by saying you're a different man now."

Jenny darted an irritable glance at him. Gelzer blinked through the winding smoke of his cigarette.

"I'm sorry. I speak that way because it's so long since I was him. Until all this began, I had come almost to believe that he was a separate person from myself. But I understand your feeling.

"*I* was the only son of Hermann Gelzer, a well-known Stuttgart doctor, and his wife, Anna. My parents were middle-aged when I was born, so I was made much of. I was too young to have anything but the vaguest memories of the First War. After it was over, Mother and I were able to go to the country each summer. Father would join us for a few weeks in August. You'll perhaps be surprised to learn that nothing terrible happened to me as a child, nothing traumatic. I lived a very pleasant life. Of course, my country was in deep trouble, but children know little of economics and politics. I had no idea that we were in the midst of disastrous repercussions from the war, that people were actually starving.

"I went to a reasonably select academy for young gentlemen. I was bright enough, learned quickly, took a special interest in the sciences. Hardly surprising. My father's study was filled with medical journals and textbooks and the equipment that he used. I saw that my father made people feel better when they were sick. That seemed a fine profession to me. I can hardly remember a time when I did not wish to be in medicine myself.

"My father died when I was thirteen. A heart attack, quite unexpected. Fortunately, he left us well-provided for, and his death only made my mother more determined that I should follow in his footsteps. I was quite agreeable to that. Still a schoolboy, still living my sheltered life, I had a great interest in the First War by then. Every boy I knew was the same. We played with model soldiers, pretended to be cavalry when out riding. There was a sense in those days that something had 'gone wrong' with the war, that there had been a betrayal, otherwise we should have had victory. Even as a boy I was aware of this feeling. There was a history teacher who had served at the front. He had lost an arm there. Germany had been brought down by conspiracy, he would tell us, when his pain was particularly bad, but she would rise again and smite her enemies. He seemed a very romantic figure to us, since we were boys.

"The real world began to impinge on my consciousness fully when I went to university. It was there that I mixed with men of all kinds. And I soon realised that things I had been reading about in the papers were far more real than I supposed. I had been so – not self-centred, but perhaps work-centred, that I hardly noticed anything outside. Now I found there was a new mood. Does this sound like a history lesson? If it does, you must remember that I lived through it. And no one was more surprised than I by the interest my fellow students were taking in the National Socialist Party. This was shortly before Adolf Hitler became Chancellor, you understand. Many people at that time still regarded him as a joke. A little man with a little man's arrogance. But the movement he represented was a different matter. There was much support for the idea that Germany had been wronged by the world, and that the only way to regain our self-respect and some measure of national confidence, was by taking back what was ours."

"What about the Jews?" David said.

"What of them?" Gelzer asked frankly. "You'll probably find

it hard to understand, but in those days, I did not think of Jews in the same breath as the rest of humankind. No one did. It was the common attitude before the Second World War. Not just in Germany. Look at your own history, some of your writers from the early years of the century. Buchan, Kipling; you find many disparaging remarks about Jews in them. A mild anti-Semitism was part of the upbringing of the upper and middle classes. As for the working class, well, ask yourself how tolerant they are of blacks and Pakistanis now. Nig-nogs, Packies, Chinks, Slant-eyes. I've heard all these terms used by perfectly ordinary looking people. In those days, it was the same with the Jew. The vast majority of people born of my generation grew up with the attitude ingrained. There were Jews at my university; some tutors, some students. They were treated largely like everyone else. Except that Jews were not allowed to join certain clubs and societies, and other men would not have considered mixing socially with them. The same thing goes on today in America, I notice. Certain clubs will reject a membership application from a Jew. It's no longer respectable to be openly anti-Semitic, but in those days it was.

"If you ask me if I felt this was right, I have to tell you that I never thought of it in those terms. It simply *was* so.

"But enough of that. I shall not pretend to have been concerned with such things then. Even though you will read in the books that the political system of our country was in upheaval, ordinary people did not have much to do with it. Ordinary people never do. I was far too busy with my studies. I went on to medical school in Hamburg, and one of my tutors there was Walther Seidler, a very great surgeon. In medical circles, he was a legend. A big, grey-haired man with the manners of a bear.

"He was also a Member of the National Socialist Party, a staunch supporter of Herr Hitler, and a rabid anti-Semite. Those few of his pupils who, by their achievements, gained his attention, became like a select society. Many of his 'special students', once they had qualified, took positions under him in the hospital. He took such an interest in me, and it was he who turned me from general medicine to surgery. I did not much care about his political beliefs, but I knew he was a brilliant technician of the human brain, and I wanted to learn everything he had to show. But being a part of this 'inner circle' meant that you had to socialise with him and his other favourites, and listen for hours on end to his rant.

"Do you know, I never took it seriously. I knew Hitler was in charge of the country, and that there were certain excesses, but I thought little of them. Isolated incidents, I thought, not to be treated with too much panic. Just as you might look at a headline concerning police brutality to a gang of black youths. I remember there was a day when all Jewish shops and businesses were to be boycotted. I recall it because there were posters everywhere, telling people that the Jews were trying to destroy Germany, that we must not buy from Jews. That was the one time I can recall when such persecution was widespread. But it lasted only a day, and I hardly noticed it going on, because it was a Saturday.

"One thing did become clear to me, however. It was one evening at dinner with the Professor. There were six of us and our host, and they were talking of party matters. It suddenly occurred to me that I was the only one who did not belong to the National Socialist Party. As if he had read my thoughts, Seidler turned to me and said: 'And why is it, Gelzer, that you haven't yet joined us? Don't you believe in the aims of the Leader?'

"I was ready to make light of it, as you might if asked whether you voted at the last election. I made some joke about being more interested in medicine than politics.

"It was a mistake. I was such an innocent that I misjudged the mood completely. My comrades began to look very serious, because they saw how black Seidler's expression grew.

"This is not politics," he said, coldly. "We speak of the future of our people."

"The subject was dropped immediately and pleasant chatter resumed, but I sensed a new coolness around me, and the next day, when I passed Seidler outside a laboratory, he cut me dead. I knew exactly what it meant, and what I had to do. I joined the party."

"Just like that," David said.

"As you might join a particular club, for the people you would meet and the advancement you would gain from it."

"That isn't the same thing at all."

"Not now, perhaps. But *then*. This is what you must try to see. Hitler was just a politician then, and the . . . Nazi Party just that – a party. No one knew then what would happen later, no one could foresee where it was to lead. You make the same mistake everyone does, attributing foreknowledge to a nation."

"Are you telling me you had no idea of what they were like, what they believed in?"

Gelzer's face coloured. "Most people believed in putting their country back on its feet."

"By blaming it all on the Jews."

"The Jews, the Jews. You talk as if that was the only policy they had."

"I know that Hitler made speeches about it right from the beginning."

"Yes, you know. Because you have read it in history books. But I was a young man, younger than you, and I could not pick up *The Rise and Fall of the Third Reich*, because it was not written then. Do you see? Ask the ordinary people of Uganda if they wanted Idi Amin to run their country and butcher thousands of his enemies? They had nothing to do with it. They were busy earning a living, no one consulted them. Herr Hitler and his colleagues never came to my door and said: 'This is what we intend to do.'" He slumped back in his chair, panting a little. There was a pause, then David said:

"I knew this was just a chance for you to run out the old excuses."

"I make no excuses. I only wish to explain it to you."

"And put yourself in a kindly light."

"That is not my intention. And if you will listen further, you will see that I have much to be ashamed of."

"Go on, then."

He got up, a trifle unsteadily. "Not now. This is more trying than I thought it would be. In the evening we continue." He drew himself up, as if to reinflate his self-esteem, turned and went out. The door was not locked.

David felt cheated. Despite his scepticism, he wanted to hear more.

Jenny ran a hand through her hair, replacing the strands which had worked loose from the band. She shook her head very slowly.

He said: "You didn't know, did you?"

270

She closed her eyes, making a small laughing sound that had no humour in it.

Then she rose and left him.

When dinner was over the father, daughter and prisoner reconvened. Now that the drugs had entirely worn off, David was irritable with pain. Gelzer was solicitous of his well-being. He offered pain killers. David refused them, being more afraid of unconsciousness. Since the shoot, the clamouring in his brain had died away. He could think clearly again, and did not want to lose it.

He watched as they seated themselves. Homed in on Gelzer, wanting to catch the old man in a lie.

Gelzer said:

"I told you how I came to join the Nazi Party. Despite what you said, David, I was not attempting to provide excuses for myself, only doing my best to make you see that hindsight is a very useful thing when dealing with these matters.

"I became a member of the party in late 1933. Immediately my position as one of Seidler's special group was restored. It meant that I was invited to party functions as well as social ones. And, of course, it brought me into closer contact with those who were deeply involved with politics and the Leader's mission to restore the glory of our country.

"I saw him speak at a rally in Munich in 1934. I was no more impressed by the man in person than I had been by his photographs and newsreels. But when he began to speak, I understood how he had come so far in so short a time. The films they have preserved do not do him justice. He was, in a terrible way, impressive.

"As far as the beliefs he expressed and the policies his party promoted, well, I could see much good in them."

David snorted. "Good?"

"I was hardly the only one. Many of your people thought so too."

"I don't have a people," David said. "*Your* people killed them all."

"I'm sorry." Gelzer began to roll an unlighted match between finger and thumb. "I was still a young man, and I confess it, I was impressed by the lights and the music and the sheer theatrical power of the man himself. The people around me were joyous, not frightened. Although I was a solitary man then, as always, I could be caught up in their enthusiasm, as you relax when you drink. His stated aims, most of them, seemed no more than common sense. Yes, he blamed the Jews for our troubles, and I could see that he might be right. Knowing nothing, I was willing to consider any explanation for the troubles in the world. I was brought up in a society where Jews were a race apart. They were strange to me, and I was rather of the opinion that they should remain so.

"So, I continued my studies and learned about the things that really trouble most people: sickness and death. I worked very hard, and mixed with men who put on uniforms in their spare time so that they might better serve their land. There was no getting away from them. To avoid the spread of what you would call the Nazi menace would have meant locking myself in a cell. It was the system in our country, the background to my real life. Just like millions of others, I lived with it because it was there, finding some things acceptable, others less so."

"And never protested?" David said.

"Tell me something. Do you agree with the leaking of nuclear waste from power stations in Britain?"

Warily, David replied: "No."

"Have you ever done anything about it?"

"No."

"Why not?"

"Because it wouldn't do any good."

"Because Government is powerful, and you are one man, yes?"

He turned his head away so that he would not have to answer, and caught Jenny's eye. She was so damn silent. Why did she ask no questions?

Gelzer went on: "Oh, I soon knew from experience that there were regrettable incidents. One afternoon in Hersfeld Strasse, I saw a gang of brownshirts smash up the premises of a Jewish butcher, and there were plenty of beatings carried out on those who disagreed with Hitler's aims. A man I trained with had his ribs and jaw broken simply for standing up during a meeting and asking whether Herr Hitler was a man of any real intelligence. He left shortly after.

"I had a career to build. I did not make waves. I did as

272

people always do in times of trouble: I kept my head down and got on with my life. Even when Jewish doctors and surgeons who had been on the hospital staff for years were removed, even when text books which had formed the basis of our training were burned. It is amazing what the human organism can come to terms with if events progress slowly enough. I suppose I was afraid to go against the grain. Correction: I *know* I was afraid. It does not make the shame of it any the less now, but we all cling to the world we know. I did not have a friend or relation or colleague who was not enthusiastic for at least some of the New Germany. My mother, who was ailing in those years, thought Hitler a common little man. They say that the generals and politicians who first gave him the support that allowed him to take over the country regarded him in much the same way. They believed he was a jumped-up little egomaniac who could be subtly disposed of when the time was right.

"I attended a few meetings, went to some rallies, said all the right things. It was dangerous not to.

"I want you to believe me now, both of you. I was indifferent to Jews: I would never have thought of taking one for a friend – to me, they were simply not a part of the world I moved in – but I was not an anti-Semite in any real sense. I never wished them harm, any more than I would wish the poor or the crippled harm. I was burrowing blindly towards my own ideas of success in a world which I could not even see was coming apart at the seams. I was like the old librarian in the story. The battle rages back and forth outside his workplace, then someone comes to tell him he must find safety from the war. He takes his nose from a book and says: 'What war?' "

There was further silence. Through the open window, there came the sound of an aircraft booming slowly across the twilight sky.

Without the drugs, David descended in dreams to the familiar places again. Three in the morning, he began to shout for his grandfather.

Jenny came out in the corridor, pulling on her dressing gown. Paul was already at the bedroom door, actually holding a pistol.

"For God's sake . . ." she hissed, elbowing him aside.

273

"Well, shut him up," Paul warned.

She went into the room. David lay on his side, reaching for something beyond the table. He was drenched with sweat, no longer speaking, but grunting as if someone were hitting him under the ribs. After an instant of reluctance, she grabbed his hands and started pushing them back against his body, whispering: "Stop it. Stop it now."

He struggled and said: "Luba?"

His helplessness made her angry again. "Stop," she repeated, and struck him across the face.

His eyes opened wide in the dark of the moonlit room, breath stopped. He saw her, began to breathe again.

"You're all right," she said. "You're having a nightmare."

"It's always that place in the end," he panted. "Always the camp."

"Stop it. You're safe."

He smiled oddly. "Depends how you define the word."

"Just calm down."

"I'm sorry."

She realised that one of his hands was still holding hers. An echo of the evening in Cornwall when he had clasped her fingers while she cried. She pulled away.

"I really am," he said.

"Never mind."

"I didn't ever mean to hurt anyone. It was only that everything got so confused when Grandfather died. I just wanted to find out the truth."

"Well, you're finding out," she snapped. "And so am I. You should be happy now."

He raised his head off the pillow. "If I'd known you before, what you were like, I couldn't have done it."

She couldn't help being sarcastic. He did not know how much his betrayal had blasted her. "I'm very grateful," she said. "Go to sleep, for Christ's sake. Otherwise we'll never find out the rest."

She was almost at the door when his voice came low once more.

"Do you believe him?"

She waited with her hand on the door.

"He makes you want to believe him, doesn't he?" David said. "I just don't know whether that's something he's good at."

274

"Wait until you've heard everything," she answered.
"I don't have an awful lot of choice."
"Neither do I."

36

In the morning, he told them of the years between 1935 and the outbreak of war. He told them how he qualified to practise medicine, how he gained a place on the staff of his mentor's hospital. Throughout his own story, there were the increasing incidents and evidences of what was happening to his country: the passing of the Nuremberg Laws; the Jewish doctor who was sent to a concentration camp for giving a transfusion of his own blood to a non-Jew. The transfusion had saved the patient's life, but the doctor had committed a crime under the new laws.

"Concentration camps," David said. "You took your time mentioning them."

"It was the first time I heard of them," Gelzer said. "Oh, I know now that they were in use much earlier, but don't forget that they were not specifically connected with Jews. In the days before the war, they were simply places to send political prisoners. At first, I think you'll find, Jews were far outnumbered by other kinds of prisoner. And there was nothing about systematic killing then. They were just camps for detaining undesirables. Your country had similar places during the Boer War, I believe."

"How did I know you'd mention that?"

"Shall I tell you what I did in the years before 1939? I worked extremely hard as a junior doctor, gaining experience. I like to think I was good at what I did. I learned everything Seidler had to teach me, and read what I could of the work going on in other countries. It became difficult, of course, because any new technique or spectacular achievement in my field – or any other – was only published in Germany if a non-Jew was responsible. There was so much we missed then, only because a Jew had discovered it. And some brilliant men whose only crime was their race languished in internment camps. Many of them, I'm sure you will tell me, died there.

"That was when it became a nightmare. When I saw that the

275

things happening around me had passed far beyond the bounds of any reason. With all the trappings of childhood with which I was burdened, I could almost see sense in the idea that Jewish profiteers were to blame for the war, and that they ought to be eradicated. But when I saw that it extended even to denying a truth only because a Jew had been the one to uncover it, then I knew it was madness."

"And you did nothing," David said. "You didn't even try to leave."

"My mother was sick. She could not travel. Would you have left this country if your grandfather was unable to go with you? My work was there, my whole life, just as yours is here. You have a house, a business?"

"Used to," David said. "You messed that up for me."

"Pardon me?"

"The whispering campaign. It went along with beating up private detectives and getting me delayed by the police while you had Grandfather killed."

The old man bit his lip. He lit a cigarette and blew a thin trail of smoke over their heads. David glanced at Jenny. He wanted to see what she was thinking as these things were revealed.

Gelzer said: "I told you I did not kill your grandfather."

"Not you personally. One of your boys, or maybe someone I don't know about."

"You see a conspiracy of some magnitude, David. I'm just an old man with a family. I have some friends with a degree of influence, people who helped me to be sure that you were out of the country. And they failed me even in that. Do you really think that I have some phantom network of spies and murderers at my beck and call?"

"Someone killed my grandfather."

"His injuries killed him. I saw his reports, and I can tell you, the only surprising thing in his death was how long it took to come . . . Jenny, I'm sorry. We should not talk about the accident."

"I'm all right."

"Did my daughter tell you anything of her husband, David? When you two were . . . alone in Cornwall?"

"A little," he said, and received a dark look from Jenny.

"Ask her if she thinks Richard was the kind of man who would have driven over an old man just to please his father-in-law."

"I never said that."

"You are not far from it. I gather you would propose an underground organisation of ageing Nazis, pledged to help former SS men escape justice."

"It's been suggested."

"The stuff of fiction, David. It belongs with those tales of cloned replicas of the Führer and black magic rites to raise him from the dead. It's not the real world. I've been in Scotland for over forty years, practising my trade and doing a little business, and the only time I've seen a power-crazed Nazi in disguise is in films. This is the real world: my job, my family, our house in Stinton, this lodge and the countryside around it. Could you see anyone with sense jeopardising all this by being involved with war criminals?"

"If the person were a war criminal himself."

"Ernst Gelzer is on no list."

"Because he's supposed to be dead."

"He is dead."

"Oh, not again, please."

"Shut up," Jenny said, cutting through the rising note of anger. "Both of you shut up." She ran out of the room, slamming the door behind her.

The men subsided. Gelzer tapped the ash from his cigarette away and drew hard on the smoke. David rubbed his shoulder.

"I wish almost anything had happened," Gelzer confided, "before I had to tell her these things."

David drank a glass of water, watching the faraway look in the old man's eyes.

"When I first came to Britain," he said, "I thought that a normal life was denied me for ever. Marriage, children. I was sure that no man with my secrets to keep could endanger the lives of anyone he loved with such a past. I'd seen so many children die . . ." His voice cracked. "I believed I could never face bringing more into the world, for fear that by some twist of fate they might fall victims to a similar end.

"But time and a little peace do wonders. I stopped having dreams every night, began to feel in some measure safe. Then I met Jenny's mother. Such a fine woman, very like Jenny is now. I had told myself love was for other people, but she changed everything, and gave me my boys and my girl. I still dreaded that I would have to confess everything to them, but

277

it only became necessary much later, when I told Paul and Alex.

"Somehow, though, I always prayed that Jenny would not have to know. Why do you think that is?"

David shook his head. He felt the old man drawing him into his confidence. It was strange, and he was wary, but when Gelzer was telling his story, it seemed so convincing.

"I wish I knew whether you were telling us the truth," he said.

Gelzer did not falter. "Only you can judge that. To be honest, I worry more that she will not believe me. She is my daughter. I don't like being separated from her this way."

That evening she came to the room alone. He was surprised to see her, especially as he was by the wardrobe, searching through his clothes. She turned, as if she might call down to someone, but then she came in and shut the door.

"Should you be out of bed?"

"I don't think there's a rule."

She picked up his jug. "Came to see if you needed any more water."

He returned to the bed and sat down awkwardly. "Well-provided for, as you see."

She moved round the room, searching for things to straighten or put away. He kept an eye on her, knowing she was uneasy.

"No one to talk to?"

"I suppose you'd like to re-create old times," she said. "You were such a good listener before."

He let that pass, indicated a chair. Reluctantly, she sat down. Then there was a long silence, broken only by the wind billowing the curtains.

"Everyone's told me lies," she said at last.

"Maybe he still is."

"Not just him. You too."

"I had to," he said. "I had good reasons."

"Perhaps Father did too. You think of that?"

"I don't know. That's been the whole trouble with this from day one. I *never* knew where I was."

"It gives him such pain. Could anyone as bad as you thought he was suffer so much?"

"You've got me there. I used to think that you might know about him. That was why I came after you."

"Not me. You know the trouble? We never check the facts of what our parents tell us about themselves. We just believe them. Mind, I was always gullible. I'll believe anything if someone says it with a straight face."

He knew she was talking about him. He flushed.

She said: "He's not an evil man. I can't believe anyone could do the things they did in those places then just live ordinary lives forever after. He's authoritarian, yes, he likes to be obeyed, but that doesn't make him bad. He's saved lives. It's been his work. I just can't believe there's a monster lurking under his skin."

"Maybe we'll find out tomorrow. He has to get to it then." Paul's heavy footsteps went by outside. Neither spoke until he had passed. "What'll you do if he says he personally gave the execution order on ten thousand people?"

She looked up at him, clenching her hands together on her lap.

"I don't know," she said. "Do you?"

37

The low background thump of music from below; Alex playing Whitney Houston on a big portable stereo.

Gelzer said:

"When the war came, I was drafted into the military. The SS. This was a special privilege accorded me because of my association with Seidler. At least I was not forced into fighting. I believed in my country, right enough, but not in its leader. In a way, I had hoped I would be posted to some battlefield where there would be no time to think. The Eastern front would have been the right place for me then. But because of Seidler, whose influence was strong, I was placed in comfortable positions where my only patients were generals. In an odd way, war is a good time for surgeons and doctors. With a constant influx of wounded, they often have the opportunity to try out things which would never be allowed in peacetime.

279

When you consider that I was chiefly interested in the brain, a stint with fighting forces, with the incidence of head wounds, would have been useful to me.

"However, as I say, I was kept in readiness to help Seidler with whatever projects he might light upon. I looked forward to this possibility almost with enthusiasm. So little I knew of what was occurring.

"It was in the summer of 1943, I think, that I 'received the call'. Seidler was engaged in very important work for the Reich, and he wanted the best of his special students to assist him. My orders were to go immediately to Poland, to a place called Auschwitz . . . I did not even know what was there to warrant Seidler's august presence.

"On the journey, I encountered a fellow doctor, also making the trip. He was quite different from myself. Ambitious not just in medical matters, but also in the SS. We rode towards our destination in some stinking train, packed together with other officers, and he lectured me on the great opportunities for advancement which Auschwitz provided. It was he who told me about the great camp there, about the use of imprisoned Jews for slave labour. Did you know, incidentally, that many famous industrial names had works in the area of the camp? I. G. Farben, Siemens. Almost to its last day, Auschwitz was a profitable concern. Somehow, the great firms which used its cheap labour never were brought to book for their part in keeping it running. But then, let us not forget also that the Coca Cola company of the United States of America never for one moment stopped selling its product and making profits in Germany. Business goes on, even while the world is coming to pieces.

"So, I arrived at the camp. All I knew was that Seidler demanded my presence.

"It took me perhaps two days to realise just what was happening there." A long, aching pause while he added another butt to the pile in the ashtray and fumbled the lighter to a fresh cigarette.

"There was a saying then: 'The Führer Commands, We Follow.' It was not a slogan, it was meant in earnest. I was as much a part of this as any of the men I saw working in that camp.

"Before, I had heard rumours. War is rife with rumours,

because so much is kept secret. There were stories, which I always attributed to our enemies. I regarded them much as the tales which both sides were told in the First War: soldiers bayoneting babies, various atrocities. I knew that almost all Jews had disappeared from daily life before the war, but the official explanation for that was deportation. I believed it then because reason still dictated that it was the only possible way.

"I gained my first glimmering of the truth when I saw a trainload of people arrive at the camp station. I was supposed to consult Seidler before beginning my duties, and went to find him at the train. He was there, with other doctors I had known, selecting the healthy prisoners.

"You could not believe such a sight as this unless you had seen it. Herds of ill-dressed, half-starved people, men, women and children, milling around beside a train which seemed to stretch a mile or more. And in the midst of it all, a relatively few uniformed men, organising everything. I've been unable to bear crowds since then. I always see the wasted faces and huge, dull eyes of those people. I don't know where they came from, but I found out soon enough where the larger proportion of them went.

"I did not believe it. Not at first. No one had prepared me for the sheer size of what was going on. The very idea that the methods of the production line could be applied to killing was new to me. I know that I went to my quarters as soon as I could get away, and I just sat there for hours, trying to comprehend what it all meant. It's a cliché now to talk of the smell of roasting pork drifting over the camp, yet now when I remember it, I'm sure there was that smell in the air." His eyes were dry, but his hand shook faintly as he raised the cigarette. "It's different now. No matter how terrible the whole thing seems, if one of your generation were to come upon such a place, you would at least be able to say: 'I know this, I've imagined it, seen it.' To me, then, there was nothing to compare with. What was being done in places like Auschwitz and Belzec and Sobibor was totally new. Nothing that had happened before could prepare the mind for it.

"I was . . . like a sleepwalker for the first day. I wanted to get out, to run and find somewhere where sanity was. I had to go to dinner with other officers that evening, and I sat through the meal, gazing at Seidler and others who I knew, unable to believe their relaxed faces and healthy appetites. I had glimpsed the chambers and the crematoriums that afternoon, seen thousands of naked men and women filing towards them. Yet here there was a civilised meal, with ordinary men eating it, drinking their wine and talking of the progress of our forces, and interesting cases they were involved in. A string quartet comprised of prisoners played Mozart for us.

"I did not sleep that night. Somewhere in the camp, a machine-gun fired. A faint red glow burned in the sky off to the east. I sat by the window of my room, drinking from a bottle of schnapps and trying to read Horace, whose Latin seemed to me a power for logic in a crazed world.

"If I had been more courageous, I might have tried to escape, although there was nowhere to go. But I was not very courageous. I was a doctor who found himself in the middle of a war, with orders to be at a certain place. I suppose you would say that I showed cowardice, and so I did.

"What is almost impossible for you to understand, at this distance in time, is just how slowly the horrors had come upon us. It began as a glorious resurgence of national pride. Most of us found out too late that we had allowed ourselves to become part of a system in which brutality was the political equivalent of argument. And by then the dangers of saying 'No' were too extreme for any ordinary person to contemplate. I was, in however indirect a fashion, a soldier of the Reich. Officers obeyed their orders. You either toed the party line, or risked disappearing in the night, as others had done before. I had my tiny fragment of family, I knew what could be done to the disobedient. With my own eyes, a week after I arrived, I saw a guard, a German like myself, shot for talking about what went on in the camp. Any lapse in apparent loyalty to the Leader and to the purposes of the war was noted down. Did you read Hoess's confessions of his time as Commandant of the camp? If they are genuine, you should pay special attention to the reasons he gives for doing his job, which was mass murder, without a single word of complaint. He never considered there was any other course. If anyone protested, he was liable to disappear immediately and be replaced by someone who would do the job anyway. All the protestor gained was his own death.

"So I did my best to keep my sanity as the true magnitude

of the operation at the camp became obvious to me, and I attended Seidler as he took me on a tour of the hospital barracks to explain the work he required me for."

The afternoon sun darkened as clouds passed over. The room descended into grey gloom, then emerged again. Jenny and David waited for him to go on, but he was having difficulty finding words.

"I saw . . . everything. All of Mengele's favourite cases, the twins and the dwarves; and the patients being used for Seidler's particular line of study . . . I evinced a proper scientific curiosity, but I don't believe I heard a word of what Seidler told me.

"You'll know about what went on in those special barracks. Nothing they put down in words is anywhere near the horror of it. And yet I know that for children under a certain age, and many adults, their use for experimental purposes was a lifeline to survival. Mengele was very careful with his patients, and Seidler no less so with his. I . . . I saw the cases he was working on at the time, and I realised why he was in such a place. In Auschwitz, there was no delicate matter of professional ethics. Work that should have taken years in peacetime could be undertaken in months. No laboratory animals necessary. He could have as many guinea-pigs as he wanted. He could try techniques that would never have been allowed outside, and if the patient died, he just pulled another from the pool. Who needed to test their theories on rats and mice, when human beings – even if Jews and gypsies were subhuman – were freely available?

"He regarded it as an unparalleled opportunity to stride forward with his research, and most of the doctors I met were the same, the enthusiasm, the sheer normality of their attitude was beyond belief.

"That was the beginning of my time in hell. Oh, I know that my suffering was nothing compared to the prisoners. But it was bad enough for an unprepared and sensitive mind. I was as much a prisoner as anyone there. Held by my cowardice, by orders, by the inevitability of it all." He gazed at them, and his eyes were shiny, but tears did not fall. "This is the point where I can only ask that you try to see it as I saw it then, not as you look on it from this safe distance. And I have to pray you believe me, because there is nothing I can offer as proof.

283

"I was there to assist my old teacher in his work, but I also had to perform the duties I was given. I soon realised there was no way in which I could avoid doing my share of the selecting when the trains arrived. And in the middle years of the war, those trains hardly ever stopped. Hundreds of thousands of people spilled from cattle trucks and sealed coaches, and it was sometimes my task to go out and choose those who lived and those who died, keeping a straight face throughout, pretending that all was for the good of the new arrivals. I did what I could; I tried to spare people who should by the rules have gone to the chambers, and I did my best to actually treat the sick prisoners who came into the hospital barracks. It was a drop in the ocean, and even that a terrible risk. I gathered together my own batch of prisoners for experimental work. I took as many as I could for that, and I did my best to see that no serious harm was ever done them. I found jobs for them, worked hard to get them better food. Millions passed through to the gas and I was sparing handfuls, but it was all I could do. In the end it seemed better to do something, however small, than nothing at all.

"Even that won me enemies. I was investigating new methods and treatments of brain disorders, actually learning something. After the war, the experience I had gained meant I was ahead of my contemporaries, could do things that were in advance of the time. But in the camp, there were colleagues who were jealous, who would have been glad to see me removed. They pounced on any chance to discredit me. I know that towards the end, when even the die-hard believers realised the war would be lost and they would have to answer for their conduct to the world, there were attempts to place blame for particular abominations on me. A man called Hotteller spread the rumours through guards to the prisoners. He was covering his own tracks. There was little loyalty in the final months. Everyone who could see past the rant from Berlin was considering how best to save his own skin.

"So there were tales about me, and I was aware of the fact that anyone who had been part of the official machine at the camp would be looked upon with little sympathy. When they started pulling down the chambers and evacuating the remaining prisoners to other camps, I decided I must get away. I could not see anyone who came to the place now being very eager to listen to my explanation. I ran, heading south, hoping to escape somehow through to Africa. Then I was captured, and they started to bring me back, but the train I travelled on was bombed. I changed identities with a man who had been killed in the attack. It was the only thing I could see to do at the time. Everything was in chaos, there seemed to be no rules left except to survive. I did what I could, and I think I never had time to consider the rights and wrongs of it all until I was already here," he wiped his eyes, "caught up in the lie."

Jenny was leaning forward, she looked as if the story had been dragged from her as well as from her father. David picked at the corner of his bedclothes, head bowed.

"I tried to preserve one little piece of sanity," Miller said. "But there is no sanity in a country where, eventually, even the children would threaten each other with the words: 'You'd better shut up, or you'll go up the chimney.'" He stared hard at David, almost reaching to touch him. "I was a coward, I did not do enough, but I didn't know how to stand against my friends and workmates, let alone an entire nation gone mad. Since it ended, I've done what I could. Spent the rest of my life trying to help people, trying to give my children and other people's children a better chance. I learned such things about myself that no one should have to learn, and I've tried to make some kind of amends. Can you understand that? I don't ask you to forgive or to forget. No one could do that. I just need you both to understand. Can you do it?" He switched to Jenny. "Can you?"

38

There was a long time after he left the room when neither said a word. Jenny did not move and David was distracted. He kneaded his shoulder until the ache grew hot, but he hardly noticed. The bedroom was lit now by a table lamp, and the window was blue-black. He wanted to talk, but was afraid that any words he spoke might be a betrayal of his mother and grandfather.

He turned his head and saw that she was looking at him, waiting for him to meet her eye.

"Well?" he asked.

"There's a natural predisposition to believe what our parents tell us," she said, getting up. "I kept thinking one thing."

"Tell me."

"I didn't get it at first, couldn't remember. But then I realised." She opened the window wide, breathing the night air. He watched her, thinking how lovely she was because it was easier than thinking of important matters. "The look he had. It was the same when my mother died."

"Maybe he's a good actor. After all, he fooled everyone for a long time."

She showed no anger, just said: "Do you really believe that?"

"I don't know."

She returned to the bedside, sat on the edge of the bed close to him. He felt nervous. "Do you believe me?"

He nodded.

"Well, that's something."

"Not enough, though. Not to include him too."

"I just wish there were some evidence we could pick up and say: 'This is the truth.'"

"Maybe it exists somewhere."

"If it did, they would've come after him before now."

He groaned. "If only everything was simple again. I thought it was, I had it boiled down to one easy notion. But it's not like that any more."

"It never is. You only make things easy by ignoring ninety per cent of them."

"You sound like a defence lawyer."

"I want him to be what he says. Of course I do."

"I'm sorry. This must be hard for you."

"I've had easier things to deal with."

"*Is he* telling the truth?"

"I think so." She shrugged helplessly. "I wish I could tell you for certain. All I know is I believe him because I only ever saw him look so hurt once before. I don't think he could lie to me now without me seeing it." A door closed somewhere downstairs. "It's down to me and you, isn't it?"

He smiled. "I wanted to kill him," he said.

"I wanted to do the same to you. I was wrong about you, because I didn't understand why you did the things you did. Maybe you're wrong about him for the same reason."

"Have to think."

"I'll leave you alone."

She went out of the door. He wanted to call her back: being alone was the worst thing now. But he let her go, lay back with his eyes closed, thinking of her honesty, and the ways in which she resembled the old man.

What would you say, Grandfather? If only I could talk to you.

She went downstairs and poured herself a large measure of brandy. Alex and Paul were playing cards at the coffee table by the window, and at first they did not pay any attention to her. She shot soda into her glass and lifted it, drank a little. The brandy and the bubbles burned the dryness in her mouth. Alex glanced up, smiled at her. She felt grateful for it, but said nothing. Paul shoved forward a pile of twopenny pieces and Alex returned to the game.

She wandered out to the kitchen, opened the back door and stood on the threshold, watching the moonless night above the hills.

Someone came in behind her. She turned and saw Father.

"I wanted a glass," he said, almost awkwardly. He went to the sink. She studied how he moved, and knew he was old, and wanted to cry.

He turned and started for the door again. She said:

"Dad – "

In another second she had her arms round him.

When they returned, he sensed the atmosphere of a courtroom. Jenny came first, and called her father when she saw David was ready. Miller entered with all the strength of his pride burning on a low light. He still looked strong, but Jenny was right; there was something hurt about him. Perhaps it was the look of someone who has had to face again unpleasant truth about himself. He wondered if he had the same look.

He waited until Jenny sat down. He still wanted to take her hand, because he was alone and they had at least shared this experience over the last few days. She folded her hands on her lap, sitting close by him. Her presence gave him a little more strength. He faced Miller, whose eyes were boring straight into his as before. He seemed calm.

"You have decided what I must do?" he said. The way he asked made it seem as if David were in control of the situation now.

"There's not much evidence, one way or the other," David said.

"No. Because it was believed I was dead, no one has ever spent much time collecting the facts of my part in those days."

"There might be people still alive who remember. My grandfather thought you were important enough to get killed trying to confront you."

"I know that. And I understand it. Why should the victim be interested in the finer points of his persecutors' explanations. Everyone in the camp knew our names, even if they never had any contact with us."

True, David thought. There was no reference to Gelzer in Grandfather's notebooks. *He* was the one who had put Gelzer's face on the young doctor who murdered his grandmother, who stood in the special barracks that day and discussed techniques as one child cried and his mother shrivelled in her own body. No evidence that Gelzer ever spoke to his mother. Nothing but the obsession.

"I'll tell you the truth," he said. "I want to believe you. I want it to be over. I don't know what Jenny thinks, but I want to put a proposition to *you* now."

Miller murmured: "Yes?"

"You've explained something to me I never understood. You've made it more real to me. Why don't you come out in the open and tell everyone else? Not so you can be punished, but so other people can understand too." He could not tell how this was received, and plunged onward. "I know it'd be awful for you and your family, but if you told it the way you did to us, it might help."

Miller nodded thoughtfully. Jenny said nothing.

"If what you've said is true," David went on, "it needs to be heard."

Miller reflected his scrutiny. His expression was impossible to decipher.

"Dad?" Jenny said.

"I'm . . . It is . . . not easy. It's a hard thing to contemplate."

288

"You won't do it?" David said.

"Please, I have kept my shame secret for so long. It's not easy to think of telling the world now."

"You have to," David said. "It's the only way."

"I see what you mean. But you must allow me a little time. Just tonight, then I can give you my answer in the morning. Is it so much to ask?"

David thought about it. Jenny was all but asking him to allow the time. He saw the urgency in her face.

"All right," he said. "Think about it, but if you really meant all the things you told us, you've got to tell."

"Yes," Miller said. "Jenny, do you agree with David?"

She shrugged. "It's not my decision."

"Very well." He got up, stretching the stiffness from his limbs. He spoke to David. "I will think hard now. Thank you."

David was embarrassed by the old man's earnest gratitude. He drank a little water, busying himself until Miller had gone.

"You're asking a lot of him," Jenny said, lingering by the door.

"It would prove he means it."

She nodded. "He'll do the right thing. I know he will."

When he was alone, he limped into the bathroom and stared at himself in the mirror. He was bearded and there were lines around his eyes. But he thought there was a degree of peace now which had not been there before. He knew that he could not have everything back as it was, but that was no longer what he wanted. He knew that when he was done with this, it would be necessary to speak to those who knew the religion he had been raised in. Grandfather had been sustained by faith, and he needed that now. But there was Jenny too. He realised that they were on opposite sides of a very high wall. Even though reason said no, he wished there were some way of knocking it down.

Father was in his study when she went downstairs. Paul and Alex were in the sitting room, reading. She passed through to fetch a book, saying nothing, and neither brother spoke. It was just like an ordinary visit to the lodge. She went into the kitchen to put some used glasses in the sink, heard Father moving about his study. As she climbed the stairs to have a bath, she wondered what he was going through.

289

It was easy for David to say: "Confess to the world," but she knew how much her father relied on his air of self-sufficiency and strength. It would take an enormous amount of his pride to admit such failings to everyone. And everyone would know, because it would be huge news.

She entered the bathroom at the end of the passage and turned the taps on, fetched a fresh towel from the airing cupboard and laid it over the rail. Steam began to rise and the old pipes groaned and rattled as brown-tinged water ran into the bath. She went to her bedroom to change.

There was no getting away from it. No matter how innocent he might be – and that did not seem the appropriate word – it was obvious that the newspapers and television would make a meal of him. Millions of people would see his face and judge his actions depending on how much information the reporters could be bothered to give.

She slipped out of her clothes and put on her red bathrobe. Oh, no, nothing would be the same again. However it turned out, they would become like zoo specimens. People who knew half the story would write crank letters, friends and colleagues Father had known all his life – all of it as George Miller, anyway – would suddenly cut him dead.

But it had to be that way. She could imagine that, if Father did not agree to tell, David would go ahead with it on his own. And she agreed with him. Only she was afraid of the consequences, and the hurt that it would cause.

The bathroom was clouded in white fog when she returned. She leaned over and opened the window a notch. The night air was cool and dry as a bone. It spilled in, clearing the view a little. She poured bath oil in the water and watched it foam, switched off the hot tap to let a trickle of cold continue. It was nearly ready. She turned to lock the door, glancing round for her book. It was not there. She slipped out and looked for it in her room, but it was nowhere to be seen.

Cursing under her breath, she crept past David's room and back down the stairs. Father was on the phone. She heard her brother's voices droning under the thrum of Mozart's Serenata Notturna in the sitting room. She found the book in the kitchen, picked it up with damp fingers and started back.

As she passed the study, the music from the sitting room

ended, and she heard Father say: "So, we have to do it after all."

She was conscious of stopping, although it took an age for her foot to come down on the carpet and forward movement to cease. Sick fear opened like a wound in her stomach. The words were open to interpretation; the tone was not. She reached for the wall, needing support to prevent herself from collapsing. The book almost fell from her hand.

Father spoke again. "Yes, it's a pity the boys didn't finish him on Trap Law the other day. But it wasn't simple like the Grandfather." He listened for a second, then said something in German. She did not understand all of it, but caught the word "Juden".

"No, I'm quite sure I can't persuade him. He seems set on it . . ." Another burst of German. She could hardly stand, was terrified that Paul or Alex would come out of the sitting room. But she had to listen.

"There's no other way. I'm not having one little Jew ruin everything now. And remember, if I am discovered, the wolves will descend on everyone I know to hunt for clues. You won't be safe. You know how tenacious the Wiesenthal people can be . . . Yes, I have something in mind. Our people finally discovered how he got into the country. There must be a boat moored somewhere on the coast. I thought I might tell Mr Kalska in the morning that I have decided to do as he says, then we arrange to drive him wherever he wishes to go. Once away from here, I'll persuade him to tell me where the boat is, and we can arrange some kind of accident on the high seas."

She felt her mind sliding into the fear. His voice was so precise, he sounded as though he were discussing business. Only the lapses into German were out of character. She wanted to be sick, or to scream, but she did neither, because he was talking once more.

"Yes, she could be a problem, but not straight away. She will see him leave in a perfectly civilised manner and that will be the end of it for a while. If the Jew's death comes to light, well . . . she is flesh and blood. I can't honestly see her betraying me and her brothers . . . I can deal with her. I am her father."

Someone got up in the sitting room, came towards the door. She thought: I can't move, but she did move. Silently to the stairs, pulling herself up them, reaching the corner as Paul came out, talking casually about fishing.

Up the rest of the stairs, shaking uncontrollably. She stumbled towards the bathroom, threw herself inside and locked the door.

All lies.

She sank down on the toilet seat, dropped the book, covered her face. She told herself she would not cry, but then tears came shuddering out and she could not stop them. She could not look at herself in the bathroom mirror, for fear of the part of her which was her father. She doubled up over her knees, trying to keep the sobs quiet.

Water from the bath began to overflow in a gentle stream.

39

He was sleeping heavily when a hand touched his shoulder. He came awake in the dark, squirming over to see who it was.

"Don't say anything," Jenny whispered, inches from him. "Just get up and put your clothes on."

"What? What's wrong?"

In the gloom her face was a puffy mask. "Never mind now. Just do what I say."

He peered at his watch. It was three thirty-two. "I don't understand. What's happening?"

She was close to breaking. "Will you shut up and get dressed for Christ's sake."

He scrambled out of bed and felt for the wardrobe. His leg twinged, but it worked well enough. He pulled his clothes on while she listened at the door.

In a minute he was standing by her side, still groggy. She pulled him down so her lips were almost touching his ear. "Not another word. You have to get out. Understand?"

He started to ask why, but she covered his mouth.

She opened the door and looked out along the passage. It was cold blue, empty. She ventured out, taking him by the hand. His heart began to race, but there was no time for working things out. The simple fact was clear enough. He concentrated on following her through the unfamiliar house, not walking into anything, keeping his foot from dragging.

From one bedroom came the grate of Alex snoring. Jenny led him, her hand like stone. They edged down the stairs, Jenny indicating where a riser might creak, where the ceiling came low at the turn. A clock ticked gravely in the hall, there was no other sound. He wished he were carrying some kind of weapon, but she gave him no opportunity. She hurried across the hallway to the front door.

Her breath ceased as she touched the handle. She searched a table under the coatstand in the alcove. The door was locked, the key not there. She turned and pointed back beyond the stairs, slipping by him to show him the way.

They reached the kitchen. David made to find a knife, but she tugged him away. She found the lock, flicked the catch, slipped the chain and opened it. Cold air stirred on his face. He followed her outside, waited as she closed the door. He could see little of the country around him. The night was black, faintly lit with a few watery stars. He noticed that the lodge, which he had not seen from the outside before, was a squat, square place built out in the open on the wide step of a hill. Beyond the groan of wind blowing down from the glens to the north, there was no sound. They were far from safety.

"Go careful now," she whispered, close to his ear. "The yard's gravelled. We have to get round the front and take one of the cars. Stay close to the house where the flower beds are."

Eyes adjusting, he watched where she trod, pushing down blooms that had no colour in the dark. She still gripped his hand, tugging him forward.

They rounded the side of the house. Three cars were parked out front. A Range-Rover, his own hire car, and a Ford Sierra, which faced the drive. She moved cautiously over the gravel towards the Sierra, digging in her pocket for keys. Each footfall shifted fragments of stone, made them crack and shift. He looked back at every step to the windows of the lodge, but no lights appeared. She lifted the keys out in a clenched fist to stop them jangling, slotted one into the passenger door, unlocked it. She gestured to him to get in, to turn the interior light out as soon as he could. While he did his best to open the door silently, she crept to the driver's side. He reached in and switched out the yellow bulb, stretched across and lifted the lock on the driver's door. She leaned in, released the hand-brake and was out again, bracing herself against the door and turning the steering wheel hard left. She began to push. He took the wheel, glancing back at the lodge. Now they were making noise. The tyres muttered over gravel as the car moved towards the drive. Jenny kept pushing until she was sure their motion would not be stopped, then she leapt in, pulling the door to without shutting it.

The car gathered speed as it rolled onto the track that led down from the lodge. Without lights, there was only the sketchiest idea of what lay in front, but she knew the road.

He could not see her well. Her hands were locked on the wheel. The car coasted faster. She was a tense curve, hunched over the steering wheel, staring hard out of the windscreen.

"What happens?"

"This track runs downhill for about two miles. Once we're that far off, we start the engine and drive like hell."

"And then what?"

She all but screamed at him: "I don't know."

They bumped over a little bridge, the car slowing for a second then picking up again. The slope was levelling gradually with perhaps another quarter-mile to go before they would have to switch the engine on. Outside was nothing but black sky and moorland running away on either side. Ahead, the road dipped between two hills. No cover, no one to run to. He looked back, but the lodge was hidden momentarily by the curve of the hill.

"Did you lie too?" he asked.

"Everyone's lied all the way through," she said. "I believed you, and that was no good, then I tried my father, and that was a big mistake. Oh, God, I wish this would end."

"I should've killed him," he said. "I knew it."

"You're all mad." Her voice was savage, but she kept driving, lifting the keys toward the ignition. "You and Paul and Alex, fighting old men's battles for them. You're all crazy. It happened nearly fifty years ago."

"And it'll happen again if someone doesn't stop them."

"Oh, shut up, will you, and let me out of this."

The car was losing speed. She thrust the key in the ignition.

"At least you'll soon be out of it," she said, and twisted.

294

Nothing happened. She tried again, same result. The car slowed below twenty miles an hour as it entered the valley. He watched her try the key twice more, then looked over his shoulder.

She swore and hit the steering wheel. "They've done something to it."

"Worse than that," he said, gazing back at the windows suddenly burning on the hill. "They know I'm out."

The car had little more travel in it.

"Torch anywhere?"

"In the box behind my seat," she said.

He rummaged the torch and a shifting spanner out of a mass of spare bulbs and fuses. "Try to get her round the next bend."

The road swept to the left just ahead, sliding out of sight beyond an outcrop of rock. She did as he said, managed to curve the last few feet.

"Swing her over and open the bonnet," he said.

The car came to rest with its nose on the verge, tail sticking out across the track.

He got out, lifted the bonnet and saw the problem in about five seconds. The distributor cap had been removed. There was nothing he could do. He slammed the bonnet in fury and hurried round the car.

"Where're you going?" Jenny said.

He jogged back round the bend, saw headlamps jabbing down the hill. It would not take them long to catch up. He returned to the car. Jenny was waiting, holding herself tight against the chill night air.

"You'd better stay," he said. "No reason to come with me."

"You can't run."

"Not a lot of choice. Where do I head for?"

She turned her head this way and that. "I don't know. There's a village," she pointed west, "over the hills there."

"Safer than the road, anyway."

"But it's miles."

He darted forward and kissed her cheek. "See you."

She started after him. "David."

"Stay here."

He left her standing in the shadow of the outcrop, wishing he had remembered to tell her to keep away from the car. In the dark, he could hardly see where he was going, tripped and stumbled over the rocks that clad the lower slopes of the hill.

The sound of the Range-Rover grew more distinct. They might take another three minutes to reach the bend; as long as Jenny did not warn them, they might wreck the car in a collision. If not, they would have wheels to outrun him. They would not be able to follow him directly, but they were familiar with the country, while he knew nothing.

He ran into a sudden upthrust of rock, slamming his knees on it, fell down and waited for the pain to recede so he could go on. Clouds drifted to cover the few stars that gleamed, there was no chance of a concealing mist or rain. He peered back into the valley. Two hundred feet down, he made out the car, but no sign of Jenny.

Jenny saw their headlights tracking over the hillside, heard the engine bellow as it surged round the corner. The Sierra was directly in their path.

The wheels locked, tearing into the road surface. The Rover mounted the verge on the left, slammed the Sierra's tail, slewing the lighter car round like a cardboard box.

A moment of stillness as the engine died. She waited.

Alex staggered out of the passenger side. Paul climbed down to see what damage had been done.

"Still movable," he said.

Father was not with them. She had thought she was far enough away, but Alex noticed her sitting on the hill above them. Paul clambered up. She watched him approach, said nothing. He grabbed her, lifted her to her feet.

"You stupid bitch. Why didn't you warn us?"

She refused to answer, tried to shake him off.

"Where did he go?" He almost hit her, but settled for dragging her down the hill to the car.

Down on the road Alex was searching for tracks.

"Got him," he said, sweeping the torch beam over scuff marks in the grass. "He's making for Pitcorey."

"That right?" Paul demanded of Jenny. No answer again. "Oh, get in there." He pushed her into the back seat and called Alex to join them.

"Shouldn't one of us go on foot?"

296

"He can't stay on the hill. He'll have to go for Pitcorey. We can run him down long before that."

As Paul restarted the engine, Alex asked her if she was all right.

"Did he hurt you, kid?"

She laughed at him.

He saw a single headlamp moving again. No way of telling from a quarter-mile off how many were after him, whether they had split up. He followed the line of the hill to the top, then scrabbled into cover below the crest to look for a star as guide. He was exhausted already. The battering he had taken on Trap Law and the days in bed had made him weak. He massaged his legs, wishing he could see the light of a single house in the whole world.

Then he was up and making his way down the hill. A flock of sheep got up in a flurrying panic, and for a second he did not know what they were, and threw himself down in the heather. He got up and went on. The outlines of the land before him were as vague as the sea. Curving expanses of moor, small hills, glints of what might be water here and there. He saw no roads, but it did not mean there were none. The only advantage he had was that he ought to be able to see them in the car long before they spotted him.

He stumbled down to the foot of the hill, checked the bright white star that was as near to west as he could identify. The moor stretched ahead. There was nowhere else to go.

He fell again. A tussock of long grass brought him down. Then he strayed into a bog and had to haul himself out of four feet of stinking water. If this was Jenny's idea of an escape route, he could have done without it. He picked himself up, hanging on to the mass of pain which his shoulder had become from the twisting and pulling. How much ground had he covered? There was still nothing but the night before him, more uphill climbing. Nowhere to hide. If he was out here when daylight came, he would be as easy to spot as a church tower in the fens.

Listening hard, he picked out the roar of the car's engine. Direction was impossible, but they were not far. He imagined Miller sitting in the back of the car, directing the operation. Miller? Who was he? This was, after all, the Gelzer he had known all along. Whatever Jenny had discovered made it clear that Gelzer was still alive and eager to do in at least one more Jew.

Damn it, if only he had a gun.

He saw a smear of light glow and die behind a rise. They were close.

Nothing to do but keep running. He would not stop to make it easy for them, let them herd him towards slaughter. That was over and would never come again.

He ran.

"We've got to get onto the moor," Alex said. "That's where he is. He won't touch this road."

"Can't drive it," Paul changed the gears as they swung round a tight corner.

"Stop it," Jenny murmured. "Why don't you stop?"

The men went on shouting at each other over the engine noise.

"Mustn't get too close to the village," Alex said.

"We'll manage."

"How can you talk like this?" She sat forward, poking her head between the front seats. "This isn't grouse shooting. How can you talk about killing someone?"

"Eye for an eye," Alex said.

"Don't you understand? Dad was lying. He did all those things."

"What?" Alex exploded incredulously.

"David was right. I heard Dad talking."

"Oh, rubbish. He explained that years ago."

She turned to Paul. "You know, don't you?"

He drove on, showing no reaction.

"You knew all along, didn't you. *Didn't* you?"

"I'm going to throw you out of the car if you say one more word."

"Why don't you listen? You're just carrying on what Dad started . . . Stop it!" She reached over and tried to wrench his hands off the wheel.

He rammed his elbow back and caught her forehead. Dazed by the blow, she slumped across the back seat. "Enough," he snarled, catching the wheel just in time to control the car past the entrance to a cart track on the right.

"Hold it," Alex said. "Stop, stop quick." He was almost quivering with excitement. "Back up to the track."

Paul brought the car to a standstill. In a moment he was reversing. The track they had seen was no more than an imprint in the grass, a memory of a road.

"We can get him at the old camp," Alex said.

Paul slammed her into first and accelerated up the new path.

Coming over another rise, he stopped. There was something below, something man-made in the wilderness. He tried to make out what it was. Cloud was thinning, the starlight picked angular shapes out of the grey. An arrangement of low buildings, like chicken sheds.

A farm, he thought. But Jenny had mentioned no farm. Perhaps she had forgotten. No lights showed, but it was something to aim for. It was no more than five hundred yards away. He guessed he could make it that far.

Feet pounding the rough ground, pain every time they struck. He took deep lungfuls of the sweet, heavy air as he ran.

Another flock of sheep started up from slumber, the young ones bleating madly as they ran. He was almost there. The buildings were a long, flat mass in front of him, with one taller construction some way off to the north. He was thinking that chicken sheds usually had a light on somewhere. Then his feet struck ground that was not turf. He bent down and touched it with his fingers, swivelled and gazed about him. When he looked hard enough, he could see the straight lines of the concrete running out far across the plain of cropped grass.

It was a runway. The buildings were an abandoned RAF camp.

He swatted the disappointment down, but could not stop anger from welling up in a stream of curses. Moving slower now, he continued towards the buildings and entered the camp's eastern side.

There was nothing left of it but three rows of barracks; a collection of dilapidated brick huts with their windows long smashed out and even the doors removed. He limped miserably along the remains of a path, looking to left and right at the gaping darkness and crumbling plaster. He wanted to yell for the hands to reach up out of the soil and take him.

No movement except the clouds above, no sound but the wind crying far back in the gloom of a barracks.

He fell down, scraped his knee, did not bother to get up. He sat back on his haunches, and the pain did not matter. The barracks surrounded him, mocking. Grandfather felt very near, his whole family were just the other side of a curtain he had no strength to lift.

Are we done? he asked. After all this, are we finished?

The sound of an engine reached him. He lifted his head. It was coming closer. A wavering dab of light crosshatched detail into the grass between two barracks fifty feet away, then was gone as the car took a corner. They were coming for him.

They passed what remained of a gate and sentry box.

"Main entrance," Alex said. "Switch your lights off and drive down there between the first two barracks. We can hide the car."

Paul, unfamiliar with the camp, did as suggested. In a moment they drew up beside what had been the guardroom. Alex jumped out and took a quick look round inside. Paul went round the back and took a big multi-purpose torch from the confusion of tools, spares and fenceposts lying there. He marched into the guardroom and chose a window facing east to the hills. He switched the top light on and placed it on the sill.

"What're you doing?" Alex hissed.

"A light in the window to guide the weary traveller," Paul said, returning to the car for his rifle. "He's more likely to come if he sees it. Now, take a look round and make sure he didn't get here before us." As he snatched the rifle from the floor of the car, Jenny looked up at him. Her eyes were burning with accusation. He shook his head with distaste and slammed the door on her.

"I'll watch for him here," Paul said. "Shout if you spot him."

She pulled herself up to the window and looked out. Alex moved away towards the barracks. There was enough reflected light from the east to get a reasonable idea of what was going on now. She saw him clutching his gun across his belly as he sprinted towards the first row. Paul went round the corner of the guardhouse, profiled faintly by the torch, then was out of

300

sight. He was taking up some position where he could watch the hills through field glasses.

David might be out there now, seeing the faint signal of what he would think was hope. He had wanted to murder her father, who had been responsible for mass slaughter, and the men trying to kill him were her brothers. She felt as if her own power to make a decision were locked in the back of her head. She was unable to see what she should do for the best. That was the worst of it. There was no best, not in this situation. Only variations on the worst.

She closed her eyes and pressed her face against the cool leather of the seat. Wished they would all go away.

He lay on the damp earth at the corner of a barracks, listenir.g. The car had stopped, he had picked up the low murmur of men's voices. After that, nothing. Were they just checking the place, or laying a trap? He huddled closer to the wall, very conscious of his exposed position. If someone were to approach from behind, he would be simple shooting. But the car had arrived from the south. He turned his head this way and that, hoping to catch something more than the rustle of the wind.

Someone flashed by at the far end of the barracks. Running low, gun ready. Impossible to be sure who in the dark. He scuffed backwards a little, keeping the figure in view. Alex, he judged, by the size of the silhouette as it joined the black outline of the last hut on the right. He took a moment to be sure whether it had gone behind or merged with the shadows in front. Then there was a chinking of cartridges in a pocket that led his eye to Alex's bulky form as it ducked into the doorway of the hut. A dull yellow glow shimmered at a window. He had to be nervous, David thought, to use a torch in a situation like this. But, of course, he knew that his opponent had no gun.

The torch went out. Alex reappeared, skulked toward the next hut. David looked for Paul, but there was no sign of him. The likelihood was that they were conducting the search from opposite sides of the camp. That did not leave him many choices. Alex entered the second hut. David got to his feet and heard the cloth of his trousers rip near the ankle. Reaching down, his fingers came in contact with a jagged length of metal, some kind of piping. He felt all the way down to where it was buried in the earth, grasped and tried to pull it free.

Alex finished with the second hut, moved on to the third. There were six more in the row.

David exerted all his strength to get the piping loose, but it would not budge. A sudden clattering made him start back to the corner. There was a repetition of the sound, like something wooden skittering across a floor. Alex came out of the third hut limping slightly. He must have run into something inside.

Leaving the pipe, David crept along the side of the barracks until he came to a window. The frame was still there, but it gave way to his pulling in a second. He lifted himself over the sill and dropped onto a floor littered with dirt and crunching splinters of glass. He straightened up, squinting into deeper gloom. The barracks was a long, low space with blue-grey rectangles to show windows and doors. Whatever he found there, it would have to be by touch. He edged along the wall, hands outstretched. Alex would be on the fourth or fifth hut now. There was little time to come up with something.

His boot touched something metallic, shifting it a couple of inches. He gritted his teeth at the grinding row it made, but squatted down to find it. The bent lid of a discarded can sliced his fingers and he leapt back, sucking on his own blood.

Alex ran to another hut. Where was he now? Seventh, eighth? Old newspaper crumpled under his fingers as he worked towards the far corner. When the RAF abandoned the place, they had taken everything useful. He had hoped whoever owned the sheep used it as a store of some kind, but the hope seemed misplaced. The hut smelled of diseased wood and wet plaster. It was cold as winter. It looked as if it was going to be a trap after all.

Alex's boots skidded as he made the distance to the next hut. Had to be the eighth. David had lost count. He groped towards the corner, eyes almost closed.

A pause while Alex searched. Then the sound of his footsteps coming out. Another rest. He was close now. David heard him panting.

His fingers closed on a cold strand of metal. He dragged, but something held it. He reached for it with the other hand, grunted as a spike punctured the flesh of his palm. Barbed wire, scaled with rust.

Alex moved again, and he knew that the last hut had been the eighth. The sound of the footfalls changed as they crossed the concreted path between the rows.

He followed the wire hand over hand to the corner, discovered why it was stuck. It was a roll as thick as a child's wrist and the circumference of a serving plate. It was jammed in the corner. Knowing Alex was coming, he yanked the wire free, looped it over his shoulder, then turned, still squatting, to face the door fifty feet away.

Alex was already there.

As he sprang to his feet, the torch beam jabbed out. He was too far away to throw the wire. There was no other door, only the windows on the far side of the hut.

The beam pooled in the opposite corner, and he started to move. Alex must have realised he was there in that moment, because he made a gasping cry of alarm. David kept going, heading for the nearest window, hoping he was correct and that the frame was gone. It happened too fast for thought. The torch went out and Alex was swinging his gun up. David was a few steps from the window. Alex was tracking him, trying to lead him like some item of game. The only saving grace was the darkness. He had to leap for it, there was no time for climbing. Still carrying the barbed wire, he threw himself headlong at the rectangle of open air.

The gun made a great flash and thunder.

Paul dropped his field glasses and came out of the guardhouse. The explosion of the gun echoed queerly away over the airfield and lost itself in the hills.

Jenny sat up quickly and put her hand to the door of the car.

"Stay in there," Paul said, and he looked as if he would have killed her as easily as anyone. "Lock yourself in and don't move till we've nailed him, understand?"

She said. "You don't just know, do you? You approve."

He scowled at her. "Fucking Jew lover."

Then he was gone, and she remained in the car, fighting the battle of her own, begging for the choice to be taken from her hands.

*

Pellets scarred the wall like gravel hurled at a fence. But he was through. He hit the ground outside with his hands, trying to roll head over heels to his feet. The wire got in his way and he crashed onto his side. Alex bellowed furiously in the hut and backed out of the door. David heard him coming, scrambled to his feet. Two choices: through the window of the adjacent hut, or bluff; back the way he had come. He chose the bluff, jumping and heaving himself back over the sill. He just made it. Alex came round the corner, stomping down between the barracks like a charging bull.

David crouched close below the window as the big man passed, heard him pull up abruptly as he tried to work out where his quarry had gone. Ragged breathing as he turned this way and that, then the scrape of boots on metal as he clambered over the sill of the adjacent hut.

Stillness. He remained where he was. The walls were solid, they were safety. Reason told him to get out in the open, but dawn was coming, he would be a target on the open airfield. Fear froze him in place. He told himself to move, but he was locked.

And there was something else. He could no longer hear Alex.

Nothing was happening. Alex must have discovered there was no one in the next hut, so where was he? He was not barging around with gun blazing. The other hut had swallowed him up. Was he waiting for his brother, or was Miller himself to have the pleasure of the kill? Uncertain, he rose, keeping his back pressed to the wall.

A bird made a mournful wailing cry somewhere. It was all he could hear except for the grating of barbed wire strands as he eased the roll off his shoulder into his hand.

Still nothing. His head ached to the thumping of his heart, his left shoulder pricked with the heat of blood oozing from old wounds.

Nothing.

Get out of the hut, he thought. Get out before you're stuck in here with all of them.

Nothing.

Get out, for God's sake.

On the impulse, he turned to the window.

And Alex rose up out of nowhere, shouting triumphantly as he brought the gun to bear.

He was still circling round, the wire in his right hand. He took in the fact that Alex was very close. The barrels of the gun that swooped towards him were only inches from his face. He got his left hand up and grabbed for them, caught them and pushed with all his strength to lift them above his head. Straining to bring them down, Alex fired.

The explosion was solid, like a heavy safe striking a cement floor. David was stunned by the volume, the violent kick of the barrels numbed his hand, but he kept hold of them, hauling backwards to bring Alex closer. Alex braced himself to resist, lost a couple of inches in the first struggle. He wanted the gun back, but it was hampering him. David got him right up against the window, then he lashed upwards with the wire.

Alex howled and let go of the gun. He clawed at the left side of his face. David let the gun fall into the barracks and grabbed him by the head, yanking him across the sill and driving up with his knee. He heard the muffled cry and felt the nose break on impact.

A piece of his conscious mind – like the reasonable being who oversees the drunk – thought: What am I doing? This isn't right. But adrenalin blotted out consideration, gave the physical impact of bone on bone a kind of joy. He brought his fist hard down on the side of Alex's skull. Alex grunted and flopped over the windowsill, neither in nor out of the building. Breath came bubbling through shattered nose. He was done.

David sank to his knees and picked up the gun. It was so heavy and cold. He needed cartridges. He dug in the jacket pockets; Alex moved weakly but was in no state to fight. David took a handful, moved away to a safe distance and broke the gun. The spent cartridges described a beautiful arc and clattered on the floor. He started to reload.

And heard the click of the hammer coming back.

"Now then," Paul said.

"Don't close the gun. Don't move one inch. I've got you."

He was in the doorway, and the dreary blush of coming dawn showed the rifle at waist level, perfectly aimed for a belly shot. The outlines of the barracks were coming into focus.

305

"Drop it," Paul said.

He let it go.

"And the cartridges."

They fell.

"Now come toward me – Slowly."

Alex's ragged inhalations filled the quiet. David walked towards the door.

"He'd better not be seriously damaged," Paul said. "Stop there."

David stopped. Ten paces separated them.

"Now I couldn't miss you if I tried," Paul said, stepping a few inches through the doorway. "But I won't try." His smile flickered in the darkness of his face. A gleam of white teeth. When he spoke next, he did so with deliberation, accentuating every word. "You dirty, rotten, stinking, pus-brained little Jew." He lifted the rifle.

Grandfather's voice reciting the Kaddish.

"Bye-bye," Paul said.

Something hit him. David saw the descent of it. There was the thick, flesh sound of it striking full in the back, then the brother staggered and sprawled on the floor. The rifle flew from his hands, skittered in the dirt.

Shaking surprise, David jumped him, but there was no need. The force of the blow, and the crack when his head met the floor, had put him out.

He went for the rifle first. Nothing would have kept him from it. When it was safe, he spun towards the door.

Jenny appeared there, a thick fencepost hanging from one hand. The other was clutched to her mouth. She stared down at her brother as if someone else had laid him out.

David forgot the rifle. He went to her.

She dropped the post, drew the other hand to her mouth. She was shaking, fighting to breathe through the words that were jerking out of her mouth.

"Oh, God, I had to do it, Oh, God, I had to."

She kept receding from him as he reached the door, shuffling back as he came on. Standing outside, her body contracting and trembling, she lifted her gaze from Paul and flicked to him. He reached for her. She flinched, muttering the words compulsively. He grasped and pulled her hand from her face. She twisted quickly and he threw his arms round her to keep her there. She struggled for a second, then ceased. Exhaustion hung in his arms.

"No more," she said. "You're free. No more now."

He held her close. "Where's the car?"

"Guardhouse." He let her go then. She saw what was in his mind. "No, David. Please."

He shouldered the rifle with an effort and started walking. He hardly knew where he was going, but he wanted the car.

She followed, hurrying to keep up. "Don't. I know he deserves it, but please . . ."

He turned the corner at the end of the barracks, spotted the torchlight in the guardhouse and the Range-Rover beside it. Jenny was still with him, dragging at his sleeve.

"Can't you be content? You've beaten them, you're alive. You have what you need. Why not get out while you can?"

No more listening. He knew there was only one way to be sure now, and the confrontation with the brothers had given him the necessary lust for it. He had a rifle, and the old man was alone. If he had skipped from the lodge, then he would be found. It was only a matter of time. No more doubts. The smell of blood and fear had finished them.

"Please!" Jenny cried, and attempted to take the rifle from him.

He was gentle with her, had no wish to hurt her. He took her by the shoulders and put her away from him.

"I'm sorry," he said, and stroked her cheek with the tips of his fingers. She was so beautiful, he wanted to say he loved her. It was too much.

He ran for the car, knew she pursued him, but he reached it first, and the keys were in the ignition. It started first time, and he had the doors locked before she could get there. He stabbed at the pedals, squealed the car into reverse, seeing her running after him in the single pool of the headlamp. She pummelled on the window, inches from him, but he put the car in first and skidded away from her over the rank earth.

In a minute even the shape of the camp had disappeared from the mirror, and he was driving hard for the lodge.

307

40

Morning was a dull grey shine behind the eastern hills. The road slithered out beneath their deep plunges and shadowed heights. He drove foot to the floor, almost by instinct. Conscious thought was given to working on his rage, preserving it for the thing to be done.

This was the second bite. He had messed up the first one by turning soft. Not again. Miller was not Miller, he was Gelzer; he always had been. Nothing had changed the corruption, and he had passed it to the sons.

And not the daughter? He saw Jenny pleading for it to end, forced her out. She would only distract him. It was Miller. Miller was Gelzer; end of story.

He reached a bend which seemed familiar, recognised it just in time to swerve round the stranded hulk of Jenny's car. The Range-Rover lurched through its own skid marks, but he controlled it, steered back to the road and took the bend beneath the outcrop at good speed.

The lights of Gallow Lodge blinked into view on the black hill.

He lifted his foot from the accelerator, let the car slow to a more relaxed pace. There must be no alarm in its approach. With luck, Gelzer would think it was his boys bringing back the carcass. He might come out to receive the good news: another Jew gone. He wished he had a pistol, the rifle would be clumsy to fire from the car. Gelzer had carried a pistol, all through the war, but he probably never shot anyone. A doctor involved in 'experimental work' had no need of it.

He came to the bridge, scraped the walls going over it, then changed down the gears to climb the hill. The lodge waited, open and unguarded, exterior lamp illuminating the yard. He rummaged in the glove compartment, found a bulky penknife and slid it in his pocket.

"Think of God not as good or bad," Grandfather once said. "Think only of a force of control. That's all it is. Something to stop the universe flying apart completely."

Almost there. Just the last curve beneath the yard, and up onto the gravel. He breasted the rise, and pulled in beside the hire car. He turned off the engine, grabbed the rifle and slipped out on the passenger side. It was a moment's work to slit the tyres of the hire car, then he scurried to the rear, peeked round the tail-gate. No movement in the house. The heavy oak door was shut. The Range-Rover ticked as it cooled, a fresh breeze from the west stirred bushes in the flower beds.

He retreated to the edge of the yard, ducked below sight of the windows and circled. Out of the lamp's glare, he moved up the hill beside the walled garden, stopped at a corner where he could see the back door.

Still no sign from the house. Yet he heard music. Beethoven's Eroica, blaring from the lounge. He crouched behind the wall, eyeing the darkened rear windows suspiciously. Was the old man already celebrating the kill?

Ten yards to the back door. No creeping now. There was no time.

He leapt from cover, jumped the wall and ran full pelt for the house, firing all the time. The noise was incredible. The rifle jumped in his hands and one shot smashed an upstairs window. There was no answering fire, only the weep and rush of Beethoven's music from the lounge. He made it to the wall, slid one arm across and tried the handle.

It was unlocked. The latch lifted out of its housing with a whisper of rust. The door swung inward. He tried to catch it, but it was beyond his grasp. It creaked wide open and bumped gently against a kitchen unit.

He waited, rifle up and ready. The music made it difficult to pick out anything. What now? How to proceed without getting his head blown off? He jabbed the rifle barrel across the doorway. No one fired, nothing moved. Gathering his courage into action, he sprang round, covering the kitchen with the rifle.

A bar of light from the hall showed a coffee cup on the table, the kettle with a thread of steam winding from its spout. He moved inside, stopping to drink handfuls of water from the tap. He had not drunk for hours. It made him retch. He was frightened. Beethoven, the sense of a room just vacated. He went on to the hallway, edging the door farther ajar with the rifle barrel. Every moment he expected gunfire to shatter the wood, but it did not come. He peered down the brightly lighted hallway. The music roared from the room on his left. Incongruous: the race that made these sounds also built the gas chambers. It spoke of faith and victory, all he could taste was fear and hate. He kicked in the lounge door, saw the red lights of a stereo's display jolting with the volume. He swept it from its table. The music died instantly. It left an aching well of silence. Another empty room. Back into the hall, pulse beating in his throat. So hard to stay calm. Quick would be better. This searching shrivelled him. The study was empty, the hall narrow, only the front entrance and the stairway to be guarded. The stairs were enclosed by walls and ceiling. You had to be at the bottom before you could see up. He pressed against the opposite wall and moved along it an inch at a time. The top step of the first flight slid into view. It was dark up there, the shadows like ink. He tilted his head, craning to see further.

The flash came first, then the deafening impact of the charge in the confined space. He went down, hit the floor and piled into the alcove on the other side of the stairs. It provided space enough for him to hide in, no more than that. Panting in reaction, he looked back at the wall and saw the hole where the bullet had gone in.

Gelzer spoke from beyond the curve of the stairs.

"I didn't get you? No matter."

The voice cut him. He bobbed out of the alcove and fired a wild shot. It was louder than the pistol but just as useless. Unbalanced momentarily, he saw Gelzer's hand snake round the corner. He ducked back as another slug lodged in the front door. Christ, what was he into here?

"I think this is a good place, David." The old man's voice was level, but hoarse as if with shouting. "The advantage of this lodge is that the windows are too small to admit an intruder. Its disadvantage is, of course, that I could not get out of them. Neither could I guard every side of the house, and I'm obviously too old to outrun you. So, this is not so bad."

"Bastard," David murmured. "Miserable, lying bastard."

Gelzer said: "You may as well go. I've called for assistance, and I think I can protect myself here until it arrives . . ." When there was no reply, he called: "David?"

"You lied," David said. "You did it so well. You even took me in."

"I know. Are Paul and Alex . . . ? Have you – ?"

"Don't be shy. The slaughter you've done, you should be able to talk about it."

"Are they all right?"

"You won't know."

He swore in German. Then: "I insist you tell me."

"Insist away," David said.

The pistol went off again. It took a chunk of the corner from above David's head. He lunged out to try another himself, but Gelzer had disappeared into safety. Too fast.

"All the things Grandfather believed about you, they were right, weren't they?"

"It's impossible to say now. All so long ago. I have seen myself blamed for things I never did, forgotten when I should have been remembered. It's history now, you understand? All history."

"Except you carry it with you."

"I carry nothing."

"Not even regret?"

"I did what millions of my countrymen did."

"Are you ashamed?"

"No."

He saw the toe of the old man's shoe. He fired, missed. Gelzer replied with a shot that splintered the coatstand. Cat and mouse, both of them darting out to let off an unaimed round and flick back into hiding.

"What you don't realise," Gelzer said, "is that this outrage, this condemnation of what we did is hypocrisy."

"Too late for excuses, old man."

"No excuses, David. Look at the world now. Is there a race upon this planet that doesn't hate the other races? It is the natural instinct. Like animals. Black hates white, white hates black, one tribe wishes to remove another. All the talking simply avoids the truth."

"Forty years, and you still believe."

"I see people. I read the papers. The Polish government 'apologised' not long ago for past excesses of anti-Semitism. Not during the war, mind you. In 1967.

"When the remnants of your people tried to return home

311

after the war, many were killed by Poles. Not Germans, Poles. They did not want to mix with the alien seed. We gave them the chance to be honest about it."

"To murder," David said.

"It's as old as the human race. Political parties in South Africa and France use images borrowed from the National Socialists."

"And I bet your people support them."

"My people. I heard a man on the radio the other day. He sells 'fascist-style' clothing by mail order. You know his biggest market? Japan! Do you think all this is the result of some old men who escaped after the war? See sense."

Listening, he had slumped against the alcove, slipped forward until his arm hung in view of the stairs. The pistol smacked again and a bullet zipped past and embedded in the floor.

"People behave as if racism were a crime," Gelzer said. "It's as natural as breathing. You have it in you too."

"I didn't help to run Birkenau."

"But you would now, wouldn't you? If you could put me there, you would do it. It's only a matter of situations."

David stuck the rifle round the corner and fired. Gelzer replied with a different pistol. There could not be many more rounds left in the rifle's magazine, and he had taken no more ammunition from Paul. Gelzer's 'assistance' might turn up any time. The cat and mouse had to end. But how?

"It's all around you, David. It is always mild when the times frown upon the showing of it. Scotsmen dislike Englishmen, Americans distrust Mexicans. But when crisis occurs it comes out of the dark. Jews hate Palestinians, Muslims hate Sikhs. That's what international politics is: civilised racial hatred."

"For you. The rest of us just get on with living."

"You tell me that honestly? Were you taunted at school, a boy with a strange accent and different blood? I think you were. If the rules were a little less strict, your playmates might have torn you to pieces."

"You murdered all those people, didn't you?"

"Not I. I was a doctor. There was no murder in the hospital barracks. Only experiment. They were going to die anyway. At least we put them to some use."

"I know the uses."

312

"You weren't there."

"If I had been, you'd have X-rayed my balls and cut my head open."

"Dramatics."

"You killed those people."

"People?" Gelzer spat. "Not people: Jews."

David resisted the urge to let off a hail of shots. He tried to keep anger from part of his brain. To think.

"Can you justify yourself like this to Jenny?"

"You will not speak of my daughter."

A small lever. He knew what he must do, no matter how dangerous it was. The game would go on until someone else stopped them, unless he went ahead with the plan that had come to him as the old man protested.

"I *will* speak of her," he said. "We share something concerning Jenny. We both betrayed her."

"What I kept from her was necessary to her happiness."

"You say you're not ashamed. You told the boys, but you couldn't tell her." He fired a wild shot that never even reached the top of the stairs. But it would keep Gelzer round the corner for a while.

"You don't speak of her. Scum like you laying hands on my daughter. I should have killed you myself for that."

He shifted silently onto his right knee, moved into the open and took up a careful firing position, rifle to his shoulder, eye behind the sight. He did everything properly, knowing that if Gelzer should chance one now, he would catch him in full view, unprepared and vulnerable.

"You haven't asked me where she is," he said.

"What?"

"She helped me get away, old man. She found out about you. But you don't know where she is."

"If you've hurt her . . ."

He settled himself. His arms felt easy as he gripped the rifle. His finger settled on the smooth metal of the trigger. He was lined up, aimed, ready.

"Hurt her?" he said. "What if I did?"

"No."

"Your daughter for my mother and grandfather. What if I hurt her badly?"

"No."

Sour bile in his mouth. "What if I killed her?"

"No!"

Gelzer ducked into sight at the bend of the stairs, the pistol switching up to squeeze off a shot. It was a tiny instant, but he realised with sudden horror that his enemy was fully exposed, a sitting target on the floor below. He started to correct his aim, but he was not fast enough. David had prepared for this fraction of time. He did not allow himself to think that he might be hit. He pulled the trigger.

It caught Gelzer in the forearm, six inches above the wrist, smashed the bones and sprayed his blood across the wall behind. He screamed and the gun fell from his hand.

The sight of the blood tipped David into panic. He had done this violence, put a bullet through a human being. He had not known how it would feel. Real blood, real agony. He flung himself up the stairs as Gelzer scuffled backward. Life and death narrowed to a point: the finality of the kill.

He turned the corner. The old man was propelling himself up the stairs on his backside, clinging to his ruined arm, moaning through his teeth at each kick.

David saw the spare pistol and the cartridges round it. He swept them away, grasped Gelzer by the bad arm and hurled him at the bend in the stairs. Gelzer hit the wall and slid down it, body twisting awkwardly in the little space of the landing. David fell upon him, clasped the sinewy throat.

Gelzer fought. He was strong, but he was old, and one fine surgeon's hand was crippled. David blocked him, sprawling half down the stairs as he sought a position of advantage. He dug at the windpipe with his thumbs. Hate, the age-old feeling of life going out under his hands. The old man started to choke. There was a sound like running. He knew he must finish Gelzer before they finished him. But Grandfather was saying, No.

He couldn't believe it. The flesh under his hands flickered like a moth dying. His mother said, No. Their voices grew and burned in his head. He ignored them, applied more pressure. The sweet, endless reality of Gelzer's existence. They screamed, No. A door burst open somewhere. The sound was outside him.

"No!"

He looked down the stairs and saw Jenny.

*

314

"Please, David. Don't."

His grip loosened slightly. Concentration wavered. Gelzer wheezed, he felt the blood pumping back in the old man's veins.

She was bedraggled and filthy, barely able to speak from running. She collapsed on the stairs and put out her hand, trying to reach them.

"Don't make yourself the same."

"We're all the same," he said, holding Gelzer down.

"No. Not you, not me, not everyone. Please. I know he's my father, but that isn't why. I'll tell everything. We'll go to the authorities, and I'll tell everything he's done. He won't go free."

Crazed, upturning eyes in the blackening face.

"You hear me, Father? You kill him and you'll have to do the same to me." She looked in David's eyes. "Don't kill."

Grandfather said: I never wanted revenge. Only justice.

Luba said: This isn't why we stayed alive.

Jenny clawed up the stairs. Not looking at her father. Not pleading or begging. She was stronger than either of them. She got a hand to David's arm.

Voice low, speaking reason. "Not me, not you. Please now."

He let go of the old man, who no longer had the strength to move. He reached and pulled her up the last step, and she drew his head to her breast. Her own face came to rest on his shoulder. Children of past horror, they cried together.